D1499162

GABE

Alvarez Security Series

Maryann Jordan

Gabe (Alvarez Security Series)
Copyright © 2015 Maryann Jordan
Print Edition

This book is a work of fiction. Names, characters, places, and incidents either are products of the author's imagination or are used fictitiously. Any resemblance to actual persons, living or dead, events, or locales is entirely coincidental.

Cover Design by: Andrea Michelle, Artistry in Design
Editor: Shannon Brandee Eversoll
Format: Paul Salvette, BB Ebooks

ISBN: 978-0-9864004-3-8

Acknowledgements

First and foremost, I have to thank my husband, Michael. Always believing in me and wanting me to pursue my dreams, this book would not be possible without his support. To my daughters, MaryBeth and Nicole, I taught you to follow your dreams and now it is time for me to take my own advice. You two are my inspiration.

My best friend, Tammie, who for nineteen years has been with me through thick and thin. You've filled the role of confidant, supporter, and sister.

My dear friend, Myckel Anne, who keeps me on track, keeps me grounded, and most of all – keeps my secrets. Thank you for not only being my proofreader, but my friend. Our friendship has grown and changed and you mean more to me than you can imagine.

Going from blogger to author has allowed me to have the friendships and advice of several wonderful authors who always answered my questions, helped me over rough spots, and cheered me on. To Kristine Raymond, you gave me the green light when I wondered if I was crazy and you never let me give up. MJ Nightingale and Andrea Michelle – you two have made a huge impact on my life. Anna Mychals, EJ

Shorthall, Victoria Brock, Jen Andrews, Andrea Long, A.d. Ellis, ML Steinbrunn, Sandra Love, thank you from the bottom of my heart.

My beta readers kept me sane, cheered me on, found all my silly errors, and often helped me understand my characters through their eyes. A huge thank you to Denise VanPlew, Sandi Laubhan, Barbara Martoncik, Jennifer Alumbaugh, Anna Mychals, Danielle Petersen, Shannon Brandee, Stracey Charran, Leeann Wright, Lynn Smith, Kelly Williams and Tracey Markin for being my beta girls who love alphas!

Shannon Brandee Eversoll has been my editor for the past five books and what she brings to my writing has been amazing. She and Myckel Anne Phillips as my proofreader gave their time and talents to making Gabe as well written as it can be.

My street team, Jordan Jewels, you are amazing! You volunteer your time to promote my books and I cannot thank you enough! I hope you will stay with me, because I have lots more stories inside, just waiting to be written!

My Personal Assistant, Barbara Martoncik, is the woman that keeps me going when I feel overwhelmed and I am so grateful for not only her assistance, but her friendship.

The cover was created by my dear friend, Andrea Michelle with Artistry in Design, and her talent is evident in every detail. Thank you for working with me, planning with me, laughing with me, and understanding me.

As the owner of the blog, Lost in Romance Books, I know the selflessness of bloggers. We promote indie authors on our own time because we believe fully in the indie author community. I want to thank the many bloggers that I have served with, and who are assisting in promoting my series.

Most importantly, thank you readers. You allow me into your home for a few hours as you disappear into my characters and you support me as I follow my indie author dreams.

If you read my books and enjoy them, please leave a review. It does not have to be long or detailed...just that you enjoyed the book. Reviews are essential to indie authors!

Author Information

Maryann Jordan

I am an avid reader of romance novels, often joking that I cut my teeth on the old bodice rippers. I have been reading and reviewing for years. In 2013, I created a blog, Lost in Romance Books, to promote and showcase indie authors. In 2014, I finally gave in to the characters in my head, screaming for their story to be told. From these musings, my first novel, Emma's Home, The Fairfield Series Book 1 was born.

I am a high school counselor having worked in education for thirty years. I live in Virginia, having also lived in four states and two foreign countries. I have been married to a wonderfully patient man for thirty-two years and am the mother to two adult daughters. When writing, my dog or one of my four cats can generally be found in the same room if not on my lap.

Please take the time to leave a review of this book (on Goodreads). Reviews are the lifeline for indie authors.

Feel free to contact me, especially if you enjoyed my book. I love to hear from readers!

Facebook:
www.facebook.com/authormaryannjordan

Facebook:
www.facebook.com/lostinromancebooks

Booktropolous:
booktropoloussocial.com/index.php?do=/profile-1765/

Email:
authormaryannjordan@gmail.com

Blog:
www.maryannjordanauthor.com

Dedication

When my parents retired, they decided to remain active devoting a great deal of time to the homeless population in our area. They sat outside a restaurant every Wednesday night to pick up the bread that had not been sold so they could take it to their church where on Thursday nights it was served with dinner to the homeless.

Over the years, they hauled and delivered thousands of pounds of bread that would have been thrown out and gave it to those less fortunate. This book is dedicated to them for their selfless acts and for all who work for the betterment of others.

PROLOGUE

THE AIR WAS thick; the wind swirled the dust up from the ground threatening to choke the men moving through the darkness. The night-vision goggles provided as clear a view as possible, but visual cues were limited. But that was all right. Each man in the Special Forces Team knew what to do in any circumstance. The dust storm would only confuse the enemy...not them.

Gabe Malloy trusted his brothers implicitly. There was no one he would rather be with than them at this moment. Their team was tasked with the missions that often involved search and rescue and right now, they were sent in to rescue the son of a local chief, sympathetic to the United States. He had been snatched from his home, after his father led an insurgence team against the enemy and was being held virtual hostage with his son kidnapped.

Locating the building, team leader Captain Tony Alvarez gave the order to move around to the side. Each man brought their own specialties to the group but were all cross-trained to perform every duty when needed. As the Medical Sergeant, Gabe would not be the first in the building, but with the condition of the child unknown, he had to be ready for anything.

Jobe, their Weapons Sergeant, moved to the back of the mud-brick building, scaling the wall to the roof. In a minute, he reported the visual he was obtaining. There were two boys in the room. One was the identified target and the other...wearing a suicide bomb vest.

Fuck. Gabe knew that he was not the only one of their team with that thought. In fact, he would bet that all twelve men had that on their minds at the exact same instance.

Tony and Assistant Commander, Chief Warrant Officer Bryant, quickly coordinated the rescue movements. Their Engineer Sergeant scaled the wall to where Jobe was located, to gain a visual as well. Eliminating a child was never what any of the men wanted to do, but if there was no other way, they would follow their mission to the letter.

Gabe's twin brother, Vinny, passed him heading to the roof as well. Trained as a Weapons Sergeant, he was also their back-up Medic. Vinny quickly aimed and shot the boy wearing the suicide vest with a tranquilizer. It would not knock him out completely, but would give them just enough time to grab the chief's son and make their escape. The child slumped to the ground unable to move and the others quickly entered the building, securing their mission.

As last man out, Gabe's eyes swept the inside of the

building landing on the child still laying on the dirt floor. The boy's dark eyes showed fear...and resignation. In a flash, Gabe realized that the child would die, knowing the insurgents would not let him live for failing to alert them to the rescue. The boy, who could not be more than ten, slowly moved his hand toward his vest, his eyes locked on Gabe's.

Gabe started toward him, but training took over instinct as the order for him to evacuate immediately came though his ear-piece. Turning, he ran out just before the explosion demolished the building behind him and shook the ground. Knocked to the dirt, he quickly pulled himself up and ran to the rendezvous, each man identifying their location and condition. They all made it out and he could hear the Communications Sergeant calling for their transport.

He could not help but do a visual scan of his eleven brothers, just to make sure they were all right. Vinny was in place, treating Jobe who took several wood splinters in his shoulder and neck, the latter causing quite a bit of bleeding. Gabe took over and quickly stopped the bleeding while Vinny checked out the terrified rescued boy.

The helicopter landed and the team members jumped on board, securing their mission, and taking off just as the insurgents were coming over the hill firing their weapons at the team.

The men were quiet until in the air and on their way back to base. The adrenaline that flowed with a successful rescue was palatable. Gabe continued to sit quietly, ignoring the pointed looks from Vinny and Tony.

They landed and were met with military personnel who whisked the child away and the twelve brothers-in-arms moved into their headquarters for the debriefing. Several hours later, the men made their way back to their barracks for showers and food before sleep. The others, still high on their success, hit the showers quickly, but Gabe found himself haunted by the eyes of the other boy. No matter how much he studied the enemy, he would never get used to their using children to try to kill them.

Vinny, his twin always in tune with him, walked over. "You okay, man?"

Gabe began stripping off his dusty, sandy fatigues. Rubbing his dirty hands over his gritty face, he sighed. "Yeah."

Tony walked into the room, looking at the identical twins in front of him. Gabe saw the captain give a head jerk to Vinny, who nodded and left the room toward the showers.

"Problem?" Tony asked. The captain was a man of few words.

"No, Sir," Gabe answered honestly.

Captain Alvarez said nothing but continued to stand in front of Gabe. Knowing the captain was not going to leave unless he was satisfied, Gabe sighed.

"Saw his eyes, Sir. Right before I realized he was

going to detonate." Silence filled the room, neither man saying anything. "Fuckin' hell," Gabe cursed, shaking his head.

Looking up into Tony's hard face, he saw the understanding eyes of his commander. "I'll never get used to them using kids, Sir."

"Good," came the captain's clipped response. "You do your job. You do it better than anyone else. You take out the enemy when ordered. But...," he speared Gabe with his penetrating stare, "you never forget that you care."

With that, Tony walked out of the room leaving Gabe alone with his thoughts. The room quickly began filling up with his teammates, scrubbed clean and ready to eat. Not wanting to miss their company, he hustled down the hall to the showers, letting the hot water pound his muscles and sluice over him. *Washing away the sand is easy. Wish I could get that fuckin' image out of my mind as easily.*

The camaraderie over the meal returned to the crude jokes, laughter, and dreams of beer-nights at bars filled with hot women. That night as the others slept, Gabe lay awake...the dark eyes of the desperate boy right before he reached for his vest haunted Gabe's thoughts. *Give me adults to work with,* he thought. *But keep kids out of the line of fire.*

THREE YEARS LATER

JARRING AWAKE, GABE sat up with sweat pouring off of him. Rubbing his hand over his face, he forced his breathing to regulate, not willing to give into the nightmare. His mouth was dry and his head pounded, both a result of the amount of whiskey he had drunk the night before. A moan startled him as he focused his eyes on the unfamiliar room. *Where the hell am I?* Glancing down at the naked woman sprawled out on the bed next to him had the memories rushing back.

His friend BJ's bachelor party. When the party was ending at the bar, he and a few other single friends stayed, drinking more while scoping out the eye-candy hanging around hoping to catch one of them.

"Who have you got in your sights, bro?" asked Vinny, knowing Gabe's penchant for leaving with the most gorgeous woman around.

Gabe looked at his twin and shook his head. "Just not feeling it tonight." If he was honest, he had not been 'feeling it' for a while. He had watched his detective friends Shane and Matt settle down and marry fabulous women and now BJ was marrying his friend, Suzanne. The constant search for a quick fuck was no longer holding the appeal that it once did.

"Jesus, you finally slowing down?" Jobe asked, a stunned look on his face.

"About time," came the sardonic voice of their employer, Tony.

6

With Jobe and Vinny's attention diverted by the prowling women who approached their table, Gabe glanced over at Tony. His boss smiled as he stood from the table, nodded to the others and then headed out into the night.

A heavily made-up blonde with huge tits showcased perfectly in a bustier made her way over to Gabe. Sliding down into his lap, she wasted no time expertly maneuvering her ass to bring his dick to life. Throwing her arms around his neck and pressing her boobs into his chest, she drug a long talon down his cheek. "Hey, big boy. You feeling lucky tonight?"

Oh, fuck it, he thought. Standing, he grabbed her hand and began stalking toward the door. Hearing the hoots from his brothers in the back, he threw up his hand in response as he left with the blonde.

Now it was the next morning and the sour taste of booze mixed with morning breath had him choking back a gag. *How much did I drink?* He never stayed with a woman all night so he was surprised that he was still there. Looking down at…*what the hell is her name?*

As if on cue, the woman stirred again and rolled over toward him before beginning to snore.

What looked sexy in the bar with a significant amount of whiskey was no longer what he wanted. Standing up, he grabbed his pants and then shrugged his shirt on.

Thirty minutes later, standing in the shower at his apartment, he washed off the stench of the bar and the woman's overpowering perfume. His mind rolled back to the times when he was washing off the sand and the stench of death. Of all the missions, none bothered him. Except one. And the dark eyes of the boy. A boy who was not even supposed to be part of the mission. A causality of war is what the report read. But in his mind, the boy would never be a casualty…but a child.

CHAPTER 1

T HE DARK NIGHT was brightly lit by the chandeliers hanging in the ballroom. Several men in tuxedoes walked around the perimeter of the room, eyes alert, in constant contact with each other through their state-of-the-art communication devices. As employees of Alvarez Security Agency, they took their roles seriously. The owner of the agency, Tony Alvarez, started his security business when he left the Special Forces and hired several of his brothers-in-arms. Their services included private security for special events, installation of security systems, and they worked closely with the Richland Police Department in several cases of search and rescue.

Tony's agency had been hired to provide private security at the gala, the celebration of the release of a movie that had been filmed in the capital city. Senators, congressmen, local and state dignitaries, as well as a host of Hollywood moguls, were on site. The men in dark tuxedoes provided the perfect backdrop for the swirl of colors in the evening gowns of the women in the gathering.

Jobe, uncomfortable in his tux, moved around the

perimeter, smiling as he saw Vinny moving among the beautiful actresses in the crowd. His eyes cut over to Gabe, who on the outside looked every bit the Hollywood hunk as the stunning star of the movie clung to his arm possessively. But Jobe knew what his brothers knew—Gabe was on alert.

Alicia Morgenstern always asked for Gabe to be her personal escort and he had agreed. She saw him the first time she was in town for the pre-filming event. Pissed at her co-star, she assumed hanging onto a gorgeous bodyguard would be the best way to make him jealous. It did not take long for her to quickly pick up on the handsome twins and she did not care which one she claimed. As Vinny was assigned to the director, she had no problem draping herself around Gabe. They fell into the habit of a quick fuck whenever she could get him alone and now that the filming was over, this might be her last time for a while.

Gabe looked over at Alicia as she moved from clinging to desperately trying to make him jealous. Sure, she had been a decent fuck on the occasions that she made it plain that she wanted him, but jealous? It took some kind of emotional investment to feel jealousy, and Gabe saw her for exactly what she was. Spoiled. Stuck-up. A prima donna. And right now, a pain in his ass.

Nodding toward Jobe, he spoke into his microphone. "Break. Move in."

Distancing himself from Alicia, he moved toward

the back door leading to the kitchens as Jobe maneuvered over to take his place on the watch. The kitchen was hot, with a multitude of staff moving in and out quickly. Looking at the crew as he walked through, he nodded to the kitchen manager as he pushed open the outside doors, moving into the cool of the night.

The air hit him like a blast, but he welcomed the crisp slap of the breeze blowing through the alley. Standing against the brick wall, he leaned his head back fighting the urge to pound it against the surface.

The last time he had to escort Alicia to an event, her blatant attempts to get him to sleep with her made him angry. He was tired of the one-night stands. *There's got to be more. If some of my friends are finding it, then...*

A noise coming from the dumpsters brought him instantly to alert as his body tensed and he pushed away from the wall. To his amazement, a child popped from behind the dumpsters carrying a box. Watching carefully, he saw the child deftly jump around the trash cans and move toward the kitchen doors. Wearing an old jacket with a hood pulled over his head, it was hard to distinguish his features.

"What do you think you're doing?" Gabe barked out, startling the urchin.

A squeak came from the child as they dropped the box and stumbled backward, tripping over some of the debris in the alley and landing on their ass. The hood flew off of their face and a mass of long, yellow blonde curls unfurled around the pixie face of the…*girl?*

Priding himself on his steel nerves, Gabe stared dumbly at the vision in front of him. The heart shaped face, with porcelain skin tinged with pink cheeks, stared up at him from the clearest blue eyes he had ever seen. Blue eyes that were staring at him in…anger.

Before he could reach out a hand to assist, she had quickly scrambled up dusting off her jeans. Breathing hard, she looked up at his face, furious at his intrusion.

"What I'm doing is none of your business," she huffed, bending over to retrieve her box, presenting him with a perfect view of a delicious ass.

He now knew this was no girl, but a full grown woman. His dick began to stir, surprising him. *Jesus, I've been around Alicia all night and all I've felt is disgust. I take a look at this tiny creature and I'm thinking…*

"What are you staring at?" she questioned, her blue eyes snapping. A gust of cold wind whipped down the alley causing her blonde curls to blow across her face. Setting the box down, she grabbed her hair and expertly twisted it into a messy knot at the back of her head and pulled her hood up once again. The wind also sent the empty box skittering several feet away, landing at Gabe's feet.

Before she could move, he scooped it up and held it. She walked over with her hand extended. He stared down into the blue depths of her eyes as though looking into a pool of swirling water, both crystal clear and leaving him wondering what lay beneath its surface.

"What do you need this box for?" his voice rumbled.

Stopping a few feet away from him she had to lean her head way back due to the height difference. "Again, a question that is none of your business," she stated daring him to differ.

Before he could reply, the kitchen door opened and Gabe found himself instinctively stepping in front of her for protection.

"Hey, have you seen a woman out here?" asked the kitchen manager, carrying several bags.

Before Gabe could respond, the woman moved from behind him. "Hi Carlos, I'm here. If this big oaf would move out of the way, you could see me!"

Carlos smiled at the woman before his eyes darted up to Gabe's. "Where's your truck?"

The smile left her face as a look of disgust rolled over her. "It died. But I've got someone who says they can get it running again soon. So for now, I'm on my two good legs."

"Dios girl. You shouldn't be out at night without at least that hunk of junk. If you wait a while, I can get you home."

"No need. I've got it. I know I can't take as much tonight without the truck, but if the giant here will give me my box, I'll take what I can and be on my way." Snatching the box from Gabe, she held it out to Carlos.

The strange exchange had Gabe speechless, a condition that he was not used to, nor liked. He watched as Carlos carefully placed several bags of food in the box before handing it to the woman. A smile lit her face that had Gabe swearing he had been punched in the gut. Her expression shone with beauty and her blonde curls once again escaped their bun and swirled around her pixie face. Her ears stuck out ever so slightly at the top giving her an otherworldly look.

She turned to walk away when he was jolted into action. "Wait," he called out. "You can't walk to wherever you're going. I'll take you home."

Just then the kitchen door crashed open once more, as Alicia stumbled out with Jobe right behind her. Gabe's angry eyes glared at the interruption and he grabbed Alicia to keep her from falling.

Jobe's equally angry look was explained quickly. "Sorry, man. She realized you hadn't come back and pitched a fit to get to you saying she was going to sue Alvarez if she couldn't find you."

Alicia looked at the girl with the box and turned her drunk gaze over to Gabe. Draping herself over him again, she crooned, "Baby, I couldn't find you. What if someone got to me while you were out here talking to...who is that?" Turning her attention to the other woman, she continued, "God, you look like some kind of alley trash. Do you actually live in the dump?"

The woman gasped and Gabe jerked on Alicia's arm, swinging her around to him.

"Shut the fuck up, Alicia."

"What? You're out here chatting with some garbage-crawler and not doing your job escorting me and I'm supposed to be all right with that?"

Before Gabe could answer, the woman turned quickly, hustling around the corner out of sight, carrying the heavy box.

"Baby, it's cold," whined Alicia as she pulled on his arm.

"You should have stayed inside then," he growled as he maneuvered her toward the kitchen door. Jobe moved ahead of her, holding the door as he saw that Gabe had stopped to talk to the other man standing there.

Before Gabe could speak, Carlos had turned to one of the kitchen staff barking, "Follow her, Jim."

A bald, barrel-chested man, arms covered in tattoos nodded and headed down the alley. Gabe swung his eyes back to Carlos in question. Carlos caught the look and just said, "She'll be fine. She's a regular and Jim'll see her safe."

"Gabester, come on," came the drunken whine from the kitchen.

Furious with Alicia, himself, and the entire fucked-up encounter, he stalked back in. Walking brusquely past her he headed back to the ballroom leaving her to wobble on her heels to catch up, with Jobe taking the rear.

Re-entering the gala, the other men of Alvarez Security could see the anger in Gabe's eyes, although to the rest of the gathering he played the bodyguard host perfectly. By the end of the evening, he had pried Alicia's grasping claws off of his arm for the last time, depositing her with her manager.

"I need you to see me to my room, Gabie dear," she purred with a wink.

"My shift is over Ms. Morgenstern." Looking at her manager, he said, "And if you check your contract, I believe that you will find that Alvarez Security has fulfilled its obligation."

"But James," she pleaded, turning to the man standing behind her. "I'm not safe. You know I have someone after me."

The beleaguered manager looked up at the wall of testosterone that had approached, swallowing several times.

"Is there a problem?" Tony clipped.

Her eyes narrowing, she bit out, "Yes. I want to be escorted up to my hotel suite and I want Gabe to do it. It's in my contract for me to have access to him and if I need to, I'll call my lawyer."

The men looked with disgust at the woman standing in front of them. Tony, not moved by threats, loomed over the statuesque woman but focused his comments to the manager. "You will find that Alvarez Security has fulfilled their obligations to the letter. If you feel unsafe, then you need to call the police and discuss it with them." With that, the men turned and walked away from the steaming woman.

"I can't believe you'd just walk away. You know who I am. I can break your little security business you know. One word from me and no one will want you."

At that, the men laughed out loud, their mirth angering her further. "Fine, the next time your dick gets lonely for me, don't come calling," she called out loudly gaining the attention of several bystanders.

With a quick scan, Gabe assured himself that there were no press nearby, but with cellphone cameras everywhere he forced himself to stay as calm as possible while stalking back over to her. Leaning down, so that only she could hear, he whispered, "Banging you was the biggest mistake I've made in a long time. You were a convenient fuck and we both knew it at the time. And truthfully, not a good fuck at that. But hear me now and hear me well—I don't take to threats. My dick doesn't come at your beck and call. And if you don't turn and walk away, then you'll get a public scene that'll not be good for your career. You get me?"

With one last pull on her arm, her manager managed to drag her across the room to the doors. Gabe stood there for a moment, trying to gain control of his anger. *I shoulda' never fucked her.* It had seemed so easy at the time and they had only been together three times. *Never shoulda' done it the first time and sure as shit, never shoulda' gone back.*

Feeling a hand on his shoulder, he looked up to see Vinny standing there, concern on his face. "You okay, bro? Forget her."

"Yeah, well your dick didn't just get the agency in trouble."

"No trouble," came Tony's response. "Our contract was for escorting and providing security while at the events only. What you do or don't do on your time is your business." With that, Tony, Jobe, and the others headed out.

"You coming?" Vinny asked when Gabe made no move to follow them.

"Nah, you go on out. I'm going to check in on something in the kitchen." He turned and walked back into the kitchen, which was in full swing of the evening clean-up. His eyes landed on Jim, but before he could walk over to him he was intercepted by Carlos.

"She's fine."

Gabe eyed the man. "Who is she?"

"What's it to you? With that tux and that actress on your arm, what do you care about the girl in the alley? Not exactly your type, is she?"

Not used to being questioned, Gabe moved in another step. "Just want to know her story."

Carlos stared at the large man in front of him, seeing the questions in his eyes. He was good at reading people and had to admit to himself, this man gave off a trustworthy vibe. Nodding slowly, he jerked his head to the side before turning and moving toward the kitchen doors again.

Gabe followed him out then waited, not so patiently, while Carlos lit a cigarette and took a long pull on it.

"She comes some evenings and gets bread and food that hasn't been used. Occasionally, I'll slip in something special, but mostly she just comes for the bread. The manager knows and approves so I give her what she needs." With that he smiled, looking over at the alley.

"Bet you'd give it to her whether the manager approved or not," Gabe observed.

"Yeah," Carlos said, taking another long drag. "She usually takes more when her old junker truck is working, but like tonight," he shrugged, "she comes on foot if she has too."

"What does she do with the bread?" Gabe asked, intrigued now more than ever.

"Don't know. Don't ask. But I got a feeling it isn't for her." At Gabe's raised eyebrow, Carlos continued. "Jim's followed her a couple of times when she was on foot and said that she gives some of it away to homeless people on the way."

At that, Gabe reared back. "What the fuck?" The thought of the tiny woman moving among the streets at night, offering something to unknown people, floored him. "Is she crazy? Does she have any idea how dangerous that is?"

With one last drag on his cigarette, Carlos dropped it and crushed the butt under the heel of his boot. "Got a feeling that little one knows what she's doing. And as long as she comes here looking for handouts, I'll give 'em to her." Turning, he walked back into the kitchen, leaving Gabe standing in the dark alley.

Pulling up the collar of his tux, he walked toward the parking garage and his new truck, thoughts of the pixie swirling through his mind. *Pixie?* He suddenly remembered a story his mother used to read when he and Vinny were young, about a pixie fairy flying out of the woods to help a boy who had been captured by a witch. While he couldn't recall the details of the story, he vividly remembered the pictures. And the woman from the alley with her blonde curls blowing wildly around her perfect face and her slightly protruding ears, she looked exactly like the drawing in the book.

Walking into his apartment, he tossed his keys on the table in the entrance hall. Pulling off his tux as he headed through the bedroom and into the luxury bathroom, he turned on the shower. A few minutes later he walked back through the large apartment to the refrigerator, snagging a water bottle. Taking a long drink, his mind continued to play the meeting with the mysterious woman over and over. And once again, his dick was coming to attention.

What the fuck am I doing? It was a chance encounter. A one-time meeting. That's all. Trying to force the thoughts of her out of his mind should have been easy. His Special Forces training had him prepared to clear his thoughts in an instant to re-focus on the mission at hand. Unfortunately, his mind was not prepared to let her go. As though *she* had become his mission.

JENNIFER'S ARMS WERE aching by the time she made it to the first floor of her building. An older man was standing by the back door as she turned into the alley.

"Miss Jennifer, I was afraid somethin' had happened," he exclaimed as he hustled to her aid.

"Oh, the stupid truck wouldn't start and I had to walk. I didn't get as much," she explained as she handed the box to the older man. "It's the best I could do, Henry."

He bestowed her with a benevolent look, smiling as he took the box from her arms. "Lordy girl, this box is heavy." Hesitating for just a moment, he looked at her beautiful but tired face. "But it's appreciated."

Gifted with her smile, he just shook his head. "Go on up. Ross is waitin' for you."

With that incentive, she took the stairs two at a time, all the way to the third floor. Walking down the well-lit hall, she ignored the peeling paint and worn tiles. Getting to her apartment, she tapped out the special knock on the old wooden door and heard the sound of several locks being unlatched. Throwing open the door, she was almost knocked over with a bear hug from Ross.

"I missed you," he effused.

Laughing she replied, "I wasn't gone that long, you know."

"I know, but I can't go to sleep until you get

home."

Lifting one eyebrow, she asked, "Well, are you ready to head to bed now?"

"Oh yeah." He grabbed her hand and led her toward the back of the small apartment. Hopping into the bed, he grinned as he turned toward her.

She walked over, love shining in her blue eyes, and grabbed the covers to pull them up. Tucking him in, she whispered, "I love you, Ross."

"I love you too, sis," came the reply. "Tell me a story."

Piling up on the bed with him, it only took a few minutes for her to regale him with tales of dragons, little boys being rescued, beautiful fairies and tonight she couldn't help but add in giants. In a few minutes, he fell asleep and she gently stood from the bed, careful not to wake him.

Kissing the top of his blond head, she left his bedroom making sure the night-light was on. He may be eight years old, but Ross still liked having some light at night.

Walking back into the kitchen, she ran a glass full of tap-water. Taking a large drink, her mind wandered back to the man she encountered in the alley. *Arrogant giant*, thinking of him standing there in his immaculate tuxedo. *Well, gorgeous, Greek god-like arrogant giant*, she admitted to herself. He was huge and even though most men seemed large to her five foot, two inches petite frame...he was larger than most by far. His muscles were hidden beneath the expensive fabric, but she had no doubt that they were there if his square jaw and thick neck were anything to go by.

A warm feeling began to curl in her stomach and descend as she imagined what it would be like to be held by him. Then the image of the woman who was a dead ringer for Alicia Morgenstern came to mind. *Arghhh…she called me alley trash! What a bitch.* Glancing down at her apparel, she paused. Jeans that she had had for years and were worn at the knees and seat. A jacket that had been given to her for the purpose of staying warm on the nights she went to pick up bread, but it too had seen better days. The image of the woman in her sky-high heels, black evening dress with a slit up to her thigh showing off impossibly long legs, and her boobs. *Good Lord, those things looked like they needed their own zip code.*

Sighing, she walked around the bar toward the tiny bathroom and stripped as she ran the water into the tub. It was an extra small tub, but it was a feature of the apartment that she loved. Turning, she looked into the mirror. Long, tangled blonde curls hung down her back. Pulling it up on her head, she noticed her slightly pointy ears giving her the elfish look she always hated. Clear skin, blue eyes. Glancing down, she knew she had curves that were generally hidden under large clothes, but nowhere near the monster curves of the woman clinging to the giant.

Forcing herself to put him out of her mind, she

took a quick bath and then climbed into bed. She normally fell asleep thinking of all of the things that needed to be done the next day, but tonight was different. This night, a handsome giant filled her dreams.

CHAPTER 2

THE MORNING SUN peeked through the old blinds and pretty pink curtains in Jennifer's bedroom as her radio alarm began blasting country music. Slamming her hand on the snooze button, she needed the extra ten minutes. Ross had other plans.

"Jennybenny," he yelled from the bathroom. "You gotta get up."

Weren't kids supposed to want to sleep late? Maybe the alarm is wrong. Sitting up in bed, she pushed her sleep tousled curls out of her face and looked at the clock. Nope, it was six o'clock. Time to begin their well-ordered morning.

Ross was dressed and out of the bathroom by the time she made it in there. Her morning routine was simple; quick shower, moisturizer and mascara, and she hopped in her slacks and blouse. Sliding on her basic two-inch pumps she remembered the sky-high heels of the lady from last night. *That woman had to be almost six feet tall without the heels. And I bet those shoes cost more than my month's salary!* Those thoughts had her quickly thinking of the mystery man from last night. As tall as that woman had been, he had been taller. *No*

25

wonder he looked like a giant. That thought was followed by the realization of what she must have looked like.

Grimacing, she moved to the kitchen where Ross was eating his cereal with the TV on. The local anchorman was talking about the huge gala event last evening to celebrate the completion of a movie filmed in Richland. Recognizing the name of the hotel as the one she was at last night, she turned to see the screen just as glamorous Alicia Morgenstern was alighting from a limo, her arm on…the giant in the tux.

She could not stop the desire to see him once again as she walked closer to the old, small TV. *Yep, he was just as gorgeous as her memory recalled.* Seeing Alicia turn and latch onto his arm had Jennifer clicking the TV off. *So out of my league.* A giggle erupted from her as she realized that the famous movie star had called her alley trash. *Wow, I was insulted by someone famous,* she thought wryly.

Glancing at the clock, she was glad Ross had gotten up on time since she could not seem to get her act together this morning.

"Got your homework, sweetie?"

"Yeah. Oh and you need to sign this," he said as he pushed a piece of paper across the counter toward her.

Looking down at the school form, she saw a description of an upcoming field trip and a place for the parent/guardian to sign. Her fingers rested on the word as her mind slid back to just a year ago when her mom would have been excited to have signed the form.

She looked up and caught Ross staring at her.

"Are you okay, sis?" he asked with more concern than most eight-year-olds have to muster.

Ruffling his hair, she smiled. "I'm good. Just took a little trip, that's all."

Ross grinned in understanding. That was their mom's saying for when her mind wandered. Jennifer signed the form and watched him put it in his backpack, making sure to zip it closed.

Walking him to the corner, she waited until the school bus pulled up and saw him safely aboard before she turned and went back into the center. Walking into the kitchen area of one of the city's elder centers she found Henry.

"Good morning," she called pouring two cups of coffee. Handing him one, she splashed a liberal amount of cream and sugar in hers before taking a swig. "Mmmmm," she purred. "Now my day can begin."

Henry laughed as he stirred the huge pot of oatmeal that they would be serving. His wife, Cora, came from the back with some of the bread that Jennifer had brought in last night from the restaurant.

"Hey darling," the older woman greeted. "These rolls are gonna be such a treat with some honey and jam and the oatmeal this morning."

"She walked since her truck wasn't working," Henry tattled to his wife.

"Girl, you know better than that," she exclaimed,

looking at Jennifer as though she were a recalcitrant child instead of a woman used to making her own decisions.

"Oh it was fine and I could tell that Carlos sent Jim to make sure I was all right," she added, although her mind wondered what it would have been like to have the giant escort her home. Shaking her head to stop the musings, she moved with practice to the serving area of the center, taking a stack of bowls with her.

The elderly residents walked through, the women first and followed by the men. Greeting each person coming through the line with a smile and a hearty helping of breakfast, the hour passed quickly. Walking around the tables, she differed their thanks back to Henry and Cora, who ran the center and reminded the residents that they would need to assist with clean-up. One of the men told her that he would be taking a look at her truck to get it running for her. Smiling her thanks, she glanced at the clock on the wall before hurrying to the back to grab her purse and briefcase.

"Bye, see you this afternoon," she yelled as she hustled to the corner to catch the bus. It took thirty minutes to get to work, changing buses twice. With her head buried in her Kindle, she never noticed the stares of the men around, but her innocence only added to her attraction.

Hopping out of the bus, she headed into the tall, government building that housed the Department of Social Services. Settling her things in the small cubicle, she began clicking through emails and then piles of records. She was combining her specialties having written her thesis on the increasing homelessness of the elderly.

"Hey girl," a cheery voice came from behind.

Smiling, she looked up at Sybil walking over to toss her oversized bag into her cubicle, followed by Roy, who was already pulling out his cell phone.

"Baby pics," the two women squealed as Roy turned his phone around to show them his new twins. Having been on paternity leave for several weeks, this was his first day back. Cooing over the pictures, the group did not hear their boss, Chip, walking over.

"Meeting at nine," he said as he walked by.

"I swear, grouchy-pants must not be gettin' any," Sybil quipped. Turning her eyes to Jennifer, she grinned. "But then if you would agree to go out with him, maybe he wouldn't be such a grouch!"

"Oh no," Jennifer said, rolling her eyes. "I've told you I have no time to date and on top of that, I would never date the boss."

The three settled into their work, but Jennifer could not keep her mind on the files in front of her. Tall, strong jaw, short hair. Eyes that seemed as though they would miss nothing. It was obvious that the tux had been tailored for him. If she had moved closer to him, her head would have fit under his chin. *And if he'd wrapped those arms—*

"Jennifer!" Sybil shouted, startling her. Jumping,

she turned to her friend. "What?" she questioned.

"I've been calling for almost a minute. We've got our meeting."

"Oh, I was…um…reading the files," she explained, not able to control her blush.

"Uh huh. With that look on your face girl, you weren't thinkin' of no file!"

Shushing her friend, they made their way to the small conference room.

BLOCKS AWAY, GABE walked into Alvarez Security. He was running late; sleep had eluded him the night before. A year ago he would have come out of Alicia's hotel suite after a night of fucking. As he headed home from the gala, the idea of dipping it in her again turned his stomach. And on top of that, his night was filled with thoughts of *the mystery girl. What woman goes out in the night to pick up bread to take to homeless people? Who goes searching for a box in a dumpster?* He wanted to be suspicious, thinking that she must have an alternative purpose. His detective friends had worked a case where the drugs were hidden in dumpsters for the next person in the chain to pick up.

Is that what she was doing? But Carlos trusts her. And the manager knows what she does with the bread. As his mind had been trying to figure her out, his dick had responded to the call of the wild. He hadn't been able to get her beauty out of his mind. Pure. Ethereal. So unlike Alicia's carefully crafted looks.

Shaking his head, he entered the building from the underground employee parking garage, making his way to the hub of the agency. Customers coming through the front doors would be met by a pleasant receptionist and then escorted to one of several conference rooms. But behind the steel-reinforced wooden doors near the back that needed a security code to enter, was the agency's actual work area. There were offices, a conference room surrounding a large open area filled with communication devices, computers, large screens mounted on the walls, and everything else that they needed to assist them in their missions.

Greeting the others, his twin smiled as he pointed to his watch. Flipping him off, Gabe just kept walking. Straight to Tony's office. Knocking twice, he waited until he heard the call "Enter". Walking in, he found himself standing at attention before relaxing.

Tony looked up and grinned. "Old habits?"

"Yes. They die hard," he added as he fought the urge to call him Captain.

Tony nodded toward the chair and let Gabe take the time to get settled. The silence hung for just a moment, each man comfortable in the knowledge that the words would come at the right time.

"Tony, I wanted to thank you for the opportunity to work for you," Gabe started. "I know that last year I agreed to take whatever assignments you had for me, but I'd like to make a request if possible."

Nodding, Tony said, "I'm listening."

"I let things get out of the realm of professional with Ms. Morgenstern and last night showed that kind of error put this agency in a bad situation."

"I agree that sleeping with a client isn't what I think is the best thing to, but you were off the clock and I'm not going to dictate to my staff who they can and can't see."

Shaking his head, Gabe responded, "I appreciate that, sir. Do you think that there will be any ramifications from her camp?"

Tony bark out a sound. "Don't sweat it. We fulfilled our contract. Her manager will take care of her and reign her in. We only have one more contractual obligation with her and that is for the premier in several months." Looking at Gabe's sudden uncomfortable expression, Tony said, "Ah. Is that the request?"

"If possible, I'd rather not be the person that escorts her for that event."

Tony laughed as he said, "Not a problem. I have several people that can easily supply that coverage."

Nodding, Gabe stood and turned to leave. Walking back toward the others, Vinny came over.

"Bro, you okay?"

"Yeah, just needed to apologize to Tony about the Alicia fiasco."

Jobe strolled over, hearing the last comment. "Jesus, that woman was a piece of work. I used to envy you, man, until I had to spend some time with her last night."

"I was a dumb fuck to ever cross the professional line with her and let her get her claws in me."

"Tony okay with you?" Vinny asked.

Nodding, Gabe answered, "Yeah, he's cool. We only have one more assignment with her, but that's in several months so maybe she'll have someone else she can pester by then."

"Who was that woman in the alley last night?" Jobe asked.

"Woman?" Vinny complained. "You never mentioned a woman last night other than Alicia. You holdin' out on me bro?"

Giving what he hoped was a nonchalant shrug, he replied honestly, "Don't know. Never saw her before."

Seeing the men standing around waiting for a more complete answer, he just said, "She was out there waiting to get some food from Carlos."

Just then, Tony called a staff meeting and Gabe was glad for the distraction. Walking toward the conference room, he felt Vinny's hand on his shoulder.

"Don't think you're getting off that easy. You may have them fooled, but remember I'm your other half," he said.

Gabe hung his head as they continued walking. *I should have known it. No way he's not going to notice I've got this girl on my mind.*

Vinny used his spare key and walked into Gabe's apartment. Moving over to the fully stocked kitchen, he made himself at home grabbing a beer out of the refrigerator. A few minutes later Gabe came up from the exercise room.

Vinny's apartment was in the same building and the amenities were one of the reasons both men lived there. A gym and indoor swimming pool, plus the security, made it a perfect place to relax after work or a mission. Saving money from their days in the Special Forces and then with the excellent pay they received from Tony, they decided not to scrimp on their living conditions.

Gabe walked past Vinny, moving toward the refrigerator where he grabbed the ingredients for a protein shake. Once they settled on the oversized sofas in the living room, Vinny finally broke the silence.

"So, are you going to tell me about the girl in the alley or not?"

Gabe considered for only a second keeping it to himself, but knowing his twin would see through him, he acquiesced.

"Hell, brother. I don't even know what to say. I went outside to get away from Alicia and get some fresh air. Caught what I thought was a kid in the dumpster. Turned out to be a woman."

"In the dumpster? What the hell was she doing in

the dumpster?"

"Getting a box."

"A box? What the fuck did she need a box for?"

"It seems she comes to the restaurant sometimes to pick up the bread that was baked but not served. I talked to the kitchen manager and he said it would have just been thrown out. She comes and gets it, but I don't know what the fuck for."

Vinny looked at his brother carefully. "There's more. What are you not telling me?"

Gabe looked out of the window for a moment, trying to gather his swirling thoughts. "There was something about her. Something...I don't know. Jesus, this sounds so ridiculous. I mean, we've both pounded any woman that was willing for the past few years, but recently I've been...wanting something..."

"Like what Shane, Matt, and BJ have?" Vinny asked, referring to their friends who had recently gotten married to amazing women. "So what about this woman brought out those thoughts? I mean a woman crawling around in dumpsters at night doesn't exactly bring to mind a happily-ever-after feeling," Vinny quipped.

Gabe shook his head, saying, "I don't know. She was gorgeous. She kind of looked like a little elf. Tiny. Dressed for comfort but not shabby. I startled her when I caught her but then there was the most amazing look on her face.

Vinny laughed. "Oh yeah, that look that says I

want to jump this guy?"

"No! Not at all," Gabe said, seeing the disbelieving look on his brother's face.

"What then?

Rubbing his hand over his face again, he said ruefully, "More like she wanted to tell me to get lost."

"Well, that'd be a first," Vinny joked. After a moment of mirth, he sobered looking as his twin grappled with his emotions. "Do you...want to see her? Again, I mean?"

Gabe looked over, the corner of his mouth quirking. "Yeah. Yeah, I do."

"So where will you find her?"

Gabe laughed and answered, "I guess the only place I know that she'll be."

"The dumpster behind the restaurant?"

"Yep. I'm heading there tonight."

THE NIGHT SKY was clear with the stars piercing the darkness. There was a full moon giving illumination to the alley, as well as the dim street lights. Gabe made sure that Carlos knew he was there but refused his offer to wait in the warm kitchen. He preferred to see her immediately when she came. And if he was honest he did not want her in the alley alone.

But she didn't come. Not that night. Nor the next. Nor the next. By Thursday, Gabe's frustration was at an all-time high and Vinny finally cornered him after work in the gym.

"Bro, what the hell's been wrong with you all week? The only person you haven't snapped at is Lily and that's only because you know the rest of us would chew your ass if you did."

Gabe's answer was a glare as he continued on the treadmill, his leg muscles corded with definition and his shirt soaked with sweat.

With a flip of his hand, Vinny pulled the emergency switch on the treadmill, causing Gabe to slip backward, barely catching himself from falling on his ass.

Rounding on his brother, he growled, "What the fuck are you doing? Tryin' to kill me?"

Calmly sitting down on the nearest weight bench, Vinny smirked at Gabe and said nothing. Just stared. And continued to smirk.

Gabe tried to ignore him but finally heaved a huge sigh and said, "You know you're a pain in my ass?" while sitting down on the other bench.

"Yeah well, it's one of my more endearing qualities," he said laughing.

The silence rested between the twins for a few minutes, each comfortable with the quiet and waiting.

"Is it the girl?" Vinny finally asked.

"Yeah," was Gabe's only reply, shaking his head.

"Look, you've been back to find her and she's now under your skin. But bro, you don't even know her.

And by the description, she's not your type."

At that, Gabe looked up sharply. "My type?"

"Oh, come on. You've always gone for the tall girls that you don't have to bend so much to kiss. Or fuck standing up for that matter."

Gabe lifted his eyebrow, saying sarcastically, "Anything else you want to enlighten me on about my type of woman?"

"Okay fine. You like 'em tall and built. You like tits and ass and long legs. From what you said, this girl's got none of those!"

"You're crazy, Vin. I don't have a type and...I...oh hell. I don't know what it was about her that's got me so tied up."

Vinny stood and pulled Gabe up with him. "Go shower and get cleaned up. I'm taking you out tonight and we'll find some fun. Go to a bar, pick up a girl, and get your rocks off and that'll get this unknown girl out of your head."

"You fucker, I've got no interest in getting' my rocks off, as you say."

"Fine, then we're still going out. Have some drinks and have some fun. Anything to get you out of this morose mood you've been in all week."

Two hours later, the twins sat at the bar drinking and Gabe found himself relaxing for the first time in days. *Maybe this is what I needed, after all.*

Their muscular frames were perfectly showcased in jeans that stretched over their trunk-like thighs and collared shirts with sleeves rolled up, partially exposing their corded arms and tattoos. The women in the bar began to swarm around, wondering who was going to get lucky that night. Vinny charmed several of them, but Gabe found himself unable to get interested.

A noise from the other side of the bar caught his attention and looking over saw an elderly man, obvioulsy drunk, being propped up on his bar stool by one of the bartenders. The head bartender came over saying, "Mr. Courtland, we've made a call. Someone's coming to get you now." Turning to the other bartender he growled, "Why didn't you cut him off earlier?"

"He hadn't drunk that much," came the defensive answer.

Gabe and Vinny pushed past the group of women and walked over to see if they could help. "You need any assistance?" Gabe asked as Vinny moved over to steady the man.

"Thanks, but we got it. There's someone we call who comes and gets him home when this happens. I'll move him over to one of the booths so that he won't fall."

Without creating too much attention, Vinny and Gabe assisted in making the man comfortable in a discreet booth. The bartender smiled and poured them a round on the house. The ladies began circling again like vultures and it didn't take long for Vinny to have a red-head poured into a tight, almost not-there dress on his lap with her breasts pressed into his chest.

Rolling his eyes, Gabe was turning back to the bar when the red-head's friend, a busty brunette decided that she'd just take what Gabe hadn't offered. His lap.

Throwing his arms around the woman before she slipped off of him and landed on the floor, he ended up with her half across his lap, her arms around his neck pulling him close.

At that moment, the bartender looked up and smiled, saying, "Hey darlin'. Glad you could come. Do you need some help?"

"No, but thank you. Henry's got my old truck outside, but if we turn it off it may not start again," she laughed.

Gabe startled, recognizing that voice. Whirling around on his bar stool, almost dumping the woman in his lap, he saw her bending over the old man in the booth. Her long curls were pulled back in a low ponytail with loose strands flowing around the beautiful face that had haunted him since he met her. Tonight, she was wearing yoga pants that showcased a delectable ass and a worn t-shirt that pulled slightly between her full breasts. *You? What the fuck?* He did not realize that he spoke his thoughts out loud until she turned and looked at him.

Jennifer stood numbly staring into the handsome face of the man from outside the restaurant. In an instant, she took him all in. From his square jaw with a slight stubble, to his corded neck, down to the shirt and jeans that strained to contain his muscles. And holy hell, the edge of a Celtic tattoo peeked out from his sleeve. *Him? My giant?* And draped over that amazing body was…a barely dressed woman glaring back at her.

Whirling around to the booth again, she could feel the blush rising from her chest to her hair. Her cheeks warm, she wished she could just run out, but it did not look like the elderly man was going to cooperate. "Come on, Mr. Courtland, you've got to help me," she pleaded, trying to grasp him under the arms.

Suddenly two large arms came from behind and gently moved her to the side. Twisting her head around, she looked up into his face. *Wait. Not his face!* Before she could question what was happening, she felt someone take her by her arms and gently pull her over once again. This time, it was the face that she saw in her dreams.

Standing to her full, if not consequential, height she put her hands on her hips looking back and forth between the two giants. *Oh my God, twins. Damn.*

"Hey darlin', I'm Vinny and this here's my brother, Gabe."

Gabe. His name is Gabe. The blush remained but before she could speak, Mr. Courtland began to stand reaching for her.

"Oh, sweet girl. Dish ya come fer me?" he slurred.

"Yes, Mr. Courtland. Let's get you to my truck. Henry's outside keeping it warm for you. Let's go now," she spoke sweetly.

Before the elderly man could lean his weight on her, Gabe stepped in and took him while Vinny claimed his other side. Between the two men, they deftly maneuvered him outside where a beat-up old truck sat idling, leaving her to follow behind.

Henry jumped out, opening the passenger door. "Oh dear, oh dear, Rupert. Now let's get you home and in bed where you can sleep this one off."

Gabe and Vinny managed to get Rupert into the truck and buckled in before he slumped against the window. Jennifer stood awkwardly to the side, unused to assistance. When they finished, she walked over, leaning her head back to look the two men in the eye.

"Thank you, I...um...well, I usually just...um. Well, thank you," she stammered while shaking Vinny's hand.

He lifted her hand and kissed it before handing her to Gabe. Gabe also held her hand, but he didn't let it go. Rubbing her palm with his fingers sent tingles throughout her body. Jerking her hand back quickly, she once again felt the blush rise from her chest to the roots of her curls.

She moved to get into the truck when Gabe realized that not only was she leaving, she was going to be squished in the middle of the old truck seat.

"I'll take you home," he said. "We'll follow and then I can help you with Mr. Courtland."

Vinny, having figured out that the tiny beauty in front of them was the woman that had his brother tied up in knots all week, just smiled. "That's a wonderful idea, darlin'. Let Gabe escort you home."

Shooting his twin a quick look of gratitude, he was about to pull her closer when suddenly the two women from the bar moved over, grasping the twins.

"Honey, did you get that drunk man of yours?" the red-head said slyly.

Her friend, the busty brunette giggled as she grabbed Gabe's arm. "Come on in, Gabe."

Vinny and Gabe growled simultaneously, trying to disentangle themselves from the grasping claws of the two. Sending them back inside, Gabe turned just in time to see the woman between the two older men in the truck as it pulled quickly from the parking lot.

"Fuck," he bit out. "I just found her only to lose her again."

Vinny, rid of the bar trolls, moved up beside him slapping him on his shoulder. "Yeah, but this time, bro, you've got more than you had." Smiling at Gabe's questioning look, he continued, "I got her license number."

Sighing deeply, Gabe smiled. "I owe you, man. I owe you."

CHAPTER 3

HENRY LOOKED UP as Jennifer headed toward the back door. "You don't have to go, you know," he called out.

Turning, she smiled, rolling her eyes. "I'll be fine. Cora is watching Ross and now that the truck is running, I want to get more food." Walking to the door, she gave a wave and headed out into the night.

The old truck rumbled into the alley behind the hotel and she pulled as close to the kitchen door as possible. The driver's door screeched horribly as she opened it to hop out. The door became stuck so she leaned her weight against it to close it all the way. She glanced over at the dumpster and saw several boxes stacked neatly as though someone had known she was coming. *Carlos must have left them for me,* she thought, grateful that she did not have to dig through the trash. A sudden memory washed over her as she remembered her encounter with the handsome man when she was here the last time.

Hearing a noise near the kitchen door, she turned expectantly. Eyes bright, her exclamations of greetings were stuck in her throat as a figure moved out into the

44

light. Gasping, she stepped back. *Him! Jesus is he everywhere? What's he doing here?*

Gabe, having come for the past two nights only to go home disappointed, found his heart pounding at seeing her again. The blonde curls were tucked under a knit cap this time, but some had escaped and blew around her cheeks. Dressed similarly to the first time he saw her, he noticed the warm but worn jacket. And her eyes…sapphire crystals focused on him.

Giving his most charming smile, he pushed off of the brick wall and walked over to her truck, careful not to move too quickly nor too close. He snagged the boxes from the ground, asking, "Are these good enough for what you need, Jennifer?"

Stunned into silence, she just nodded before she quickly reacted. "How do you know my name? And what are you doing here?" Walking to the back of her truck, she stood next to him, glaring up.

He saw her stalk over, both admiring her courage and strangely angered at her lack of concern in talking so boldly with a large stranger in a dim alley. While he would never hurt her, she could not know that. Leaning against the truck, he casually crossed one tree-trunk leg over the other.

"Thought I'd come help you out," he said, turning on the charm once again.

Jennifer gave an unladylike snort and rolled her eyes. "Aren't you missing your movie star friend? Or wait, maybe the half-dressed woman from the bar?"

Irritation flashed through his eyes for a second, then he answered, "Nope. I'm here to see you tonight."

"Me? What makes you think I could afford you even if I did want an escort?" she said indignantly, pushing by him to move toward the kitchen door.

"Afford?" he asked, eyebrow lifting in confusion. "What the hell are you talking about?"

Not even turning to look at him, lest her eyes give away her interest, she said, "I heard what your movie star said. She said you were her escort, so I figured she paid you to do…um… that."

Laughter rang out from the kitchen door as Carlos came out. "Escort service? Oh Gabe, that's a good one," he cackled. Turning back to her he asked, "You ready, Miss Jennifer?"

Nodding to Carlos, she started taking the food bags from his hands and turned to walk back to her truck. And slammed straight into a brick wall. Or rather a human wall. Of muscle. Named Gabe. *Jesus, he's big. Probably big everywhere.* Feeling the blush creep up her face again, she chastised herself. *Get over it girl. That hunk isn't for you and you certainly aren't for him.*

Seeing her stumble again, Gabe reached out his arms and deftly steadied her by the shoulders. "Seems like you keep wanting to land on your ass, when I'm around," he joked, as he noticed the flash of interest in her eyes.

She peered up at his face, noting the dark shadow of his beard stubble on his jaw. His eyes were an unusual shade of green with flecks of gold that caught the lights coming from the open kitchen door. "You never did answer my questions," she said, trying to get her thoughts back on track.

"It's simple. I looked up your truck registration from the tags because I wanted to meet you."

She stared numbly as she turned and looked at his face, her mind trying to process both pieces of information. "You...you looked up...my..." Her confused look turned angry as she placed the bags in the back of the truck and then stalked over to poke her finger in his chest. "You looked up my tags? Is that even legal?" her voice rising with each word.

He threw his head back in laughter feeling her tiny finger poking him. "Yes," he replied looking back down at her angelic face. "It's public record. Anyone can look it up," he explained gently as though speaking to a child. He saw her eyes narrow with concentration, then fly open wide as she processed the rest of what he had said.

"What do you mean you came here to meet me?" she asked incredulously. *This man hangs out with movie stars. Or women in bars that look like they could be in movies. Well, playing the trashy slut in a movie. What the hell does he want with me?*

Gabe, mesmerized by her blue eyes, could see the questions flying through her mind. He slowly reached out his hand and cupped her face, feeling her cold cheek pressing against his hand. "I wanted to meet you." Seeing her about to retort, he continued, "I work for a security company and was on duty providing security services for the event. And yes, that included making sure that Ms. Morgenstern was safe. I was on my much-needed break when I saw you out here."

Jennifer felt his callous thumb rub over her frozen cheek and couldn't help but slightly move her head toward the warmth. For an instant, she allowed herself to forget that she was there to pick up food for the center, or that she was only a city social worker not a socialite, or that Ross wasn't home waiting...*Ross! Shit!* Jerking back suddenly, she turned and tossed a few more bags into the back of the truck shouting her goodbyes to Carlos as he went back inside.

"Wait," Gabe moved forward stealthily, taking her arm and gently turning her back around to him. "What's the hurry? I'd like to help."

"Help?" she asked, confusion marring her perfect face.

Nodding toward her truck, he said, "Yeah. With the food. With whatever you're doing." Seeing the doubt in her eyes, he hurried to keep talking. *As long as she's not walking away from me, I've got a chance.* "Look, I know we didn't meet under the best circumstances. In fact, it was pretty fucked up," he admitted shaking his head at how the scene must have looked to her. And then he thought of the scene outside of the bar and he visibly cringed.

Taking a deep breath, he rose to his full height and

moved back a step, putting his hand out toward her. "Good evening, Miss. I'd like to introduce myself. I'm Gabriel Malloy. I work for Alvarez Security Agency and I would very much like to make your acquaintance."

A giggle erupted from her perfect lips and she could not help but take his huge hand in her much smaller one, noticing how he held it delicately as though he did not want to crush her. She knew she was blushing again, but somehow the look of uncertainty on his face was endearing. "It's nice to meet you Gabriel. I'm Jennifer Lambert." Trying to pull her hand back, her face shadowed with doubt as she accused, "But you knew that, didn't you?"

He held fast to her hand saying, "Yes, that's true. But I promise I'm no random stalker. I just..." Finding himself uncharacteristically not in charge, he floundered. *How can I tell her that after years of meaningless sex that I want something more? And when I saw her, I felt something. Something deep inside. And since then, I haven't been able to get her off of my mind?*

Focusing back on her face, he saw the doubt moving back in and noticed her taking a step backward toward the truck.

"I'm not a stalker but I wanted to meet you. And the two times we met have been completely fucked up. I'm not like what you saw. At least not anymore. At least not now."

"Gabriel, look I have no idea what you are trying to say to me or why you wanted to meet me so much. I don't know what you think I am, but—"

"What do you mean, what you are?" he asked sharply.

"Look, if you're looking for a little woman to save, I'm fine. I get the food for people who need it and work hard to make sure the arrangement works. But if you are looking for some kind of rescue, I assure you that in spite of what some think, I'm not alley trash!" she exclaimed, throwing Alicia's words back in his face.

Growling, he moved into her space slowly pressing her back up against the door of her pickup truck. "Those were not my words." Tipping her chin up with his fingers, he leaned down until his lips were a breath away from hers, noting that she did not move away. Instead, her eyes widened as her pink tongue flicked across her lips, making him impossibly hard. With no resistance in her eyes, he moved closer capturing her mouth in a kiss. Initially, he just wanted a taste. Just one taste. But as soon as she opened her mouth in a groan, he lost all semblance of control. His muscular arms wrapped around, lifting her off the ground and he growled his approval as he felt her legs wrap around his waist allowing his cock to nestle deeply between her legs. Taking the kiss deeper, he plunged his tongue into her mouth, savoring the taste and feel of her.

Jennifer lost all control as the gorgeous man holding her tightly pressed his massive chest against her and she could feel her nipples pebble into hardened points. One of his hands held her ass and the other was wrapped around the back of her head as though cradling her. Kissing him back as though her breath depended on it, she tangled her tongue with his, loving the rumble she felt deep in his chest. She began rubbing her jean clad pussy against his huge erection, wishing that the material between them was not in the way.

"Ah-hmm," came the interruption from the kitchen door.

Jennifer jerked her head back, instantly missing the heat of Gabe's kiss and mortified at having been caught making out with a complete stranger in an alley. *Carlos! Oh my God. I can't believe he saw me do that. I never do that!* Squirming to get down, she was grateful when Gabe complied, although he growled again; only this time it did not sound like he was happy.

"Sorry guys. I just have this one last bag, Jennifer. It's got some roast and ham I thought would be good. And a couple of goodies I thought your Ross would like."

Rushing over to take the bag out of his hands, she rose on her tiptoes and kissed his cheek. "Thank you so much, Carlos. He'll love them, I'm sure." Turning she rushed past Gabe, who was still trying to get his dick under control, and placed the last bags in the truck. Moving quickly around him, she opened the door, wincing at the screech. As she was closing the door, it did not move and she saw that Gabe had his hand on it.

"Jennifer, I'm sorry. I didn't mean for..."

"No, it's okay. That shouldn't have happened. I'm not that...I don't...this isn't something that I do. That's just not me. I'm sorry." Pulling the door closed she began to start the truck, hearing it sputter. *Please start, please start. Oh, thank God,* she breathed a sigh of relief as the truck finally turned over and began to run. Pulling away from the alley, she spared a glance in the rear-view mirror seeing the handsome giant standing there, staring back.

She felt tears stinging the back her eyes, blinking hard to keep them at bay. *He's not for me. He's so out of my league. Even if my life allowed for the distraction of someone like him.* Lifting her fingers to her lips, she could still feel the tingle and taste. *God, he can kiss!* And as she drove through the night, she realized that if that kiss was all she could ever have with him, he might have ruined her for any other man.

GABE SAT WITH Carlos at one of the tables in the kitchen area of the hotel. Expensive brandy sat in glasses between them. So did the silence.

Finally, Gabe said, "So you gonna tell me anything about her?"

Carlos stared deeply at the man in front of him, measuring him. "Why are you so interested? A man like you...got fuckin' movie stars wantin' your dick."

"Not a fan of having my motives questioned, but

since you don't know me well, I'll give you that," Gabe growled. He sat in silence for another moment, gathering his thoughts. "What can I say, man? I'm tired of the meaningless non-relationships that I've been in for years. Time to settle down. Time to find something real." He rubbed his large hand over his face before leaning back in his chair and taking another swig of brandy. He looked up into Carlos' face, making direct eye contact as he admitted, "Don't know how to explain it. I saw her and felt a goddamn punch to the gut. I went from thinking I'd found a street urchin, to realizing it was a gorgeous woman, to wanting to kiss the hell out of that pixie, to wanting to paddle her ass for being out in the cold, dead of night in alleys."

Carlos barked out a laugh, earning a glare from Gabe, which he ignored. "Right there, you just earned my trust," Carlos said as his laughter stilled. "Any man who feels all that is a good man in my book." Sighing, the older man said, "Although I can't give you a lot of info. She's some kind of charity worker. I just know that she has permission to come get the bread and some of the food items that were not served and would be thrown out. She always drives that god-awful pickup truck and takes whatever she can."

Gabe continued to stare, willing the man to give him more.

Carlos took a swig and smiled. "I remember the first time I saw her here about a year ago. I thought I was going to have to deal with some snooty society bitch and here came this…what'd you call her?" he asked looking up at Gabe. "A pixie? Yeah, that's just what she looked like. A good-lookin' woman with a heart of gold. Her old truck's crapped out on her a couple of times and I sent Big Jim after her to watch over her."

Carlos caught Gabe's incredulous look and chuckled. "He may be scary lookin', but I trust him to see her home safe."

Gabe stood and reached over to shake the older man's hand. "Thank you, man. I appreciate it."

Carlos took his hand and then pushed up from his chair as well. "There's one thing though that I'll let you know. I'm pretty sure she lives with a man named Ross. She's mentioned him liking some of the pastries from here, but she's got no wedding ring. Now she doesn't seem like the type who'd be living with some man and then kissin' you like she was. But, hey – what do I know?"

At this information, Gabe growled once again. *The way she kissed me tells me this Ross either isn't kissing her the way she needs to be kissed or her heart isn't into that relationship.* One way or the other, he was more determined than ever to find her. And if he had his way, making her his was top of his priority list.

THAT NIGHT AFTER Jennifer had delivered the food to

Henry, given Ross his treat from Carlos and then re-tucked him into bed, completed some work on her laptop, and took a long bath she finally settled into bed. For the past two hours, she had managed to push the thoughts of Gabe out of her mind. Or at least to the back of her mind. But now in the quiet of the dark bedroom, she lay there and images of him came to the forefront. Closing her eyes, she could see his huge, body-building physique standing there staring at her. Square jaw, corded neck, thick chest that tapered down to his...*don't go there!* Thighs as large as her waist. With his brown eyes and the smile that drew her in, she wanted to taste more of him. *Taste him? Oh my God, I kissed him. Up against my truck. Jesus, what a floosie...I never do that!* But as much as she wanted to chastise herself and was mortified that they'd been caught by Carlos, she could not get her giant out of her mind.

Listening to make sure that Ross was indeed asleep in his room, she leaned over and opened her nightstand, pulling out her pink vibrator. Using it, she quickly realized that it did not hold the same appeal that it had before. *A poor substitute for the real thing,* she thought ruefully.

"LILY," GABE SHOUTED as he entered her work area. "Got some time for me?" he queried.

"Sure, what do you need?" she asked swiveling

around in her chair to face him. Lily was the software engineer for Alvarez Security and wife of his good friend, Detective Matt Dixon.

"I need a favor. I've got a name and license plate number and I want to see what you can pull up. I've pulled up the address, but I want to see what else you can find."

"Okay," she said eagerly as she took the paper from his hand and turned back to her computer station. "Is this one of the cases you're on?" Silence greeted her. Lily twisted her head around to see Gabe rubbing the back of his neck with a guilty look on his face.

"Um…not exactly," he said awkwardly.

Just then BJ, one of the other computer experts of Alvarez Security, came into the room. "Good morning," he greeted. "What's Gabe got you working on, Lily? Finding out about that new girl he's interested in?"

At that, Lily's hand slowly moved away from her keyboard and she swiveled back around, her eyebrow lifted in question. "Girl…?" she asked, drawing the word out.

"Um…well," Gabe stammered, glaring at BJ.

"Sorry, man," BJ countered, "I thought she knew."

"Knew what, gentlemen?" Lily asked.

"You haven't noticed how morose Gabe's been the last couple of weeks. Met some girl that won't jump all over him and now she's got him so tied up in knots that he's resorted to stalking her."

"You want to shut the fuck up, BJ?" Gabe growled.

Laughing, BJ walked out of the room calling over his shoulder, "Talk some sense into him, Lily. He's been a grumpy-ass lately."

The silence hung between the two co-workers and friends for a minute before Lily finally sighed and patted the empty chair next to her. Gabe settled his bulk into the seat and looked at her, resigning himself to talking.

"So...you met a girl? Someone you really like and you want me to dig into her background?" she asked. "Is she in trouble?"

"No!" Gabe answered vehemently. "She's perfect. Pretty...nice...real caring."

"And...?" Lily prodded, then saw her friend uncharacteristically quiet. "What are you not telling me, Gabe?"

"I've never done this. You know...actually liked a woman. Lily, you know me. Hell, you know all of us. We don't mind having fun for a night, this girl's different. Seems special. And I don't want to screw it up."

"Okay. So just talk to her. Ask her out. Have a conversation. Find out what she likes and doesn't like. Come on, Gabe, don't be a wimp."

With that, he leaned back in his chair exhaling loudly. "A wimp. Man, you know how to go for the jugular."

Laughing, she patted his leg. "Look, Gabe...here it

is from a woman's perspective. If I found out that Matt had been using subterfuge to find out about me before just talking to me, I'd be livid. A woman doesn't have to have wine and roses. If she's as nice as you say she is, then talk to her. A woman wants a man who takes a real interest in her." At that, she noticed the gleam in his eye and she quickly amended, "And not just interested in sex!"

"Yeah, you're right," he drawled. "Jesus, who knew this would be so hard."

Lily threw her head back, her eyes sparkling. "Go get 'em, tiger," she joked as she turned back to her computer to begin her day of work.

ACROSS TOWN, JENNIFER stood outside State Senator Reno's office, waiting impatiently. He and his wife had always been supporters of her work with the elder housing. Watching some of the stylishly dressed women walking by in their sky-high heels and business attire, she smoothed her hands down her grey pencil skirt. Rubbing a scuff mark from her black pumps, she noted that they were beginning to look a little worn. *Okay, next month if there is money left over at the end of all the bills I'll buy a new pair of shoes.*

Just then his door opened and another stylishly dressed woman, arms full of papers and files, walked out with her head down as she was reaching into her purse. Jennifer stood too quickly, colliding with the other woman causing files to scatter on the floor.

"Oh my God, I'm so sorry," she exclaimed, stopping to pick up the papers.

The other woman also apologized, "No, no. I wasn't watching where I was going." As she looked up, she exclaimed, "Jennifer?"

"Sherrie! How long has it been?" she asked as they bent to their task. In just a couple of minutes, the files were gathered and placed in some semblance of order. As they stood, they continued their greeting.

"Are you still working at the law firm?" Jennifer asked.

"Yes. Are you here for your elder housing?" The two women had met earlier when Jennifer was canvasing some of the legal firms, looking for anyone willing to assist with the legal needs that some of her elderly clients had.

"I'm heading in to do some more shameless begging as usual," Jennifer explained, laughing. "It seems like all I do is find new places to beg for money for our programs."

"Well, I'd love to grab coffee sometime and find out how your programs are going."

Beaming, Jennifer gushed, "Oh, I'd love to also."

The women traded business cards before parting ways and Jennifer hurried into the congressman's office.

"Ms. Lambert," he greeted warmly.

Walking over to shake his hand, she smiled genuinely and asked about his family.

"I've got new pictures," he said proudly pulling out his cell phone. He quickly scrolled through a few new photos of his children and wife. Inviting her to have a seat, she perched on the edge of his comfortable leather chair. "What can I do for you today?" he asked solicitously.

"I'm just touching base with some of our statesmen to make sure that we are still on track for the continued funding for our centers. I know budget time is coming up and I'm afraid that the plight of our elderly often gets shoved to the side."

"You know my office is always willing to fight for your funding."

"Oh, Senator Reno, I know and it's so appreciated."

The two continued to chat for a few more minutes before his door opened and his assistant walked in. "Oh, excuse me sir. I didn't realize you had someone. I don't have an appointment for you at this time."

Jennifer noticed the man's eyes held no warmth when looking at her before sniffing dismissively.

"Oh Monty. You haven't met Ms. Lambert, from DSS. We were just chatting after our appointment time, catching up a little. This is my assistant Montgomery Lytton."

Jennifer stood and greeted the assistant, who continued to look as though she were unworthy of the congressman's time.

"Well, I'll be leaving sir. Thank you so much for seeing me today. Give my best to your wife."

Walking out of the office, she was surprised to see that Monty had followed her to the door.

"Ms. Lambert, the Senator is a very busy man and it would be best if you remember to stay on your designated appointment time in the future. He may forget to look at the clock, but for you to continue to have access to him, you need to remember."

Smiling her most charming smile, she said, "I think in the future, Monty, I will continue to let Congressman Reno let me know when he's available. And if you think you'll keep me from making appointments, I'll just talk to him and his wife when I see them at the elder-care functions." With that, she turned and walked to the elevator.

Fuming, she left the building and walked to the bus stop. The wind had picked up, causing her to pull her scarf around her neck a little tighter. On the ride back to her building, she began to calm. *He's just the assistant to the Senator. He doesn't threaten me! And if he thinks to intimidate me, then he's got another thing coming.* By the time she made her way back to the office, she felt much better.

Greeting Roy and Sybil, she wrote up notes on her meeting with the Senator, making sure to include him in the next elder-care publication she was working on. Smiling to herself, she decided to add his wife to her mailing list. *Take that, Monty.*

CHAPTER 4

MICHAEL GIBBONS SAT behind his large, polished mahogany desk in the spacious office at the top of his office building. Pewter framed photographs of his wife and children sat at the edge, in clear view of any visitors. The corner office afforded him a view of the revitalized downtown Richland as well as the river that meandered through the city. His silk suit jacket was carefully placed on his suit-tree, as he preferred to work in comfort with his sleeves rolled up unless he was expecting guests. A real-estate mogul, he had made a fortune in buying old, dilapidated buildings and turning them into prime real-estate. He regularly dined with the mayor, the governor, and numerous other politicians from city councilmen to senators.

Michael's grandfather had raised him to attain the highest social standing possible while making sure his many businesses were secure, whether through legal means or not. Working to keep the legitimate business in the spotlight, he found that the under-belly of Richland's society began to come to him...for money, advice, protection. It did not take long to realize how much more money could be made by following in his grandfather's footsteps while keeping the lawful business in the forefront. Extortion and fraud were extremely profitable and so far he had been successful.

A self-made man, Michael believed in hard work, arriving at his office by seven a.m. every morning and staying as late as needed. If his wife was unhappy, she knew not to complain and since he kept her in jewels and her country-club estate, she was very satisfied.

A side door to his office opened and his mistress walked boldly in, straight to the back of his chair, and put her arms around his neck. Running her ruby-tipped fingernails down his chest she leaned forward, pressing her breasts against his shoulder as her hands found their way to his crotch.

A flash of irritation crossed his face, but her expert hands soon had him deciding to admonish her for the surprise visit at another time. Theresa had become more assuming and if there was one thing he wanted in a mistress, it was for them to know their place. She had been his paramour for almost two years, replacing the previous mistress that had been with him for the five years before that. His former mistresses were well satisfied as was his wife; he rewarded their loyalty with a home, cars, and plenty of money to live the rest of their lives comfortably. They understood that when another woman came that caught his discriminating eye, he would set them up and move on.

Theresa was becoming greedy. No longer willing to stay in the shadows, she was hinting at wanting to escort him to functions instead of his wife. Michael had worked too hard to establish his business interests as legitimate to have a pussy fuck them up. But for now, she was still compliant and her hands on his swollen dick at the moment did distract him.

He unzipped his pants allowing her to slide between his legs and suck him off. Sliding his hands down the front of her low cut dress, he grasped her breasts firmly, pinching her nipples. He came hard, spilling into her mouth just before his private phone rang. Glancing at the name he zipped his pants up quickly and picked up the phone.

"Mr. Gibbons? Just wanted you to know that she was here."

"Are we going to have a problem with her? You know what I want."

"Yes, I know. I'll take care of her."

"Well for God's sake, don't fuck it up. I don't want my name in it and I don't want any publicity."

Wanting to continue the conversation in private, he jerked his head toward the door, indicating to Theresa that she should leave. Pissed at being dismissed before she was able to be taken care of, she stood and gave a stiff smile. She walked over to the door leading to a small hall and private elevator. Unbeknownst to him, she did not leave immediately but instead pressed her ear to the door, trying to overhear the conversation.

"Okay, we can continue," he added. "My private investigators tell me that this one building in the two block area is in a prime location and the only hold-up is that the apartment is for old folks. We could force them out, but this bitch is in our way. Hear me well, the last thing I want is for her to end up in the newspaper championing the cause of these old geezers. And for fuck sake, I don't want other groups involved."

"I got it."

"Keep an eye on her and let me know if she comes back."

"Yes, sir," came the expected response.

Ending the private call, he pressed for his secretary. Immediately, a distinguished woman entered, ready to assist. She was his cousin's wife and completely trustworthy. *What was it that grandfather always said? Keep your family close if you want to keep your enemies at a distance.*

Concluding their legitimate business, he asked for her to send for his private investigator whose office was in his building, as well as his head of security. As she left, he mulled over the file open on his desk. *The fucking Elder Care Housing Grant. And the equally beautiful Jennifer Lambert that had spear-headed the project.*

His eyes scanned the latest report. Her grant had given the group enough money to have a five-year lease on the building. Rubbing his head, he considered the ramifications of taking her on publicly. *No, not happening.*

A knock on his door indicated that his appointment was there. Santo Mancello, head of security walked in first. Tall, dark and ruthless, the Mancello family had served Michael's family since the time of their grandfathers. Following Santo, Michael's nephew Frederick, his private investigator, walked in and took a seat. Frederick was still learning the job, but being a quick study and eager to please, Michael was satisfied that his nephew would do well in the family business. As the men sat down in the dark leather chairs, they began their meeting.

By the time they had considered their options, he announced, "I've had someone make inquiries to the owner of the building, Mr. Stuart Mason. He's an old man, lives alone. Seemed as though he would be willing to sell. So, I want Ms. Lambert watched. Discreetly. I want to know who she sees and what she's doing. If we can provide an incentive to have her bow out of the project, that would be perfect. If not, then perhaps she will open up a door for us to encourage her to abandon. And if not that, then lean on her. But not until I give the order. Someone at The State Capitol is reporting to me and will try to sabotage her efforts there.

"Sir, we also have someone at her workplace that will be reporting to me as well," Santo said.

"Is there any way that they would agree to move? If you had another cheap building that you didn't want – would they want to move and then you would avoid the hassle," Frederick said.

"All the money from their grant has gone into their

own renovation and the lease. It also keeps the old geezers in the neighborhood that they were from. Our contact at The State Capitol has indicated that it would still be a public relation nightmare to force the issue. Not to mention that would indicate that I am willing to buy out instead of force-out. And that would be suicide for my reputation as a man who gets what he wants, how he wants it."

"So for now, keep our eyes open?" confirmed Santo.

Nodding, Michael stood indicating that the meeting was over. "Remember, I don't want her to know she's being watched. Not until I give the order to move in."

As the men left through his office door, his secretary stepped in. "Sir, if there is nothing more, I will say goodnight."

Turning, he smiled. "That will be all, Eloise. Please kiss your children for me and tell them that we will have you over for dinner soon."

His secretary beamed as she closed the door. Standing in front of his wall of windows, he looked out over the night skyline of the city. A smile crossed his face as he saw many of the buildings that he had made millions from renovating. The smile left his face as his eyes moved to the distance, on the other side of the river, knowing that a huge block of buildings were ripe for the picking if it was not for the old folks and their beautiful, meddling champion.

CHAPTER 5

THE AFTERNOON WAS cold and Jennifer was about to meet Ross' bus at the corner. An old man, in a worn coat, stood at the bottom of the stairs. Looking up at her, he asked, "Do you have any food here?"

Sighing deeply, she answered, "We're not a homeless shelter. There's one a few blocks over. I can show you where as soon as I meet the school bus."

"Oh, I got a place to stay. I was just hungry, that's all," he said, keeping his eyes on her.

Looking at him with compassion, she added, "Okay. Go straight through the main hall into the kitchen. Tell the woman in there that Jennifer said to give you some food."

The old man climbed the stairs as she came down. Stopping her with his hand on her arm, he thanked her.

Bestowing a smile on him, she nodded and then jogged down the street, trying to stay warm as she hurried to the bus stop. *Oh, I hope I'm not late.*

The bus stopped on the corner and out bounded a bundled-up child, jumping the last step onto the sidewalk, looking around.

"Ross, Ross," she yelled, waving her arms. "I'm here."

"Jennybenny!" the child yelled as he threw himself into her arms. "Sis, the field trip was so cool!"

Greeting her brother, she pulled the scarf off of her neck and wrapped it around his neck. "Where's your scarf? And for that matter, where are your gloves?"

"I don't know. I may have left them in the museum."

"Ross, honey. You have to be more careful. Here put mine on," she said calmly, pushing his hands into her knit gloves.

"I'm sorry, sis. I'll get more with my allowance when we go to the dollar store," he said.

"Oh that won't be necessary. Just try to keep up with the next ones, okay buddy?" she smiled, kissing the top of his head. "Come on, tell me about the museum."

The two walked back to their building, chatting and laughing, oblivious to anyone watching.

Sitting in one of Alvarez's SUV with darkened windows, Gabe smiled as he watched the scene in front of him unfolded. *Jesus, I'm such a stalker, but I just had to know.* Gabe knew he had a reputation as a player, but he had never been with a married woman or a woman with a significant other. It just was not his play. *But Ross? Her brother.* Continuing to smile, he started the vehicle pulled into traffic. *Beautiful. Jesus, she's so beautiful.* As he replayed the scenario in his mind, his smile lessened as he thought about her giving up her scarf and gloves and the child's comment about the dollar store. Glancing down at his expensive, leather gloves and feeling the heat pouring out of the vent of his new Jeep, he vowed to not waste any more time getting to know her.

DRIVING TO THE restaurant, Jennifer wondered if he would be there. Her giant. *That's such a childish way to think of him. Gabe. His name is Gabe. Stop making him more than he is. Just a man. A player. An over-confident player.* As she pulled the old truck to the dumpster, she saw him step from the shadows, a smile on his face. *Okay, an incredibly gorgeous, well-built hunk of a player.* Licking her lips nervously, she looked up in his face as he stepped up to open her door. Wincing at the screech she noticed that he did not seem to pay attention to the old jalopy.

"Hello, Jennifer," he greeted as he assisted her down from the truck.

She couldn't help but smile. He helped her down from her rusty, old junker as though she were alighting from the carriage to the ball. "Hi, Gabe."

"I've already been inside and gathered everything that Carlos had for you."

Looking over, there were several cardboard boxes filled with bags neatly stacked by the kitchen door. Before she could comment, he turned and lifted them easily, walking to the back of the truck.

"That looks like more than I usually get," she said. "Are you sure that's all for me?"

Gabe smiled down at her as he set the boxes carefully in the bed of the truck. "Well, didn't know how far you had to carry them, so I put less in each box to make them lighter."

Turning her stunned look up to his face, she said, "Wow, thank you. That's really...thoughtful. I just...well, I...Gabe, why are you doing this?"

Looking down at his boots for a moment, he rubbed the back of his neck trying to figure out what to say. "I just want to get to know you, Jennifer. It seemed like helping you was the best way."

She searched his face, trying to determine his motives, but found nothing but sincerity. Shaking her head slowly, she confessed, "I don't know what you think to gain. I'm...nobody."

His head lifted, cocked to the side, confusion in his eyes. "Nobody?"

Her eyes snapped and she placed her hands on her hips. "Gabe. Seriously. Look at me. Do I look like some movie star? I'm just me. Just the real me."

"I don't want a movie star. I want to know you. Just you. Just the real you," he countered quickly.

"This makes no sense," she said, her hand moving back and forth between them.

"I'm a man who finds someone that sparks something deep inside, something that hasn't been sparked in a long time, and I want to explore it. And I know you felt it too if that kiss was any indication. That makes sense to me," he said softly, stepping closer.

She stood there with her head leaned back to peer into his eyes and her heart racing, pondering his words. *What am I doing? This is crazy.*

He saw her eyes dart between his as though trying to see inside of him, looking for a lie. Or something to believe in. *Come on, baby. Give me a chance.*

Not used to having to work so hard, he found himself holding his breath, hoping she would give them a chance. He saw her eyes drop to his lips and her breathing increase.

Absently pushing her wind-blown curls out of her face, she sucked in her lips before looking down at the ground. Sighing deeply, she looked back up, resignation on her face.

"Gabe, I...I'm a social worker for DSS. A low-level city employee working my butt off to get by. My life isn't really...um...conducive to dating."

"Then let's just take time to get to know each other. Let's just see where it goes." He took one more step closer, reaching out to gently place his hands on her shoulders, noting that she did not pull away.

"What do you suggest?" she whispered, her eyes on his lips.

Gabe leaned down, his lips a breath away from hers, and said, "I'd like to kiss you."

Unable to form any words, she found herself rising

on her tip-toes to capture his lips with hers. She heard moaning as he deepened the kiss, then realized the sounds came from her. Opening her mouth to his, she reveled in the feel of his tongue plunging inside. She drank him in. His taste, distinctly him, filled her senses. Winding her arms around his neck, she was barely aware of being lifted as the kiss took on a life-force of its own.

One hand on her ass and the other arm wrapped around her cupping the back of her head, he held her easily. Amazed at how perfectly she fit in his arms, he groaned as his cock swelled, pressing in his jeans painfully. *Always thought a man my size needed a big woman, but this. Is. Perfect.* Her breasts pressed into his chest and her ass fit perfectly.

The kitchen door opened, shedding a bright light into the dark alley, as Carlos looked out at the lip-locked couple again. "Damn you two. What do y'all do, just come to this alley to make out like teenagers?"

They broke the kiss and Jennifer began to squirm to be let down.

"Not letting go yet, babe. Just hang on," Gabe rumbled. Turning with her in his arms, he nodded to Carlos. "That it?" he asked, indicating the boxes still by the door?

Laughing, Carlos nodded. "Yeah, man. That's it." He paused for a second before calling out, "Ms. Jennifer? You okay?"

She smiled his way and said, "I'm fine, Carlos.

Thanks for the food." She watched him wave and then head back into the kitchen, closing the door behind him, once again casting them in shadows.

"Oh my God," she said. "That was so embarrassing."

"Nothing wrong with a man kissing a beautiful woman in the moonlight, although I'd prefer it not be in an alley with the smell of garbage floating through the air."

At that, she giggled and he gently let her down, keeping his hands on her shoulders until she was firm on her feet. Blushing she looked at the ground, not willing to look up at him.

Gabe tilted her head up with his fingers on her chin. "Let's get this food in the truck and then I'm going to follow you home." Seeing the question in her eyes, he quickly continued, "I don't want you out at night by yourself and yes, I know you've been doing it for a long time." Kissing her forehead, he made short work of the boxes, loading them efficiently.

Assisting her into her truck, he waited patiently as she worked to get it started. *She needs a new set of wheels*, he thought, frightened at the thought of her breaking down on the side of the road late at night. She finally moved out of the alley and he pulled in behind her, driving to her building.

He noted with irritation that she pulled into the alley behind a four-story brick building, in an older section of town, a block from where she had met with her brother. She hopped out of the truck before he was able to get out to assist, a habit of hers that he wanted to change.

A back door flung open and an older man was calling out a greeting by the time Gabe made it to her side. The man hustled over ready to protect her. Gabe was impressed with the man's loyalty but unhappy that he was the only line of defense that she had if there was a problem. Something that he wanted to rectify as soon as he could.

"Hey Henry, it's okay. This is a…friend of mine, Gabe Malloy. Gabe, this is Henry. He runs the center here."

Gabe stepped up and shook Henry's hand. "Good to meet you, sir. Why don't you and Jennifer go inside where it's warm and I'll bring the boxes in." He noticed Henry glanced to Jennifer, then watched approvingly as Henry hustled her in out of the cold.

Stacking the boxes, he brought them into a warm if old, well-lit industrial kitchen. Seeing Henry pat the counter, he set the boxes down, watching Jennifer immediately dig in. Unsure what to do next, he stepped back and watched her in action, admiring the look of joy on her face as she opened the bags. She had thrown off her old jacket and for the first time was able to admire her body. Her sweatpants were worn but cupped a delicious ass, every bit as marvelous as he remembered the one time he was able to ogle her in the alley. As she turned away from the industrial-sized freezer, he saw that her figure was indeed stunning. Tiny, but curvy. And in all the right places. Suddenly the idea of a tall, scrawny model with fake tits seemed unappealing. But the vision in front of him—blonde curls framing a fairy face with a petite body to die for— was perfection.

"Are you back, girl?" a female voice called from the doorway. "Do you need something warm to drink?" An older woman headed into the kitchen, bustling with energy, stopping quickly when she saw Gabe.

"Cora, this is a friend of mine who helped me to-night. This is Gabe. And this wonder-woman is Henry's wife, Cora.

"Pleasure to meet you Cora," he said smoothly, offering his hand.

She shook his hand, her eyes moving quickly be-tween his and Jennifer's. "I didn't know you had anyone helping you dear, but I'm so glad you do." Turning back to Gabe, she said, "I'll make some hot chocolate."

He looked over at Jennifer, seeing her smile light up the room.

"You've never tasted anything like Cora's hot choc-olate," she effused.

Cora blushed and patted her hand. "I'll take some up to Ross."

Jennifer's smile dropped and a look of panic crossed her face. *Ross? Oh my God, I can't introduce him to Gabe. Not now.*

Gabe saw the expression change and knew what was going through her mind. As much as he wanted to stay, he moved over and said, "Hey, I know it's late. I'd better be going."

"No," she said quickly. "I mean, not if you don't want to. Ross is my brother and he's…"

"Upstairs and almost ready for bed. We'll just go check on him," Cora finished, pulling Henry out of the kitchen with her.

Gabe looked down, seeing the look of uncertainty in Jennifer's eyes. "You can go to him if you need," he said softly as he walked over to her. Cupping her tiny face in his large hands, he tilted it upwards so he could see her eyes. Crystalline blue eyes framed by blonde curls, peering at him. He saw them dilate with desire and that was all he needed. Bending down he placed a soft kiss on her lips. Chaste. Not hungry. Just a gentle touch.

She felt the slight pressure on her lips and before she could stop, a moan came from deep inside of her. All of her being was tied up in that moment just at the touch of their lips and the feel of his hands around her face. Suddenly the idea of him leaving was unbearable and she reached up to grasp his arms, her fingers wrapping around his sleeves feeling the muscles below. Opening her mouth, she licked his lips, eliciting another moan, this time coming from him.

Losing all sense of control, Gabe growled into her mouth as his tongue plunged into the sweetness, exploring deeply. Meeting her tongue, they began a duel deep inside of her warm mouth. He picked her up as though she weighed nothing and set her on the kitchen counter without breaking the kiss. One large hand continued to hold her face while the other one crept around her back pulling her close.

With her legs spread apart at the edge of the counter and his massive body between them, she was at the right height to feel his erection pressing against her core. She began to rub herself on him, desperate for the friction that was sending electricity throughout her body. Feeling herself become wet, she increased her undulations while his hand slowly slid from her back around toward her breasts.

Gabe's hand stopped directly underneath her breasts, waiting for permission to continue their exploration. He felt her moan again as she continued to rub herself on his swollen dick. *Jesus, she's going to undo me*, he thought as he tried to maintain composure. But his cock had other ideas. For a military man trained to have his body under complete control, he felt all semblance of control slipping.

Moving his hand upwards to cup her breast, he felt its heaviness as he palmed it, feeling the nipple harden. He rolled the nipple through her shirt and bra, desperate to have her naked and underneath him. *Soon, very soon.*

Jennifer began to feel the tension building deep inside radiating from her pussy outwards. *More, I need more.* Her hands had moved from his huge arms to his neck and then higher to cup his stubble covered jaw. His lips, soft and yet unyielding continued to kiss her senseless until her only thought was to reach the pinnacle.

She felt his hands move from her breasts down to her pants, sliding them under the waistband. He hesitated, giving her control. She had no control. All she wanted was to feel. For just a little while to feel. No responsibilities. Nothing but pleasure. Grasping his head, she pulled him back for another kiss.

He slid his hand down the front cupping her mound, loving the gasp that escaped her lips. Moving the wispy material of her panties to the side, he found her wet as he slid his fingers through her lips and circled her clit. Her gasp became a desperate plea for more. Moving a thick finger inside, he plunged it into her waiting pussy.

Not able to think about anything other than the feelings radiating throughout her body, she raised her legs, wrapping them around his hips pulling him closer. He added another finger inside her tight pussy and began scissoring them, touching her in places that had long been dormant.

Climbing higher and higher, she knew she was close and every fiber in her being screamed for that elusive release.

Watching her face with her eyes closed and her blonde curls hanging about her shoulders had Gabe entranced. He knew she was close and wanted to watch her as she fell apart. *Jesus, I've never cared about watching a woman before.* Other than the male satisfaction of knowing he had brought a woman to orgasm, he was never concerned about watching them, but now found that he would not have been able to take his eyes off of her if his life depended on it.

Crooking his finger deep inside, he felt the slick walls of her pussy contract as her fingers dug into his shoulders, holding on as though he were the only thing keeping her intact. "Let it go, baby. Just let it happen," he softly ordered as he watched the blush form at the top of her breasts and rise to her face.

Feeling the heat of her blush, Jennifer obeyed and let go. The orgasm rushed over her taking her with it. With her head thrown back, she felt the sparks radiate from her pussy outwards. Her mind void of everything other than the avalanche of feelings, she collapsed forward, her head pressed to his chest.

Gabe slowly pulled his fingers out and slid them into his mouth, loving the taste of her. She watched him through barely open eyes, amazed at how erotic it was to have a man taste her. He moved her panties back into place and pulled her head back up to see her eyes.

"I want to see you, baby. I want to make sure you're all right," he continued to order.

She raised her face to his, stunned at the concern she saw in his eyes. "I'm good," she said shyly. A small giggle escaped as she admitted, "I'm really good."

"Oh, baby. You were more than good." He leaned in for a kiss and she could taste herself on his lips, another first for her.

As the high of her orgasm began to slowly fade, realization crept in. *Oh my God. I'm sitting on the kitchen counter where anyone could walk in and see me. Jesus, what is wrong with me?*

Gabe felt it the second that she began to doubt what she was doing. Cupping her face, he stilled her. "Baby, listen to me. Don't regret what happened. Please. It was too important. Too important to both of us."

His words settled in, but she looked at him in confusion. "Important? Gabe, I'm not the kind of woman who just does this. Ever."

"Baby, look at me."

She lifted her eyes to his, searching for sincerity.

"This was important to me too. You're different. You're someone I wanna get to know. I wanna take care of. In all ways."

She licked her lips, taking in his words as her eyes dropped to his waist. Seeing his jeans, straining at the crotch, she suddenly blurted, "But you. We didn't take care of you."

"That's okay, baby. This was about you. This was all about you tonight."

"Gabe, I don't understand what's happening. I just met you and we've made out three times. This is so not me. I'm nobody. You see where I live...in a building where I pay a low rent because I help out with the center. These elderly people depend on me. I have... responsibilities. Ross. My job. I can't..."

"Shhh," he scolded, placing his fingers on her lips. The same fingers that had just been deep inside of her. She could still smell herself on them, eliciting another slight moan.

He watched her face, knowing the emotions were overwhelming. *Hell, they're overwhelming for me too. Never done that. Just got a woman off and was willing to walk away without getting off too. And fuck. She was perfect. Is perfect.*

"Don't overthink this. We feel something. Something big. Let's just let it go and see where it takes us."

At this, she gave a small nod. "Yeah," she whispered. "I'd like that."

"Good. Then I'll say goodnight. When can I see you again? Do you have plans for Saturday?"

"No," she said shaking her head in thought. "But Gabe?" Doubt crossed her face again.

"What baby?"

"There's a lot you don't know. About me, I mean."

"We've got time. Nothing but time to learn all about each other," he said gently.

"No, you don't understand. I've got Ross. He's my brother and well, he's only eight years old. I've never had him around men. I mean a man that I was...um...whatever we're doing."

He watched her struggle but, *Damn, she's adorable*

when she's confused. "I get it. I really do. But I'd like to get to know both of you."

She lifted her eyes to peer deeply into his. "I can't risk having him grow attached to you, knowing that you could walk out at any moment."

He felt his chest squeeze at the love she had for her brother. "Jennifer, there are no guarantees in life, but I'll promise you this. I'll never just walk out. I'll never just leave him, or you, hanging."

Sucking in a deep breath, hoping she was not making a mistake, she smiled up at him. "Okay. Then I'd love to see you on Saturday."

Giving her a quick kiss, he reached over to her bag and pulled out her cell phone, quickly entering his number and memorizing hers. Lifting her off the counter, he linked his fingers with hers as he walked to the door. "See you Saturday, babe," he said as he captured her lips once more in a kiss. This one was slow. Soft. Gentle. Full of the promise of things to come.

As she shut and locked the door behind him, she quickly finished in the kitchen and hurried up the stairs. Cora was just coming out of the apartment, having heard Jennifer on the stairs. With a smile on her caring face, she asked, "So, did you and your young man have a chance to talk?"

"Well...I have a date for Saturday," she confessed.

Cora grabbed her in a hug, pulling her close. "Oh darling girl, I'm so glad. It's about time you took care of you and not just everyone else."

Saying goodnight, Jennifer slipped inside the apartment and checked on Ross, who was already asleep. Looking down at his boyish face resting in slumber, she hoped she wasn't making a mistake. *Oh Ross, I hope this is a good thing for you. He seems like such a good man and I'd love for you to be able to be around someone like him.*

Closing his door, she got ready for bed and slipped between the sheets. Her mind wandered to the evening, amazed at how it ended. And for once, she didn't need her little pink vibrator. Still sated from her orgasm, she smiled as she drifted off to sleep. And this time the giant in her dreams became the handsome prince.

ACROSS TOWN, GABE headed into the shower, his thoughts full of the evening as well. The smile never left his face as he remembered the look on her face as she flew apart in his arms with his fingers deep inside of her. Leaning one hand on the shower wall, he grasped his cock with his other hand working it until he came, the thoughts of being buried deep inside of her making his hand seem like a poor substitute.

As he lay in bed, unable to sleep, he began to plan his date. A date. It had been a long time since he went on a real date with a woman he was interested in. *Dinner? Definitely. Somewhere really nice? Yes. Wait, no. She lives simply and I don't want to overwhelm her. Okay, casual dinner. Flowers? No, that may be too much. Jesus, who knew this would be so difficult!*

As he lay there, conflicting ideas racing through his head, he forced himself to think of her as a military mission. *Know your enemy. Hell, she's not the enemy.* But that thought continued and he realized that he needed to think about what she would like. *What does she do on Saturdays?* An idea began to form, and a slow smile crept across his face as he formalized his assault. His mission? Meet her on her own field and show her the man he wanted to be.

Finally with a plan in place, he closed his eyes and let sleep overtake him.

CHAPTER 6

J ENNIFER SLAPPED HER hand on the alarm. *Oh, what I wouldn't give to sleep late one Saturday morning.* Her dreams had been filled with erotic images of Gabe with his hands on her. She started to slide her own hand down but was halted by the sounds of Ross already awake and in the bathroom.

"Jennybenny, come on. Cora and Henry need us."

Where does he get that energy? Was I that energetic at the age of eight?

"Coming Ross, just give me a minute." Pulling herself out of bed, she quickly donned her jeans and a t-shirt. Running a brush through her tangled mane of blonde curls, she quickly pulled it up into a sloppy bun secured with a chopstick.

"You ready?" she asked, checking to make sure he had combed his hair and washed his face.

Tugging on her hand, he pulled her toward the door. "Come on. I want pancakes," he called. "As soon as we serve them we can have them too." Saturday mornings were special to Jennifer. She and Ross got up early and helped Henry and Cora prepare breakfast for the residents. The food was donated or bought with their grant and helped to stretch the residents' meager budgets. For some of them, it may be their only meal of the day. They usually had pancakes, Ross' favorite, and scrambled eggs and bacon as well. Ross accepted the duty of serving food, then loved to sit with the residents as he ate with them.

She smiled at her tow-headed brother as he dashed into the hallway toward the stairs. She could hear his feet stomping down quickly as he headed to the kitchen. *Little boys. Do they ever walk?*

As she neared the kitchen, she could hear Ross' chatter and a deep male voice answering. Rounding the corner she stopped, stunned. Standing in the industrial kitchen wearing an apron and talking with Ross...was Gabe. His eyes looked across the room, capturing hers and his mouth split into the most glorious grin. Before she could ask what he was doing there, he turned back to the counter where the bowls of pancake batter were being mixed.

"Hey, that's my job," Ross shouted. "Are you going to help me?"

Jennifer saw Ross' expression of awe at the giant of a man in the kitchen. Nor could she miss the smiles on Henry and Cora's faces.

"Looks like we've got some extra help today," Cora announced unnecessarily. "Ross, you'll have to show our new helper how it's done."

Gabe bent down to Ross' level and stuck out his hand, introducing himself. "So, you're Ross? Nice to meet you. I'm Gabe."

Ross stared at his hand for a moment and Jennifer was just about to prompt him to greet Gabe, when he suddenly put his small hand in Gabe's and shook it enthusiastically. "I'm Ross. That's my sister, Jennifer, but sometimes I call her Jennybenny, but I'm the only one who can call her that. Are you going to help make breakfast? I mix the pancake batter, but you're bigger and can do it faster. Can I watch?"

"Ross," Jennifer admonished as Gabe burst into laughter. "Let the poor man have a moment to see that the whirlwind that just blew in is really a little boy!"

Gabe stood as Ross up scrambled up on the stool next to the counter. "All right Ross. How 'bout you show me how it's done." He winked at Jennifer before returning to the batter.

Jennifer locked eyes with Cora and motioned for her to follow as she walked into the pantry. Rounding on her friend she hissed, "What's he doing here?"

Cora smiled as she replied, "Honey, he just knocked on the back door about twenty minutes ago and said that he'd like to help. Now you know, I'm not going to turn down an offer of help."

"I know. I just...well, I'm not sure...oh, I don't know," she said nervously.

Cora stepped closer, tucking one of Jennifer's curls behind her ear. "What is it honey? I don't know him, but he seems like good people to me. The way he looks at you and showing up here? Seems like you've got a great guy interested in you. What's confusing about that?"

Looking to the side, she bit her lip as she tried to organize her thoughts. Sighing, she turned her gaze back to the woman who had been like a mother to her for the past couple of years. "Honestly? There's Ross to consider. I'm his guardian, not some twenty-four year old who has no responsibilities. It's not fair to have him around a man that may up and leave at any time. Ross has already dealt with loss – I don't want him to have more if I let someone in and then they leave."

"Oh darling girl. You're doing a wonderful job with your brother. You can't protect him from all loss and I think it would be good for him to have a younger man to be around instead of all of us old folks."

Jennifer glanced at the kitchen door, hearing the laughter of Ross mixed with Gabe's patient voice. Sucking in her lips, she looked back at Cora. "He's…or was…well, he says that he's not—"

"Girl, spit it out," Cora laughed. "We've got breakfast to fix."

"He's a player, Cora. He's been surrounded by gorgeous actresses and women. I've seen him. First of all, I have no idea why he's even hanging around me and second of all, I refuse to be another one of his conquests."

This outburst caused Cora to stop laughing and pull Jennifer in for a hug. "Honey, I have no idea what that young man in there has been like, but I'm a good judge of character and he gives me the impression of someone who really wants to get to know you. I think you'd possibly miss out on something really special if you let this chance pass you by."

Hugging Cora tightly, she took a deep breath and nodded. "Okay then. Let's go make breakfast."

For the next thirty minutes, Gabe worked alongside Jennifer, Ross, Henry and Cora as they prepared food for the almost forty residents who began to trickle down to the dining room. Ross ran ahead, already visiting with them. Cora and Henry began the serving, telling Jennifer and Gabe to bring the next batch of pancakes when they were ready.

Suddenly finding herself alone in the kitchen with Gabe, she couldn't help but glance over at the counter where they had made out the night before.

He caught her eyes looking over and grinned. "Thinking of something special?"

Blushing a deep red, she rolled her eyes. "Please don't remind me. That was so…"

"Hot?" he interjected.

"I was going to say unlike me," she retorted.

Gabe took a step forward and stared down at the beauty in front of him. Barely any makeup, hair pulled in a messy knot on top of her head with a few curls falling down. Cheeks naturally blushed. Jeans and a t-shirt. *Well, jeans that have me growing hard every time she bends over and a t-shirt that makes me want to peel it off and discover the treasure underneath.*

"I'm glad it was unlike you," he said.

Cocking her hip, she narrowed her eyes as she said, "Oh? And why is that?"

He reached over and cupped his hand on her face. Her skin felt like pure silk and he couldn't help but brush his rough thumb over her cheeks, noting with pleasure that she leaned into his palm. "Because you're special. And I want to be special to you."

Sucking her lips in, she suddenly felt very unsure, but before she could back away he interjected, "I know you don't trust me yet. I have to earn that. But you will trust me, darling. I promise to show you just how special you are."

He leaned down and placed a gentle kiss on her lips. Soft. Not demanding. Then it was gone as he turned with a large platter in his hand and walked into the dining room. She stood there for a moment, dazed by the events of the last twelve hours. Giving her head a little shake, she picked up another platter and followed the others as well.

For the next thirty minutes they, along with Henry and Cora, served the residents. As Jennifer greeted each by name, they were all curious as to the handsome man standing next to her. He charmed the women and earned nods of approval from the men as he heaped their plates with the nutritious food.

Ross wanted to stand next to Gabe and kept up a running dialog the entire time. "That's Mr. Simmons. He's funny. Sometimes he'll take his teeth out just to make me laugh. Maybe he'll do it for you. Do you want to see him take his teeth out?" he asked, twisting his head way back to look at Gabe. Before Gabe could answer, Ross had moved to the next description. "That's Mrs. Portal and she's standing next to Mr. Zimmerman. I think he likes her because he always hurries to stand next to her in line. Isn't that what you'd do if you liked someone? I try to stand next to Chrissy, who's in my class. I like her because she smells pretty. You're standing next to my sister. Do you think she smells pretty?"

Gabe burst into laughter, as he ruffled Ross' hair. Jennifer finally moved over to Ross saying, "Honey, you need to slow down. You're going to wear Mr. Malloy out with all your chatter."

Ross had started serving but after a few of the residents begged him to sit with them, he bounded over to sit with them.

Gabe smiled at him and then turned to look at the beautiful woman standing next to him.

"I'm sorry. He gets so excited and sometimes it's hard to keep up with his train of thoughts."

"Don't apologize. I think he's great."

Jennifer beamed with pride as she looked first at Ross and then up at Gabe. "Thanks. He's pretty special."

"You two going to eat with us old fogies?" called one of the residents.

Smiling, the two fixed their plates and sat down at a

table surrounded by residents, all questioning 'Jennifer's young man'.

"He's awfully handsome, Jennifer. Where have you been hiding him?" one lady quipped.

In answer to one of the men's queries, Gabe replied, "I was in the Army, sir. Special Forces." The table became quiet, as the man sitting across from him stood up and leaned over the table with his hand extended. "Sergeant McBride, U.S. Army. Served in Vietnam."

Gabe, momentarily stunned, reached across the table and grasped the older man's hand while rising from his chair as well. At that, several other men stood as well, introducing themselves by their military rank.

Jennifer looked on, moved to tears as she saw the men bonding with Gabe over their military service. She realized that she did not know anything about him and perhaps dismissing him as a player had not been fair. He seemed embarrassed by the attention but also appeared genuinely impressed with the former soldiers around him.

Gabe sat back down, moved but also nervous. *Jesus, she thinks I'm an attention hound and this probably just confirmed it.* He warily glanced next to him, unsure of what her reaction was going to be. "I'm sorry, Jennifer. I didn't come here to be the center of attent—"

"That was really nice," she said softly, glancing at the tables now filled with men smiling as they began conversing among themselves about their military careers. Her eyes swept back to his as she said, "I know you didn't plan that."

He was surprised to see her smiling shyly at him. *God, she's so beautiful.* Before he could say anything, Ross called out to her and he watched her walk over to her brother. She bent down to roll his sleeves up his arms to keep them out of the syrup, laughing as she kissed the top of his head. On her way back to their table, she stopped casually among the residents. Assisting one, picking up the dropped napkin of another, refilling coffee cups. He rubbed his hand over his heart, feeling it ache.

The breakfast ended and the residents all rose, taking their own plates to the industrial-sized dishwasher in the kitchen. Gabe watched as they moved with a purpose, each seeming to be glad to have that purpose. Ross grabbed a bucket of soapy water that Henry handed to him and began wiping down the tables. As Jennifer bustled by, Gabe snagged her and whispered, "What should I do?"

Looking confused for a moment, she replied, "Nothing. You helped cook breakfast so you can just rela—" She was interrupted by the sound of a bucket of soapy water hitting the floor and a surprised Ross standing in a puddle. Sighing, she began to walk over when Gabe stopped her.

"You keep doing what you were doing. I'll take care of him," he said.

She watched from the kitchen door as Gabe deftly

lifted Ross out of the puddle and sat him on a dry table. He took the mop out of Cora's hands and began to clean the floor. Within a few minutes, the floor was clean and the tables were wiped off. She heard Ross' laughter and he and Gabe chatted over spilled water.

Jennifer jumped when she felt a hand on her shoulder and turned to see Cora standing right beside her.

"Seen a lot in my days. Seen a lot of good and my share of not so good," Cora commented as she held Jennifer's eyes. "But I know the difference between fake and real. And I'm telling you that that young man out there is real. Not saying he ain't had his fair share of problems or mistakes. But girl, that man is real."

"I know," she replied in a whisper. "But is it fair to have him around Ross to only take a chance on him leaving?"

"Honey, there's no guarantees in life. You know that. Ross has already known loss and he's gonna know more before his life is over. You're not doing him any favors by trying to shelter him from that. And he needs to know some good men in his life." Jennifer's eyes quickly found Cora's but before she could retort, Cora continued. "And I'm talking about more than just us old geezers around here. Good men all of them too, but Ross needs more."

Jennifer turned back to see the glow on her brother's face as he peered up at Gabe.

"And darling girl? You need more too. So do both of you a favor and take a chance." With that, Cora gave her shoulder a squeeze and walked back into the kitchen.

By that time, the dining area was scrubbed and Gabe had removed Ross' wet shoes and socks. "Come on, buddy, let's go find you something dry," he said while bending down low. Ross scrambled onto Gabe's back and they walked over to Jennifer.

"Did you see that?" Ross began enthusiastically.

Laughing, Jennifer replied, "Yes, I did. Are you sure you didn't make that mess just so someone would help you?"

"No," he protested loudly but could not stop the grin.

She reached her arms up to him, saying, "Let's go. I'll get you cleaned up and we can let Mr. Malloy get back to his Saturday."

Gabe lifted one eyebrow, saying, "Trying to get rid of me so soon? I've got him. Just show me the way."

Jennifer nodded, secretly not wanting him to leave, and proceeded up the stairs. Halfway up, she turned suddenly, a look of concern on her face. "I'm sorry. Here I am letting you carry him and we live up several flights. Let me have him for a bit."

Gabe, towering over her, frowned down at her. "Seriously? Babe, I carried packs heavier than him all day long in the desert. Think I can handle a child."

"Oh," she mumbled. "Just thought I would help."

With Ross still on his back, he leaned down as though to whisper, "The day I have a woman, any woman but especially one as tiny as you, carry a load for me is the day I give up my man-card."

Ross giggled as he asked, "What's a man-card?"

Rolling her eyes, she turned and continued up the stairs. "Men," she grumbled.

Gabe grinned to himself as he watched her move ahead of him. Many of her blonde curls had escaped the chopstick holding them and falling down her back. Then his eyes dropped lower. *Hell, that was a mistake.* Instantly his dick reacted, making the rest of the climb uncomfortable. Focusing on something besides his hard-on, he quickly scanned the interior of her building. It was old, but he was pleased to see that it was well-lit. The first two floors seemed to have been renovated and he knew that those were the studio apartments for the elderly residents.

As they entered their apartment, Gabe set Ross down then tried to discretely adjust himself, hoping to hide his hard-on. Ross ran back to his room and Jennifer turned around looking nervous.

Sweeping her hands around, she said, "It's not much, but it's home."

His eyes scanned the room quickly taking everything in. The room had new paint, with some family pictures hanging on the walls. The wooden floors were old and scarred but like the rest of the space, it was scrubbed clean. A small sofa and bean-bag provided the only seating in the room and faced a wall with an older TV on a stand. Bright blue curtains hung on the window, matching the blue pillows on the sofa.

As his eyes moved, he saw the tiny kitchen. It was furnished with a small refrigerator, small stove, and very little counter space. More blue curtains hung at the small window over the sink and over the window that was next to the dinette set.

His eyes went back to hers and he could see the doubt filling them. Taking the two steps that it took to place himself right in front of her, he smiled as he lifted his hand to cup her face. "It's nice, babe. You've made a really nice home here for yourself and Ross." Just as he leaned over and noticed that she was rising on her toes to meet his lips, they were interrupted.

"Gabe, come see my room," Ross called out.

Gabe sighed as he touched his forehead to hers, then felt her step away.

"Coming buddy," he called as he turned and followed the voice down the short hallway. The end of the hall led into a tiny bathroom that he could see. Glancing to the left, he saw a small bedroom with a twin-sized bed covered in a floral print. *No way that closet can be hers*, but then Ross popped out of the room on the right and grabbed his hand pulling him in.

"See? This is my room. It's kind of junky, but sis only makes me clean it on Saturdays and I haven't done it yet. But I will," he promised looking up at Gabe, smiling. Leaning in, he whispered, "I don't really mind, but she gets cranky if she can't find something. I told her to just ask me and then she won't have to waste time looking. I really want a dog, but we don't have room here. One day when I grow up and get big like you, I'm gonna get a dog."

"Makes sense to me, bud. But your sister works real hard, so maybe it's best to keep things picked up."

The room had a few sports posters on the walls and navy curtains with footballs and baseballs printed on them adorned the windows. A matching bedspread was sloppily tossed on the bed showing an attempt at making the room seem neater. *Probably didn't fool his sister,* Gabe thought with a smile. Some toys and books were scattered on the floor, but there was not much floor for a boy to play on. With a small chest of drawers and a bookshelf nightstand, the small room gave Gabe little space to move. He felt her presence behind him before she spoke.

"Ross, it's Saturday. Why don't you go ahead and get your room picked up so that Mr. Malloy won't think that you live in a zoo."

"But I don't want to miss Mr. Malloy. What if he leaves before I get to come out?"

Her voice carried authority, but sweet with love. Gabe turned to see her standing in the doorway, still looking uncertain. Wanting to take that look away, he walked over and touched her face. Calling over his shoulder, he said, "Buddy, I'll be out here talking with your sister. I'll still be here when you get finished."

Ross, suddenly filled with a purpose, began hurriedly putting things away. Gabe laughed as he followed

Jennifer out of the room. Taking a closer look into the bedroom across the hall, he knew that she had chosen the smaller room for herself. Barely bigger than a closet, he wondered how she managed. *Most women I know have walk-in closets filled with clothes that are bigger than her room.* As he rubbed his chest again, he realized once more, *but then she's not like any woman I've known before.*

They moved to the sofa where she sat on one end and noticed how much space he took as he sat on the other. A giggle escaped causing him to look over quizzically.

"I'm sorry. I'm just not used to having such a large man in here on my small furniture."

"Oh, and what size of man are you used to having?" he asked, only half joking.

She tucked an escaped curl behind her ear as she blushed, saying, "No men, large or small, actually."

He could not help but swell with caveman pride at hearing that. He placed his arm on the back of the sofa, bringing his hand close enough to touch her curls. *Soft. So fuckin' soft.*

"I want to thank you," she said.

"For what?" he asked, surprise on his face.

"For breakfast. For helping. For greeting the men downstairs and allowing them to reminisce about their military days. I know that meant a lot to them." She paused, looking around before her eyes found his again. "Especially for talking to Ross. He hasn't had many men to be around other than the men downstairs."

"He's a great kid, Jennifer. Don't thank me for any of that. Not when you do it every day," he said honestly. His eyes landed on a picture on the end table of a family of four. He recognized a resemblance.

She turned to see what he was looking at and answered his unspoken question. "That's my parents. They were Peace Corps. Ross was born when I was sixteen. Their last assignment was overseas of course, but that wasn't where they were killed. They had come back to visit and raise more money here in the states when their car slid on some ice and was hit by another truck. Killed instantly, so I was told."

The silence in the room was deafening. Gabe wanted to say words of comfort, but they seemed inadequate.

"I'm so lucky that Ross wasn't with them. He had come over here to visit when we got the news. So...I petitioned the court, became his guardian and it's been us two for the past year."

"I'm sorry, Jennifer. So sorry." He looked around at the tiny apartment, barely big enough for her much less a growing boy.

"I'm really lucky to have this place," she commented as though she could read his mind. "I live here virtually rent free since I work with the center downstairs. That allows me to save a lot of money for Ross."

"Your parents didn't have...um..." Gabe stumbled uncharacteristically over his words.

"Insurance?" she said for him. Shaking her head, she said, "Not much. Enough to pay the funeral expenses, but Peace Corps employees don't make a lot of money." Smiling at him she shrugged. "But we don't need much. I gave him my bedroom since I knew he would need more room and we live pretty simply. I know he misses them, but he's adapted really well. And the folks downstairs have all adopted him," she said laughing. "Sometimes I think he gets into more mischief with them around!"

Gabe's fingers continued to move through her silky curls as he watched her face as she described her brother. His mind wandered momentarily to his childhood with his twin Vinny. They had been raised by loving parents in an upper-middle-class neighborhood. Not spoiled, but definitely given more than what they needed.

"I suppose it seems pathetic to some," she said defensively, "But to us, it's home."

Using the hand tangled in her curls to pull her over gently until his lips were just a whisper away from hers, he said, "Baby, what you do and what you've done...perfect. Just perfect."

With that he lowered his lips to hers. The kiss started slow, just the moving of lips as they molded to each other. Then with a single moan from her mouth, he pulled her closer as his tongue slid in, tasting the sweet syrup from earlier. Like nectar, he couldn't resist. He wrapped his arms around her tiny form, dwarfing her in the process.

In just a few seconds with his tongue tangling with hers, she melted into him. All else slipped away as she allowed herself to be swept away in a rush of passion. Her breasts felt heavy as her womb clenched. She knew she was becoming wet and she squirmed slightly to ease the ache.

"Sis, I'm finished," came the call as Ross bounded into the room. "Eew," he exclaimed. "Are you kissing my sister?" he asked in surprise.

The two jumped apart as Jennifer was mortified to think that she lost herself in Gabe's embrace with Ross in the next room. *Jesus, I was practically dry-humping him.* Her blush rose across her face, but before she could think of a response Ross jumped in again.

Plopping down on the coffee table right in front of the couple, he said to Gabe, "I thought about kissing Chrissy, and I was just going to give her a little kiss. Not like the big kiss you were giving my sister. But then when I tried, she moved away from me and looked like she was going to yell. So I didn't kiss her after all."

Laughter erupted from Gabe as he watched Jennifer cover her face with her hands in embarrassment. "Well, Buddy, I think it's a good thing that you stopped. Remember, a man never forces himself on a woman. When Chrissy wants you to kiss her, she'll let you know."

"Oh," Ross replied, his sharp mind working. "So that means that sis wanted you to kiss her?"

Jennifer's head shot up as she glared at Gabe, quietly admonishing, "Will you please not talk about kissing to my little brother? He's only eight."

Giving the back of her neck a little squeeze, he replied laughing. "Baby, a man's never too young to know about women. And are you going to deny wanting to kiss me?"

Her eyes bugged out of her head as she turned to Ross, seeing the question in his eyes as well. Sighing, she agreed, "Yes, Ross. I did want to be kissed, so Mr. Malloy was not doing anything wrong at all."

Gabe stood, pulling her up with him. "I'm gonna head out now. Got a date to get ready for," he said with a smirk. Looking down at Ross he said, "Buddy, I'm taking your sister out on a date tonight. Is that all right with you?"

Ross smiled up at the giant in front of him holding his sister's hand. "Yeah. Can I come too?"

Before Gabe could answer, she jumped in. "Not tonight, Ross. Cora and Henry are going to watch you."

Ross face fell until she added that they were taking him out for ice-cream. "Cool," he said. "But can I come some other time?"

Jennifer saw hope written all over his face. *I can't promise what I don't know. What if there's not another time.*

Gabe saw it the instant it hit her face. Doubt. Fear. Uncertainty. Giving her hand a gentle squeeze until she looked up at him, "Absolutely, buddy. There'll be lots of next times and on some of them, we'll all go."

Her huge blue eyes widened as she stared up at him. He wanted nothing more than to kiss the worry out of them but knew there would be time for that later. Walking to the door, he gave her a quick, chaste kiss then stood and nodded to Ross. "Later, Buddy."

Ross called out his goodbye, then ran to his room. "I'll be back to pick you up about six," he said. Jennifer leaned in and Gabe took the invite to kiss her once again. This time, less chastely. The trip down the stairs had his dick just as hard as it had been going up the stairs. *Damn. Time for a cold shower.*

CHAPTER 7

GABE STEPPED INTO his apartment and halted immediately. The space that seemed so comfortable when he left this morning now seemed huge. *All this for one person,* he thought ruefully. Looking around he realized that Jennifer's entire apartment could fit in the space of this living room and dining room. Taking a deep breath, he grabbed his phone making a call.

"Bro? You home? Need some advice. See you in a few."

Within a few minutes, Vinny and Jobe walked through the door. "Hope you don't mind if I crash? I was down in your gym when you called," Jobe said. "But if it's private, then I'll head down to Vin's apartment."

Gabe looked over at the two men, one a brother, and both brothers-in-arms. "Nah, it's all good," he said. "But I need advice."

"On what? I know it's not about girls," Jobe quipped. The silence in the room reverberated among the men. With eyes raised, he said, "Seriously? You asking us about woman advice? What gives? You make a date with two at the same time and need us to take

106

one off your hands?"

Giving his friend a death glare, he could hardly call him out. A few weeks ago that would have been exactly why he called them.

Vinny watched him carefully. "Something tells me this is about the woman you've been chasing for the past few weeks. You finally caught her and don't know what to do with a real woman?"

Gabe nodded, "Yeah, something like that."

A whistle erupted from Jobe's lips. "Well, I'll be damned. It's about time the great Gabe fell. I was beginning to think that Shane, Matt, and BJ found all the good women."

Gabe tossed them each a beer before settling down on his sofa. A sofa he noted, not only held his bulk, but the bulk of his twin with room to spare.

He gave them a quick run-down on Jennifer and her situation, finishing with, "I've finally got a date and now don't know what the fuck to do. Where do I take her? Hell, I hardly ever go on dates that are more than meet in a bar and make small talk enough to go back to their place and bang for a couple of hours."

"You've been a real romantic, haven't you?" Jobe joked. He turned to Vinny and said, "But then you've been no better." Turning back to Gabe he said, "So you called twin, 'Mr. Bang-Em-And-Run-Away' for advice?"

"You got any good advice or just here to bust our chops?" Vinny complained.

"You two, shut the fuck up. I really don't know where to take her. She's not going to be impressed with a fancy restaurant. Jesus, I was going to take her to that new place downtown, Chef Molene's. Expensive as shit but the food is supposed to be out of this world."

Vinny said, "You don't think she'll like it?"

Gabe sighed. "Bro, she lives in an apartment smaller than this room and gets restaurant food not sold to take back to feed the elderly residents that live in her building. Somehow, I don't see her being comfortable in that setting, knowing how much the food costs and how much goes to waste."

"Hell, give her a chance to get all dolled up and go out on the town. She may really like that since it sounds like she doesn't get a chance to do that. You know, put on the skimpy dress and throw on the heels. What woman doesn't like that?" Vinny asked.

Gabe looked at his twin and said honestly, "I doubt she owns a cocktail dress and probably hasn't had any money to spend on shoes in years. If ever. I don't want to make her feel out of place."

Jobe looked between the two twins, both admiring their relationship and realizing how out of their element they were. "I swear you two can be dumb-fucks." This gained the angry attention of the twins.

"Look, what do you admire about her? Her looks, her giving personality, her hard work and her dedication, right?" Jobe asked. At Gabe's nod, he continued. "So, give her what she doesn't have but wouldn't mind having."

Seeing the raised eyebrows of both men, he just shook his head. "I'm one of four kids. We grew up happy but poor as shit. So we learned early how to have fun on little and we appreciated it more than you can imagine."

"I'm listening," Gabe said, leaning forward.

"She works all day for the city. She goes home where she takes care of her brother and the residents. She goes out at night and gets hand-outs for food to give to others. What she doesn't have is time for herself to just have fun. So, I don't know her man, but you're getting to know her. Give her something just for her. Just for fun. To maybe take the worry off of her shoulders for just one night."

Gabe felt the pain in his chest once again as he thought of Jobe's words. *Just fun.*

"Fuck man, how'd you get so smart?" Vinny asked.

Jobe ducked his head and laughed. "Y'all know me. Know where I came from." And they did. There was nothing the team had not known about each other that was not learned in hours together in training, in the field, on a mission. They knew Jobe had grown up poor. He knew hunger. He knew want. But he also knew love and that was the gift his parents gave him and his siblings. Shrugging, he rose from his seat and walked over to Gabe, who stood to meet him. Clapping his hand on Gabe's shoulder, he said, "You're one of the best men I know. You've been pissing your time away waiting on finding someone who could make your heart really beat. Sounds like you found that. So don't fuck it up trying to impress. Just work at making her life a little better. Haven't met her yet and hope to. But for now, just give her some fun and I bet you'll find some of that yourself." He walked toward the door and nodded as he let himself out.

The two brothers looked at each other, words not necessary. It had often been that way; growing up they found that it was as though they shared the same feelings and emotions as well as looks.

Vinny walked over looking at his twin. "You okay, man? You know what you need to do?"

"Yeah. Just gotta figure out what would be the best."

Nodding, Vinny pulled him in for a hug. "Can't wait to meet her, man." Then throwing is head back in laughter, he continued, "And mom's gonna flip, you bring home a girl." With that he followed Jobe out of the door, leaving Gabe in the middle of his massive living room trying to figure out what to do.

JENNIFER RAN DOWN the stairs with Ross in tow.

"Lordy girl, where's the fire?" Cora called out.

"Ross, honey can you go in with Henry and the others and watch basketball?" Jennifer asked.

"Yay!" came his response as he charged into the

room, quickly settling down with the men circled around the TV.

Jennifer grabbed Cora's hand and dragged her into the kitchen. Grabbing the coffee pot, she quickly poured them both a cup.

"Girl, what has got your feathers all ruffled?"

"Okay, you know I have a date tonight, right?"

"Oh course," came the simple reply. By this time, several of the women residents wandered in to see what was happening.

Biting her lip, Jennifer said, "I don't know what to wear. I have nothing to wear. I have no idea…oh, this is such a bad idea."

"Now slow down, child. This is not a bad idea, you having a date with a nice young man. And you look pretty no matter what you wear."

"You don't understand. He's used to…women that wear cocktail dresses and hang out in bars."

One lady piped up, "Well, that doesn't sound very nice."

"No, no. I don't mean seedy bars." *Well, I don't actually know where he picks up his dates. Oh Jesus, this is a mistake.*

"Well, I think you should wear one of those little dresses like you see on TV, where you can show him how lucky he is," another one added.

"Certainly not," exclaimed another. "He'll think he's out with a floosie. Now in my day, we dressed in our Sunday best to go out on a date."

"Bertha, you are so full of it," came the retort. "Don't think I don't know you were at Woodstock, probably dancing nude in the mud!"

"Well, I never," she replied.

One tiny lady appeared at Jennifer's side, placing her hand on her arm. "I think you should borrow some of my high heels. I have some packed away from when I used to go dancing with my husband. Your young man is awfully tall and might like to have you a bit taller."

"I'm telling you, a black cocktail dress with pearls is the only way to go," declared another.

"Lucille, she doesn't want to look like Jacqueline Kennedy," another woman said. "Just wear your hair down, a tight pair of jeans, and make sure to pack a condom."

Seeing the panic on Jennifer's face, Cora stepped up. "Quiet, you old hens. Now you listen to me, young lady. He may have been used to escorting some beautiful women around, but they've got nothing on you. I've often told Henry that I've never seen another woman so beautiful in my whole life. And sweet? Lord have mercy, girl. You'd make any man proud to have you on their arm."

Jennifer looked into the eyes of the woman who had been like a mother to her for the past several years, seeing nothing but sincerity in her gaze. The other women around nodded their heads.

Taking a deep breath, she let it out slowly. Just

then, her phone chimed with an incoming message. Looking down, she read it and smiled.

"From him?" one of the women asked.

"Yes. I texted him and asked what I should wear. He just answered: Comfortable and warm."

"Well, there you go. A practical man. I like him," announced Bertha as she walked out of the kitchen, followed by the other women, leaving just Jennifer and Cora.

"You're about to talk yourself into a tizzy. Honey, he seems like a good man. This doesn't have to be forever. But neither does it have to be just one date. Just go. Have a good time. Have some fun. Forget for just one night that you have all of us to take care of."

Kissing the old woman's cheek, she called out to Ross but he was engrossed in the game. Cora told her to go on and get ready, they'd take care of Ross for the evening.

Running up the stairs, she kept thinking, *Warm and comfortable. That, I can do.*

NOT WILLING TO wait at the apartment and certainly not wanting Gabe to wade through the throng of residents peeking out of the activity hall to see him, she waited on the front stoop. Wearing jeans with blue, knit leg warmers over them, she had donned a warm pair of boots. Her blue sweater was covered in a wool coat, with a matching blue knit scarf. Her blonde curls were tamed from the wind with a knit hat, all compliments of one of the residents who knitted as a pastime.

Just then, Gabe drove around the corner, seeing her standing on the stoop in the cold. Her hair, mostly tucked under a hat, had blonde curls escaping and framing her perfect face. Her cheeks were red from the cold and he cursed himself as he looked at the clock in his Jeep Wrangler. *What the fuck is she doing out here in the cold? I'm actually early.*

Parking quickly, he was almost out of the vehicle when she came bounding down the stairs. Her hand was on the door handle when he rounded the front of the Jeep.

"Don't touch that handle," he ordered. Surprised, she looked up at him in question. He walked closer and opened the door. Giving her a hand up, he assisted her into the seat. He grabbed the seatbelt and moved it across her body. Leaning in for a kiss, he explained, "My mama taught me to always open a door for a lady and I'm not about to disappoint her now."

The Jeep was warm and she smiled as she looked out of the passenger window at the faces peering down at her from her building. Giving a little wave, they took off down the street. After a moment, she squirmed feeling her ass getting warm.

"You okay, baby?" he asked, looking at her in concern.

"I swear it feels as though I am sitting on a heating

pad," she said blushing.

He chuckled, saying, "I've got the seat heaters on for you." Looking at her confused face, he realized that she had never had that in a car.

"Seat heaters?" Laughing she said, "I'm afraid my old junker truck doesn't have those. You'll just have to suffer if we go out in it," she joked.

"Good to know."

"So where are we going? I hope I'm dressed all right," she said, her voice slightly laced with uncertainty.

Reaching across the seat, he took her gloved hand in his. "You're gorgeous, darlin'. And dressed perfectly."

Driving downtown, he found a parking spot and growled as he saw her hand reach for the doorknob. She pulled it back before he could say anything, grinning as she said, "Oh yeah. I almost forgot about your mama."

He laughed as he rounded the Jeep and assisted her down. The downtown area was beautiful in the March night with lights twinkling from all of the trees. Tugging on her hand, pulling her closer, he wrapped his large arm around her tiny frame and they began walking down the street, noticing how snugly she fit into him. *Funny, I always thought that a man my size had to have a tall woman with curves to fit into me.* At that moment, he realized that nothing had ever felt so right. The spring warmth had not come yet and he was glad he told her to dress warmly.

"So where are we going?" she asked, twisting her head up to look at him.

"We're there," he announced, smiling down at her expression.

She turned in the direction that he was facing, but all she could see was a horse carriage in front of her.

"Mr. Malloy?" the carriage driver called, as he stepped down with his hand out. "Your ride awaits."

She gasped in surprise, turning quickly to look up at Gabe again. "A carriage ride? Really? Oh my God, I've never done this," she squealed in excitement. Bouncing up and down, she could barely contain herself as Gabe escorted her over.

He laughed as he assisted her up into the leather seat, thinking at that moment he could see the resemblance between her and Ross.

They settled in the comfortable seats and the driver handed them a blanket. "It's a chilly night so wrap up," he advised. Gabe gladly draped the woolen blanket over their legs, tucking it in tightly around her. Throwing his arm around her once again he pulled her close. The carriage began its journey around the downtown area, including the large park by the river running through town.

He looked at her, seeing her sparkling eyes as she took in their surroundings. Her smile was infectious as she looked up at him and he felt the piercing in his heart once again.

"Gabe, I've never done this before. This is amazing!" she said, leaning into him.

"I couldn't agree more. Never wanted to do this until today," he admitted.

She whirled around looking at his face. "Never? You've never…"

Seeing where her thoughts had taken, he said, "No, baby. I've never done this. Ever. You're the first." He watched as her smile came back and felt her settle into him once more.

After a little while, he leaned down and set a basket onto their laps. Opening it, he pulled out a bottle of wine, two glasses, and some chocolate covered strawberries.

"Oh my goodness," she exclaimed, taking the glasses while he poured. Sipping the delicious wine, she leaned back and he held out a strawberry to her. Biting into the chocolate juiciness, she moaned in delight.

He watched her mouth surround the strawberry, eyes closed in ecstasy, the little moan escaping. *Fuck, I could come right now.* Shifting in the seat to try to accommodate his erection, he hoped she had not noticed.

A small trickle of juice lingered on her lips and he leaned over capturing it with his mouth. She tasted of wine and sweetness, eliciting a moan from himself. He slid his tongue inside as he set his empty wine glass on the seat and cupped her face in his large hand. Taking the kiss deeper, he became lost in the feel of her mouth, her taste, her body pressed next to his.

She wrapped her arms around his neck, holding on as though she would drown if she let go. He angled his head so that the kiss became more demanding, invading her senses. Pulling him closer, she let go and let him in. *No more doubts. No more caution.*

He felt the change in her as she gave herself over to him and he reveled in the knowledge that this amazing woman was giving him all she had. Pulling back, he leaned his forehead against hers. He looked into her crystal blue eyes staring into his. Answering her unspoken question, he said, "The carriage has stopped baby." Catching her surprised look toward the driver, he laughed, "It's okay. I'm sure he's used to this."

They thanked him as Gabe turned and lifted her completely out of the carriage, holding her pressed tightly to his front before slowly letting her down. Turning, he tipped the driver and then took Jennifer's hand as he led her down the street. Ushering her inside a small family owned Italian restaurant, they were shown to a corner table near the back.

She quickly pulled off her gloves, scarf, and hat then shook out her curls. Gabe stood behind her assisting with her coat, before handing them to the hostess. Her cheeks were pink and eyes sparkled in the candlelight. He helped her to her seat and then sat at a right angle next to her.

They ordered and sipped the wine while waiting for their food. Comfortable with each other's company, the conversation flowed. He regaled her with tales of growing up with a twin.

Laughing at the stories of how they switched places in school sometimes to confuse their teachers, she asked, "So are you two really that identical?"

"We were then. Now, he's got his hair a little longer and sometimes grows a beard."

"Hmm, a beard? Maybe I'm out with the wrong twin," she joked.

Growling, he found himself thinking of her with anyone else but himself and did not like the idea at all.

"So you two never changed places for a date?" she prompted.

At this, Gabe blushed.

"Oh my, I think I finally made the big man blush," she exclaimed. "Did you two really change places?"

Rubbing the back of his hand over his neck, he looked at her amused expression. Sighing, he admitted, "Yeah. When we were younger. I...well...I...sort of...hooked up with two women for the same night. He stepped in and met up with one of them. Jesus, this is embarrassing."

Throwing her head back in laughter, she said, "So if you make a date with me and with someone else at the same time, I could end up with Vinny?"

He leaned over and gently pulled her to him with his hand on the back of her neck. "First of all, baby. You will never be going out with my brother. Second of all, as far as I'm concerned, there is no other woman but you."

Her laughter died down as she peered into his eyes. "Gabe—"

"No, babe. Don't even say it. You are the best woman I have ever met and I'm willing to take this as far as it will go." Seeing her eyes widen, he continued, "And don't start goin' inside of your head thinking of all the reasons we won't work. Take it one day at a time, baby. Just one day at a time."

With that, he leaned in to kiss her once again, taking her mind off of everything other than his lips on hers.

With his lips a whisper away from hers, he said, "You with me, Jennifer?"

"Yeah. I'm with you," she said just as softly.

The food arrived and they once again settled into easy conversation. "So tell me about your place," he said.

"Well, you've seen how we operate. It's a bare-bones operation, but we make it work. My job with the city is to work on programs for the elderly. I started out just driving around checking on them, but they often end up with no one to care for them and many lose their housing. I received a grant and with the help of Senator Reno and his wife, who's amazing at fund-raising and we had enough to open the center. It provides very low rent studio apartments for qualified seniors. We offer one meal a day, free of charge to the residents. We also have the open hall for movies, social gatherings, things like that."

Gabe watched her face as she talked and he found himself rubbing his chest again. *So fuckin' gorgeous. Outside of his close circle of friends and brothers-in-arms, she was the best person he had ever met.*

"I just hope we can keep going," she said. Seeing his question, she continued, "The area is slowly being renovated and some of the buildings have been bought. I know they're cheap…well, cheap if you have several million to buy and renovate. I've heard that there's someone who's wanting to buy our building, and that would turn all the residents out. But so far, I'm holding on and I'll fight anyone who tries to take this away from them."

Seeing the passion in her eyes, he found himself wanting all that passion turned his way. *Buying the building out from under her? I'll have Lily and BJ check to see what they can find out.*

The meal finished too quickly and he knew he needed to get her back to Ross. Standing, he assisted as she slipped into her coat and with fingers laced they walked outside. The night sky was clear and filled with stars. The wind had died down, leaving the early spring chill not as biting as earlier.

As they drove to her building, he parked outside. Turning to each other, they both began talking at once. Laughing, he said, "Ladies first."

"I just wanted to thank you. Gabe, I haven't had so much fun in a really long time."

Fun. That's what Jobe said to give her. Smiling, he said, "I'm glad. Babe, I hope it is the first of many, many days and nights of fun."

"One day at a time, right?" she said softly.

"Yeah, baby. One day at a time."

He walked her inside and up to her apartment. Slipping inside as Cora hugged them both before going into her apartment, Jennifer walked down the hall to check on Ross. Coming back into the living room, she said, "He's sleeping."

"He's a great little boy," Gabe said truthfully.

"I know. I just hope that…well, that I can do right by him." Seeing his lifted eyebrow, she continued, "I'm not a man."

At that, he chuckled. "I think I got that part figured out, sweetheart."

Giggling, she said, "I mean, I worry about when he gets older."

"You're doing great. You're giving him love and those men downstairs will give him attention and wisdom." Stepping right up to her, he pulled her in close reveling in the feel of her body next to his. "And now you've got me. And with me, comes Vinny and my friends." Leaning down, he kissed her, sweet and soft. Full of promise. Full of hope. "I've got you covered." With that, he took the kiss deeper before gently pushing her back to arm's length.

"I want all of you. But we're gonna take this at your speed, at your pace. Goodnight, baby. I'll call you tomorrow," he promised.

With that, he walked out after making sure she locked her door.

She went into the bathroom and pulled off her clothes, taking a quick, warm shower. Drying off, she looked into the mirror and for the first time in a long time saw a woman looking back with a relaxed smile on her face. *He put that there. He gave me that. Was it only this morning that he stood in the kitchen making pancakes?*

Crawling into bed, she fell into a peaceful sleep with a smile on her lips.

Across town, Gabe walked into his large apartment, noting his security system. *Hers is shit. Worse than shit, because it's nonexistent.* Vowing to talk to Tony on Monday, he planned on asking if a security system could be placed in her building. Taking a shower, he thought of her sweet body pressed close to his. *Soon baby. I hope you're in my bed soon. But only when you're ready.*

CHAPTER 8

THE NEXT WEEK found Jennifer at work, smiling as she went through her day. Sybil and Roy surrounded her at lunch clambering for information.

"Give it up, girl," Sybil said. "You've had a goofy grin on your face all week."

Roy looked up from texting his wife and said, "Yeah, it's getting on Sybil's nerves."

Sybil punched him in the arm and said, "Ignore him. I just want to know who he is."

"Who?" Jennifer asked.

"The man who's the reason you're grinning like you are," she retorted.

"Okay, okay. I have met someone and he's everything I thought I would never have."

"Oh girl. Why did you think you'd never find that someone special?" Sybil asked.

Looking at her two co-workers, she shrugged. "I live and work with older people. I don't go to bars or parties. After work, I'm with Ross. I'm not complaining," she added quickly, "But let's face it, there just isn't a lot of time to meet a man."

"Well...," Sybil prompted.

"He's huge. A former Special Forces Sergeant and is now working for a security company."

At that, Roy's attention was sparked. "Security?"

"Yeah, I think it's called Alvarez Security Agency."

Roy whistled. "I've heard of them. High priced but supposedly the best. Impressive, girl."

The lunch discussion was tabled as their boss' secretary popped in to tell them that there was a meeting being called.

"Jeez, can't Chip let us know ahead of time he wants to meet?" Jennifer grumbled, packing up her sandwich.

At the meeting, Chip asked about the possible loss of funding for the elder care building, drawing the ire of Jennifer.

"This is so ridiculous. We have a five-year lease and are only two years into it. This shouldn't even be an item for us to be worried about."

"Well, it appears that the state is looking at the budget and ways to cut back. And if someone comes along and makes an offer on the building that brings in much-needed cash, they may pull the grant funds."

"Well, I'll just start going back to the State Capitol once again," she groused. "I can't do my job properly for having to keep the sharks at bay."

"From a practical standpoint, the owner of the building can take it back any time a payment isn't made, so if your money dries up, be prepared to vacate the building."

"What'll we do if that happens?" she asked, fear in her voice for the first time.

"That's your job and your problem," came the sharp retort. "Now moving on."

The meeting droned on for another thirty minutes, but Jennifer did not hear anything that was being said. Her mind raced with ideas to keep the real estate moguls out of her business and out of her building.

Walking back to her desk, Roy and Sybil noticed her determination. "What are you going to do?" Roy asked.

Smiling, Jennifer said, "I've got a couple of ideas."

"Plan on sharing?" he asked.

She patted his arm. "Not yet. Let me work on them first and see what I can do."

That afternoon, she made a call to one of the reporters for the Richland Times that had done an article on the overworked-understaffed Department of Social Services a few years ago. "Frank? Jennifer Lambert here. Got some time for me? Sure, I can meet you. Tomorrow morning sounds good."

Smiling, she hung up her phone. "Nothing like a little public support to keep things in line," she chirped.

BEHIND HER, SOMEONE overheard. And noted. And walked away. And made a call to Santo.

"Sir, she's on her way out of the building, probably to The State Capitol again."

"Thank you. I'll notify them that she is coming," came the sharp reply. "I want intervention."

"Yes, sir. I'll work on it on this end."

Santo clicked off his phone. Impatient, he was growing weary of his boss' reticence to act. Michael had heard from the building's owner. It seemed the old geezer made an impromptu visit disguised as a homeless man and the intrepid Ms. Lambert welcomed him in. And now…Mr. Mason refused to consider any sale.

All it would take would be one visit from him to Ms. Lambert and she would not be a problem anymore. No one holds a cause dearer than their own lives or their own family.

He had been thrilled to have worked up to the honored position with Michael and had been rewarded for his loyalty. But…the older ones began to get soft in their older age. Moving away from the window of their high rise, he placed another call.

"She's on her way. Boss wants intervention. You know what to do."

Clicking off after his terse instructions, he went back to the window and pondered his options knowing he needed to plan carefully. Deciding that perhaps a small taste of fear might just be what the good Ms. Lambert needed, he made another phone call.

GRABBING HER BAG, Jennifer headed out of her building and toward The State Capitol. Upon arriving, she made her way to Senator Reno's office, hoping that he would be in and Monty would not. No such luck.

Monty looked up from his desk and stood, moving slightly to stand in front of the Senator's door. "May I help you?"

"Yes, I was hoping to speak to Senator—"

"He's not in," came the abrupt reply.

"Well, then perhaps I can wai—"

"That won't be convenient for the Senator. He won't be back this afternoon."

Monty had shifted slightly closer until he was standing right in front of her. Stepping back a few feet, she realized that he was maneuvering her away. Sucking in a calming breath, she looked up into his face. "Well, then I will make an appointment."

"His calendar is very busy this week. I can fit you in next week. Tuesday? At ten o'clock."

"Fine, that'll be fine." *Damn, over a week away.* Plastering a false smile on her face, she purposely stuck out her hand as she said, "Thank you so much for all of your…help."

Monty looked down at her hand for a moment before taking it in his own. Pulling her in ever so slightly, he said, "The Senator is very busy you know. You really should not just drop in. If you can't stay away, call before you come next time." His voice carried a tone of warning as his hand gave hers a slight squeeze.

Pursing her lips, she jerked her hand away before turning on her heels and walking off. Halfway down the stairs she heard her name called. Turning she saw Sherrie. Trying to smile, she walked over to her.

"I would ask how you're doing, but you seem fit to be tied," Sherrie said. "Are you all right?"

Jennifer glanced up the stairs and saw Monty standing there staring down at her. Turning quickly, she grabbed Sherrie and said, "Oooh, that man makes me so angry." Seeing her friend's quizzical look, she explained her encounter with Monty.

"That's funny, he's always so polite when I drop papers off for my law firm."

Jennifer said, "He never gives you a hard time?"

"No, but then I'm just dropping things off. Perhaps it's because you actually need to see the Senator." Seeing Jennifer's angry face, she asked, "Come on, let's grab that cup of coffee you promised me last time."

That earned a smile from Jennifer and the two women headed to the coffee shop down the street.

SOMEONE WAS STILL watching. And continued to follow. And made a phone call.

"She's going to make things difficult which may need to be dealt with sooner rather than later. Keep me abreast of what she's doing. And for fuck's sake, stay off of her radar," Santo ordered.

Santo then walked to Michael's office, nodding to Eloise at her desk. "Can you ring me in?" he asked politely.

Smiling, she checked with her boss before indicating that he could go in. Michael was coming out of his private bathroom and Santo knew that Theresa had just visited. He had a bad feeling about that one, wondering how long she would be satisfied to stay out of the light. That was another poor decision Michael had made, letting her lead him by his dick.

He almost commented on his fears but held himself in check. If Michael made a mistake and had to step down from the head of the family, Santo knew he could be next in line.

"She went out with some big security guy the other night."

Michael looked at Santo, anger replacing the satisfaction of fucking Theresa from behind as she was bent over his desk just a few minutes earlier. Taking a deep breath, he asked, "Is there a way to give her a warning, without fucking ourselves over?"

"I'm working on it."

Michael smiled, his good humor back. "I knew I could count on you."

Santo moved out of the exclusive office, thinking of the time when it might be his.

AT THE END of the week, Jennifer arrived home to a hive of activity. Several large, black SUVs were parked in front of the building and the residents were buzzing around. Stepping off of the bus, she made her way to the door seeing Gabe installing a camera near the door.

"Hey honey, what are you doing?" she said running up and grabbing him around the waist.

"Huh," came the surprised reply. "Well, hello beautiful." Gabe turned around and locked his arms around her.

He leaned down to kiss the top of her head and she looked up wanting his lips on her own. He looked like Gabe but wasn't. Gasping, she suddenly stiffened as she jerked back, but his arms held her tight. "You...you're..."

He threw his head back and laughed, but before she could react they heard, "Get your fuckin' hands off my woman."

Both turned and looked at an angry Gabe coming around the corner. She threw up her hands and pushed on Ga...someone's chest. *Vinny! Oh my God. This is Gabe's twin. And he was going to kiss her!*

Gabe arrived at the top of the stoop and gently pulled her into his embrace. Vinny was still laughing and said, "It's nice to see you again, Jennifer. I'm sorry darling, but when a beautiful woman comes up and grabs me for a kiss, I just can't help myself."

"You kissed her?" Gabe growled, taking a step toward his brother.

She quickly stepped between the two giants and said, "No, he didn't. Well, the top of my head."

Vinny smiled his panty-dropping smile and said, "Well hell, little one. That was the only thing I could reach."

She giggled, knowing it was true.

"Gabe! Jennybenny!" came a yell from down the street and as they looked up, Ross came jumping off of the school bus. Running full speed he did not stop until he took a flying leap in the air toward Gabe, who caught him easily.

"Hey, big man. How's school today?"

Ross' face scrunched as he answered, "Same old thing every day. Except for..." he looked around cautiously, "Chrissy sat next to me in art class."

"Good man, you're making progress!"

"Gabe, stop encouraging him. And Ross, where are your manners, jumping up like that?" she gently reminded.

Just then, Ross looked over and saw Vinny. His eyes grew wide as he looked back and forth between the two men.

"You...you look just like Gabe," he exclaimed. "How'd that happen?"

Gabe set Ross down on the ground and said, "Ross, this is my identical twin brother, Vinny."

Vinny knelt down and shook Ross' hand. "Good to meet you. I see you've been hanging out with Gabe here."

"Yes, sir. We're buds. When the weather gets warmer, he's gonna show me how to play football. I kinda know, but I'm not very good." Leaning in closer, he whispered loudly, "Sis tries to show me but she's not very good either."

The two brothers laughed as Jennifer shooed Ross inside to the kitchen to find a treat. She then looked around and asked, "What are you all doing?"

"Installing a few cameras and basic alarm system. You've got a great thing going here, babe, but there's no security."

Her eyes grew wide and she sucked in her lips. "Gabe, honey, I've got no money for this. I'm working as hard as I can to keep it running."

Vinny's mirth disappeared as he looked at the woman that had stolen his brother's heart and smiled in approval.

"It's on us, darlin'. Tony does a few charity cases each year. Don't worry about it. He can take it as a tax write-off."

Gabe wanted to kiss the worried look off of her face but planned on that later. In fact, if she was willing, he had a lot planned out later. When he had come into the center earlier to talk to Henry about the installation, Cora had cornered him. A direct-speaker, she got right to the point.

"I'm thinking that you'd like to have more time alone with Jennifer. Henry and I had already planned on taking Ross out to visit our daughter this weekend.

She's got a couple of kids his age and he really likes to visit. Now…you could come over here and have a nice date, but I gotta warn you…there's lots of old biddies around who'd love to get in your business. So I'm thinking that you might want to take her out and well…it was easy pack a small bag for her."

He raised his eyebrow and rubbed his hand over his face. "Ms. Cora, I appreciate that more than you can know because that tells me that you trust me. But, this has got to be at her pace. Her time."

Cora stared at him long and hard, then nodded. "Knew I had you pegged right from the start. A good man. But let me tell you, she needs a little push. That girl's got a heart as big as they come and if she shines that light on you, then you'll think you've been burned it shines so bright. But she needs someone to care for her too, and I don't mean just us in this building. I think you're that man. So I trust that you won't take advantage of her, but will take care of her needs…and I mean *all* of her needs." With that, she handed him a small bag and turned with a wink.

Now he stood on the stoop with her in his arms. "We're almost finished here. You head on in and say goodbye to Ross. I understand he has a little trip this weekend and I've got plans for us."

She turned her head up sharply to see him smiling down at her. Licking her lips, she asked, "What have you got in mind?"

Wrapping his arms around her, he pulled her in

tightly so that she was completely engulfed in his embrace. Dropping his head down to a whisper's breath away he said, "Nothin' you don't want. But everything that you do." With that, he kissed her, then gave her a squeeze before walking back down to Vinny to complete the job.

WHEN SHE CAME out later, she allowed him to assist her into the Jeep. "So, where to tonight?" she asked.

"I thought we'd do dinner at my place. Is that okay?" he asked, glancing over hoping to see interest in her eyes. He was not disappointed.

Sucking in a deep breath, she nodded, a smile curving her lips. "Yeah, it's fine. Actually, more than fine."

Linking his fingers with hers, he drove them to his apartment. Getting out in the underground garage, he grabbed the bag of items from Cora and was glad that she had discreetly stored them in a grocery sack. They headed to the elevator and Jennifer's eyes grew large. "Oh my God, Gabe. I had no idea you lived in a place like this. It's so…um…fancy."

He glanced nervously down at her hoping that she wouldn't hate his place. "There's a lot of room here and a great gym downstairs. I found out about this place from a detective friend of mine. Matt used to live in this building until he moved into a house with his wife, Lily. She works with me at Tony's. Several of us live in the area and actually, Vinny lives a few floors below me."

Quirking an eyebrow, she quipped, "Convenient for when you need to change dates?"

Whirling her around so that she was plastered to his front, he groused, "Baby, I'm not sharing you with anyone, especially my twin."

Laughing, they entered his apartment and he showed her around. She was amazed at the amount of space he had. He watched her as she silently walked around the living area and into the huge kitchen, finally stopping at the windows taking up most of one wall. She stopped and looked at the setting sun over the city skyline.

He walked up behind her and wrapped his arms around, pulling her back in tightly to his front. "Whatcha thinking?"

"Honestly? I've never seen an apartment so large! It's beautiful, Gabe."

"But…"

She twisted around to face him, her head leaned way back. "No 'but', honey. I admit it's kind of overwhelming. I've seen places like this in magazines, but I've never been in an apartment that's this big."

"I know we're still new, but baby, I want to give you the world." He leaned down to kiss her, but she stopped him.

"Honey, all I need is you. You and Ross…that's the world to me."

With those words, he took her mouth and took charge of the kiss. Deep. Wet. He lifted her in his arms, holding her tight. Her breasts were pressed against his chest and he could swear that he could feel her nipples through her shirt. The desire to taste them was overwhelming as he held her up easily with one hand on her ass and the other snaking around to the underside of her breast.

Hearing her moan was his undoing. "Babe, you say the word and we stop."

"No, don't stop." All she felt was his lips and his hand on her ass and she wanted more. She grasped the bottom of her sweater and pulled it quickly over her head.

Her breasts were pushed up in a pink, lacy bra right at his head level. His knees almost buckled, but not from her slight weight. He moved his lips from hers and trailed kisses down her neck to the top of her breasts. Moving from one to the other, he sucked her nipples through the lace until he thought he would go mad with want. As though she read his mind, she slid her hands from his shoulders to her chest where she pulled the cups down, exposing the perfect rosy-tipped mounds.

Greedily he sucked as he backed her against the wall, bringing one knee upwards to take her weight so that he had both hands free. He quickly divested her of the bra and filled his hands with her as he molded the fleshy orbs, taking one nipple deeply into his mouth before giving it a gentle bite.

She began to writhe against his jean-clad knee, needing the friction to seek the relief that she desperately was looking for. She wrapped her legs around his waist, pulling him tighter, feeling the distinct bulge in his pants. A very large bulge. *Oh lordy. It's been a really long time,* she thought.

He pulled back away from her breasts and looked into her eyes. "You want this, baby? I gotta know 'cause you're no fuck against the wall. You want this, Jennifer…it's you and me. You're in my bed and in my life."

"I. Want. You." She pulled his face in for a kiss, plunging her tongue in tasting all that was him.

Growling he stalked into the bedroom, bending with her still in his arms and throwing the comforter back. Laying her gently on her back he stood over her partially naked form. Heavy breasts beckoned but before he could answer the call, she moved to unzip her jeans. He took over, sliding them down her legs, taking her pink, lace panties with them.

He stood, looking down at her, stunned that she was finally in his bed. "Perfection," he said. His hands reached for her tiny feet and lifted them in his hands. Sliding up her legs, he pulled her them apart, exposing her pink folds. Kneeling on the floor between her legs he kissed from her knees upward until his mouth covered her pussy. Sucking hard, he licked between her nether lips, lapping her juices until he pulled her clit into his mouth. *Jesus, I could come right now. What about this woman makes me lose all control?*

She arched off of the bed and he reached one large hand up and placed it on her pelvis holding her still. She began to writhe more, her hips undulating upwards, seeking sweet relief. He added a finger into her pussy while still sucking on her clit. The feelings were overwhelming and moans escaped her as she felt herself climbing higher and higher until she cried out his name as the tremors overtook, shattering her into a million pieces.

He lapped her juices and then raised up from the floor, placing his finger in his mouth, not wanting to miss a single taste. He grabbed the back of his t-shirt and pulled it over his head. His hands went to his jeans, unbuttoning them as quickly as he could.

As he shucked his jeans, her eyes traveled down from his wide shoulders to his naked chest. A Celtic cross tattoo was inked directly over his heart, matching the Celtic symbols around his bicep. She could not wait to trace the intricate design with her tongue. He was powerfully built with massive chest muscles, chiseled abs, and a tight stomach that ended in a perfect V that traveled downwards. By the time her eyes had moved to the end of the V, his jeans and boxers were off and her eyes feasted on his cock. *Oh my God. The college boyfriend that I had was nothing like that. And he's been the only one.*

He saw her expression go from sated to afraid.

Leaning over her, he placed his hands on either side, surrounding her with his presence. "What's going on in that gorgeous mind of yours, baby? We don't have to do anything you don't want to."

She looked up into the face that she trusted with her life. *How could I have fallen so far in love in just a few weeks?* "I was just…well…it's kinda been a long time. And…there was only one other." Her eyes looked down as her hands raised to rest on his chest. "I know you had…um…a lot…"

Her expression almost broke him. She looked so little. So lost. So unsure. *My fuckin' reputation finally came back to bite me in the ass, just like Tony warned.* His captain and boss told him and Vinny that the fuck 'em and leave' em attitude would one day haunt them. Looking down on her doubting face, he wanted to kick the man that he had been.

"Baby, look at me," he pleaded. "I've never once been in love. I've never loved any woman. My past is fucked up and is just that…the past. There's no comparison with anyone else."

"Gabe," her small voice said. "You've been with…famous women."

Sucking in a deep breath, he lowered himself gently to her side, pulling her in tightly with him. "You gotta understand baby and hear me well, or we've got no chance of getting past this. I have never, and I mean never, been with any other woman that meant something to me emotionally. So whoever I was with, famous or not, they were just pussy. That's all. It was just sex. A physical release. I know to women it means something different, but right or wrong there it is. For me, it was just physical. But with you, babe? It's everything. It's my world."

She leaned her head off of his chest and sought his eyes, seeing sincerity blazing from them. "What are you saying?" she whispered.

"I'm saying that I love you. I think I loved you from the moment I saw your pixie face popping out from behind the dumpster."

Giggling, she moved her hand over his chest up to cup his cheek. "How can I love you having only known you a few weeks? Is it real?"

"You love me, baby?" he asked softly, nuzzling her ear.

"Yeah. I love you, Gabe."

He looked deeply into her crystalline blue eyes, seeing the light that was her, shining out on him.

Cora's words came back to him. *If she shines that light on you, then you'll think you've been burned, it shines so bright.* He felt that light. *Fuck yeah.*

Laying on his side with her next to him, he began to explore every delicious curve. Jennifer felt the electric shock from her nipples to her womb and down to her pussy once again. As he moved his finger through her slick folds, he lifted himself over her placing his engorged cock at her entrance.

"Babe, you said it had been a while. How long is a

while? I don't want to hurt you."

Lowering her eyes in embarrassment, she replied, "Um, about three years."

His eyes widened in shock but quickly recovered, not wanting to embarrass her further. *Fuck yeah,* he thought once again. First in feeling her light shining on him and now knowing that light had not been shared with anyone intimately for a long time.

He gently entered her slowly after rolling on a condom. Filling her a little bit at a time, he allowed her to adjust to his size. She moaned at the feeling of fullness and the pressure that immediately began to build. With a final push, he was in all the way and began to pump slowly.

"More, I need more," she said in a whisper and that was all it took for him to begin moving faster. The delicious feeling of friction was soon sending her over the edge again. *Two orgasms in one night. I've never had that,* she realized as the shock waves pulsated from her inner core outwards.

He felt her pussy walls grab his dick and her natural juices made the pounding easier. He captured her lips once more, imitating the motion of his thrusting with his tongue. He could feel his balls tighten and knew that he was close. He watched her hands move up to cup her breasts, tweaking her nipples. *Jesus, fuck.* He'd seen women play with themselves during sex, but it had always seemed so fake—as though it was just for his benefit. But Jennifer? Her eyes were closed and the pleasure that covered her expression was all it took. Throwing his head back, he powered through his orgasm, pulsating deep inside as her pussy tightened around him once again.

Falling down to the side of her, he rolled her on top of his sweaty body, still shaking with the intensity of the moment. *Never... never. I've never fucked like that. Jesus, is that what love does?* he wondered.

Neither of them spoke for several minutes, the emotions of the act too overwhelming. Too important.

As their breathing slowed down, she lifted her head and looked down at him, noticing the name **Malloy** tattooed into Celtic cross design as she traced it with her finger. "Wow," she said softly.

His chest began to move with chuckling, bouncing her up and down. "Yeah, baby. You can say that again. Wow."

"I just didn't know it could be like that," she said honestly.

He stared at her face for a moment, also realizing that he'd never met anyone as honest as her. No pretense. No faking. Just real. Just her.

He tightened his huge arms around her, enveloping. Protecting. Needing.

"Baby, I may be many things, but I'll always lay it right out there. I want you, in my bed and in my life." Seeing her about to protest, he continued. "I know you've got Ross and we'll go slow. But I'm in love with you and in love with him too. We'll figure it all out together."

A gentle smile rolled off her lips and he swore once more that her light pierced his heart. "Together? That sounds good."

She watched as his handsome face broke into a grin. *I've never seen anyone so heart-stoppingly gorgeous in my whole life.* She ran her fingers over his strong jaw, loving the feel of the rough stubble underneath her fingertips.

He pulled her head down to his and kissed her once more. This time soft. Gentle. Full of the promise of home. "Yeah, baby. Together."

Later that night, after they ate Chinese take-out, he asked her to stay. She grinned and held up her oversized purse. "I hoped you would ask. I even packed a few things just in case."

He threw his head back and laughed as he held up the grocery bag that Cora had packed.

Her mouth opened in an 'O' as she peered into the bag. "Well, that sneak."

"I prefer to think that she's just a romantic at heart, darlin'."

Pulling her in close as they lay in bed, he wrapped her in his arms, feeling warm and sated. And both slept…images of handsome giants and elfish princesses filled their dreams.

CHAPTER 9

GABE WALKED INTO the break room, grabbing his coffee and greeting the others gathered there before their Monday morning staff meeting.

"So…?" Vinny asked.

BJ, Jobe, and a couple of the other men looked up, used to Gabe and Vinny's weekend sexual escapades.

"Not going there," Gabe growled.

"Hmmm," Vinny taunted. "Something tells me the great one has fallen, just like our friend BJ here."

Gabe said nothing but just kept drinking his coffee. Lily walked in, noting the strange atmosphere. Looking around, her eyes landed on Gabe. Lifting her eyebrow at him, she asked, "Good weekend?"

"Yeah. Great weekend, thank you," was his polite reply.

Walking toward the door, she stopped and placed her hand on his thick arm. "Well, if it involved that beautiful, new woman that has finally captured your attention, then I wholeheartedly approve." Giving his arm a little squeeze, she walked out of the room, calling over her shoulder, "Meeting in five minutes, gentlemen."

Jobe slapped him on the back as he moved out, following Lily. BJ walked by next, laughing. "I know, man. When you fall, you fall hard." BJ had found the love of his life and they were expecting twins.

Vinny walked over to his brother and stood directly in front of him, placing his hand on Gabe's shoulder. "She's a real beauty and a helluva person to boot. I'm glad for you, man."

Gabe grinned, glad for his brother's support.

"Can I ask about her brother? You ready to take him on as well?" Vinny asked, true concern on his face.

Nodding, Gabe replied, "He's a great kid. There's something about him that just pulls at me. You know, when a kid looks up at you as though you're supposed to have all the answers."

"Gabe," Vinny growled softly. "You're not—"

"No," he bit out. "It's got nothing to do with what happened over there." Rubbing his hand over his face, he startled when the twins realized that Tony was standing in the doorway.

Tony walked over, "Sorry to listen in. Gabe, you'd be a fool to not face the fact that part of you wants to save her brother just like you couldn't save those kids in Afghanistan. That doesn't make it wrong. You love the sister and you love her brother, then it's all good."

Nodding, Gabe and Vinny followed him out of the break room and into the conference room. Walking in they were surprised to see their detective friends, Shane Douglas and Matt Dixon, sitting at the table. Greetings abounded all around before Tony took charge of the meeting.

"Matt and Shane have something that they're looking into and wanted our input."

Matt spoke first, saying, "Vice is looking into rumors of possible extortion. So far, we've got nothing but hints of gambling and money laundering. We're sure there's an organization behind extortion, but can't prove anything. Seems like someone's into buying some real estate cheap and selling big."

Gabe looked up at that. "That's not a crime, is it?"

"Not if you do it legitimately and not use extortion and threats to get people to sell."

"What my partner hates to say is that there's the fuckin' possibility that whoever is behind this has got their hand in the pocket of some of the police. So the chief asked if we could contract Lily and BJ again to take a look and see what they can find out."

Tony looked over at Lily, giving her a slight nod. "You available?"

Smiling, she looked at her husband Matt, and joked, "I've always got time to help the police." Looking back to Tony, she said, "And that's the truth. It doesn't take me too long to do some computer digging."

Finishing up the last of the assignments while Shane and Matt went back to the station-house, Tony reminded them that they had a company picnic coming in another two weeks. "The weather's supposed to be nice and we want to make sure all of you can come."

They finished the meeting and as they dispersed to their various assignments, Tony asked Gabe to stay. Vinny looked over at them and Tony nodded to him as well, indicating that he could also stay.

"Gonna get to the point. Gotta letter from Alicia Morgenstern's attorney. We are contracted for one more security detail for the film company when they are back in town in a couple of months for the opening of the movie they made. Seems like Ms. Morgenstern is requesting that Gabe escort her to the event. I have already replied that he will be engaged elsewhere but that we will, of course, provide our normal security for the event."

Gabe hung his head for a moment. He had not thought of her in weeks...not since meeting Jennifer. Looking up at his boss, he said, "I appreciate it, Tony."

"What a fuckin' bitch," Vinny bit out, protective of his brother.

"Yeah, she's a piece of work but this is our last dealings with her or the movie company." He looked at Gabe for a moment. A private man, he respected the privacy of the men under him but wanted to keep a pulse on them as well. "I understand you may be bringing someone special to the picnic?"

Gabe's smile told Tony all he needed to know. It was obvious, the big man had fallen and by the look on his face...fallen hard.

"Yes, sir. She's a social worker for the city and runs

an elder residence for those who might find themselves homeless. She's also the guardian of her eight-year-old brother. Will it be all right for him to come too?"

"Hell, you don't have to ask. I want to meet the woman who brought one of the big twins down," he laughed.

"You will, sir. You will."

"HOW DID YOU get so big? Do you eat a lot? Jenny says you eat a lot, but then she's just a girl and she's kind of small, so she thinks everyone eats a lot."

Gabe laughed at Ross' endless questions. In the past week, he'd visited almost every day, getting to know her brother and finding that he was a really smart child…and genuinely caring.

He stood just a few feet from him; after showing him how to hold a football they began to toss it to each other. Ross was a quick learner and although he was young, Gabe patiently worked with him.

"My brother and I were always big, I guess, and if you can believe my mother, we did eat all the time. She says she almost went broke trying to feed us."

Ross stopped and looked up at his friend. "Do you got any sisters?"

Gabe shook his head, "Nope, just my twin brother."

Ross wrinkled his nose for a moment as he thought.

"I used to think that I'd like to have a brother, but I've just got a sister instead. She's nice though…even if she can't throw a football. She works real hard. Gabe?" Ross asked. "Do you think she works extra hard just because of me?"

Gabe squatted next to Ross, putting his large hand on the boy's shoulders. "Your sister is nice. And she works hard, too. But buddy, don't ever think that she doesn't want to do anything and everything that she can do for you. She wouldn't have it any other way."

"You like her don't you?" Ross asked.

"Yes, I do like her. Is that okay with you, bud?"

"Sure! If you marry her, do I get you for a brother?"

Gabe wondered about how to answer. *Hell, I'd love to tell him I'd marry her tomorrow if she'd have me, but I can't say anything to him before Jennifer.* "Well, buddy, it's a little too early to talk about marriage. But I do plan on staying with your sister and you definitely come with the whole package."

That seemed to satisfy the curious child and they resumed their tossing.

"Hey guys," came the sweet voice of Jennifer from nearby. Both turned to see her jogging over to them. She ran to Ross first, bending over to kiss the top of his head before turning to throw her arms around Gabe. Leaning her head back, she raised up on her toes to meet his lips halfway. He bent to give her his lips but kept it chaste with Ross present.

"You all having fun?" she asked.

"Gabe's teaching me how to throw a football. I told him that you're good at a lot of stuff, but you're not so good at football."

"Humph," she groused, pretending to pout.

Gabe laughed and threw his arm around her, leaning in to whisper, "But you're so good at other things." Blushing, she slapped at his arm playfully. He loved seeing the blush on her face, imagining it starting at her breasts. *Damn, shouldn't have let my mind go that way.* He discreetly adjusted himself while Jennifer picked up Ross' jacket.

They walked back to Gabe's Jeep and Jennifer buckled Ross in the back before Gabe assisted her up. As soon as they made it to their building, he escorted them in.

"Can you stay for dinner?" she asked hopefully, as Ross ran to his room.

Wrapping his strong arms around her, he pulled her in closely. Breathing her in, he leaned down for a kiss. With a glance toward the small hall, he heard Ross playing in his room. Taking the kiss deeper, he slid his tongue into her mouth. Tasting sweet nectar, he wanted more. Pulling back, he chuckled at the little sound of disappointment that escaped her perfect mouth.

"I wish I could, baby, but I've got some surveillance tonight."

Her eyes grew wide as she realized that there was so much about his job she did not know. "Is that dangerous?" she asked.

"Nah. I'll be with Jobe. BJ was scheduled, but his wife is being threatened with bed rest because of the twins so we are covering his night shifts. What about you?"

"I'm helping fix some sandwiches tonight for the residents to have for lunch tomorrow. Other than that, just hanging out here with Ross."

"Okay, babe. I'll call you tomorrow."

With a kiss goodbye, she watched him head down the stairs.

GABE AND JOBE sat in the car, watching the night security cameras that they were checking on. It was almost midnight and they were ready to head home. Gabe's phone vibrated and he looked down hoping it would be Jennifer with a good night for him. Instead, he saw a number he did not recognize.

"Yeah?" he answered brusquely.

"Mr. Malloy?" a woman's voice asked.

"Yes. Who is this?" he asked softer.

"This is Cora. I'm sorry to bother you so late, but Miss Jennifer needs your help."

His blood ran cold. "What's wrong?"

Jobe looked over in question.

"She got a call and went after that old drunk, Mr. Courtland. She always takes Henry, but he's ailin' tonight and took cold medicine that has him out like a light."

He looked over at Jobe, who was on the phone talking to someone. Jobe looked over, mouthing, "Where are we going?"

"Ms. Cora, can you tell me where she is?"

"I assume it's the same bar he always goes to. I just felt horrible for her to go out alone."

"I'm heading there now. Don't worry, I'll bring them home." Hanging up, he told Jobe which bar they were going to and heard Jobe relay it on the phone.

Looking over, Jobe just said, "Called Vinny."

Nodding, Gabe knew that his brother would want to know. They drove quickly, arriving at the bar about the same time that Vinny did. Gabe was out of the vehicle before Jobe brought it to a stop beside Jennifer's old truck. Vinny grabbed his shoulders just before he went inside.

Rounding on his brother he barked, "What?"

"Be cool. Take a deep breath and go in there cool. Just like any mission. You're thinking with your dick…oh hell, you're thinking with your heart and not your mind. Got it?"

A quick breath later Gabe nodded as Jobe joined them. Walking inside the dimly lit bar, the calm flew out of his head. Jennifer was leaning over Mr. Courtland attempting to get him to stand. The bartender that always called her was standing nearby but was outnumbered if things got ugly. And from the looks of the punks in the back, standing to the side, leers on their faces…it would have gotten ugly.

Gabe's vision was filled with red as he made a move toward the back. Vinny and Jobe grabbed him, pulling him over to the side where she was.

"Help. Her," Vinny barked, turning back to the group of younger men, now not so cocky with a wall of muscle bound testosterone standing in front of them.

"Boys, don't you think it's 'bout time y'all called it a night?" Vinny drawled. The now nervous looks passing between them had them edging toward the door. "And boys, this little lady is protected by *Us*. You get what that means?"

Their heads began to bobble and each took several steps back. Vinny turned back toward Gabe to help, now knowing he needed to calm his brother. Jennifer was still on one side of Mr. Courtland and Vinny overheard Gabe say, "Girl, get over here and let us carry him or swear to God, I'll—"

"You'll what, Gabe? Turn me over your knee? Isn't that what the big, bad alphas say? Well, news flash, Mr. Giant. That may work in my romance novels but here in real life, you don't scare me. I've got to get him home, in bed and call one of my social worker friends tomorrow to see if we can get him in a detox program. Then I'll have to clean out his apartment and get it ready for another person to move in because our waiting list is a mile long. I don't want to have to do it, but I've got no choice…" she choked out a sob and angrily turned away, wiping her tears.

Now that the threat was gone, the fight fled out of Gabe as he pulled her over to his massive chest, wishing that he could take away her responsibilities and pain. Vinny and Jobe approached, silently moving past the couple standing next to the booth. Each man easily lifted Mr. Courtland between them and carried him outside.

Jennifer wiped her tears and looked up at Gabe. "I'm sorry, I shouldn't be crying."

"Babe, you're human doing a super-human job." Pulling her tight, he apologized too. "But baby by coming out here alone, you put yourself at great risk and I can't have you doing that. If something happened to you, I...well, think about Ross."

Wiping her nose, she quipped, "That's a low blow."

"Not meant to be. But you cannot take care of all of the Mr. Courtlands of the world."

Sniffling, she pulled back and sighed. "I know. I just couldn't leave him here."

"You should have called me. If I can't come, I've got a whole pack of Mr. Giants who can come to your rescue."

She could not hold back the giggle that escaped, "There's only one Mr. Giant for me."

He kissed her lips gently, saying, "Glad to hear it. But they're there if you need help and I want you to call on me." He cupped her face, tilting it so that his eyes were fastened on hers. "And baby, I know you're independent and capable...but never, I mean never, come out to a bar alone again. You got a mission, then you have people who have your back. Anything less is a suicide mission. Got me?"

She saw the fear and concern in his eyes and nodded. "Okay. No more Lone Ranger."

He threw his head back and laughed. "Jesus, you're a nut," he said as he escorted her over to Vinny's truck.

Once at the center, the three men quickly got Mr. Courtland into his studio apartment, out of his clothes and into bed. Cora came down from keeping an eye on Ross and bustled around attempting to help while trying to fuss at Jennifer. She finally headed back to bed to check on her husband, leaving the other four in the foyer.

Jennifer looked over at the men, standing around talking with the easy camaraderie of men who had had each other's back over the years, both in the military and now in their jobs. She could not help but smile thinking that she and Ross had that now. *But...I owe them an apology.*

Stepping up to them she looked them in the eyes as she admitted, "Guys, I really screwed up. I should have never gone there by myself and I know that now. So I'm sorry—"

Vinny interrupted her by taking a step forward, leaning down low to get right in her face with his hands on her shoulders. "Darlin' girl, no apology necessary. You've got my brother's back and we all have yours."

With that he kissed her forehead and then turned to Jobe saying, "I'll ride with you and let Gabe have my truck."

Jobe nodded, bent low to kiss her forehead too and then followed Vinny outside. She glanced up at Gabe saying, "I like your friends. And brother."

"What about me?" he asked as they began the climb up the stairs.

"Oh, I like you too," she teased.

He swooped her up in his arms and she giggled as she grabbed around his neck. "What are you doing? You shouldn't carry me up the stairs; you'll break your back," she whispered as they neared her door.

"Baby, how much do you weigh?"

"That's a rude question to ask a lady," she retorted.

"Well, whatever the answer is, I've had rucksacks and weapons heavier than you. So carrying you around is just good exercise," he whispered in her ear as he used her key to enter.

"Can you think of something else you can do with me that's good exercise?" she purred as he slowly lowered her, letting her slide along the front of his body.

The feel of her breasts pressed against his chest and his cock answering the call of the wild had him dipping his head to take her lips. Backing her up against the door he angled his head as the kiss deepened, his tongue plunging into her sweet mouth. He lifted her back up in his arms, this time trapped between the door and his large body.

The kiss became consuming, both tongues vying for dominance. He captured her moan with his mouth, feeling his dick swelling painfully. She rubbed her aching pussy on his jean-clad knee, needing the friction as she felt herself begin to lose control.

Ross! I can't do this here in the living room where he could walk in.

Pushing back on Gabe's shoulders, she forced him back. He regretted the separation but understood where her mind had gone.

"I know we have to stop, babe," he sighed, lowering her until her feet met the floor. She looked at him, indecision marring her lovely features. "What're you thinking?" he asked, rubbing his thumb over her brow.

Quietly taking his hand, she led him past the small kitchen toward her bedroom. Opening Ross' door she peeked in, seeing him sound asleep. Closing the door gently, she continued to pull Gabe into her room before shutting and locking her door.

Now it was his turn to look at her in question. She gave a little shrug, saying, "Can you be quiet?"

"Are you sure?" he whispered, hope mixed with desire flaring on his face.

Smiling, she pulled off her shirt in answer to his question. Her white lacey bra glowed in the moonlight that slipped through the blinds. Sliding her yoga pants and panties down her legs, she said, "Does this answer your question?" Her bra was quickly divested and tossed onto the floor.

His breath caught in his throat as he perused her perfect, tiny body. Curves, calling to his hands, filled her petite frame and her rosy tipped nipples begged for his mouth. Taking one step backward in the small bedroom brought her knees to the bed. His eyes glanced behind her and he stopped moving.

"What's wrong?" she whispered, wondering what had him halting.

"That bed," he said, looking at the tiny twin-sized bed. "There's no way it'll hold me."

She twisted around to see how small her bed really was and then looked back at him. *He's right. We'll never fit.*

Disappointment filled her face as she heaved a sigh.

No fuckin' way am I leaving her like this. "Babe, are you up for being a little creative?"

Her face lit up immediately. "Absolutely, as long as we can be quiet," she reminded him.

"I know, sweetheart. I'll be quiet but what about you?" he teased. He quickly divested himself of his clothes as well, pulling a condom packet out of his jeans and tossing it on the bed. "Lay back with your sweet ass right on the edge. I'll take care of you," he promised.

She did as she was told and he dropped to his knees between her legs. Smoothing his hands over her feet and calves, he lifted each leg over his shoulders opening her up to him. Leaning forward he slid both hands over her mound, up her stomach to her breasts. Palming the fullness, he lowered his head to her slick folds, licking and sucking as Jennifer began to writhe under the sensations. She clapped one hand over her mouth to keep from crying out loud as his hands slid back down and under her ass to lift it higher.

His tongue plunged into her wetness and lapped like a starving man. *Every time with her is like no other,* he thought as he realized that years of fucking for fuck's sake had never felt like this. *I've never felt so connected.*

He pushed all thoughts out of his head as he concentrated on giving her pleasure. One hand maneuvered back to her nipple and he rolled it between his thumb and forefinger.

"Gabe," moaning as softly as she could, she begged, "please." At this, she felt him move to her clit, sucking it deeply into his mouth and biting down ever so gently. "Aughhh," she cried out with her hand still covering her lips, desperately trying to not wake Ross as her orgasm threw over the edge. As the tremors subsided, she dropped her hand just as Gabe leaned over the bed, his weight on his arms. He kissed her and tasted of the heady combination of her juices and his essence.

"What about you?" she asked. "How are we going to make this work?" she whispered, licking her lips.

His eyes dilated in lust seeing her pink tongue flick out. "Oh baby, we're not nearly finished," he growled. Her eyes sparkled in the moonlight and he held out his hand. "Come on up."

He gently pulled her off of the bed and placed his hands on her shoulders, turning her around. "Crawl on your knees, ass in the air and stay right near the edge of the bed."

She quickly did as she was told and he rubbed her ass in satisfaction. Leaning over her body, he tweaked both nipples and she gave a little yelp. With his breath tickling her ear, he admonished, "Gotta stay quiet, baby."

Giving a little moan, she nodded. She saw that he was standing on the floor, his impressive cock standing at attention.

"Good girl." Placing his aching dick at her entrance he rubbed the head in her still wet folds before plunging in. To keep the bed from moving, he grabbed her hips holding her in place. Trying to be careful, he knew she was probably going to have bruises. *Marked by me. Jesus, how caveman that sounds.*

He moved in and out quickly, building up the heat and friction to the point that she could feel herself ready to fly apart. Her body rocked back and forth as he pounded into her, his balls slapping against her ass.

"Touch yourself, babe," he ordered, smiling as she quickly acquiesced. *Fuck, that's hot.* Her innocence was more of a turn-on than any coy flirt he had ever known. Feeling his balls tighten, he growled softly, "You almost there, babe?"

"Yes, yes, please..." she begged once more as the

tightening in her core burst free, sending sparks outward from her pulsating pussy to her whole being.

Following immediately, he threw his head back while his thick neck muscles strained with the force of his orgasm. Her inner walls grabbed his cock as he poured himself into her. Peeling his fingers off of her hips, smoothing the red marks, he leaned over her body. Not wanting to crush her, he fell to the side taking her with him. They lay sideways on the small bed, legs tangled, his arms around her, breaths ragged, bodies slick with sweat, and hearts beating as one.

I want this, he thought. *Every day. Every night. In my place. In my bed. In my heart.* Turning her so that she faced him, he wanted to see her eyes. Crystal clear. Blue. Shining. *With tears?*

"Baby, what's wrong?" he asked, his thumb wiping the single tear that slid out. "Did I hurt you?"

"No, no," she said. "I just…never."

"Never what, beautiful?"

"I never thought I would have…this."

Gabe leaned up, piled the pillows against the small headboard then lay back pulling her up onto his lap. "What? What did you not think you would have?"

"This. You. Everything." Seeing his concerned face, she added, "I'm not making much sense am I?" Taking a deep, shuttering breath, she said, "I knew being a social worker was going to be a lot of work for little pay. But I wanted it. And when I focused on elder care and housing, I felt like I had found my calling." She looked around the tiny room, smiling as her mind wandered.

Gabe gave her a gentle squeeze to pull her back into the present.

Her eyes sought his and she blushed as she said, "I had a couple of boyfriends, nothing serious," she rushed to say when she saw the tight look on his face. "But I figured that it didn't matter if I had a little apartment surrounded by older people. I had friends and I was happy. Then when mom and dad were killed, everything changed in a flash. It was hard to grieve when I had Ross who was just turning seven years old.

"I gave up most things for him, and gladly did it. I wouldn't trade him for anything, but I...assumed that I also gave up on love. I mean who'd want a woman with an eight-year-old brother. I was okay with that until you. And now you're giving me something that I didn't think I could have."

Looking into his strong face with his massive arms around her, she said, "I love you, Gabe Malloy."

Sliding his hand up to cup her face, he whispered, "Oh baby. You have no idea what you've brought into my life. Smiles that could light up a room. A heart so big that it takes in all others. You care, you give, you work to make things happen. You make so many lives better just by being who you are. And when you shine that light on me? Fuck baby. I've never known anything like it."

He leaned in and kissed her lips. Soft. Gentle. A

barely there whisper of a kiss. He leaned back and held her eyes again. "And Ross? Baby, providing for the two of you will be my mission. I think I've searched for a mission since I got out of the Special Forces and I've found it with you and that sweet boy."

He leaned in and kissed her again. This time cupping both cheeks with his hands, pulling her close. Breathing her in. Living her essence.

Sliding down in the bed, he said, "I've got my alarm set. You go to sleep here and I'll leave before Ross gets up."

"Honey, you can't possibly be comfortable on this tiny bed," she fretted.

"Baby, with you in my arms, I'll sleep better than in years," he promised.

And he did. No nightmares. Only dreams of a future.

CHAPTER 10

T HE MORNING OF the picnic dawned bright and clear. Before Jennifer and Ross headed over to Gabe's place earlier, she tried to prepare Ross for the shock of seeing the large apartment, but he was all-boy when he went in. Warned to be on his best behavior, he stood at the entrance and just stared around at the open space. Watching him bounce on the balls of his feet, she knew that he was itching to take a flying run and jump onto the large L-shaped sofa.

"This is all yours? You don't have to share it with anyone? Does Mr. Vinny live here with you? Can you see the whole world from these windows?"

Gabe laughed and tried to answer the rapid-fire questions.

Jennifer stood, feeling awkward knowing that the questions would become more complicated as Ross took it all in.

Gabe glanced over at her, knowing she was trying to figure out a way to explain to Ross how one person could live in so much space and they shared such a small place. *Their parents were Peace Corps. Ross has probably never seen anything like this.*

Before he could think of anything to say, Ross bounced again and said, "Jennybenny, I gotta go pee."

"Ross, you just went and you know how to say it," she said patiently.

"But I gotta go again. To the men's room," he pleaded politely.

"I got it babe," Gabe said, deftly walking with Ross toward the guest bathroom.

She walked into the kitchen with her picnic basket and began adding the things to it that Gabe had bought. She expected the beer and wine but noticed that he had included some PBJ sandwiches for Ross.

"Hey darlin'," she heard a voice behind her. Whirling around, she narrowed her eyes. "Vinny, I swear you could sneak up on anyone."

Laughing, he kissed her forehead. "Where's our brothers?"

Sighing, she nodded toward the back. "Ross claimed he had to go to the bathroom but I'm sure it was just a ploy to see how big this place really is."

"You okay, honey?" Vinny asked.

She smiled up at the face that was almost as handsome as his brother's. Even as identical twins, she could tell them apart. "I think I'm going to be faced with the 'why can't we have a place like this' questions by the end of the day. My parents lived very frugally when they were overseas and well, he's never seen a place like this."

"Vinny!" came the yell from the back as Ross took a

leap up and Vinny caught him. "This place is huge. The bathroom's bigger than sis' room," he exclaimed.

She rolled her eyes at Gabe as he gave her a sympathetic look.

The temperature that day was going to be rising and eventually be pleasant enough for shirts without jackets. Something that Ross did not understand.

"Ross, get your jacket now. Even if you take it off later, you'll need it when we first go."

"I don't know where it is," he lied.

"Don't tell me that. You brought it in with you," she said as she placed the salad and baked beans into the picnic basket that she was packing.

Vinny smirked at Gabe, who was waiting patiently on Jennifer and Ross. He leaned his hip casually against the breakfast bar, his legs crossed at the bottom. He caught his brother's grin and smiled back.

Ross came back into the room, his jacket in his hand. "Hey," he said as he looked at Gabe and Vinny. "They don't have to wear jackets. Why do I?"

Jennifer popped her head out of the kitchen and glared at him. "Well, Gabe was just going to get his jacket and since Vinny forgot his, Gabe will get one for Vinny to wear also."

Gabe, without batting an eye, pushed off of the counter and walked to the hall closet pulling down two sweatshirt jackets. Tossing one to Vinny, he grinned at Vinny's incredulous look.

"How'd I get pulled into your little domestic drama?" he quipped.

"Shut up and put the jacket on," Gabe ordered.

Ross watched carefully and then pulled his jacket on too.

Gabe gave him a high-five and said, "Ready to go, buddy?"

With a whoop from Ross, Gabe laughed and said, "Go on with Vinny and get the football in the Jeep. Let me grab the food from your sister and we'll be right down."

She started to pick up the basket when Gabe's arms came from behind and his hands rested on the counter, pinning her in. He leaned down and nuzzled her ear, whispering, "Thanks for coming today." Giving her a kiss that was fast, hard and wet, he pulled back and linked his fingers with hers and grabbing the basket with his other hand. "Let's go before I'm tempted to have Vinny take Ross and we just stay in bed."

Locking the door, she said, "Thank you for getting your jacket. I know a giant like you doesn't need a jacket but—"

"You don't have to thank me, babe. We're in this together. Whatever you need, whatever Ross needs, that's what you'll get."

Smiling up at him, she gave his hand a squeeze as they headed to the Jeep.

WALKING UP TO the group of men standing around the picnic center, Jennifer found her knees shaking. Gabe had his arm thrown possessively around her shoulders but gave her a little squeeze as they approached the group. Feeling tiny next to the large men in front of her, she smiled as each introduced themselves. Having already met Vinny and Jobe, she was quickly put at ease as she met the two detectives, Shane and Matt. Several others were introduced, but it was Tony that made her nervous. Tall, broad, not as heavy as Gabe and Vinny, but he exuded a commanding presence that would have had her picking him out as the person in charge of any mission.

"Hear good things about you," Tony said, shaking her hand. "Both your job and the way you're raising your brother. It's good to finally meet the woman who brought one of my big men down."

Glancing down at Ross standing next to her holding her hand, she smiled as he looked up at the wall of men. Vinny came from behind and swooped him up on his shoulders saying, "Come on, little man. We've got some footballs to toss."

Jennifer gasped at the thought of eight-year-old Ross trying to play with the large men. "Honey," she said, turning quickly to look at Gabe. "He's too—"

"He's fine, babe. Let him play," he said softly.

Her worried eyes sought his. "But I don't want him to get in your way either. You can't play the way you want to if you're having to worry about not stepping on him."

"Let it go, sweetheart. It's all good. We'll be fine. He'll be fine." With a reassuring pat on her ass and a quick kiss, he ran off to join the others.

The picnic was the first time that she got to meet some of the other women from Gabe's friend group. Shane's wife, Annie, a local veterinarian, was sitting with Lily, one of Gabe's co-workers and Matt's wife. BJ's wife, Suzanne, worked in the clinic with Annie. And much to Jennifer's surprise, she saw Sherrie there.

The two women hugged and Sherrie explained that Suzanne begged her to come and get out of her apartment. Months earlier, Sherrie and Suzanne had been kidnaped by the same gang and while BJ rescued his fiancé, Tony went in to save Sherrie. Since then, she and Suzanne had become friends as well.

Annie and Suzanne were both pregnant, the latter with twins. The other women insisted that they sit while they began to set out the food. Jennifer realized how much she missed the conversations and fun with women her own age. *As much as I love Cora and the other women at the center, this is really nice. Chatting, gossiping, laughing. Talking about babies.* Her eyes glanced over at the football game, checking on Ross and seeking out Gabe. *Babies. I wonder if Gabe would want to someday have babies?*

"Don't worry about Ross," Annie piped up seeing Jennifer glancing at the game. "They'll take good care of him."

"Oh, I know he's in good hands. Gabe is great with him."

"Have you had him long?" Suzanne asked. "That is if you don't mind me asking."

"Oh, not at all," Jennifer admitted. "My parents were Peace Corps and had been overseas for a couple of years; I was already out of college. About a year ago they were stateside visiting and were killed in a car accident. I became Ross' legal guardian and we've done all right. I live at the elder housing center where a big part of my job takes place when I'm not in the office and so I save a lot on rent. Plus he has about twenty grandparents every day checking on him."

"Well, he certainly is a lucky little boy to have a sister like you," Lily quietly stated.

"Oh, I'm the lucky one," Jennifer admitted. Looking over at the game again, she confessed, "But being a woman, there is so much I don't know how to teach him. I can teach him how to be a good person but what about how to be a good man?" Throwing her hand up as she pointed to the game she continued, "How can I teach him how to play football?"

Lily quickly stood and gave her a hug, saying, "Oh honey. You're doing marvelously. And what you can't teach him, you've now given him a band of brothers that will help him."

After a while, Tony and Jobe began manning the grills. As Jennifer sat quietly for a few moments, she noticed how Sherrie watched the grills with lowered eyes as though she did not want anyone to see her. *Jobe? She has a thing for Jobe?* As Jennifer continued to watch, she noticed that Tony would occasionally look over at Sherri and then look away quickly when she raised her head. *Tony? It's Tony that has her attention. And it appears she has his as well. Hmm, looks like a coffee date with Sherri is overdue.* Before she could consider her friends anymore, the other ladies called for the food items and she jumped up to get her basket.

After a few minutes, the men ambled over from their game. She turned to see Ross piggyback riding with Gabe. A smile played on her lips as she saw the grin on Ross' dirty face. As he was set down, she started to grab a wet cloth to wash his face off, but he jerked away, looking up at Gabe.

Gabe quickly said, "Come on buddy," and headed off to the outdoor water faucet. The two of them splashed their faces and washed their hands. As the strolled back to the table, she overheard Gabe say, "We gotta be clean for the ladies. They spent time fixing the food and we want to be presentable, right Little Man?"

Ross grinned then looked at Vinny, who had sat down with his plate almost full.

"Vinny," Ross called out. "You gotta go wash up. It's for the ladies."

The laughter from the group burst forward as Vinny humbly headed off to wash his hands as well. Gabe leaned over and kissed Jennifer lightly on the lips before sitting next to her. With Ross tucked between the large men, she saw the joy on his face. *Well, maybe 'hero worship' was a better word.*

The food was quickly consumed and the friends sat around talking and laughing for a while until the setting sun made the air chilly. With goodbyes all around, Gabe helped Ross and Jennifer into his Jeep and he took them home.

As they entered her apartment, she immediately ran the bath water for Ross ignoring his grumbling. Once he was in, she walked back to the living area and saw that Gabe had put away the picnic basket.

"Thanks, honey," she said, walking straight up and wrapping her arms around his waist. He kissed the top of her head and then tugged her over to the sofa, seating her on his lap.

"You do a helluva lot, babe. I don't want you to wear yourself out."

"It's not bad," she said defensively. "Most of the work around here is done by Cora and Henry."

"That's not all I'm talking about. There's Ross as well."

"Ross isn't a burden at all." She sat quietly for a moment, thinking of her brother. Turning her big blue eyes on Gabe, she asked, "Do you think he's...all right?"

Quirking an eyebrow, he looked perplexed by her question.

"I mean, as a little boy?"

"Babe, you're just going to have to come out and

ask what's on your mind, 'cause I'm not following."

"Today at the park, I watched him with you all. I can give him a lot, but I'm…well, how do I teach him to be a good man?" she asked, concern filling her pained expression.

"Jennifer, a man learns a lot about being a good man by being around a good woman. My mom was the best there was and my brother and I learned as much from her as we did our dad."

"Yes, but you also had a dad."

"True, but you've got men in your life that can help him become the kind of man you want him to become."

"But—"

"Don't start with that, baby," he warned. "You and me are together. I'm not leaving and I promise to protect the two of you and help him learn how to be a good man."

"That's a lot to take on," she advised.

"What? You don't think I'm up for the job?" he said, jokingly lifting his crotch into her hips.

"Oh, I think you're more than *up* for the job," she giggled. Grabbing his face, she pulled him in for a kiss, plunging her tongue into his mouth knowing that he would take over immediately. And she wasn't disappointed.

With her body tucked into his, he took ownership of the kiss angling for better access. Her sweetness filled his senses while his dick pressed painfully against his jeans.

"Jenny," came the call from the bathroom.

She jerked away from the kiss, first a moan and then a sigh escaping her lips. She stood on shaky legs and walked to the bathroom door. Using her special knock, he called for her to enter.

Once he was ready for bed, he ran out to say goodnight to Gabe, who picked him up in a bear hug. "Thanks for teaching me how to play football," Ross said.

"No problem, buddy. We'll have lots of time to learn more," Gabe promised.

Ross started to run to his bedroom, when he stopped and turned toward Jennifer. "You know sis? Gabe says you're doing a good job with me. I just wanted to say that I think so too." He ran over to throw his arms around her as she knelt to embrace him.

With tears in her eyes, she looked over Ross' shoulder at Gabe smiling down on the two of them.

A few minutes later as she walked him to the door, she looked up and asked, "Did you tell Ross to say that to me?"

"Honest to God, babe, I didn't. He did that all on his own." Giving her a goodbye kiss, he reminded her, "Told you. A good man needs a good woman, no matter what age." With that he headed down the stairs.

An hour later Jennifer called Cora. "Hey, the restaurant just called. It seems that an event overbooked and they have a lot of food that was prepared that will just go to waste, including some meat and vegetables. I'm going to head over to pick it up. Will you keep an eye on Ross? He's already asleep and I shouldn't be long."

"Sure," Cora agreed. "I'll be right across the hall."

PULLING HER OLD truck into the alley, she parked near the kitchen door. Hopping out she tried to open the door to let Carlos know she was there. The door was locked, so she tried knocking. No answer. *Damn, I'll have to walk around to the front and go in that way.* Looking down at her clothes, she regretted the sloppy sweatpants and zip-up hoodie that she was wearing. *Oh, what does it matter who sees me and what they think?*

Turning to get back into her truck, she gasped as two men loomed toward her, one grabbing her arms and pinning them easily behind her back with one hand while the other clasped a hand over her mouth tightly.

"Shut up and just listen," the other one said.

Instinct took over and she reared back kicking her legs out, hitting the one in front of her. Trying to squirm, she bit down on the hand at her mouth.

"Goddammit," he cried out, jerking her arm harder while the one in front backhanded her across the face.

Unable to move, she took the full force of the hit. Pain sliced across her face and she squeezed her eyes shut as tears sprung out. She felt something run from her nose, over her lips and drip off her chin. The pull on her shoulder had her certain that it was broken. *Oh Ross, I'm sorry. They're going to kill me.* The initial rush of adrenalin was draining out, leaving her quaking in pain and fear.

"You weren't supposed to hurt her," growled the man holding her arms.

"The stupid bitch nearly kicked my balls," the other one groused, as he was catching his breath. Standing up straight his eyes bored holes into hers, as the dark face loomed in her view grabbing her throat.

"You need to—"

Just then, the kitchen door flung open and Carlos ambled out for his smoke break. The light from the door illuminated the scene in front of him. "What the fuck? Jim!" he yelled as he bolted from the kitchen.

The two men ran off before Jim was able to catch them while Carlos knelt by Jennifer. Seeing her bloodied face, he quickly called 911 before grabbing her phone and calling Gabe.

GABE AND VINNY bolted into the ER, not surprised to see Matt and Shane already there. Vinny had the presence of mind to call them as soon as Gabe called him. Pulling them to the side, Gabe asked, "Where is she? What happened?"

"Right now she's getting x-rays, but it doesn't look like anything is broken. Just…" Matt began.

"What?" Gabe growled.

"She looks bad, but her nose isn't broken," Shane said. "At least that was the last thing the doctor said."

Gabe's legs felt weak, a feeling he'd never known before. Not with all the military missions. Not with all the training. But the idea of someone hurting Jennifer had him both scared and livid at the same time.

"What the fuck happened?" Vinny asked.

Matt and Shane shared a glance. Taking a deep breath, Matt answered, "She's not saying a lot."

Gabe's eyes shot toward his friend. "She's not saying?" he bit out. *Oh Jesus, was she sexually assaulted?*

Knowing where his thoughts had gone, Shane quickly spoke up. "She was fully dressed and there's no evidence of any sexual assault."

"So why isn't she talking? Did she see who did this?" he prodded.

"We haven't gotten that far, man. We know she told Cora that the restaurant called to say they had food for her to pick up. According to the kitchen manager, Carlos, the restaurant never made the call. He just happened to go outside to take a smoke when he saw two men attacking her. Then the docs took her for x-rays just before you got here, so we haven't gotten any further."

Hearing a noise behind them, Gabe knew instinctively that Tony and Jobe had arrived. Glancing at his brother, he knew Vinny had made the call.

Vinny turned to fill them in when a doctor came out to speak to the detectives. "I'm her fiancé," Gabe spoke quickly. "When can I see her?"

The doctor turned to him saying, "She has no broken bones but several contusions. She'll be released within the hour and you can take her home." With that, he turned and headed back into the ER bay area.

Gabe followed him, with the others close behind. He stopped just outside the room. Heart pounding, he felt fear. He hadn't felt fear since…*shit don't go there.* He closed his eyes tightly for a second to clear out the memory of the fright in the child's eyes just before—

"You okay, bro?" Vinny asked, his hand on Gabe's shoulder.

Sucking in a huge breath, Gabe nodded and walked into Jennifer's room. She was sitting up in the bed, a gauze bandage across her nose, staring at him through two black eyes. Her cheek was swollen and turning purple. His eyes slid to her neck. Her tiny neck. The fingerprint bruises on her throat stood out against her pale skin.

He stopped in his tracks, unsure if his legs would hold him erect. Vinny quietly slid to one side and Tony the other, offering support as they walked him over to the bed. Gabe sat down on the edge of the bed with her, taking her small hand in his much larger one.

Her eyes were looking down and he saw a single tear slide from the corner, making a track down the swollen check.

"Baby?" he asked softly.

She kept her eyes down, unwilling to look into his face. *Stay strong. Stay strong,* she chanted to herself. With her chin quivering, she finally lifted her eyes seeing his haunted face in front of hers.

Her eyes looked around the room, filled with his friends. Her friends now too. And the look of concern on their faces only made it worse. Her nose was so swollen that she couldn't breathe through it and with her bottom lip split, it hurt to talk. Swallowing deeply, she managed to croak out a "Hi", as though she were greeting them at the picnic.

"Babe, what happened?"

"I don't know," she whispered.

Matt spoke, "Jennifer, we know that the restaurant didn't call. Can you describe the voice on the phone?"

Swallowing painfully again, she shook her head. "Man's voice," she whispered.

"Can you describe the men who attacked? Carlos told us that there were two. We need to know anything you can remember," Matt prodded. "Tall, short, heavy, skinny, black, white, eye color, clothes."

"I...um...don't really...um..." she mumbled, the pain medicine already making it hard for her to concentrate.

The men in the room shared a glance but before they could continue a noise at the door startled them.

A child's scream pierced the room as Ross barreled

into the room, Cora following closely. Ross launched himself toward the bed but was caught in mid-air by Gabe. Jennifer reached out and pulled the crying child from him, holding him close to her heart. With her arms around him, she began to shake as tears streamed from her eyes.

"Shhh, I've got you. I'm here," she whispered in his ear.

The men in the room looked at her and then each other, before several of them moved to a corner.

"She'll be able to tell us more tomorrow," Matt said.

"She's scared and drugged right now. We've gotten all we can tonight," added Shane.

Tony quietly spoke, "We'll get on it. Meeting at my place tomorrow at eight a.m." Looking over at Jobe, he ordered, "Make sure to tell BJ." Glancing at Matt, he just lifted an eyebrow.

"Yeah, man. I'll tell Lily. She'll be upset, but she'll be there."

With a backward look at the tearful pair on the bed and a visibly upset Cora standing next to the bed, they nodded at Gabe before walking out.

Vinny walked back over to the bed, hearing Cora exclaim, "Oh lordy, child. I'm so sorry. I'dve a never brought Ross if I thought it was this bad."

Ross turned his tear-stained face up to his sister's, taking in her injuries. Lifting his hand to her throat, he asked, "Does it hurt bad?"

"No baby. Not too bad. The nice doctors have given me some medicine that makes me feel better. I'm sure it looks worse than it feels," she lied.

"Who did this?" he asked. "Was it some bad men?"

Her eyes found Gabe's and silently implored him to assist with the explanation.

"She's going to be fine, buddy," Gabe promised. "Just had a problem with someone who wasn't nice, but we're going to take care of her, aren't we?"

Ross' tow head nodded enthusiastically. "When can we go home?"

The doctor entered the room just then, overhearing Ross' question. "She's ready to be discharged. We just need her to sign some forms. Will someone be caring for her for the next several days? She's not to drive or lift anything heavy. I'd advise her to sleep inclined upwards for a few nights to assist in the swelling in her face."

Cora stepped forward, but Gabe put his hand on her gently. "She'll be coming home with me."

Jennifer looked up sharply. "I can't leave Ross," she croaked.

"Of course not," Gabe replied. "He'll be coming with us."

She looked conflicted and searched Cora's face for her advice. Cora leaned over, saying, "Darling girl. I don't know what happened, but right now I think you should spend a few days with Gabe. We would easily take care of you, but I think that young man needs to be with you to see for himself how you're doing."

Jennifer nodded, knowing that it was for the best. Moving stiffly to the edge of the bed, she gasped as Gabe lifted her easily and gently to the floor. Turning to Cora, he said, "Why don't you take Ross back to the waiting room. We'll be out in just a minute."

Cora nodded and took Ross' hand as they walked out. Jennifer could hear Cora comforting her brother as they walked down the hall.

Looking back at Gabe, she blushed, although with the bruising it was hard to tell. "You could have taken Ross and let Cora help me dress."

Grinning, he kissed the top of her head. "Yeah babe, but then I'd miss your beautiful body."

An unladylike snort followed this statement and she just shook her head, wincing in the process.

Immediately contrite, Gabe turned to pull her clothes out of the plastic bag provided by the hospital. She discovered that leaning over caused her head to pound, so he leaned her back against the bed so that he could slide her pants up her legs. He knelt to pull her socks and shoes on as well. He pulled out her sweatshirt and eyed the narrow opening at the top. *Jesus, how can she pull this over her swollen face without it hurting like hell?* Tossing it to the side, he pulled out her worn, zip-up hoodie. *With her blood on the front. Fuck, that won't work either.*

The last item was her bra, which he assisted her in, sliding her arms through and fastening in the front.

Jerking off his own jacket, he pulled it on and buttoned the front.

Standing, she glanced down at the jacket that hung to her knees. "At least I'm covered," she said ruefully.

He pulled her in gently to his chest and held her tight. *She fits. Right here, next to my heart.* He tried to still his racing mind, but the anger at what happened took over. *Someone's gonna fuckin' pay.*

Vinny met them outside, already making arrangements. Cora turned to her and asked, "Honey, why don't you let Ross come back to the center and stay with me and Henry until you feel a little better?"

Vinny and Gabe were about to agree, but Jennifer shouted, "No!" Her eyes were filled with fear as she muttered, "He stays with me."

A look passed between the two men as Gabe assisted her into the SUV. Cora hugged her tight and promised to see her the next day. Vinny buckled Ross into the front while Gabe settled in the back with Jennifer.

Little was said on the drive to his apartment and Vinny helped Ross get settled for the night in Gabe's second bedroom. Gabe walked in to make sure he was all right, when Ross asked, "Where's sis going to sleep? Is she sleeping with me?"

Vinny's eyes opened wide as he stepped back for his brother to answer. Gabe easily said, "No, buddy. She's got to be propped up and we want her to get plenty of rest. I've got her in my bed right now, with a bunch of pillows."

"So where are you going to sleep?" Ross asked.

"I'm going to be with her, making sure she rests and that way I'll know if she needs anything during the night."

The explanation satisfied Ross, but he then looked around the room in concern. "Do you have…um…"

"Whatcha need, buddy?" Vinny asked.

"Well, I have a nightlight on at home," he said in a small voice.

Gabe looked at the small boy in the strange bed, his eyes wide having just seen his sister in the hospital, and realized how young he was. Ross' eyes stared at his, but instead of having a haunted look they were filled with the look of someone who trusted him to make things all better.

"Don't have a nightlight, but I've got a small lamp in the study that we can put in here."

Vinny volunteered to get it and soon Ross was settled in and fell asleep. Gabe propped Jennifer in his bed with lots of pillows and with the pain medicine making her comfortable, she was also soon asleep.

Gabe met Vinny in the living room, plopping down on the sofa, taking the offered beer. He took a long pull on the beer before looking at his brother.

"What are you thinking, bro?" Vinny asked.

"Man, I'm so torn between being scared and pissed, I don't know which way to go," he said, rubbing his hand on the back of his neck. He took another long pull from the beer before looking back at his brother's worried face. "She's holding something back."

"Yeah, that's what we all thought as well."

"That's not like her. She jumps in to right a wrong quicker than anyone I've ever seen and sometimes without thinking about herself at all."

"You think she's just scared?"

Gabe nodded. "Whatever those fuckers said to her spooked her. And I'd be pissed as hell if it were a random attack, but they called her there."

Vinny settled back on the sofa. "You might as well know that we're convening a meeting here tomorrow about her. Tony knows you don't want to leave her, so he's bringing the whole gang over including Matt and Shane."

"Appreciate it, man. Hopefully by tomorrow, she'll be more likely to be able to answer some questions. I think tonight she was just in shock."

Vinny hung his head in thought for a moment before a chuckle erupted. "I'm sorry man, but when Ross wanted to know where she was going to sleep, I almost lost it. I was in a panic over how to answer him, but you were real cool."

Gabe smiled, "Well, he's a cool kid. I didn't want to make things worse, but I couldn't lie to him either."

The two men sat quietly for a few minutes finishing their beers before Vinny spoke again. "You're really doing this, aren't you bro?" At Gabe's questioning look, he continued. "Her. Ross. Making it work for all of you. You're willing to take her on, knowing that includes helping to raise her little brother."

Gabe shook his head while smiling. "What can I say? I saw those huge blue eyes looking at me from that fairy face and I was a goner. Tried to tell myself that it was just because I was tired of the meaningless fucks but honest to God, my chest sometimes hurts when I look at her. And as I got to know her? Goddamn, there is nothing but goodness in that tiny woman. Got a heart as big she is and I know…just know…that there's no one else for me."

They stood up together as Vinny left for his apartment. After Gabe locked the door, he began shutting off all of the lights. As he was turning off the lamp on the table near the hall, he stopped. Remembering Ross' comment about being afraid of the dark, he decided to leave it on. He peeked in on Ross and was glad to see him sleeping peacefully.

Moving on to his room, he stopped by the side of the bed and stared down at Jennifer. He gently leaned over to maneuver the pillows to the side of her, helping her to rest easier. Quickly taking care of business in the bathroom, he slid under the covers and awkwardly moved as close to her as possible without disturbing her sleep. *Hell, with those pain meds in her, she wouldn't wake up if a bomb went off.*

He lay, listening to her breathing through her mouth and his anger rose to the surface again. *Some fucker's gonna pay. And when I get my hands on them…*

CHAPTER 11

WAKING THE NEXT morning, Jennifer was aware of a stiff neck and her face feeling tight. Sluggishly she tried to move, but something heavy was holding her legs down. *Where am I?* Her eyes felt swollen as she tried to open them and then slowly the memories began to come back. *The alley. The men. He hit me after I kicked him.*

Her breathing became rapid as the memories flooded back and she felt the movement in the bed instantly.

"Baby? Are you in pain?" Gabe asked as he jerked himself up. He saw that the ice pack was thawed and said, "Stay here, I'll get a fresh one and your pills."

"I don't mean to be crude," she croaked, "but I have got to go to the bathroom."

Nodding he assisted her into the spacious room and closed the door as he left. She avoided the mirror as she headed to the toilet. Walking to the sink, she washed her hands with her head staring down at the water. *Stop being a wuss. If Ross is going to see your face, then you need to know what he's looking at.* Taking a deep breath, she lifted her eyes to the large mirror…and gasped. Her left cheek was swollen and purplish and her eyes…*I look like a raccoon.* And on her neck was the purple imprints of the man's fingers.

Taking a shaky breath, she remembered the night's events. *They must have been there to rob someone. But who would be there at night in the alley. Oh my God, I must have stumbled across some...some...something illegal. Wrong place at the wrong time,* she thought as she promised to have Carlos wait outside from now on.

Deciding to take a quick shower to rid herself of the sweat, fear, and the hospital smell she turned on the huge shower. Stepping inside she quickly washed her hair and body, feeling the cleansing power of the water as the warmth enveloped her. Stepping out, she saw Gabe leaning against the counter, one large leg crossed over the other. Wearing jeans hanging low on his hips, he was shirtless and the expanse of muscles never ceased to draw her in.

"You didn't want to join me?" she asked, trying to take the scowl off of his face. Walking over, she placed her hand on the warm skin of his chest, feeling the power underneath her fingertips. "I'm really okay, honey," she said. "Just the wrong place at the wrong time."

His eyes flashed anger, but he quickly held it in check. "Let's get you dressed, baby. As much as I'd love keeping you naked all day, I'd lose my resolve to be a gentleman while you're injured." He held up her bra and assisted her in fastening it. He gave her a fresh t-shirt of his to put on, seeing that it hung to her knees.

Damn, love seeing her in my shirt.

"Is Ross awake yet?" she asked. "He's usually an early riser."

"Yeah, he's up and having breakfast with Vinny. I told him that we needed to let you rest and then you'd be out to see him."

She wanted to smile, but her lip hurt too much and all she produced was a wince. Gabe reached behind her to grab some pain meds and handed them to her with a glass of water. Satisfied after watching her drink, he placed his hands on her shoulders and said, "Baby. I gotta let you know that there's going to be a meeting here in just a little bit. Everyone's coming over to talk to you, 'cause last night at the hospital you were already out of it from the shock and medicine. Matt and Shane will be here and so will Tony and the gang."

Nodding her understanding, she looked up sensing that there was more that he was not saying. Placing her hand on his firm jaw, she asked, "There's more, isn't there?"

Sighing, he agreed. "Yeah. It seems that it wasn't random." At her sudden intake of breath, he continued, "But you're going to be safe. I'll make sure of that."

Confusion crossed her face as she tried to make sense of his words. *Not random? They were after me? But…that makes no sense.*

Before she could process more of what he was saying, she heard Ross coming into the bedroom.

"Jennybenny, you awake?"

Skirting quickly around Gabe she opened her arms, welcoming her brother's embrace. His usual enthusiasm was gone, replaced by a very soft hug. Looking down at his reticence, she knew that Gabe had warned him to be careful.

"Hey, sweetie. Did you sleep okay?"

"Yeah! The bed was huge but Vinny and Gabe gave me a light that I could keep on all night so it wasn't scary! And the bathroom! They had a light on in there too 'cause it's so big."

His voice continued to rattle on, but she had stopped listening. *He gave Ross a light for his room and one for the bathroom as well.* With Ross still in her arms, she leaned her head way back to look into Gabe's face. "*Thank you,*" she mouthed.

He just smiled and herded both of them to the kitchen, knowing that the group would be coming soon. Out in the kitchen, Vinny handed her a cup of coffee which she took gratefully. "I ran by your place this morning to get some things from Cora." He held out her robe, which she grabbed. Even with a bra on and Gabe's t-shirt hanging to her knees, she felt exposed. She tied the soft robe on, belting it at the waist.

As comfortable and beautiful as she looked, Gabe couldn't help but notice the worn material and could not wait for the day when he would buy her new things. *But not now. She'd never accept them right now.* Pride was as important to her as it was to him, but he longed for the day to claim her completely and then shower her with all the things that she had never had.

A knock on the door signaled a change in the comfortable atmosphere. Vinny opened the door and in walked a wall of masculinity…and one small woman, carrying her laptop case. Lily rushed over to hug Jennifer, as the other men's faces registered shock and anger at the evidence of her assault.

Jennifer knew that she was going to be questioned and needed to move Ross from the group. Signaling her intent to Gabe, she walked Ross back to the guest room and turned on the large, flat-screen TV hanging on the wall. With assurances that the grownups had to talk, she left him wide-eyed, watching TV.

The group had settled in the spacious living room, the furniture suitable for the large-framed men. Gabe walked over and escorted her to a place on the sofa next to him and threw his arm protectively over her shoulders.

Matt and Shane began their questions, taking notes as she carefully described the night's event from the time she received the call to the time Carlos ran out to chase the men away. Her recollections were detailed and the two detectives were pleased with her thoroughness.

When she finished, she looked at the group and said, "Gabe told me that it may not have been random, but we didn't have a chance for me to find out what you know." Licking her swollen lips, she added, "What can you tell me?"

Shane leaned forward, placing his arms on his knees as he held her eyes. "We interviewed Carlos last night and found out that he never made a call to you. That wasn't him on the phone. The call did come from one of the kitchen phones, but there's no way of telling who made the call. The kitchen is filled with employees, many who use the phones a lot. You were set up, honey."

Her eyesbrows pulled together as she tried to take in this new information. "But...but why? I don't have anything of value to rob."

"We don't think it was a robbery," Matt added.

Her eyes shot around the room at the other men sitting there intently listening before she twisted around to look at Gabe. His eyes held warmth for her, but his jaw was tight and ticked with anger. "I don't...understand."

"We don't either, baby," he answered. "But that's why we're here."

"Jennifer, what all are you working on?" Tony asked, pulling her attention over to him. She could tell he filled the role of boss with the same intensity as he must have in the military.

"I...um...well, I'm hired by the city as a social worker with the Department of Social Services. I..." giving a little laugh, she continued, "I'm nobody. My focus is with elder housing." Seeing the somewhat blank looks from the assembly, she said, "As a nation we're having a serious shortage of affordable housing for older people—the ones who can still take care of themselves and live independently, but the cost of living is beyond their ability. I've worked to receive grant money and keep the center going. It's only one, but I hope to see more like it develop. You know, a lower-cost apartment building that's just for the elderly.

"Because I devote a lot of my time to this particular center, I get to live there practically rent free and well…" she smiled, "I love it." Her face sobered as the thoughts of last night came flooding back. Looking directly at Tony, she added, "So don't you see? I'm nobody. Not rich, not famous. I don't have anything of value. There is nothing about my life that is special."

Tony's eyes softened as he listened to the woman in front of him with his friend's arm around her shoulders and said, "I wouldn't say that, sweetheart. I think we'd all agree that you're nothing but special."

His face hardened again and he said, "But something is happening and we're all here to find out what that is."

The group began to brainstorm over the possibilities. A feminine voice broke through the noise. "She does have one thing of value," Lily said. The others in the room looked over, giving their full attention to her.

"You all asked if I could look into some of the possible extortion cases being used in some real estate dealings in the city. I honestly haven't come up with anything concrete, but let's face it. Jennifer's got her hands on some prime real estate."

"My old building? I know my boss said that some-one wanted to possibly buy it, but we've got a five-year lease from my grant. And by the time it is up, we should have more centers available."

"So someone is looking into buying the building from its owner? If they want it bad enough, then maybe trying to scare you away would fit into the extortion that they are used to using."

Shane looked over at Lily giving her a wink as he said to his partner, "Matt, you married a brilliant woman." Matt just smiled at his wife, saying, "Don't I know it."

Vinny queried, "So who's behind these dealings?"

Lily frowned saying, "I haven't figured that out yet. Whoever is doing it is burying themselves really well. It appears that there are layers and layers of real estate and sub-companies all hiding behind each other."

"Good work, Lily," Tony said. Turning back to Shane he asked, "So we keep working this end?"

The two detectives nodded and the discussions once again surrounded Jennifer as she sat quietly in Gabe's embrace. She felt his arm tighten and she turned her face back toward his.

"You're gonna be fine, babe. You and Ross are staying here with me."

She nodded absentmindedly then said, "But only for a while. I've got responsibilities and a job to do."

"Let's take it one day at a time, okay baby?" he

whispered, pulling her close.

She left the room to check on Ross, finding him still entranced in the movie on the huge TV. *I've got to be careful here. I can't have Ross getting used to things that I can't give him.* She kissed the top of his head and went back out into the room just in time to say goodbye to everyone.

The next several days passed in a blur as she slept a lot and entertained phone calls from Chip who wanted to know when she was getting back to work, Sybil who warned her that Chip was hinting at getting rid of the center, Cora who assured her the center was fine, and then a visit from Sherrie.

By the time Sherrie saw her, the swelling had gone down and the bruising was more yellowish than purple. Sitting at Gabe's table, she poured coffee for them before they began to talk about the assault. Sherrie reached across the table giving her hand a squeeze and said, "Jennifer, no one deserved this less than you. I can't believe it happened. You know, I was at the Senator's office the other day delivering more files when he asked how you were. I think he was as shocked as anyone to hear about it."

Jennifer laughed, saying, "Well, his wife certainly took care of things," as she pointed to a huge bouquet of flowers from them.

"Oh, they're gorgeous. When I told him I was visiting, he wanted me to let you know that his backing of your grant is still his top priority." Giggling, she said,

"I couldn't help but notice that he said it right in front of Monty."

"Oh, I'll bet that went over well," Jennifer laughed. "If anyone would be glad to see me fail, it would be that man."

"Have you been back to work yet?" Sherrie asked.

"Not to the office, but I have been back to the center. Lordy, I was mauled by the residents with promises of cookies to make me feel better, advice on how to make the bruising go away, and several of the men volunteered to join with Gabe to 'kick some butt' as they said."

Gabe walked in later, seeing Jennifer and Sherrie laughing and talking. *Good, she's needed this.*

After Sherrie left, Jennifer walked up to him as he was changing in the bedroom. Running her hands over the corded muscles of his back, she smoothed them up to his shoulders and then down his arms.

Looking into his face she saw want in his eyes. Want. Need. *Love?* Sucking in a deep breath, she simply said, "Make love to me, Gabe. I need you."

His heart stumbled at her words. With one hand on her back pulling her toward his chest, the other moved to cup her face. Her delicate features called to him, proudly claiming her as his while the urge to protect surged through his blood. Leaning down to kiss her, he started with a touch of lips. A barely there kiss, but one filled with all the love he could pour into it.

She raised up on her toes to take the kiss deeper

and he needed no more encouragement. With the hand around her waist, he lifted her easily and carried her to the bed. Stripping her gently, he found himself quickly trying to shed his boxers when the sight of her naked body called to him.

She took him by the hands and pulled him toward her as she backed up to the bed. With a gasp, she felt him lift her as they fell on the bed together. The slowness of earlier dissipated as their hands began a battle of who could discover each other the most.

He moved his large hands over her full breasts plucking the nipples, eliciting a moan from deep within her. She explored his muscular chest and abs, until sliding down lower to grasp his cock in her hands. Her fingers moved up and down feeling the firmness beneath the silky skin. A drop of pre-cum appeared and she gently spread it around with the light touch.

He inhaled sharply, desperate for her to continue while wanting to make sure she was taken care of. Rolling toward her, he kissed her gently, careful of her injuries. Trailing kisses down her throat, he sucked at the pulse pounding at her neck. Making his way to her breasts, he pulled one deeply into his mouth, alternating between nipping and soothing.

After giving each breast attention, he continued his trail of kisses down her stomach and over her pelvis toward the prize. Moving his head between her legs, he latched onto her clit sending her hips up off of the bed. Smiling, he held her in place with one large hand, before plunging his tongue into her depth, tasting the sweetness that was purely her.

Jennifer's head fell back to the mattress as her hands grasped his hair. She'd been watching him lick her, feeling his tongue against her sensitive skin, hearing the rumble of pleasure from deep within his chest, but it was too much. *I've held back for so long. Felt as though I had to be strong for everyone. But this...I want to give myself over completely to this.*

The warmth that started in her pussy radiated outwards until she felt every nerve tingle and then tighten. "Please," she begged, wanting more but not knowing exactly what she wanted.

He smiled up at her, licking her juices off of his lips before plunging his fingers deep inside while sucking deeply on her clit once more. That was all it took for her to come flying apart, the inner spasms pulling at his fingers until she lay still on the bed unsure if she could move.

As he crawled up her body, her eyes latched onto his watching them light up as he kissed her breasts once again before kissing her lips gently. She tasted herself on him and suddenly wanted him inside more than she could imagine.

Sensing the desperation in her and feeling it himself, he settled his cock at her entrance and plunged inside. Torn between wanting to take it slow and pounding out his fear that had not dissipated since her attack, he tried to hold himself in check.

She sensed the reticence in him and wanted none of it. She grabbed him by his massive shoulders and pulled him forward. "I need you. All of you," she pleaded.

Realizing that her need was as strong as his was all it took. He began to move harder and faster, building up the friction that sent shock waves through her and had his balls tightening. *I've never felt more alive than I do at this moment with this woman.* He'd had sex, but this was more. All consuming. All powerful. Driving into her, he could feel himself coming home. Before he could let her know that he was coming, she cried out his name and he felt her pussy grab his dick as he poured himself into her.

She felt the warmth spilling deep inside and she clung to him tightly, afraid of letting go. *I'm living. Finally living,* she thought with a smile on her face.

They lay tangled together, hearts beating erratically until finally as their breathing slowed, their hearts began beating in unison. She turned her head to face his and his breath washed over her.

"I love you, Jennifer Lambert," he whispered, staring into her crystalline blue eyes. Her blonde curls lay against his pillows and he knew that was where she belonged forever.

A sweet smile crossed her face as she held his eyes. "I love you too, Gabriel Malloy."

That evening after getting Ross put to bed, she climbed once again under the covers with Gabe snuggling close. Making love once more, he pulled her back to his front and held her as she fell asleep. *This. This I could do forever.*

SEVERAL WEEKS LATER, walking into the kitchen of the center, she called out to Cora, "I'm running up to my apartment. I need to water the plants and get a few things." Once there, she looked around, stunned at the smallness of the rooms. Smiling to herself, she had to admit that she loved this tiny apartment and the memories it held. Grabbing some of her and Ross' things, she headed back downstairs.

Standing in the kitchen, she stood next to the counter lost in thought.

"What's on your mind, honey?" Cora asked.

"I'm kind of…well…lost."

"How so? You've got a good man who's good to you and your brother. You've moved out of this tiny place filled with us oldsters and into somewhere nice. What's there to be lost about?"

"That's just it. We only moved there temporarily while I was recuperating, but that was two weeks ago. I'm fine now and it feels weird to still be there. Like I need to come back here."

"Whatever for?" Henry asked, coming into the kitchen. "I can't see Gabe wanting you to move back here."

"I know, but this…" she said waving her arms

around, "and you are a big part of my job. And my life. And Ross'."

"Lordy girl. You're not moving to the moon. You're still over here almost every day," exclaimed Bertha, following Henry into the kitchen.

Cora turned to the women standing in the door-way. "You old busy-bodies. Can't you let someone have a private conversation?"

"No," piped up Lucille. "At our age, there's nothing private anymore. Life's too short to not get our two cents in!" Looking at Jennifer, she said, "Darling girl. You lived here because it was cheap and easy. Nothing wrong with that. But you've got Ross to think about and you've got a chance to build a future with a good man. So move your stuff out of here and get back to him!"

Laughing, she kissed them all before jogging back out, feeling lighter than she had in a long time.

CHAPTER 12

THE NEXT COUPLE of weeks passed without incident as Gabe, Jennifer, and Ross settled into a routine. Rising early, they all had breakfast together before she dropped Ross off at school and went to work. Some days she went into the office, some days she headed to meetings at the State Capitol or City Hall to continue to push for the elder housing causes, and usually ended her afternoons at the center where she continued to take care of any issues that Henry and Cora could not handle.

Her evenings were spent with Gabe and Ross watching TV, going to get ice-cream, or hanging out with Vinny. And night time, after Ross had fallen asleep, she and Gabe worshiped each other's bodies in the shadows of the city lights coming through his windows.

One morning, sitting in her cubicle at work, she realized that she had left one of her reports in Chip's office where they had been meeting earlier. Walking down the hall, she saw him and his secretary stepping into the elevator before she had a chance to call out. With a puff of exhalation that blew a few escaped curls out of her face, she glanced at his office noticing that his door was still open. *Perfect, I'll just grab the file and get out.*

Walking in, she rolled her eyes at his messy desk. Files and papers filled the desktop, the filing credenza behind his desk and the small table to the side. *How does he stay organized?* Walking over to where she thought the file would be, she began shuffling papers around. Finding the file on the side of his desk near his phone, she could not help but notice his phone-notepad next to it, with the words **Elder Care Center** scribbled at the top along with doodles made as though he were writing while on the phone. Curious, she leaned over the desk to see the pad more clearly. **Buyout break lease threats** He had just written words, not full sentences, so she had no idea what he was talking about or who he had been talking to.

She read the words again, trying desperately to make sense of them. A cold feeling began to slide over her as the realization that this must be tied into her assault somehow. Or if not, it was damn suspicious.

"Can I help you?" came a voice from behind, startling her.

Whirling around, she saw Chip standing in his doorway with a sandwich in his hand. His questioning eyes looked at the file in her hand. "I'm sorry, but I left this in here earlier," she said as she held the file out for him to see. "I need it for my data report."

Nodding, he moved into his office and around his

desk, sitting in his squeaky chair, laying the sandwich down...next to the phone-notepad. She saw his eyes glance down to the pad and then back up to hers. Smiling her most charming smile, she turned to leave saying, "I'll just get back to work now. Enjoy your lunch."

On shaky legs, she made her way back to her cubicle where she found Sybil. Leaning in closely, she told her friend what she had seen.

"What do you think it means?" Sybil asked.

"I have no idea, but it's suspicious, don't you think?"

"Honey, what I think it means is that you'd better stick close to that Mr. Hunky of yours," Sybil replied. "And for God's sake, be careful."

The one thing both ladies forgot was that cubicles were not conducive to private conversations.

SANTO SAT AT his desk, thinking over the conversation he had with Michael earlier. The Ms. Lambert situation should have been handled so differently. Frederick's men had completely bungled the job of scaring her in the alley when they panicked. Manhandling her was one thing, but to hit her and then run away...Jesus, fuck. And now her security boyfriend, the police, and the Alvarez Security Agency were not only protecting her, but investigating as well.

The day after the attack, Frederick had reported the incident to Michael Gibbons and himself...

Michael sat perfectly still in his chair, saying nothing as Frederick related the previous evening's disaster. Santo, not speaking, watched Michael's face. Not a muscle moved, other than the pulsing of a vein running down the right side of Michael's forehead.

"Was she injured?" he asked.

"Not seriously," Frederick had reported. "But she did go to the hospital. Our contact at the hospital said that she had sustained facial injuries."

The silence in the room was deafening.

"Facial injuries. You send two large men to simply scare a woman and they resort to hitting her? In the face?"

"It appears that she kicked one of them and he retaliated."

Silence.

"I have seen a picture of Ms. Lambert. She is quite a tiny woman," Michael stated.

Silence.

Michael's eyes cut over to Santo. "And now?"

"According to her tail, she's now staying with her boyfriend, who works for Alvarez Security and has the protection of the Richland Police."

Michael's voice, steady and even, continued, "And the police?"

"Not ours," Santo said. "It appears that she's friends with several of the Vice Detectives who have now taken a particular interest in the case."

Santo could feel Frederick's eyes on him, but he never

let his eyes waver from the boss'.

"And do either of you have any information to offer me that will make this fucked-up situation any less fucked-up?" Michael asked, his voice taking on a hard quality.

Frederick spoke up again, saying, "We're hoping it appears that she was just in the wrong place at the wrong time. A robbery or drug deal gone bad. There's nothing that ties us into her attack. And our contacts at the newspaper made sure it wasn't in the news."

Michael nodded but kept silent. The silence stretched out for several minutes but felt much longer.

Finally speaking, Michael simply said, "I'm not pleased."

Frederick broke out into a sweat while Santo continued to sit calmly, knowing that Michael was not going to make a rash decision. And Frederick was Michael's family...

"I want the two men taken out of action. If they can't discern the difference between enforcing and a simple act of scaring...they're not ready for my organization."

Frederick stood quickly, nodding to Michael and left the room.

"Your suggestions Santo?"

"Sir, her grant is coming under review with the new tighter budget from the state. Our person in The State Capitol is working behind the scenes to make the money go away. I would also suggest that we look at an angle of getting in her building, seeing what we can do from the inside. Or find out to use as leverage. And with our contact at DSS, we can sabotage her from her workplace as well."

Before Michael could respond, his private door opened and Theresa strolled in. Barely glancing at Santo, she made her way to Michael's desk. Santo watched his boss carefully, to see if he was dismissed.

Michael's eyes cut sharply over to Theresa and he lifted his eyebrow in question.

"I've been at home alone for the past two nights," Theresa pouted.

Michael said nothing.

"I want to go out tonight, baby. Where can we go?" she continued to whine. Leaning over his desk, she presented her ass to Santo and he knew his boss was getting an eyeful of her cleavage.

"I have been with my wife for the past several evenings and will be with her again tonight. You will return to your residence. The parameters of our arrangement have not changed, Theresa, and this will be the last time I explain it to you. You do not accompany me to events. Those are reserved for my wife."

Theresa bolted up and glared down at the man sitting behind the desk. "Well, the cow can't keep your dick hard or you wouldn't be coming to me for your fucks."

Santo's eyes cut sharply to Michael, knowing that Theresa had just crossed the line. His boss might allow his mistress many favors, but there was a limit to what he would put up with.

Michael stood slowly from his chair, eying Theresa coldly. "No. More," he stated firmly. "You will return to your residence and I will come to you when I want. This is *your last warning, Theresa. Unless you want to find yourself on the streets, leave. This. Office. Now."*

She turned and stomped to the private door, slamming it behind her. Michael sat back down, the vein in his forehead bulging. The two men sat in silence for a few minutes.

Finally, Michael turned to Santo and with a deep breath, said, "I'm counting on you Santo. Do not disappoint me."

Santo jarred from his musings when his phone rang again. Recognizing the number, he answered, "You got something for me?"

"She's getting nosy. Starting to look around."

"And you can't stop her?" Santo bit out.

"Not without it looking suspicious," came the reply.

"Then divert her attention. Get her back to the old folk's home and get her attention on just taking care of them and not on crusading. Call in the health department. Have plumbers show up. Get goddamn creative."

"I'll do what I can."

"Make it happen. The boss doesn't take failure well."

Clicking off his phone, he leaned back in his seat rubbing his hand over his face, thinking of the best leverage to use to get this woman out of their way, without any blowback on their organization.

CHAPTER 13

GABE WALKED INTO his apartment the next Friday evening, seeing Jennifer fixing dinner in his kitchen, dancing to music as Ross sat at the table working on a school project. As soon as Ross saw him, the young boy's eyes lit up. The familiar piercing in his chest that Gabe was beginning to recognize as pure happiness hit him once again.

"Gabe! Come see what I'm making."

Gabe walked over smiling at the joy on Ross' face. *That's the way every little boy should look. Happy, healthy, loved.*

He looked into the kitchen as Jennifer's delectable ass shook to the music. She whirled around when she heard him and smiled. That gorgeous face with her blonde curls piled on her head, showing off the little elfish ears that he adored.

Nodding to Ross, he said, "Be right over, buddy," as he walked to Jennifer and kissed her. Hard and fast.

Giving her a wink, he turned back to Ross, who was looking at him with a wrinkled nose. Soon he was being given a lesson on the solar system, which Ross was attempting to build with Styrofoam balls and wire.

"Honey, can you help Ross clear off a section so that we can eat?"

They quickly made room for dinner and the three of them sat comfortably eating.

"I've got a trip I'd like us to take tomorrow," Gabe said casually, not showing the nervousness that he felt.

While Ross was already cheering the idea of a trip without knowing where they were going, Jennifer waited to see what else Gabe was going to say.

"I thought we'd drive out of the city tomorrow. Got a nice place I'd like to take you to and…"

"And what?" Jennifer prodded.

"Well, I've got a little restaurant I'd like to take you to."

"Yea!" Ross agreed.

Jennifer looked at Gabe suspiciously, saying, "Okay. But are you sure that's all there is to it?"

Just then, Vinny interrupted when he came into the apartment, greeting everyone. Jennifer jumped up and got another plate.

"No, you don't need to feed me," Vinny protested although he was looking at their meal with a hungry look in his eyes.

"It's no problem," she laughed. "I'm used to serving about fifty people."

Vinny dove into his meal and then said, "Hey, have you told them that we're going to mom and dad's tomorrow since mom's dying to meet them?"

"Your parents?" Jennifer asked, glaring up at Gabe.

"You didn't say anything about us meeting your parents."

"You've got parents?" Ross asked.

Gabe turned his eyes to his twin saying, "Way to go, ass...um...bro."

"And just when were you going to tell me it was your parents' place?" Jennifer demanded.

"Sorry, man," Vinny mumbled. Wanting to help, he turned to Ross and said, "Yeah, we've got parents. They've got a great little restaurant pub right on the river. It's real nice and you can see the boats from their place."

"I want to go. I want to go," Ross chanted while Jennifer continued to glare at Gabe. Turning toward the sink she began to clean the dishes.

Gabe and Vinny sat at the table for a moment longer, watching the scene unfold. Vinny looked contrite, "I'm sorry, bro. I didn't mean to upset her."

"No worries. I should have told her right off the bat. I was trying to work up my courage."

Vinny snorted. "Your courage? Hell, bro. You were one of the biggest, toughest son-of-a-bitch men in our squad and you're afraid of one tiny woman?" He glanced over to make sure that Ross wasn't listening. "I reckon that's what love'll do to you. That's why I'm not looking for it."

Gabe grinned. "Yeah, I'll remind you of this conversation when it hits you in the ass."

"As quiet as you may think you're being, I can hear

every word," came a voice from the kitchen.

Vinny raised his eyebrows. "Damn, she's good. And that is one pissed off lady."

"No shit, dumbass," Gabe replied, eyeing the back of her as she rattled the pans in the sink, sloshing water on the counter.

Laughing, Vinny headed out of the apartment after reminding Ross that they'd look at the boats the next day.

Sighing, Gabe also stood and walked into the kitchen. Jennifer turned and leaned back against the counter.

"Baby, I'm sorry. I was going to tell you. I was just waiting for the right time."

"And when was that? When we walked through their front door?"

He smiled as he walked forward and placed both hands on either side of her, effectively trapping her within his embrace. Leaning down, he kissed the top of her head. "I really am sorry. I'm new at this...I guess I'm not very good at it yet." He kissed her forehead again. So, am I forgiven?" Leaning farther, he kissed her nose. He moved down a little farther until he was a whisper away from her lips. "Forgiven?"

Lifting her sparkling blue eyes to his, she could not help but smile as she moved into his kiss. Simple. Sweet.

"Yes, you're forgiven," she said. "But Gabe, your parents? That seems...kind of..."

"Serious?" he asked, moving his mouth over hers.

"Yes, ummm" she said breathily, the feeling of his lips on hers making all thoughts float away.

"Well, I am serious about you and Ross. So, why not meet my family?"

His words moved through her bliss and she leaned back. "Serious?"

She squeaked as he lifted her up onto the counter.

"Baby, what do you think we're doing here? I'm not just playing house. I love you. I love Ross. You love me. I'm ready for you to meet the rest of my family."

She captured her bottom lip with her teeth as a worried look crossed her face.

He leaned down, peering into her eyes. "What's going on in that overactive brain of yours?"

She hesitated before blurting out, "I've never done this before. I've never met anyone's parents like this."

"You think I have?" he asked. Seeing her incredulous look, he continued. "Baby, I've never taken a woman home to meet my parents. Ever. But since I told them about you and Ross...and well, Vinny hasn't shut up about you, they can't wait to meet you."

He stepped forward, standing between her legs and pulled her into his chest. With one hand around her back and the other cradling her head, he held her close.

"I love you, Gabe," she whispered.

Smiling to himself, he kissed the top of her head. "I love you, back."

Ross popped around the corner of the kitchen

counter and looked at his sister and Gabe. "Are you two finished kissing? I need some help," he said.

Setting Jennifer down from the counter, he gave her a wink and said, "I've got to go save the solar system."

THE NEXT DAY dawned clear and bright as Gabe loaded them into his Jeep. Vinny sat in the back with Ross, keeping him entertained for the forty-minute drive, while Jennifer sat nervously wondering what would be waiting for her.

After leaving the city, they meandered along a smaller highway along the riverside. The early spring day gave hint of the beauty that was to come. The grass was turning green, the trees were budding, and cows were wandering in their pastures.

Ross was excited about seeing the farmland and Jennifer realized that she did not get him out of the city enough. *Sure, I take him to parks and to the zoo, but this…he needs this too.* She jumped when Gabe took her hand in his.

She looked over at him as he squeezed her fingers and gave him a little smile. He gave her a questioning look and she nodded her answer, knowing he was silently asking if she was all right.

Driving into a small town on the edge of the river, she was amazed that she had never heard of Riverton.

Quaint shops lined the streets and the edge of the town was on the river, with a boardwalk on the side. A harbor was at the end of the town and Ross' excitement over the boats had him straining at his seat belt to be able to see.

"Hang on, buddy," Gabe instructed. "You'll get to see them, I promise."

With those simple words, a warm feeling surrounded Jennifer's heart. *This is serious. He does love Ross.* Smiling to herself, she continued to look at the town as they pulled up to a stone building next to the harbor. *It looks just like something from...*she saw the sign hanging over the door. **Malloy's Pub***...it is a real pub!*

Vinny helped Ross out and Gabe grabbed him before he could run to the boats. Hoisting Ross on his back, they walk over to Jennifer. Heading into the pub, it took a second for her eyes to grow accustomed to the dim lighting.

A stone fireplace was in a gathering place to the left, with old, comfortable sofas surrounding it. Jennifer inhaled deeply the slight smokey smell of the fireplace that gave the pub a homey scent. Along the right wall was a long polished bar with mismatched stools lining it. In the corner was a dart board with a chalkboard to the side for keeping tallies. Toward the back were empty tables and booths, awaiting the lunch regulars.

"Boys," came a deep call from the back.

Jennifer looked toward the voice and saw a large, muscular man heading toward them wearing jeans and a *Malloy's Pub* t-shirt. A Celtic tattoo on his bicep peeked from the t-shirt, matching the one she knew so intimately on Gabe. *I knew Gabe and Vinny were huge but never thought about their parents.* The man bear-hugged first Vinny and then turned to Gabe and smiled.

"Maeve, get out here woman. Your son's brought a little monkey with him," he shouted with a smile.

Just as Ross popped his head up over Gabe's shoulder and announced "I'm not a monkey," a beautiful, petite, dark-haired woman came out of the kitchen as well, wiping her hands on her apron.

After gifting Vinny with a kiss, she turned to Gabe, seeing Ross' face peering at her. "Oh Patrick. That's no monkey. It's a wee boy who looks just like he'd love a piece of my apple pie."

Gabe swung Ross down to the floor, depositing him safely between Jennifer and himself. Placing his arm around her, he turned back to his parents. "Mom, dad. I'd like you to meet Jennifer Lambert and this little man is her brother, Ross. Jennifer, I'd like you to meet Patrick and Maeve Malloy."

Maeve stepped in front of Jennifer and took both of her hands in hers. "Oh my darling girl. You look just like a fairy princess."

Jennifer's smile faltered as she noticed tears in Maeve's eyes.

Maeve pulled her into a hug, whispering, "Thank you for loving my son. I've prayed so long that he would find someone."

"Don't mind my Maeve," Patrick said, putting his hands on his wife's shoulders. "She cries when she's happy."

Patrick stepped up to Jennifer and she had to lean way back to look into his cheerful face. "Good to have you here, darling. Maeve and I've heard a lot about you and are tickled to finally meet the woman that tamed one of my boys."

Bending down to Ross' level, Maeve said, "And Ross, I was serious about the pie. But how about we eat a little lunch first. We've got the best hamburgers and French fries, or if you just want a grilled cheese, we can do that too."

Ross looked up at Jennifer for permission and she nodded to him. Vinny led Ross to a large booth at the back and said, "Eat first and then we can go see the boats."

Gabe and Jennifer followed and they all settled down together. Ross, used to adults around, quickly acclimated and his enthusiasm for seeing the boats up close after lunch had him bouncing in his seat.

"Sis, did you see the big ones? Vinny says I can go see them up close. Are you going to come too? Can we all go? Can I ride on a boat sometime? Some of the boats are for riding and some are for fishing. Can I go on a fishing boat?"

"Shh, Ross. Not so fast, honey," Jennifer gently admonished as Patrick and Maeve laughed.

"Oh, my. He sounds just like my boys at that age," Maeve said.

As the staff brought out platters of fish and chips, Shepard's pie, and hamburgers, the group began to eat. Maeve and Patrick asked Jennifer about her work with the elderly.

Jennifer cut her eyes over to Gabe and he just grinned.

"Yeah babe, I've been talking about you," he admitted, leaning over to kiss her forehead.

Turning back to his parents, she gave a quick explanation of her job at the Elder Center. They listened attentively and then Maeve had to admit, "I was concerned at first when he told me that he had met a woman in an alley!"

Laughing, she said, "Well, I have to confess that seeing this giant," as she elbowed him in the side, "certainly gave me a fright!"

"Well, however it happened, I'm so glad he met you, my dear," Maeve said affectionately. "Now, do you have any friends for my Vinny?"

"Oh no, ma. Don't go playing matchmaker with me. I love Jennifer here...for my brother, but I'm not looking to get tied down just yet," Vinny exclaimed.

"I'll keep my eye out anyway," Jennifer said with a wink.

Patrick began asking Gabe and Vinny about their work. They discussed a few of their security cases and some of the work they were doing with the police department. Patrick nodded approvingly, proud of his sons' military careers and their present jobs.

As his eyes settled on Ross, he noted, "Son, you ate a whole plate of fish and chips. You're eating like my boys did at that age!"

At this, Ross' head whipped around with a grin splitting his face. "Do you think I'll be as big as them?"

"Our daddy was a pretty big man, sweetie, but I don't know if you'll be quite as big as them."

Ross pondered this for a moment as the adults continued to talk. After a bit, he slid out of his chair and tapped Gabe on the arm. Gabe looked down affectionately and put his arm around Ross as he leaned down.

"You need something, buddy?"

"Even if I can't be a big as you, can I still be like you?" Ross asked.

"You wanna be like me?" Gabe asked.

"Yeah. Sis says that you help people and I know you helped us. I'd like to be like that too. She says my dad helped people too so I thought that might be a good thing."

At this, Jennifer turned around and looked at the serious face of her little brother. The table had grown quiet as the adults listened to the voice of the child.

"Buddy, you can be anything you want to be and I'm honored that you want to be like me. And I promise to help you grow up to be the kind of man that your dad would be proud of. Is that a deal?"

Ross' grin was his answer as he scrambled back into his seat and looked at Vinny. "Can we go look at the boats now?"

Laughing, Vinny agreed. Jennifer squatted down to be at Ross' level and said, "Stay right with Vinny. You don't know how to swim and I don't want you going too close to the edge. Don't run away from him. Don't—"

"Baby," Gabe said, watching Ross squirm. "I'll go too and we'll be careful. Promise."

Kissing Ross' head as he bounced over to Vinny, she stood and leaned back to look into Gabe's face. Placing her hands on his strong chest, she said, "Honey, he doesn't know how to swim."

"Noted. But babe, we're not going to let him near the edge." Gabe pulled her close and kissed her chastely. Not the kiss he wanted to give, but in front of his parents, it would have to suffice.

As they were walking toward the door, Gabe turned back and said, "And the first thing on our agenda with spring break? Swimming lessons!"

Before Jennifer could respond they were out of the door, Patrick following along. Jennifer turned to Maeve, suddenly unsure what to say. Maeve quickly put her at ease, directing her to the comfortable sofas in front of the stone fireplace.

The two women sat for the next hour, talking about their families. Jennifer learned more about Gabe as a boy and recognized many of the behaviors that she saw in Ross.

"Sometimes I'm afraid that I'm not everything that I need to be for him," Jennifer confessed.

Maeve leaned over and grasped her hand. "Oh my dear. I see a normal little boy, eager to learn, happy to be around others, inquisitive and intelligent. In spite of the loss that he…well both of you have suffered, he's a wonderful boy. And you…well, let's just say that I couldn't have picked out a more perfect woman for my Gabe."

Smiling, Jennifer squeezed her hand in return. After a few more minutes of chatting, the men came in from the docks and she listened to Ross as he chattered continuously. His face was red from the wind and she wrapped him in a blanket, sitting him near the fire, as Maeve brought out mugs of hot chocolate. He started to protest until he saw Gabe sit near the fireplace too as he pulled Jennifer down in his lap.

All too soon it was time to head back to the city. They piled back in the Jeep after goodbye hugs and promises to visit soon. Ross fell asleep almost immediately and soon they were pulling into the garage of Gabe's building. After a simple supper and bath time, Ross was once again sound asleep in his bed.

Walking into the bedroom, Jennifer noticed that Gabe was in the bathroom with the shower water running as he pulled his shirt off. She had barely made it into the room before he was stalking toward her. Smiling as she backed up to the counter, she leaned back as he pressed closer. Her gaze took in his chest, the expanse of muscles that tapered down to his defined abs.

His hands slid over her shoulders, down her back, and to the bottom of her shirt lifting it over her head. His eyes dropped to her full breasts, spilling over the top of her demi-bra. *Not her usual lingerie.*

She grinned, saying, "I bought something new. Do you like it?"

Growling his answer, he unzipped her jeans and began to slide them slowly down her legs, taking her panties with them. With a flick of his fingers, the bra landed on the pile of clothes on the floor. He perused her naked body, petite with curves that begged to his hands. Silky skin that his fingers ached to caress.

Her fingers went to his belt buckle and she made quick work of his jeans as well. His erection tented out his boxers and she knelt as she pulled them off. Staying on her knees, she took him in her mouth. Sucking deeply, she could only take part of him so her hands circled the lower part of his dick and moved gently up and down in rhythm with her hands.

He moaned and threw his head back as the sensations shot through him as he wrapped his hands in her silken curls. Looking back down, he was awed that this gorgeous creature was pleasuring him when what he wanted to do was worship her body.

He could tell he was close to coming but gently pulled her up and into his arms. Kissing her soundly, he said, "Baby, I could have come right then and loved every second, but when I come tonight, I want to be buried deep in your sweet pussy."

She stepped into the shower, letting the warm water cascade over her body and in turn, watching the droplets fall off of his towering frame. He lifted her up in his arms and pressed her back against the wall, allowing the water to hit his back, keeping it from spraying her face.

She held on, first to his shoulder and then cupping his face, before pulling him in for a kiss—one that she started, but he quickly took over. What started as a soft as a whisper kiss evolved into demanding, possessive, unyielding. She felt the rough stubble of whiskers against her fingers as she held him close.

He plunged in, exploring every crevice while committing her taste to memory. He wanted more, needed more. She met him stroke for stroke, her tongue vying for dominance.

Slowly letting go of her mouth, he kissed his way across her neck as she arched her back and down to the swell of her breasts. Sucking one nipple in deeply, he tugged hard, first nipping and then soothing.

Her hand grabbed his head, pulling him closer. The feelings of euphoria washed over her as much as the warm water that slid down her body. With every pull on her nipples, she felt the zing straight to her core.

Lifting her up again, settling her on the tip of his cock, he guided her onto him gently this time. Unlike earlier, this was about slow. Gentle. Easy. Care. Comfort. Keeping her back against the shower wall so that the water was not on her face, he moved her up and down, letting the sensations flow over both of them.

Taking a wet nipple in his mouth, he sucked gently, circling his tongue around the beaded tip. Knowing shower sex was a new experience for her, he realized it was new to him as well. *It's all new with her. Everything. The sex. The feelings. Everything.*

It didn't take long for her to feel the familiar pull of her impending orgasm. Climbing higher and higher until she knew she was ready to jump off the edge, she felt him press against her clit and that was all it took for her to fly apart. Throwing her head back, she felt her orgasm roar through her as her inner walls grabbed at his pulsating cock.

With just a few more pumps Gabe joined her, as she milked every bit of seed out of his straining dick. As he emptied himself into her waiting body, he knew this was it for him. She was his forever. Lowering her carefully onto the shower floor, he leaned back to turn off the cooling water.

Snagging a couple of thick towels, he dried her off first, rubbing every part of her body. She was warm and flushed, and his attention to detail had her growing wet once again. *What is it about him? He could keep me in a constant state of need!*

He moved the towel up her toned legs to the apex,

making sure to torment her as he made sure to rub the towel against her clit. Slowly standing, he continued to dry her smooth skin up toward her breasts, where the material dragged across her nipples. Taut with need, they puckered as he captured first one and then the other in his mouth before drying them again.

"Gabe...," she cried, her need overtaking her every thought.

Chuckling, he slowly pulled the towel through her hair watching the curls spring to life. She clung to his shoulders as though he were the only thing holding her up. Tossing the towel to the side, he pulled her into his muscular chest, pressing her face against his heart and holding her tightly. For a moment they stood, each lost in the thoughts of how perfectly they fit. He bent and scooped her up in his arms.

"Gabe?" she said again, this time more subdued.

"Yeah, babe," he replied.

"If I don't run a comb through my hair now, I'll never get the tangles out later."

"Okay, baby," he said as he snagged her large comb from the counter on his way into the bedroom. Sitting her down on the bed, he crawled in behind her.

Twisting around to see what he was doing, she saw the comb still in his hand while he gently ordered, "Turn back around."

She acquiesced but told him to start at the bottom or he'd never get the tangles out. She felt the comb move through her hair. Gently at the bottom, separating tangles and then slowly moving up. The feeling of having her hair combed was like a massage. Jennifer relaxed, giving over to the feelings. When the last curl was combed, she whimpered at the loss and heard him chuckle again.

"Don't worry baby. Now that you're relaxed, I've got ways to wind you up again," he said tossing the comb to the nightstand. Laying on his back, he pulled her on top, her legs straddling his torso. His gaze dropped from her beautiful face down to her perfect, full, rosy-tipped breasts. His hand trailed from her hips to her breasts where he held the weight of them before rubbing his thumbs over her taut nipples.

The desire shot right through her again, straight from her nipples to her pussy. Deciding to take the lead, she lifted herself over his cock and without waiting seated herself to the hilt. She could have sworn that he touched her womb as his thickness filled her completely. Lifting herself up and down on him, she controlled the pace until her legs grew tired. Feeling his hands squeeze her hips he began to match her rhythm.

Opening her eyes, she looked down at him seeing his smile.

"You ready to give it over to me, baby?"

With a blush and a nod, she laughed as he rolled her onto her back. "I wanted to keep going, but my legs gave out too quickly," she complained.

"Baby, I'll give you control when you feel like you need it but never worry about handing it back over."

He kissed her hard and wet, before continuing. "Cause girl, I like control in all ways, but especially in the bedroom." Leaning back in, he captured her lips once again, plunging his tongue in at the same time he slid his aching cock deep into her warm pussy. *Perfect. A perfect fit.* He couldn't remember the last time he felt so connected to a woman. *Never. The answer is never.*

It took very little time for his hard strokes to bring her back to oblivion once again. She cried out as her world exploded in a shower of sensations, sparks flying out from her core in all directions.

He looked at the beauty under him, her lashes on her cheeks as her eyes were tightly closed. Her long, blonde curls were drying spread out across his pillow. With continuous strokes, he pumped furiously, needing to reach a secret place inside of her that he wanted to touch. Head thrown back, his thick neck muscles strained as his biceps bulged with the strength of his body emptying inside of her. As the last of his strength left him, he fell to the side taking her with him. Tucking her tightly with her head resting on his chest, he struggled to slow his racing heartbeat.

With legs tangled and hearts beating as one, he leaned down to snag the covers making sure to pull them over their sweaty bodies.

As sleep began to overtake them, she whispered, "Gabe?"

"Ummm?" he answered.

"I really like your family."

He smiled in the dark, pulling her head closer to him. "I'm glad, baby. They liked you too."

A few minutes later, she whispered, "Gabe?"

"What now, baby?"

So softly he almost could not hear, she whispered, "I wish you could have met my parents. They would have loved you too."

His breath caught in his throat as he leaned down seeing a single tear escape. Wiping it with his thumb, he said, "I wish I could have too. But if you'll have me, I'll be your family now too." He saw her smile and he captured it in a kiss. A soft touch of lips. Full of promise.

CHAPTER 14

JENNIFER MADE HER way into the kitchen of the Center the next Monday, arms loaded with bread. Henry and Cora walked in and helped her put it away before serving breakfast.

"You didn't go by yourself to get this, did you?" asked Henry.

Laughing, she replied, "Oh no. Gabe was working so he sent Jobe with me last night." Sobering, she hugged the two friends and said, "I won't make that mistake again."

"Do the police have any idea who it was or what they were doing in the alley?"

"I don't know. At least not that they've told me. I gave them a good description though. Although how, I don't know! My knees were shaking so bad that I'm surprised I remembered anything."

Giving the two a hug goodbye, she headed out to catch the bus to work. Gabe had wanted to make sure someone was giving her a ride, but she refused. She'd told him that her job had her running all over the place—hardly conducive for a driver. Then he suggested that he buy her a car. That resulted in an argument that was only resolved when he kissed her senseless and she agreed to only use the city transportation in the daylight. Since the days were getting longer, she figured that could be a promise she could keep.

Arriving at DSS, she had just set her purse down when Roy ran over. "I've been trying to call your cell. Chip told us that the budget hearing for grant continuations are getting ready to happen this morning."

She whirled around grabbing her phone and did not see any missed calls. "Do you have the right number? I've got nothing missed here."

Holding up his phone, he said, "I put in the number that Sybil gave me."

"Oh, I don't have time to figure it out now. I've got to get to The State Capitol."

As she pulled her coat back on, Chip came walking around the corner. "You're missing the chance to fight one last time for your program."

Glaring at him, she retorted, "Well, maybe if you'd let me know this was happening this morning I could have been there."

He stood his ground saying, "You've had quite a few days off in the last two weeks. Perhaps that is why you are behind."

"Days off? Jesus, I was mugged. Hardly a vacation!"

"Stop it," Sybil jumped in, thrusting some files in Jennifer's hand. "Here's your data. Go."

Running out the building, she decided to splurge

on a taxi and made it to her destination in record time. Heading into the building, she saw Monty down the hall as she was getting off the elevator. *Oh, damn!* Just then, Sherrie walked around the corner near Monty but saw Jennifer down the hall. The two women made eye contact and Sherrie gave her a nod.

"Monty," Sherrie called out. "How nice to see you." As she moved to shake his hand, she dropped an armful of files, spilling the contents over the floor. "Oh, no," she exclaimed as she dropped to the floor, beginning to gather them.

Monty dutifully squatted on the floor to assist her. Jennifer joined in a group of people walking down the hall and managed to move past the couple on the floor without Monty looking up. Grinning at the first stroke of luck in the day, she moved toward the conference rooms hoping to catch Senator Reno before he entered.

He saw her first and smiled as he walked over. "Ms. Lambert, how good to see you again. Here to check on your project?"

"Yes and thank you so much for giving me one last time to say how much the elder care projects in the city need the funding."

Holding her hand and pulling her in for a chaste hug, he said, "I'll fight for you, my dear."

Smiling up at his face, she said, "Thank you so much."

A reporter came over to her and asked, "What special interest group are you lobbying for?"

Excited to have some press, she told him and said that she would love to provide him with some information about the data she had been collecting on the effects of her projects. The reporter agreed since the Senators had retired to the conference room. As Jennifer pulled out her files she began to flip through them, but none of her data was included. It was as though Sybil had given her a file of random papers.

Looking at the reporter apologetically, she tried to set up another appointment but the reporter's attention had already diverted to someone else.

"Not having any luck today?" came a voice from behind.

Whirling around, she came face to face with Monty. And he did not look happy.

"I see you managed to interrupt Senator Reno when he was trying to meet with the press," he accused.

"I was trying to do what anyone else around here is doing—trying to fight for my program to not be cut from the budget."

"You don't really fall into the same category as the others do you?" came the cruel remark.

She could not help but look around. The hall was filled with men in expensive suits and women in their power clothes. Leather briefcases. Looking like the money their companies and special interests groups represented. Sucking in her lips, she turned her eyes back to him.

"You're right. I don't look the part. I'm an educated woman that works for an overworked, unpaid department in the city. But let me tell you something," she said, advancing on him and poking him in the chest with her finger. "I speak for those that no one wants to remember anymore. So take your snooty attitude and shove it."

He glanced down at the petite woman with her finger hitting his chest and for a second admiration seemed to flash in his eyes, quickly replaced with irritation. "Remember, Ms. Lambert. Make your appointments through me."

Quickly walking around him she hurried down the hall, blinking back tears. *Damn, I hate crying.* Turning the corner she saw Sherrie, who ran over.

"Did I help? Did it work?" Sherrie asked, a gleam in her eye.

Jennifer had to laugh in spite of her frustration. "Yes, it worked very well. I got to see the Senator before he went behind closed doors."

Sherrie eyed her critically, then threw her arm around Jennifer's shoulders. "Come on, sweetie. You look like you could use a cup of coffee." Her eyes sparkled as she said, "I have just the place."

A few minutes later, the two women were sitting in a booth at a little café drinking coffee laced with Baileys. Jennifer relaxed and confessed, "Oh my God. This is just what I needed." Looking over Sherrie's shoulder, she saw two men walking in the café and a smile lit her face.

Sherrie looked at her friend and laughed, saying, "There's only one person I know who can bring that look to your face." She turned and looked behind her, not surprised to see Gabe, but then saw Tony walking in with him.

Jennifer saw Sherrie's eyes light up when she saw Tony and also noticed Tony's gaze locked on Sherrie as well. *I wish I could get those two together. The way they look at each other, it wouldn't take much.* Before she had time to ponder their situation, the men were upon them.

Gabe leaned down to kiss her, sliding into the chair next to hers leaving Tony to sit next to Sherrie. They greeted each other shyly before the waitress came to bring them menus.

"Sherrie brought me here for some fortified coffee after my latest run-in with Senator Reno's assistant. I swear that man has it out for me."

"You need me to take him out, babe?" Gabe joked.

"Yes, actually that would make me happy," she replied. "But you'd have to take a back seat to Sherrie here. She jumped in with some subterfuge and occupied him while I made a sneak attack."

Tony's face jerked around to look at the stunning woman sitting next to him. "What did you do?"

"Nothing wrong, I assure you," Sherrie answered sharply.

"Oh, it was fabulous," Jennifer gushed. "He was in the hall and I couldn't get by so Sherrie distracted him so that I could slip by."

"So how did this distraction happen?" Tony asked.

"I did a strip-tease for him in the middle of the hall," she quipped.

His eyes widened and then as though he could not hold it back, a chuckle slipped out. "I'll bet that was a distraction."

"Well, I was a waitress in a strip bar last year, so I just thought maybe you assumed I used the skills I saw on stage."

Gabe and Jennifer watched the tableau in front of them play out, each with their own thoughts. Gabe knew that his boss and former commander had his demons, the same as the rest of them. And whether or not they wanted to admit it, those demons lived on. In their dreams. In their minds. In their hearts. *But if I can fall in love, then I'd give anything for Tony to find that too.*

Jennifer just pondered the two sitting across from her with a small smile on her face. *Maybe, just maybe.*

She went back to her office and found that Chip and Roy had gone for the day. Sybil was still there, sitting in her cubicle.

"Sybil, why did you hand me this file earlier?" she asked.

Sybil looked at the folder in her hand and said, "I thought you wanted to take your data to give to the Senator in case he needed some facts and figures to back up your program."

"I did, but there was none of that information in here."

Sybil looked surprised. "I grabbed it off the top of your desk, where I thought I had just seen you put it. I'm sorry, hun. What was in it?"

Jennifer opened up the folder and showed her some phone and fax notes. "It's just junk papers."

"Oh girl, I am so sorry. I have no idea how the files could have been mixed up."

Jennifer shrugged, "Don't worry about it. I was able to get to him before he went into the meeting anyway."

Sybil nodded as she grabbed her purse. "I'm heading out for the day. You coming?"

"Nah, not now. I'll see you tomorrow."

With that Sybil left and Jennifer sat looking at her desk. The file in question was sitting right on top of her desk, where she had left it. *So how did Sybil get them mixed up?*

THAT NIGHT AFTER Ross was tucked in, Jennifer walked into the living room and leaned over to flip off the TV. Gabe looked up in surprise.

"Are you going to tell me what has been on your mind ever since you got home?" she asked.

Gabe started to protest, but then thought better of it. Sighing heavily, he said, "Come here, babe."

"Oh. It's that kind of talk," she said with suspicion.

"Yeah." She straddled his lap, looking into his eyes wishing the butterflies would cease. "Okay, what's up?"

"Alvarez Security has a job this Friday night and I wanted you to know what was happening."

"Okaaay," she said, drawing the word out in hesitation.

"The big opening showing of the movie is this weekend and it will be held here in Richland since it was filmed here." Seeing her about to protest, he quickly continued, "I will not be providing any personal escorting. I will just be at the event providing general security."

"That's it? That's all?"

"Well, that and providing security for the party afterward at the ballroom."

"And Alicia Morgenstern? She'll be there, I assume?" Jennifer asked, trying very hard to be calm and not jump up and scream.

He dug his fingers into her hips as he sucked in a deep breath. For a moment he wished that he had taken Vinny's advice and not told her about the assignment at all. But he knew he could not do that.

"Yes, she'll be there. But I'm not her personal security. I won't even have to be around her. It will be general security. In fact, Tony has agreed to put me on the outside of the building so I won't even see her."

The room was eerily quiet as he sat watching the emotions play across her face. Surprise. Hurt. Anger. Irritation. Fear. Then back to hurt again. *Fuck, this is not how I wanted this to go.* "What are you thinking?" he asked gently, almost afraid of her answer.

"What do you want me to say, Gabe? This is your job and you have to do what you have to do. Are you asking if I'm happy about my boyfriend spending the evening around a Hollywood starlet who happens to be his former fuck-buddy? Nope, I'm not," she said honestly, noticing his wince. "But I'm going to have to deal with it because it's not your fault. But don't ask me to like it."

She leaned in and gave him a quick kiss, then moved to get off of his lap. His hands held her fast in place, but before he could speak, she pushed back gently. "Oh no. You need to give me some space. Some space to be a little pissy and a little pouty. You wouldn't like it if I was going to be spending an evening in the presence of a former fuck-buddy of mine." At that, she saw his jaw clench. "I promise my little pout won't last long, but you need to give me that."

Nodding his agreement, he let her slide off his lap and watched her as she walked back to the kitchen. He sat for a minute then thought he should give her more time to process what he had told her. He headed down to Vinny's apartment and when the door opened, it only took one look for his twin to know that the information had not gone well.

"Come on in, bro. Did she kick you out?" Vinny asked.

"No, she really did pretty good with it. Just not happy and how can I blame her? She mentioned that I wouldn't be happy to have her around a former fuck of hers and she's right. Jesus, that'd make me fuckin' crazy so how the hell did I think that she'd be okay with this."

The two brothers walked into Vinny's living room and settled down with beers in hand.

"Look, talk to Tony. Tell him that you just can't do that night. He'll let you out."

"Nah. It's our job to take the missions that come to us."

"Hell, this isn't the special forces anymore."

"Maybe not, but it's still the job. Would you back out?" Gabe asked.

"Hell no," Vinny answered quickly. After a moment of thought, he added, "But then I don't have anyone like Jennifer in my life. She's special. And she's smart, bro. She knows nothing's going to happen and then it'll be done and over with. No more even seeing Alicia Morgenstern unless you're a dumb fuck and go see one of her movies."

The two brothers laughed and finished their beer before Gabe stood and walked to the door. "Thanks, man," he said as he gave his brother a chin jerk.

Entering his apartment, he saw her sitting on the sofa, remote in her hand flipping through channels. He walked around and sat on the coffee table right in front of her. Neither one of them said anything.

She tossed the remote to the side and looked into his face. The face she loved. The face that held her through the night. *He looks like a little boy wondering if he's in trouble.* The side of her mouth quirked up in a small smile.

Her smile caused his heart leapt. Taking that as an encouraging sign, he leaned in slightly placing his large hands on her knees. "You okay, baby? I swear I'll call Tony tonight and tell him I can't do it."

Shaking her head, she just smiled at his offer. "It's okay." Sucking in a huge breath, she said honestly, "I know it's stupid. You were with her before me so I can't hold anything against you for that. I guess I was hoping that anyone you were ever with would never cross our paths again. Especially one that called me a garbage-crawler."

Gabe winced again and hung his head for a moment. *How could I have ever fucked her? Jesus, I was such a prick.* Lifting his head back up, he moved forward again. "Baby, she's a bitch. And believe me when I say, she's nothing. Not even a speck on my memory. Ever since I saw you that first night, it's only been you. And you are the only woman I have ever loved."

She leaned forward and melted into his kiss. This kiss was not hurried. It was the slow exploration of two lovers who had forever to love.

He picked her up in his powerful arms and carried her to the bedroom where he worshiped her body long into the night. Finally they fell asleep, wrapped in each other's arms. Warm. Secure. Loved.

CHAPTER 15

GABE WALKED INTO Alvarez Security the next morning and saw Tony waiting for him. A quick glance to the side revealed Vinny.

"I can take you off the security detail," Tony said immediately.

"Not necessary, Tony. It's okay. I talked to Jennifer. She was a little unhappy at first, but that's on me. When I crossed the line between my professional life and personal...well I set myself up for grief. But she's fine. I did tell her that I'd volunteered for the outside detail."

Tony nodded and went back to his office. Gabe looked over at his brother. "Thanks, man, for looking out for me, but I've got it covered."

Vinny nodded and slapped Gabe on the shoulder as they headed into the main room. Several hours later Gabe's phone rang and he saw Shane's name illuminated on the screen. "What's up?"

"Need you to be calm and not lose your shit," his friend said.

His blood turned cold with fear. Not an emotion he was used to feeling. Vinny looked over at his brother, instinctively knowing something had happened.

"Talk."

"Jennifer called 911 this morning. She saw one of the men who assaulted her and followed him."

"What the fuck?" Gabe roared, causing Tony, Jobe, and BJ to come over. They looked to Vinny for an explanation, but he just shook his head.

"She's fine. She did good, man. You should be proud of her."

"She followed the man who assaulted her and you think she did good? You tellin' me you'd be happy if Annie did that?"

"Look, she followed at a distance to keep an eye on him but called 911 and got someone there real quick. We got him. She's here at the station and he's in lockup. You need to come here to be with her, but I'm tellin' you man, lock your shit down before you get here. She doesn't need to see you like you're feelin' right now."

"On my way," Gabe clipped, shoving his phone back in his pocket. Turning, he saw the line of men behind him. Focusing on Vinny, he said, "Jennifer saw one of the men who assaulted her. She followed him and called the police. They've got him." His jaw was tight with anger.

Tony asked, "She okay?"

"Got the feeling she's scared."

Tony nodded. "Vinny, drive him."

"I got it," Gabe growled.

"That's an order," Tony retorted.

Vinny nodded and the two brothers headed out of the building and drove quickly to the station. Walking in, Gabe saw Matt and Shane first, but as they moved out of the way he could see Jennifer's frightened face peering at him. Jogging over he immediately opened his arms and she moved into them. Kissing the top of her head, he whispered, "I'm here. You okay?"

He felt her nod rather than heard her response. Pulling her back, he peered into her face.

"I'm fine. Just kind of nervous," she confessed. Looking up into his face, she knew he was angry.

Matt spoke up. "You'll be fine. They can't see you, but you will have to look. No pressure." Turning to Gabe, he said, "To aid in a positive identification, we're putting him in a lineup."

Gabe nodded to his friends and tucked Jennifer into his side as they walked down the hall. When they got to the door, Shane gave the instructions. "Gabe, you can be here for support but don't speak. I don't want her influenced at all."

"Got it," he replied.

Shane finished his instructions to Jennifer before they stepped into the room. She glanced around nervously, noting the large window in the room that led to another well-lit room with a height measurement scale on the back wall. *Just like in the movies.* Sucking in a deep breath, she, Matt and Shane stepped to the window and Gabe moved behind them.

Seven men came in from the other room and stood with their backs against the height chart. "Take your time," Matt instructed. "Look carefully."

Jennifer knew immediately which man it was, but did what she was told. She looked over each man carefully and came back to the man who had stood in front of her that night in the alley. Tall, broad shouldered. Dark hair. And angry eyes.

"Number five. It's number five," she said.

Suddenly, she felt her legs grow weak and Matt grabbed her as Gabe's arms came from the back to encircle her as Matt let go to get a chair. Sitting down, she tried to steady her breath, but all she could see was that man hitting her.

Gabe gently pressed her neck forward, forcing her head down. He said softly, "Put your head all the way between your knees, baby and breathe with me. In through your nose...out through your mouth...in through your nose..."

Through the fog, she heard someone say, "Get some water," and she felt Gabe lift her head slightly, pressing something to her lips. "Take a sip baby."

She dribbled more than she sipped, but the fog was beginning to lift. Continuing her deep breathing, she could hear voices in the background distinctly as Gabe's presence became sharper. The feel of his hands rubbing her back, pulling her hair out of her face, whispering softly to her.

With one final deep breath, she lifted her head and peered around. Gabe's face was directly in front of hers, concern had replaced the anger from earlier. Matt and Shane were on either side of him as well as a uniformed policewoman that was standing next to Shane.

"I'm sorry," she said, embarrassment flooding her face.

"Don't be sorry, darlin'," Shane said. "You did real good."

Standing on weak legs, supported by Gabe, she said, "It was number five, I'm sure of it."

Nodding, Shane said, "We got it. He's being taken to the interview room and we'll have a go at him. You managed to claw at his hand that was on your neck that night, so we'll threaten him with a DNA sample."

Sucking in a ragged breath, she looked up and said, "I really need to get to work. I made a call when I was here, but I'm buried in paperwork and have got to get into the office."

"You need to go home, baby."

"No, I can't. I've had so many days out already, I haven't even had a chance to talk to Senator Reno to see what's going on with the budget, and I need to talk to Roy and Sybil. Some strange things are happening in the office and I want to know what is going on."

Gabe's fingers flexed on her shoulders as he tried to control his frustration. He felt Vinny's presence approach. "Bro, she's safe. She's in good shape. She needs to do something normal, not be coddled."

Gabe's head swung around as he looked at Vinny incredulously. "So you're now the expert on women and relationships?"

Vinny's grin was infectious as he leaned over and kissed Jennifer's head. "No, man. Just you and your relationship."

Jennifer couldn't help the giggle that escaped when a chuckle erupted from Gabe as he shook his head.

The three of them left the station and dropped her off at work. As she entered the DSS building, she felt a strange sensation of eyes on her. Turning around, she saw the twins driving away and assumed it must have been them. Moving toward the elevators, she missed the eyes that were following her. Angry eyes. Determined. Vengeful.

SANTO TOOK THE phone call from his office.

"Cops got Frederick's man. Seems Ms. Lambert recognized him, followed him and called the fuckin' police."

Goddamn it. "How the fuck did she recognize him? He shouldn't have been anywhere near her."

"Don't know. According to his partner from that night, he may have been trying to get back in Frederick's good graces."

Santo thought for a moment, quietly deciding the course of action. "I'll take care of it," he said, hanging up and then quickly dialing again. "Frederick? Your man was picked up by the police. It seems Ms. Lambert saw him and his ass is now in jail. Take care of him. Yeah. Permanently."

"JENNIFER," CORA'S VOICE sounded weak on the phone. "I don't want you to worry, but honey we've got a problem. Some of the residents are sick...it seems that they have a stomach virus and someone from the health department is here causing problems."

"I'll be right there."

Arriving at the center, Jennifer jogged into the building and straight into the kitchen. She saw a man talking to Henry and she headed directly to them.

"Is Cora okay?" she asked Henry, ignoring the man from the Health Department.

"Yeah, just a little weak," Henry answered, the fatigue showing on his face. "The problem is this here man," he said jerking his thumb at the stranger.

She turned, putting her hand out to him and identified herself. The man looked down at her and ignored her extended hand. "You've got mice in the kitchen. I'm still identifying other problems."

"We do not," she stated definitively. "It's an old building, but we're inspected each month and there have been no problems."

"What do you call this?" he asked, holding up a bag

containing a mouse caught in a trap.

Henry shouted, "Now hold on. I was in that pantry this morning and there was nothing there. This fellow shows up and goes in there and suddenly there's a mouse in his hand. If you ask me, that's real fishy!"

The man stepped closer to Henry and Jennifer instinctively stepped in front of him. "Henry, go check on Cora and the others. I'll be in to see her in a few minutes."

Henry shuffled away and Jennifer looked up into the dark eyes of the inspector standing directly in front of her, before dropping to his name tag. "You want to take a step back, Mr. Burton? Threatening posture will get you nowhere with me." Pulling out her phone, she glanced at the numbers and placed a call. He looked at her suspiciously.

"Bob? Jennifer Lambert here. Can you come to the center now? It's an emergency. Got someone from the Health Department who just showed up and I need you. Yeah? Thanks."

The man, who had stepped back a few paces, continued to hold her stare. "Who'd you call? I represent the Health Department."

"The grant that I have to run this facility has someone from the State Health Department who comes monthly to do inspections. He knows the building and our business. He's also the one approved by the state to do our inspections. Not you. So you want to tell me why you're here? Who called you? Who sent you? And why the fuck you are messing with these people?" Her voice had risen with each word and the last was shouted.

"You okay, honey?" came a voice from behind. As Jennifer turned around, she realized that a number of the residents had come out to the see what was happening.

"All I know is that my department got a tip that there was food poisoning here and I was to investigate."

"Food poisoning? There are residents with a stomach virus which is not the same. If a doctor or hospital had diagnosed food poisoning, there would have been a lot more involvement than you just being here. And haven't you read the paper lately? The flu is going around affecting the whole area. Are you visiting all the places with flu calling it food poisoning? So. Who. Sent. You?" The last words were punctuated with a tiny finger poking his chest.

Anger flashed in his eyes and for a second she felt fear. *Something's not right.*

Before she could question him further, he abruptly turned and said, "I'm writing up a report. If possible, I'll get you closed down." With that he walked out of the back door into the alley.

She was surrounded by the residents all clambering to know what was happening. Rubbing her forehead to still the headache looming, she calmed them down, sending them back to the common area. Heading up the stairs to Henry and Cora's apartment, she knocked and entered. Cora was sipping tea, looking pale.

Both she and Henry wanted to know what was going on and Jennifer explained as best as she could. "I swear it's like someone is out to get us!" she exclaimed with frustration. Another knock on the door had Henry rising to let Bob Tolsen in. After greetings all around, he sat down at the table with the other three and they went over the morning's events.

Henry explained that there was a stomach flu that had gone through the residents but that no doctor had mentioned food poisoning. Bob nodded and took notes as he asked questions.

"It wouldn't be food poisoning. If it had been, then most of the residents would have been affected at the same time. This went through the residents slowly as though they were passing it along, just as you said…a stomach flu. I don't know who sent this man, but I'll follow up with the Richland Health Department and see what I can find out. It makes no sense that he'd just show up without the official paperwork giving him authority to investigate or inspect."

Jennifer's brain began working overtime. *What is going on? Why would someone want us out of this building? It's an old building, not worth anything to anyone else. That was one of the reasons they were able to afford to get the building with the grant.* Rubbing her forehead again, she knew the headache was coming.

"Bob, I'll walk you out." Kissing Cora and Henry goodbye, she and Bob made their way to the ground floor and stopped on the front stoop. "I don't know what's going on, but I'm afraid it seems like someone is trying to sabotage this project. And I swear if it was just me? Sure I'd be pissed, but whatever happens is affecting the wonderful people who live here."

"I'll check into it, I promise," he said, shaking her hand.

Watching him leave, she decided to make an impromptu appearance to The State Capitol once more. *And I just dare Monty to get in my way!*

FOR THE FIRST time that day, things were going her way. Monty was not at his desk and Senator Reno ushered her into his office. It just so happened that his wife was visiting as well and her friendly face made the horrible day seem better.

"I will be honest, Ms. Lambert," the Senator said. "The budget hearings are not going as well as I had hoped." Seeing her face, he quickly added, "That doesn't mean anything to you right now. I'm just letting you know that the state's budget is very tight. But, I'm fighting for you.

Mrs. Reno looked at Jennifer and the evidence of stress was on her face. "My dear, I have a perfect idea. The Senator and I will be attending a gala on Friday night for the opening of the movie that was filmed here months ago. We have two extra tickets and would love to have you and a friend attend as well. You look like you could use a night out." Smiling she added, "And perhaps there is a special young man who would like to escort you?"

"I...I don't know," she stammered. *The premier? Jesus, Gabe will be there. But so will Alicia Morgenstern. But I probably won't even see her.*

Mrs. Reno interrupted her thoughts. "I can see you are thinking of all the reasons to not attend, but I insist." Leaning in as though to whisper, but knowing her husband could hear, she added, "And these events often turn out boring for me because they usually become work events for my husband. You might be able to make some more converts for your project."

With that enticement, Jennifer's mind was made up. Smiling, she agreed. "I would love to attend. My...um...well my boyfriend actually works for the security company that will be there, but I have a girlfriend that I would love to invite."

"Perfect," Mrs. Reno exclaimed.

Thanking them both, she hurried out of the office...and ran straight into Monty. Bouncing off of him, she felt his arms reach out to grab her arms to steady her.

"Well, well, Ms. Lambert. What a surprise to see you here, unannounced with no appointment," he said sarcastically.

Jerking away, she was getting ready to retort when Mrs. Reno approached from behind. "Oh Monty, I see you've met the lovely Ms. Lambert."

Monty's eyes flashed, but his voice was even as he said, "Yes, we are well acquainted." Giving Jennifer a pointed look he smiled at the Senator's wife and returned to his desk.

"See you on Friday night," Jennifer said to Mrs. Reno in a voice loud enough that Monty had to have heard. *Take that, you bully.*

As she walked out of the building, she called Sherrie and invited her to go to the gala. Thrilled that Sherrie accepted, they made the arrangements. As Jennifer walked to the bus stop, she began to think about the event, wondering what to wear. Slowing her steps, she realized that she had nothing in her closet that even came close to formalwear. Glancing at her watch, she realized that she had to get Ross off of the bus and had no time to worry about it now. *I'll find something tomorrow.*

THE NEXT TWO days passed in a blur. Between Gabe working night shift duty and Jennifer's involvement with the center, they barely saw each other. She had managed to buy a beautiful dress at a consignment shop near where she worked. She hated spending the money on it but knew that she needed something striking. She told Gabe about attending but he was not happy about it.

He just stared for a second as she quickly explained how it came about. *Fuck, just what I need. I'll be outside and she'll be in where Alicia is.*

"Honey, I'll be with the Senator's wife. This will give me the opportunity to talk about the budget with some of the others there. Maybe I can drum up more support for my project."

Okay, he thought. *She won't even be around the Hollywood types,* but he hated the idea nonetheless.

The night of the event, he kissed her hard and wet before leaving the house. She got dressed and stood looking at her appearance in the mirror. Her mind raced with thoughts of the evening to come. *He'll be working outside and won't even see me. I'll be with Sherrie and we won't even be close to the stars so I'll never have to see Alicia.* The feeling that this evening had disaster written all over it would not leave her, but there was no backing out now.

She left Ross with Henry and Cora and was now standing in front of her mirror putting on the last touches of makeup. The doorbell rang as Sherrie was there to pick her up. The two women exclaimed over each other's outfits.

Sherrie looked resplendent in her black evening dress, one shoulder exposed and the fitted bodice tapered to a flared skirt that extended to her ankles. Her sky-high heels gave her a Hollywood appearance and Jennifer knew that her friend could rival any of the women that would be there that night.

Sherrie was staring at Jennifer, thinking the same thing. Jennifer's blonde curls were pulled up around her face and then cascading down her back. Her beautiful face with large blue eyes gave her a fairy princess look and the blue dress fitted perfectly to her figure. It too had a princess look with a jeweled bodice and layers of silk flowing to her ankles. Silver pumps completed the look. "You look like Cinderella," Sherrie gushed. Seeing Jennifer's questioning face, Sherrie quickly continued, "You're gorgeous. Absolutely gorgeous."

The two ladies caught a cab and headed out into the night.

"ARE YOU FUCKIN' kidding me?" Gabe asked, staring at Tony.

"I wish I was," came the sharp retort.

Tony had just informed him that Jobe and BJ had become ill with the same flu knocking out so many. "Both tried to come, but can barely move. I've moved some of my less trained men to the outside, but I need you and Vinny on the inside. I'm sorry, man."

Gabe rubbed his hand across his neck trying to reduce the tension building. "Jesus fuck. I didn't even tell you that Jennifer's gonna be here. And now, just being anywhere in the vicinity of Alicia...fuck me."

"You're not on her detail. In fact, she has no detail.

You're just around the dignitaries and officials. On the perimeter of the room, that's all."

Gabe nodded. *There was nothing that could be done now.* As he walked away, Tony called out, "Sorry, man." Gabe nodded once again, saying, "It's okay. We don't call 'em, we just take the missions, right sir?"

He pulled out his cell phone and tried to call Jennifer. It went straight to voicemail. *Fuck me.* Leaving her a text, he headed into the building.

THE EVENING SO far had gone without a hitch. Jennifer and Sherrie sat near the back of the theater, viewing the movie. She had wished for the scenes with Alicia to be horrible and ugly but, of course, they were not. Overall, the movie was enjoyable but it had been a really long time since Jennifer had been to any movies and she had forgotten how realistic the love scenes were. Seeing Alicia almost nude on the big-screen did not make her feel better, even though she was with an actor. Thoughts of Alicia and Gabe together made her cringe. She had shared their story with Sherrie and could feel Sherrie's sympathetic gaze on her more than once.

Finally, the end came and she heaved a sigh of relief. Looking over at her friend, she said, "Now, I can go hang out with some of the officials and see if I can talk business!"

Sherrie laughed, saying, "Go get 'em, tiger."

The two women walked arm in arm out of the theater and up toward the ballroom. Jennifer's eyes lit up when she saw Tony and she nudged Sherri to point him out. "Looks good in a tux, doesn't he?"

Sherrie's gaze cut over and her breath caught in her throat. "Yeah, he does," she whispered to herself. She diverted her eyes so she never noticed that he did not take his off of her.

Entering the ballroom, she found the Senator and introduced Sherrie to his wife. They stood for a few minutes before the Senator asked Jennifer to accompany him to meet a few others who may be interested in helping her. After about thirty minutes of chatting with some officials she had not met previously, she could tell they wanted to move over to meet the celebrities. *I guess talking about the plight of elderly homeless just isn't the conversation they want to have.*

"And what would a beautiful, young woman such as yourself be doing with these stuffy politicians?" came a smooth voice from her side. Turning she saw a middle-aged man with a perfectly coiffed woman on his arm, smiling at her.

"I...was just trying to meet some of the Senator's friends," she said awkwardly, wondering who the man was.

"Well, if I know Senator Reno, he definitely has friends that are looking more to strike up a conversation with the Hollywood elite than a beautiful hometown woman. And that tells me how ridiculous some of our politicians are."

"I'm sorry. Have we met?" she asked, looking back and forth between the suave gentleman and his escort.

"Forgive me. I am Michael Gibbons and this is my charming wife, Carmella. I own Gibbons Real Estate and can tell you from experience that some of these politicians, who are among my closest friends, truly are stodgy old men."

She laughed as she shook his hand. "Well, thanks for the warning. I can't compete with Hollywood it seems. But there's always tomorrow. Good evening." Smiling graciously, she began to look for Sherrie again when she felt eyes on her. This time it felt right. She turned and saw him across the room. Gabe. Her Gabe. Tall, huge, built. Her giant. She smiled again when she remembered what she called him when they first met.

What's he doing on the inside? He must have come in looking for me. She took him in. All of him. From his handsome face with those green and gold eyes staring back at her to his square jaw. His tux fit him perfectly and she knew it was made just for him. Her heart began pounding and her legs began moving toward him of their own will.

He had looked over and saw her from across the room. *God, what a beauty.* Her dress showed off her figure and her blonde curls framed the porcelain face that filled his thoughts and dreams. Before he knew it, she was walking toward him and he smiled as he walked to meet her, never taking his eyes off of hers.

She approached and stood a respectable distance knowing he was working, when she wanted to throw herself into his arms.

"I want to kiss you, Mr. Malloy," she said softly, smiling up at him.

"Not as much as I want to kiss you, Ms. Lambert. And kissing you would just be the start," he added, just as softly.

"I won't be staying much longer, but I wanted to tell you that I love you."

He reached out and touched one of her blonde curls framing her face. "You're beautiful, you know." His face became serious, saying, "Absolutely, fuckin' beautiful."

Gracing him with one of the smiles that took his breath away, she turned around to leave.

"Gabe, darling, I've missed you," came the seductive voice from the side.

Jennifer turned to see Alicia Morgenstern approaching Gabe. The reporters were beginning to snap photographs of the beautiful actress and the handsome man standing with her.

"You don't seem glad to see me," she accused.

"I'm not. I'm with someone now and since we were never involved, you need to just keep moving on."

"Don't tell me that little blonde doll that was just here is who you're involved with," she bit out.

"Watch it, Alicia. The reporters just might get a glimpse of the real you if you're not careful," he whispered. With that, he turned and walked away hoping like hell that Jennifer had already left.

Jennifer ducked into the ladies' room before she and Sherrie left. After finishing her business, she was surprised to look up into the mirror and see Alicia Morgenstern walk up behind her.

"Well, if it's not the little garbage-crawler. I suppose this hick town will let anyone into these events."

Jennifer's eyes flashed but, determined to maintain her composure, she dried her hands and began to walk away.

"Where did you get that dress, by the way? It looks like a Walmart special." One of Alicia's cronies giggled behind her and the two of them moved to the door.

Jennifer stood at the mirror for a long time. She knew Alicia was a bitch extraordinaire, but her words still hurt. Sighing, she turned to leave, the weight of the events of the past few weeks pressing on her.

Sherrie noted her mood and quizzed her. "I'm just tired," she said. "Are you ready to go?"

"Yes, I saw Vinny earlier and told him that we were leaving."

As the women received their wraps, they stepped back into the ballroom to say goodbye to the Renos. Hearing a commotion, Jennifer turned to see Alicia draping herself over Gabe, pretending to stumble. She saw his strong arms come around the woman and steady her. As Alicia continued to appear weak, he kept his arms around her. The cameras began to flash and

Alicia preened on Gabe's arms for the cameras.

He's just doing his job, but the memories of the film's love scenes intertwined with her thoughts of the two of them together were more than she wanted to deal with. Turning to leave, she grabbed Sherrie and said, "Let's get out of here."

Thirty minutes later she climbed up the steps to her old apartment. Entering, she heard Cora holding a crying Ross. Hurrying over, she asked, "What's wrong?"

"He's been throwing up for the past half hour. I'm so glad you're here. He's been crying for you," she said.

"Oh Cora, I'm sorry." Taking Ross from Cora, she cuddled her brother, rubbing his back. "It's so late, go on to bed," she said to the elderly woman. "I've got this."

The older woman bent to kiss her head and went back to her apartment. *Well, there's no going back to Gabe's tonight.*

Just then, Ross began to throw up again. She managed to get him to the bathroom, but some of his vomit splattered the front of her dress. Holding his head over the toilet, she grabbed a wet cloth and held it to his face.

Finally getting him back in bed, she ran into her tiny room to change. She looked in the full-length mirror hanging on the back of her door. Her hair was in disarray and her dress was a mess. A tear began to escape as she realized that at that moment she truly did look like Cinderella...after the ball, when the magic disappeared. Sighing heavily, she wiped her stray tear as she pulled her dress off. Sliding on a t-shirt and shorts, she washed the evening's makeup off of her face. With her curls pulled into a messy bun, she decided that this was how she was comfortable. *I'm no starlet. No reason to even try.*

Hearing Ross again, she quickly went back to his bed and hurried him into the bathroom. Sitting on the cold tile floor, she knew it was going to be a long night.

CHAPTER 16

J ENNIFER PASSED OUT on the foot of Ross' bed in the middle of the night so that she could be near if he continued to be sick. After getting him to bed she had scrubbed the bathroom and the kitchen, trying to disinfect the area. Feeling something shake her, she tried to pry her eyes open.

"Jennybenny, wake up," her brother's voice said.

"What is it, honey?" she asked sitting up, realizing that the sun was coming through the blinds.

"I want a piece of toast. I got the bread out of the bag but haven't toasted it yet."

"Okay, baby," she said pulling herself up. Walking into the kitchen, she plugged in the toaster and opened the refrigerator as Ross piled up on the sofa and turned on the TV.

After a moment of still trying to rise from her exhausted, foggy mind, she heard a cry.

"Noooo!" Ross yelled at the TV. Looking around the corner to see what he was upset about, she saw the morning news show with scenes from last night. And there was Gabe. With Alicia. Hanging onto his arm, pressing her body next to his. Scene after scene. So

264

much so that the local news anchorwoman wondered who the mysterious escort was and if there was a romance for Alicia blooming in Richland.

"He's not supposed to do that," Ross accused, his eyes angry. "He supposed to only do that with you."

"Honey, it's all right," Jennifer lied, burying her hurt. "That's just his job."

"Well, I don't like it. And I don't like him," Ross announced.

Jennifer grabbed the remote and changed the channel. Same thing. Another channel. Same thing. *What the fuck? There's no news in Richland except for Alicia Morgenstern's boobs?*

Ross jumped up and ran to his room, slamming the door.

Jennifer stood in the middle of their tiny living room. She could hear Ross crying, her apartment still smelled like vomit, she needed to wash his sheets, the residents were still recuperating from their stomach virus which had undoubtedly been given to Ross and she was probably next on the rotation. The paperwork at her job was piling up at an alarming rate. Someone at her office seemed to be sabotaging her. Even the gala had not provided her with the contacts that Senator Ross had seemed to think would be there. She had been assaulted, had a city inspector threaten to shut the residence down, and now she was faced with Alicia Morgenstern's boobs on her boyfriend's arm on all the news stations.

Her phone beeped. **Gabe.** *Oh hell, no.* She answered and began talking before he had a chance to say anything. "No Gabe. Just no. Don't say a word. I don't have time for this right now. I'm up to my eyes in my own problems and don't want to hear it. You were right, though. I should have never gone. And I'm sick at heart that I did. But I don't have time for you or us now. So just NO." With that, she hit disconnect and turned her phone off, tossing it on the sofa.

She battled the urge to open the door, run down the stairs and continue running down the street until she could not run anymore. Heaving a huge sigh, she stooped to pick the remote off of the floor and tossed it to the sofa next to her phone as she walked to Ross' room.

GABE STARED AT the phone in his hand, lifting his eyes to his brother.

"Didn't go well?" Vinny asked.

"Didn't go at all," was the answer. "Jesus, she's pissed and I've never heard her this pissed."

Tony walked over as the debriefing finished. "Go home, get some sleep. All of you," he said to the gathering. Looking at Gabe, he said, "Last time. No more."

Gabe nodded, understanding what Tony meant. No more of Alicia and no more escort cases like this one. *I'll face dodging bullets any day rather than dealing with the Hollywood set.*

Vinny threw his arm around his brother, getting ready to drive him home when his phone rang. "Hey mom," Vinny answered. He listened for a moment before interrupting. "Mom, mom. No Gabe isn't engaged to Alicia Morgenstern. I don't care what the news programs say. No, he's very much still with Jennifer. In fact, he's over there right now with her. Yeah. Yeah. I'll tell him, mom. Love you."

Gabe stared at Vinny. "You've got to be shittin' me? Even mom believes that load of—"

"Look, man. It's all over the morning news. Alicia and her handsome, new, personal co-star."

Gabe looked down at his shoes, not knowing who he was madder at—Alicia or the reporters who made it their business to put a spin on everything. *And if mom's seen the news…oh fuck.* Heaving a sigh, he looked up at Vinny. "What the fuck do I do now?"

Vinny looked disconcerted, running his hand through his already messy hair. "I have no idea, bro. Maybe she needs some space. Or maybe she shouldn't have any space. Oh hell, I'm not the one to ask."

"We've been on missions that have lasted for days without sleeping. Tension. Life or death. Decisions that had to be made hard and fast or someone could die. And swear to God, brother. I can't remember being so tired as I am right now."

"What are you gonna do?"

Looking in Vinny's concerned face, he chuckled ruefully. "I'm heading to her place since it's obvious she didn't go back to our place last night." Turning, he walked out of the door, the sound of Vinny's laughter ringing in his ears.

JENNIFER HAD MANAGED to get Ross to stop crying long enough to strip his soiled sheets and put fresh ones on. She once again had a bit of vomit splattered on her t-shirt but had not had time to change. The knock on the door was welcome, sure that either Henry or Cora would be offering some assistance.

She flung open the door and stared at the chest of...Gabe. Lifting her tired eyes to his, she simply turned and walk away.

"Baby," he started.

She threw her hand up in the air and without looking at him said, "No, Gabe. I told you over the phone, just no." Right then, Ross called for her again and she ran to his bed, holding his head. He was only dry-heaving at this point, but it hurt nonetheless.

"Come on, baby. I told you to just sip the water. Just a sip at a time."

"My stomach hurts so bad," he cried. He looked up at Gabe standing in his doorway and shouted, "What are you doing here? I hate you. You went on a date last night with someone else."

"Ross, I told you that's not what happened," Jennifer said, fatigue about to take her over the edge. "Now lay back down and let me run the sheets to the washing machine downstairs."

Moving to the door she pushed against Gabe's chest, moving him backward so that she could slip out of the room. Walking back to the pile of soiled sheets, she bent to pick them up. She found her arms gently pushed away as Gabe moved in to gather them.

"Gabe, I've been up all night with Ross. I'm so tired I can't see straight and the world is falling down all around me. The last thing I want to do is talk to you right now."

"Okay. No talking. But just tell me where the laundry room is," he said quietly.

She stood, trying to hold back the tears, and said, "Those sheets have puke on them. Do you really want to hold those in your hands?"

"You think I haven't washed puke sheets before? Now tell me where to go."

"The room to the left of the kitchen."

He turned and headed down the stairs. Making his way into the laundry, he shoved the sheets in with some detergent and started the washing machine. As he turned around, he ran right into Cora.

Throwing his hands up in defense he said, "It's not what you think."

She stepped closer and looked him in the eyes. "I know. You were doing a job. In fact, I told Henry this morning that you looked miserable on the TV, as though that woman was the last person you wanted to be with."

Glancing behind him toward the washing machine, she said, "You're a good man, Gabe."

"Yeah, well tell it to that stubborn woman upstairs."

"Oh, she knows. Right now, she's got too much on her plate, but I've known Jennifer for two years now. She'll sort it all out and be right as rain soon enough. But don't doubt that she knows you're a good man. Come into the kitchen and I'll fix a tray for you to take upstairs." With that, she turned and headed for the kitchen.

Fifteen minutes later, he re-entered the apartment. The small windows were thrown open and the curtains were billowing as the cool spring air blew in replacing the stale odor. He saw Jennifer come out of Ross' room and she gently shut the door.

"How's he doing?"

"Better. He nibbled some crackers and then fell asleep. I'm going to let him sleep for as long as he will." She eyed the tray. "What's that?"

"Cora thought you'd like something to eat. I was hoping you'd eat and then lay down to sleep yourself."

She walked over and lifted the cover, the scent of biscuits with butter and jam along with hot tea smelled divine. "I need to be awake in case Ross needs me."

"I've got it covered, baby."

Taking a huge bite of the biscuit with the melted butter dribbling down her chin, she said, "Oh, I don't think so. You're not exactly his favorite person right now."

Fighting the desire to lick the butter off of her face, he just kissed the top of her head instead, saying, "I'm on it. Not going to let it fester and get worse. When he's awake, we'll talk. Man to man." Seeing her raised eyebrow, he continued, "Baby, he's not too young to understand that things are not always what they seem."

She just nodded as she sipped her tea and finished her biscuit. He watched as her eyes began to droop. Taking her hand, he pulled her out of her chair and into her tiny bedroom. He lifted her t-shirt over her head and tossed it in the laundry basket. Turning to her dresser, he pulled out a clean one and slid it over her body. She crawled silently into the bed and he covered her. She fell asleep immediately. He watched her for a few minutes, her face resting in slumber. Even the dark circles under her eyes could not mar her beauty. Kissing her forehead, he went back to the living room and made himself as comfortable as possible on the sofa. Then sleep overtook him as well.

HOURS LATER SHE woke, hearing low voices in the background. She pulled herself out of the bed and glanced at the mirror before leaving the security of her bedroom. *Oh Jesus. What a wreck.* Too tired to care, she quietly opened her door. Not intending to snoop, she could not help but stop in her tracks and listen to the voices.

"But you said you love sis. And I saw you on TV. You were with some other woman and that hurt my sister."

"I know, buddy, and I'm so sorry. But when you love someone, you need to give them a chance to explain if something doesn't seem right. A chance to make things right if they can. And when you find out everything, then you can decide if you want to still be their friend. Can you do that for me?"

"Yeah," came the child's voice.

"One of the things I have to do in my job is sometimes be around people to make sure they are safe. Last night, there was a big party and Mr. Tony's men were there to make sure all the people were safe and no one was going to come in and hurt them."

"Like bad guys?"

"Yeah, like bad guys."

"What about that lady? She looked like your girlfriend."

Jennifer could hear a deep sigh and she leaned a little farther out of the room. "Buddy, there are people in this world who are not very nice. They like to make trouble for other people and they don't care who gets hurt."

"I know some kids like that. They're just mean and

I sometimes get mad when they're being mean to another kid."

"Good for you, buddy. You should always take up for those who can't take up for themselves."

"So was that lady not very nice? I didn't like the way she looked."

"No, she's not very nice. She said some mean things and was acting mean."

"So why didn't you stick up for my sister?"

"Wow, you're asking some really tough questions. And I won't always have the right answers. But Ross, I love your sister. I tried to just do my job last night, which was to make sure that the people we were hired to protect were safe, but I didn't do a good job of protecting your sister. And for that, you have no idea how sorry I am."

"I bet if you tell her that you're sorry, she won't be mad anymore."

"Well, that lady wanted to put on a show for everyone around and if I'd been mean to her then a lot of people wouldn't have understood that. But that's not an excuse. I hurt your sister. I just hope she'll hear me out the way you have."

Not willing to stay in the room eavesdropping anymore, she stepped quietly into the tiny hall. She could see Gabe sitting on the sofa, facing her way. His hand was on Ross' neck, holding him as they talked. Man to man.

A tear slid from her eye, down her cheek. Sucking

in her lips, she felt her breath catch in her throat.

Gabe's gaze looked over Ross' head and met hers. "So buddy, do you think your sister will forgive me for not protecting her last night?"

Ross, oblivious to Jennifer's presence, said, "She'll forgive you. You just tell her like you told me and she'll be okay. She loves you, you know."

Looking back down at Ross, he asked, "So are we cool again?"

In typical little boy fashion, Ross threw himself at Gabe and gave him a hug. This time Gabe was surprised. Feeling Ross' arms tighten around his neck, he felt the profound emotion of helping a child. A child that he loved. His gaze went back to Jennifer as Ross continued to hug. Slowly, as he disengaged from Ross, he stood up.

With a sob, she ran the few steps into the room and launched herself into his arms. Holding on as tightly as Ross had been, she wrapped her legs around Gabe's waist. "I love you, honey," she cried.

Gabe's heart melted as he let out the breath he hadn't realized he was holding. "I love you too, babe." He felt something against his thigh and knew that Ross was holding on as well. Gently lowering himself to the sofa again, he curled one arm around Ross as he held Jennifer close. Protected. Safe. Loved. Together.

HOURS LATER, BACK in Gabe's apartment when Ross had gone to bed, Gabe and Jennifer settled down on his sofa. Pulling her into his arms, he said, "Okay baby. You need to unload everything on me."

"Unload what?" she asked in confusion.

"All the shit that's swirling around in your head and in your life. Everything that's going on that needs to be sorted out."

Sucking in a deep breath, she said, "Oh honey, there's just so much going on. But I'll deal with it all."

"Not the right answer, sweetheart."

She laughed, repeating, "Not the right answer?"

"I fucked up big last night. I didn't take care of you and you've no idea how much that sucks for a man like me. You do so much for everyone and part of my job of loving you is to make your life easier."

She opened her mouth to protest, but he cut her off. "Nope, not hearing excuses. Just want to hear problems."

It had been a really long time since she'd had someone to unload her problems to. *Maybe, must maybe...it'll help.*

"Sometimes I feel like a juggler who has too many balls in the air. And if I'm not careful, then they're all going to come crashing down." She shook her head, sighing. "Gabe, I teach people how to problem solve and yet, I can't seem to break down my problems right now into manageable pieces."

"So let me help. Let's start with work," Gabe encouraged.

"I went to that stupid event last night because the Senator and his wife invited me, but the enticement was that I would meet some others to support the cause of elder housing. Nope. The ones I met just wanted to see the *stars*. And every time I try to go see him, his assistant Monty seems to make it his business to try to keep me from progressing."

At this, Gabe's senses began to go on alert, but he kept quiet since it seemed as though she was on a roll.

"And it's not as though my co-workers, who I might add are actually friends, are helping. Roy didn't have my phone number to call me when something was important and Sybil sent the wrong papers with me. On top of that, my boss Chip may be working against me as well. I found some phone doodles in his office that looked like he was talking to someone about the center.

"Then there was the man from the City inspectors who threatened to shut us down but when I called my inspector from the state, he didn't know who this man was. Throw in the stomach virus that has gone through the city, hitting the residents and now Ross, and top it all off with Alicia Morgenstern's boobs publicly stuck to my boyfriend...what else can go wrong?" she ended, throwing up her arms.

Sucking in a deep breath through his nose before letting it out, Gabe processed everything she had said. *Work the problem. Treat it like a mission.* Lifting her chin so that she was looking directly into his eyes, he started, "There is no more Alicia. She's done. Contract's over. No more. And Tony's not putting me on escort detail again...I didn't even have to tell him, although I did. No more nights like last night.

"The flu sucks but so far the residents are recovering and Ross will too. He's young and will bounce back quickly. We need to keep him hydrated and comfortable, but he'll get better. Right now, I'm more concerned about your work. This Monty character, your co-workers, and why the fuck didn't you tell me about this man who came there?"

"Because in the past week, we've both been so busy we've barely seen each other," she retorted.

Calming his voice, Gabe said, "Okay, give me his name and I'll do some checking." He looked at her tired eyes and said, "Enough tonight. You need to sleep and I want to be here to make sure you do. And we'll keep our door open and Ross' open in case he gets up in the night."

She looked at his face, seeing the fatigue around his eyes as well. *He's exhausted and yet trying to sort out my mess and help take care of Ross.* Blessing him with a small smile, she leaned in and kissed him, breathing him in and feeling all of the fight leave her body. "Okay."

Wrapping his arms around her as they both lay in bed, his mind quickly ticked off the things that needed to be done the next day. Number one...find the prick that came into the building and threatened her.

GABE WATCHED THE man leaving the municipal building, walking toward his car. Stepping between the man and the car, he called out, "Mr. Burton?"

The man's head snapped up, staring at the giant in front of him. "Who…who wants to know?"

"Me," came the succinct response.

"I've been doing what I was told. Ain't my fault nothin's happened so far," Mr. Burton babbled, sweat breaking out on his face.

Gabe eyed him carefully, saying nothing.

"That's what you're here for, ain't it?" he said, nervously looking around.

"You want to tell me why nothing's happened?" Gabe asked, deciding to play along and let Mr. Burton think he was someone else.

"I don't know. I just did what I was told and that little lady called in someone from the state, so I got out of there. But I did what I was asked."

"Now you want to tell me who asked you to do that?"

Mr. Burton wiped his brow as the sweat began to slide down his face. "You mean…you ain't…?"

Gabe took a step forward, growling, "Answer the fuckin' question."

"I…I…" he opened and closed his mouth like a fish out of water.

Gabe leaned in closer, clenching his hands into

fists.

"I just get a call and make a visit to wherever I'm told to go. And sometimes I write them up for some kind of violation."

"Who told you to go to the Elder Center on 21st Street?"

Mr. Burton licked his lips nervously. "I don't know." Seeing Gabe step closer, he shouted out, "I swear, I don't know. I just get a call and then afterward I get a payment in an envelope under my car seat."

"I find out you're lying to me, it'll be worse than whoever the hell is getting you to do their dirty work. And I'm telling you right now, you ditch that false report on the Elder Center or I'll use this and you'll lose your job and your pension." With that, Gabe pulled out the miniature recording device in his pocket showing the recording of their conversation.

Mr. Burton's eyes bugged out of his head once more as he stammered, "Oh, I promise. No more. I won't bother 'em no more."

Gabe shook his head in disgust and walked away. Driving back to the office he called Tony. "Got a situation. Need a meeting when we get back. Yeah. Thanks."

GABE FOUND THE conference room already filled when he walked in. Tony, Jobe, Vinny, BJ, Lily, and several others. Looking around the room in question, the answer came simply from Tony.

"You need us, we're here."

Grateful, he nodded before sitting down. "Had a long talk with Jennifer last night and there's been a lot of shit happening that seemed all unrelated until I lay in bed and started questioning it. Then did a little recon today and now…"

Vinny leaned forward, concern in his eyes. "Let's hear it, man."

Gabe began to explain about Jennifer's grant, the five-year lease that now the building's owner seemed to be nervous about, the problems with the Senator's assistant, and then the bogus inspection from a city inspector on the take.

BJ and Lily were on their laptops quickly pulling up information as Gabe was reporting. Lily's soft voice spoke up. "Martin Burton. Health inspector with the city for the past twelve years. Good record, good job performance." A few more clicks on her keyboard. "Hmm, looks like he spends more than he earns."

BJ chimed in, "About three years ago, it seems that his bank account had deposits at various intervals of significant amounts of cash. Could be when he started doing bogus inspections on the side. They correspond with some buildings that were condemned, then sold."

Lily added, "Montgomery Lytton looks fine, but I'm sure he would have had a background check and security clearance to work for the Senator." Looking up at Gabe, she said, "Maybe he's just very protective of the Senator's time."

Before Gabe could answer, BJ spoke up. "If you keep digging though, this Mr. Lytton almost looks too squeaky clean. Nobody's that clean."

Tony interjected, "You think someone cleaned up his background?"

BJ shrugged. "Don't know, but I'll keep digging."

Gabe looked at concerned faces of his co-workers sitting at the table. Most of them had sat like this, working out the details of a military mission. The addition of BJ and Lily just made the group more well-rounded. Brothers-in-arms then…and now. "I really appreciate it. I mean I've got nothing to go on more than her concerns and my gut. But, I've got a bad feeling since her attack was not random. The guy Matt and Shane got clammed up real tight. Only way someone like that doesn't cop a plea is if they know what will happen if they talk."

"You want me to pull Matt and Shane into this?" Tony asked.

"Not yet. Let's see if we can find out anything else first," Gabe answered.

CHAPTER 17

G ETTING HOME THAT night, Gabe felt better than he had in several days. He had Alvarez Security working on Jennifer's problems, he had talked to his mom, convincing her that everything was fine with his relationship with Jennifer, and hopefully he could take some of the stress off of her.

Entering his apartment, he noticed it was quiet. The kitchen light was off and there was no noise coming from the bedrooms.

He gently opened Ross' door to check on him and saw that he was fast asleep. Closing the door, he turned to his bedroom. Turning the knob, he wondered if Jennifer would be asleep also. The lights were off except for one lamp by the bed. His eyes had no difficulty finding what was in the middle of the bed. Jennifer was lying on the bed, her blonde curls spread over his pillows. Her blue eyes sparkled from her pixie face and her smile pierced him. And she was naked. *Fuckin' perfection.*

He stood there for a second, not believing the vision in front of him until she lifted her arms in the air, beckoning him to come to her. *She's not giving me shit about what I've gotta do in my job. She's just giving me her. All of her.* He stripped in record time and joined her on the bed. She reached down to grasp him, but he stilled her hand. "No baby, tonight it's about you."

And he continued to show her exactly what he felt about her. Worshiping her body, loving her soul. Giving everything he had to give without once thinking of taking for himself.

Kneeling between her knees, he spread her legs apart and dove in for a taste. He slowly licked her wet folds before moving his tongue expertly around her clit and sucking it into his mouth.

She began lifting her hips, trying to press her pussy closer to him, but he put his hand on her abdomen.

"Lie still, baby." He heard her mewl in protest, but he just grinned.

Plunging his tongue deeper, he reached up with his hand and fondled her breast, tweaking the nipple as she tried to lie still. The pressure built until she thought she would explode.

Gabe watched her in the throes of ecstasy as he kept his head between her legs. She cried out his name as she burst into a million pieces, her body shaking with the force of the orgasm. Panting as though she had finished a race, she lay on the bed, boneless. She felt the bed shift as he came up over her body, keeping his weight off of her as his muscular arms flexed with the strain.

Suddenly needing his cock deep inside of her, she spread her legs wide, welcoming him into her body.

Her slick pussy grabbed at him as she became accustomed to his girth.

He pounded into her, watching her breasts bounce with each thrust. She threw her hands above her head and grabbed the headboard. Leaning down to grasp a nipple in his mouth, he sucked deeply then used his teeth to gently bite the swollen tip. That was all it took for her to go over the edge once more.

She felt her inner muscles grab at him as he continued to pound deep inside. Suddenly he pulled out and her eyes flew open as she wondered why he stopped.

Flipping her over, he ordered, "On your knees, baby." She immediately rose up on all fours and he entered her from behind. Gabe slammed into her wet pussy, the force moving her forward. He grabbed her hips, holding her tightly, hoping he was not leaving bruises on her perfect skin. Feeling his balls tighten, he knew his release was imminent so he reached around and tweaked her clit once again. With just the right pressure, he brought her to orgasm again just as he felt his own rip from his body. He pulsated inside until every drop was gone, knowing without a doubt that she was the only woman for him.

Both breathing in great gulps of air, they lay entwined for several minutes as their heartbeats slowed in unison.

As Jennifer lay sated, she knew that she'd made the right decision. As his arms surrounded her once more, holding her tightly to his chest, she knew she had nothing to worry about. He gave her everything. More than she could ever want or need.

Sleep claimed her quickly as they lay tangled together. Used to sleeping naked, he now slept with his boxers on just as Jennifer always put on one of his t-shirts, since Ross could come into the bedroom at any time. Gabe lay there for a few minutes, tucking her tiny body into his massive one. Smiling, he thought of how his life had changed so much in the past few months. His huge, masculine apartment now had some books and video games scattered in the living room, peanut butter in his kitchen cabinets, hair care products and makeup in his bathroom, and a wonderful little boy and a beautiful, caring woman graced his life. *Jesus, I am one lucky fuck.* Pulling her in tighter, he soon joined her in slumber.

Several hours later his cell rang. Grabbing it quickly, he answered with a "Yeah, talk."

Jennifer raised up on her elbows, pushing the mass of curls from her face. She watched as his face grew hard while he just listened, saying nothing.

"Gotcha. I'll tell Tony. We've got them covered. Yeah. Both of them." With that, he disconnected and tossed his phone on the nightstand. Sitting up, he sucked in a huge breath, rubbing his hand over his face. Feeling a small hand on his arm, he looked over at the woman staring up at him, concern in her eyes.

"What's wrong?" she whispered as though trying to keep the news from being bad if she were very quiet.

"The man picked up for assaulting you was let out on bail. Not surprising. But his body was just found down at the river. He'd been shot first."

Her lips made an 'O', but no sound came out. After a few seconds, she whispered again. "Maybe he was just…"

"Babe, his hands were tied behind his back. Execution style."

This time when her mouth formed an 'O', it was accompanied by wide eyes, searching his for a reason.

He twisted his body around so that he was facing her and pulled her into his lap. Taking his large hands, he tried to cradle her with one on her back and the other on her face. "We know that you were not a random assault. They were there for you. The false call, the way the fucker shut up in questioning, and now an execution."

She head-planted into his chest, a sick feeling rising from her stomach into her throat. He slid his hand from her cheek to the back of her head, holding her against his heartbeat.

"Baby, I'm on this. We're on this. We've got you covered. You and Ross."

At that, her head jerked up, eyes wide again, this time in panic. "Ross? Oh my God, Gabe. Ross? He's in danger?"

"Baby, listen to me."

But she was too far gone. Trying to scramble from the bed, she found herself tackled by a large, masculine body trapping her underneath him.

"You have to let me go. I've got to get Ross away from here. I've got to…oh God…I've got to…"

"Baby, calm down. Look at me. Jennifer, look at me," he gently ordered.

Her wild eyes locked onto his. Searching. Hoping.

"Baby, you're not going anywhere and you're not taking Ross anywhere. You are safe in this building. It's secure and I can protect you here."

"But we can't stay here forever."

"Ross can miss a couple of days of school and—"

"Don't you dare suggest I miss more work," she argued.

Sucking in a deep breath to calm himself, he rolled off of her taking her with him. Sitting up against the headboard, he pulled her across his lap so she was straddling him. "Gonna put a man on you and Ross until this mess is cleared up."

"A man?"

"Yeah, either me or someone from Tony's will be with you and Ross. Take him back and forth to school, and someone to take you as well. No more public transportation for either of you."

She nodded slowly, then looked back into his face. "How can Tony do that? Afford that, I mean?"

"Baby, you're mine. Ross is mine. I take care of what's mine. And my brothers? We take care of each other. We've got this."

Sliding down into the bed, he gently pulled her

down with him. Let's sleep for now. In the morning, I'll talk to Vinny and Tony and we'll set up what we need to do."

She acquiesced, but sleep did not return. For either of them.

THE NEXT AFTERNOON found Jennifer and Ross accompanying Gabe into Alvarez Security. After settling Ross in the safe room and answering his non-stop questions about everything he was seeing, Jennifer and Gabe went into one of the large conference rooms. Shane and Matt had joined the assembly. Lily hugged her and then they all sat down. Gabe's arm was thrown casually across the back of her chair, but everyone knew she fell under his, and their, protection.

All eyes turned toward her, but she just stared dumbly at them. "I know...I know you all want me to have some kind of answer or reason for this, but I—"

"No Jennifer," Tony spoke up. "We just want to pull together as much intel as we can so we know who we're fighting."

Shane spoke first, saying, "The man you identified as assaulting you clammed up in the station. Wouldn't say anything and we knew he'd get out on bail. He had no priors and no record. A fisherman out late last night saw him in the water. When he was fished out, he had been shot in the head at close range, with his hands tied behind his back. Definitely an execution."

Matt took over, "We've identified him and while there is little on him, his mother did say that her son had been dressing nicely and telling her that he had a good job. She assumed he was in business, but there's no record or taxes. His face was partially blown off—"

At this Jennifer gasped and Gabe glared at him.

"Sorry, honey. We took his driver's license photo to a couple of people who have been complaining of extortion and have a positive identification that he and a partner have shown up at business or buildings."

"Extortion? I don't really know what that means, other than like in the Godfather movie," Jennifer said honestly.

Shane nodded, "It's the same thing. Someone wants something and doesn't want to have to pay for it. Or they want someone to pay them for something they shouldn't have to pay for. So they send in enforcers." Seeing her forehead crinkle in confusion, he continued, "Thugs. Someone to threaten if they don't get their way."

"Okaaay," she said slowly, nodding in understanding. "But I still don't see how that affects me."

"Some of the old buildings in your area have been sold for next to nothing and then flipped into nice buildings that are then sold or rented for a huge profit. You've already said that someone's been interested in the building you're in."

"Yes, but I don't own it. A Mr. Stuart Mason owns

the building. I've talked on the phone with him a few times and he assures me that he has no intention of selling."

"Maybe if your program is scared out of the building, Mr. Mason will have to sell because he'll need some money if no rent or grant money is coming in."

Lily piped up then, saying, "I've continued to try to run down the interested parties in her building. Mr. Michael Gibbons of Gibbons's Realty has looked into several buildings in the area for clients. His business itself appears completely legitimate. He handles real estate for many clients, generally the high-end ones who have millions to spend on big houses or condos. He also handles the real estate needs for a lot of the businesses in the city."

"I met him at the event the other evening. He was there with his wife. They seemed friendly with the Senator and his wife as well."

"Just because he's legit doesn't make his business partners or associates legit," Tony noted.

"Exactly," Matt agreed. Turning to Lily, he said, "Can you keep digging? On his clients, associates, anything to tie into the extortion."

"On it," Lily said with a smile and a wink.

Gabe's hand slid from the back of Jennifer's chair to her shoulder, massaging the tightness. She turned to look into his confident face. "Told you babe. We've got this," he said.

"Ross—" she started.

Tony interrupted, "We've got him covered too. Vinny or Gabe will drop him off at school and then we'll make sure someone picks him up at school every day. We just need you to notify the school that someone with an Alvarez Security identification will be there to pick him up."

She nodded, "Okay. I can do that. I…just don't know what to tell him."

The table was silent for a moment as they group pondered. None of them were parents, but Jobe spoke up. "Honesty's always best. Kids know when things aren't good or aren't right. Don't scare him but don't keep him in the dark."

She looked over at Jobe's handsome face, seeing wisdom beyond his years. "I think you're right." Turing to Gabe, she said, "Will you be with me when I tell him?"

His eyes warmed as he lost himself momentarily in the depths of her crystal blue ones. "Yeah baby. There's nowhere else I'd rather be, than right by your side."

Vinny smiled at his brother's good fortune in finding such a woman as Jennifer, then sobered. "Besides a security detail for the two of them and Lily and BJ digging into Michael Gibbons' clients, what else?"

Shane said, "We're investigating the extortion end of things. If you can look into anything involving Jennifer's work or the center that'd be good."

Tony added, "Gonna do some digging into this Monty character."

At that Jennifer looked up and said, "Oh I have someone who's helping me with that."

The group looked at her and she noticed Tony's eyes cut sharply to her. "I have a friend that's at the capitol building a lot. The lawyer she works for has several clients who work there and Monty's used to her. She's going to do some digging for me."

"Sherrie? Like hell she is," Tony growled, losing his normal cool.

The eyes that had been trained on Jennifer now turned to look at Tony. Recovering his composure, he explained, "Call her off. She's not trained."

Smiling, Jennifer said, "Well, I think Monty may like her so it makes it easy for her to get some information."

Tony scowled but said nothing. That seemed to signal the end of the meeting. As they stood, each moving to their own destination, Tony made his way over to Jennifer. Looking uncharacteristically awkward, he said, "You really do need to tell her to back off and let the professionals handle things."

"I'll tell her, Tony. I don't want anyone in harm's way on my account."

He nodded and walked away. Jennifer turned her face up to Gabe's and said, "You know, if he would just admit that he likes her and would do something about it..."

"The man's got his own demons, baby. Can't rush it."

They headed out of the room and down the hall to the safe room to collect Ross. Vinny was walking out of the room with Ross at his side.

"Vinny says we can go to his parents' place again and go out on one of the fishing boats," Ross yelled, jumping up and down.

Jennifer's eyes snapped and Gabe glared at his brother. Vinny threw his hands up in defense.

"Whoa, little buddy. I said we needed to ask your sister and Gabe if we could do that."

"She'll say yes, won't you sis? Especially if Gabe asks her. Gabe will you ask her? Please?" Ross begged.

Vinny had the good sense to look embarrassed. "Sorry guys, I should have asked you two first."

Gabe was suddenly filled with pride at the realization that his brother had included him in who needed to be asked when it came to Ross and Jennifer had not protested. He looked down at her, seeing her smile as well.

She turned her face to Gabe and said, "What do you think, honey?"

"I think it's a good idea. We could leave tonight and spend the night with my parents. They've got friends with fishing boats that would take us out for a little while tomorrow."

"Yay," cheered Ross, jumping up to high-five Vinny. Vinny bent down to remind him who he needed to thank. Ross turned and ran to Jennifer, throwing his arms around her waist and hugging with all of his strength. Letting go of her, he turned to Gabe and threw his arms around him as well. Gabe bent to picked him up as Ross' arms went around his neck.

"Thank you, Gabe. I love you, you know," he said, with his face buried in Gabe's neck.

Gabe's gaze caught his brother's as they looked at each other over Ross' tow head. His heart pounded with completion and as they turned he saw his group of brothers-in-arms standing behind him. Each with an expression of pride as well.

THE NEXT DAY, Jennifer nervously stepped onto the boat, *The Sea Glass*. Holding tightly to Ross' hand, she would not let go even as he squirmed. Gabe shared a look with his brother and parents. Patrick stepped up and said, "Here Jennifer, let me take Ross' hand. I'll show him the front of the boat where the men pull the nets in."

The panic on her face was vivid, so Maeve moved in to say, "That's a wonderful idea. Vinny and Gabe will be with him and then we can sit back here and chat a bit."

Leaning over, Gabe kissed her forehead whispering, "I've got him, baby."

She released Ross' hand slowly, bending to make sure his life jacket was secure. Gabe squeezed her hand in reassurance. Breathing deeply, she dropped her hands and watched as Ross grabbed Gabe's hand and the men moved to the front of the boat.

Maeve saw the tears in Jennifer's eyes and throwing her arm around her shoulders, she moved them over to a cushioned bench near the back. The warmth of the spring sun was beaming down on them as the light reflected off of the water. Jennifer relaxed as she became accustomed to the movement of the boat.

Glancing at Maeve, she said, "I know I seem so overprotective. I'm not usually like this. I realized that ever since he's been with me, we're usually at the center and I have lots of people looking out for him. He's allowed freedom, but I always knew he was with someone."

Letting out a shaky breath, she admitted, "Ever since our lives became so complicated, I'm afraid all the time."

"How was Ross after your talk last night?" Maeve asked, referring to the decision by Jennifer and Gabe to talk to Ross about the need for protection. They had done it in the comfort of Patrick and Maeve's home with all the adults around, providing a sanctuary.

"He was concerned about bad men and definitely wanted his night light on. But, strangely enough, he wasn't as afraid as I had thought. Instead, when I kissed him goodnight, he told me he'd protect me." A tear slid down Jennifer's cheek at the memory and she quickly wiped it away saying, "You must think me a mess."

"Oh my dear, I think you're doing a fabulous job in

the middle of what sounds like a mess!" Maeve exclaimed. Leaning forward, she said, "You know, my Patrick and I couldn't stop talking about you after you left the last time." Seeing Jennifer's face, she quickly explained. "We're so proud of our boys. When they were active duty, I used to lay awake wondering if that knock on the door would come. That's just being a mama, but I couldn't help it. But we were so proud. When they left the military, I felt that they were somehow a little lost."

Maeve looked out over the water for a moment, her mind seemed to wander and Jennifer waited until she was ready to speak. "Both of them had things that they never talked about – even with each other. As a mother, that just broke my heart. My boys had volunteered for missions that I knew were dangerous, but they served their country. And to think that whatever they had endured had changed them...well, it hurt. We're lucky though. They never took to drink or drugs to fill whatever emptiness might be inside. Tony deciding to open his agency was a miracle also...those men are like brothers."

"They are good friends to me as well," Jennifer said smiling. "I've never really had that before."

Maeve patted her hand saying, "You couldn't ask for better." Looking into Jennifer's face, she said, "I know my boys weren't saints when it came to women and their father and I so wanted them to find someone they could love and would love them the way they deserved."

"I do love him, you know," Jennifer said.

"Oh darling girl, that's why Patrick and I couldn't stop talking about you after we met you. We think you and Gabriel are perfect together. Now if we can just find someone for Vincent," she laughed.

By then, the men were returning from the front of the boat and joined the ladies. Ross could not talk fast enough to tell Jennifer all that he had seen and learned about fishing.

"Look what I got! The captain gave it to me."

Ross opened his hand showing a smooth piece of green glass. "It's sea glass."

Jennifer smiled as she bent to examine it, noticing her brother's excitement. "It's lovely."

"He said that glass gets thrown into the water and over time the sharp edges become smooth from the rough water and sand. Then it looks like this."

She ruffled his blond hair and smiled at the captain as she stood. The older man walked over and offered her a piece of sea glass as well. His face, tanned and lined from the wind and sun over the years, could not hold back the sparkle of his grey eyes. "I also told the little lad that people, just like the glass, can become polished and beautiful from the rough effects of life." Leaning down closer to her, he whispered, "Your Ross is fine and gonna grow up into a good man. All the things in life that threaten to beat him down will just end up polishing him into the kind of man you want him to be." With that, he pressed the small, smooth glass into her palm. With a nod, he walked back to the bridge of the ship.

Jennifer stood for a moment, tears filling her eyes, barely noticing when Gabe stepped over to lead her back to the seats.

Maeve moved over to curl into Patrick's embrace and Jennifer did the same with Gabe. The party headed toward the harbor and Jennifer discovered that she was no longer afraid of the water. Wrapped in Gabe's strong arms with Ross right at their side, she felt a completeness she had never known. *Nothing can touch me as long as we are together. No harm will come to us now.* Closing her eyes, she lifted her face to the sun, letting its warmth soak into her soul.

Gabe looked down at the princess pressed into him and the familiar pang hit his heart once again. The sunlight caught the blonde curls, sending them shimmering down her back. *How can this tiny woman have come to love me?* His gaze moved to the tow-headed boy leaning into his other side. *Jesus, I'm a lucky fuck.* Vowing to keep them safe, he joined them in closing his eyes and letting the warm sun fill him with peace.

MICHAEL AND SANTO met in his opulent office as the evening sun was setting over the city. Santo noticed that while Michael was agitated, he gave the appearance of calm, offering him a whiskey poured from his cut-glass decanter into crystal tumblers.

Settling back behind his desk, they drank in silence for a few minutes. Finally Michael began to speak, as Santo stayed respectfully quiet.

"My great-grandfather came to this country from Italy and started a little grocery store in New York in the early 1900's. His wife complained of the cold winters and so he left his business and settled in Virginia. He had nothing but the money saved from selling his little store. He was smart though. Started another little store and became successful. He found that many people during the depression had spent their money and needed credit from his store, which he gave willingly. But...found that some people needed a little persuasion to pay their bills when it was time.

"My grandfather, as a young man, proved himself worthy of his father by making sure that people were...encouraged to pay what they owed. My grandfather took over the business when he became older. By then, there were several groceries and they expanded. Knowing that war was coming, they bought up old warehouses on the river's edge that had emptied when times were tough. And having the foresight to know that they would be useful to the government during wartimes...well, let's just say that by the time America joined the Great War, my grandfather's business acquired top dollar for the old warehouses. He changed his name from Gambelini to Gibbons."

Santo continued to sip his whiskey and listen attentively.

"Being German or Italian during the war was not popular and my grandfather was a master manipulator. He buried the name change so that there was little to lead back to the original name. There were a few owners that wanted to hold out for themselves, but by then my grandfather was rather relentless in his business dealings. What he wanted he got. If someone held out...well, the men who worked for my grandfather would go in and when they were finished...there was no impediment to the buyout. The interesting thing was that my grandfather was able to hide all of this underneath his legitimate businesses. He was brilliant.

"My father had been a pacifist during the Vietnam war. He didn't want to go and from what I understood from my grandfather, my father had been a great disappointment. Not wanting to go into the family business or the war, he fled to Canada, where I was born."

At this, Santo looked at his boss in surprise. He had heard the stories from his father and grandfather, but never expected Michael to share his father's disgrace. Santo recognized the sign of extreme respect that Michael was showing to him by speaking with such candor.

"My parents were killed when I was very young and

I was shipped here to be raised by my grandparents." Nodding as he sipped, he said, "I was loved. Educated. And introduced to the family business as a young man. My grandfather wanted to make sure I did not turn out like my father. He taught me how to run a legitimate business while managing to take care of other businesses on the side. And I embraced all of that. Worked hard and built the business while expanding into legitimate real estate dealings."

Santo finished his whiskey and moved his finger around the rim, pondering the story unfolding in front of him.

"Could I walk away from the building that the old folks are in? Of course I could. But everything in me has never allowed myself to back down." Michael turned his head and stared into Santo's eyes. His voice took on a cold tenor. "I will not allow a tiny piece of pussy to be the catalyst for stopping me in what I want. Ms. Lambert has managed to thwart me at every turn and it stops now."

Santo hid his smile...he'd been wanting to take care of the troublesome woman for a long time.

"I want you to start with the old man. Get rid of him and her little old folks' empire will begin to topple."

Santo gave in to his grin at that time. "You got it boss." With that, he stood, set his empty tumbler back on the credenza and walked out.

Michael sat and continued to stare out onto the

Richland night skyline. His private door opened and a beautiful woman walked in, making her way over to him. He looked up at his new mistress. Quiet. Compliant. Perfect.

CHAPTER 18

MONDAY MORNING AFTER dropping Ross off at school and being at work for several hours, Jennifer called Gabe's cell to ask him who would be available to take her to visit Stuart Mason's home. "I want to talk to him again. I told him that I would keep in touch, but with so much going on, I really haven't. If the others are right, he may be afraid that if we move out of the building he will have to sell."

Gabe told her that Jobe had just finished a job in the downtown area and could pick her up. "Wait on the inside, babe, until you see him drive up."

She agreed and grabbed her bag.

"Heading out?" Sybil asked.

"Um, yeah. Thought I'd meet Gabe for lunch," she lied. *I hate this. I have no idea who to trust anymore.*

Jobe picked her up and drove in the direction of older neighborhoods in the city. Pulling up to a modest home in a tree-lined neighborhood they noticed that the mail was still in his box by the front door as well as several papers.

"I wonder if he went on a trip?" Jennifer asked out loud, moving out of the SUV.

The hair on the back of Jobe's neck stood up and he immediately moved out of the vehicle and stepped in front of her. "Jennifer, stay back. Let me go up to the door."

Eyes wide, she peered up at him. "What's wrong?"

"Maybe nothing, but I'm not willing to take a chance," he responded. With that, he moved to the porch that spanned the front of the house. Looking into a window, he immediately ran to the door pulling out his cell phone and began speaking.

Jennifer watched in concern and then when Jobe pulled out his gun and ran to the back of the house, she could not help herself…she moved forward and up the steps. Glancing at the front door to see what Jobe had seen, she saw splintered wood around the deadbolt. Moving cautiously to the front window that Jobe had looked into, she saw Mr. Mason on the floor. His body lying awkwardly. A pool of dark liquid under him. The front of his shirt red. And his eyes. Staring. Unseeing. Dead.

A scream pierced the quiet neighborhood and Jobe came running back around the house, his gun drawn. Seeing her on the porch, he took the steps in one leap and moved to her.

"Jesus fuck, Jennifer. I told you to stay back," he bit out, pulling her into his body. She realized that the screaming had come from her but seemed unable to stop the shaking. She felt him pull out his cell again, "Tony. Got a problem. Get Gabe to Stuart Mason's house ASAP. Jennifer's fine."

Jobe scooped her up in his arms and carried her back to the SUV. Opening the back door, he sat on the edge of the seat, holding her in his lap awkwardly, keeping his arms wrapped protectively around her. *How does Gabe do this? We're trained to protect but how the fuck do you protect someone you love?* He continued to stroke her back for a few minutes.

Jennifer was vaguely aware of Jobe's quiet voice and then the sound of sirens began to intrude into her consciousness. Vehicles began to pull in around and Jennifer felt herself shifted slightly as Jobe explained to the first responders what was happening. She heard Matt and Shane's voices in the background, as Jobe continued to press her head into his chest.

The squeal of tires resonated and she could hear Gabe's voice calling out her name. She felt strong arms lifting her from the comfort of Jobe's chest and then was pulled into the familiar embrace of the man she loved. Voices continued to sound all around her, but it was as though she was in a dense fog and everything appeared far away.

Gabe looked down at Jennifer in his arms as Jobe gave a quick, succinct description of what had occurred. Matt and Shane had already gone inside and Jobe moved toward them to answer questions.

"Babe?" she heard Gabe call.

"Sir, does she need to be checked out?" one of the EMTs asked.

Gabe walked to the back of the ambulance, carrying her in his arms. Placing her on the stretcher, he looked down at her pale face. One of the workers put an oxygen mask on her face and in a moment, the voices became clearer and her vision became less cloudy.

Gabe watched carefully as the color began to come back to her face. Her eyes sought his and she saw the angry tick of his jaw.

"I'm sorry," she whispered. "Jobe told me to stay back but it was as though I had to see what was happening. I never...never...I..."

"You're right. You should have stayed where Jobe told you, but I'm more angry with myself. I should have come with you instead of sending someone else."

Gabe helped her sit up and she pulled the oxygen mask off. They exited the ambulance as she assured the worker that she was fully revived. Licking her dry lips, she peered toward the house, now a hive of activity.

Gabe walked her to Tony's vehicle and placed her in the back seat. "Babe, I need to see what's going on. I need you to stay right there," he ordered. She acquiesced, not wanting to see anything else of horror. She watched as he moved toward the house and stopped to talk to Matt, Shane, Jobe, and Tony. Sighing, she leaned her head back again and closed her eyes.

"What the fuck happened, man?" Gabe growled.

Not making any excuses, Jobe apologized. "I'm fuckin' sorry, Gabe. I told her to stay and assumed she would. That was my error. She went to the window to look in as I ran around the back."

Gabe hung his head knowing he could not be pissed with Jobe. *Jesus, why couldn't she have stayed where she was told to stay?*

Matt spoke up. "Stuart Mason was shot three times at close range. There's nothing to suggest robbery. Honestly? It looks like another execution."

"Fuck," Gabe bit out. "The fuckin' noose is getting tighter and tighter."

"We're done here for now. Going to let the rest of the investigative team process the scene," Shane said. "Matt and I are heading over to pay Michael Gibbons a visit. If he's so legitimate, then we should be able to get the names of his potential clients out of him."

Jobe added, "I'll stay here and make sure they've got all they need from me."

Tony moved Gabe to the side and said, "Let's get her home." Gabe nodded and they quickly headed back to the vehicle where she was sitting, pale and quiet. Tony pulled himself into the driver's seat and Gabe slid into the back with Jennifer.

She opened her eyes and looked at his worried face. "I'm fine, honey. I really am. The shock sent me into a bit of a tailspin, but I'm fine now."

She thought for a moment and then asked, "Tony I hate to be a bother but can you take me to the Elder Center?"

Tony's eyes looked at Gabe's in the rear-view mirror. She caught the silent exchange and rolled her eyes.

"Come on, guys. I'll admit I grew faint at seeing the poor man's body, but the little lady doesn't need to be tucked into bed. I've got to let Henry and Cora know what is going on. They knew him from a long time ago when he lived in the neighborhood."

Sighing, Gabe nodded at Tony and he changed directions. Pulling out her cell phone, she sent a text, then tucked her phone back into her pocket. Seeing Gabe's questioning look, she explained, "I was supposed to have coffee with Sherrie today. I just texted her that something had come up and I needed to go to the Center instead."

In a few minutes, they pulled up to the front and all three headed inside to the TV lounge. Seeing Jennifer and Gabe brought a smile to the resident's faces and they stood to greet them and see who the other man was. Jennifer left Gabe to introduce Tony, bringing another round of military introductions.

She found Henry and Cora in the kitchen. Diving in, she quickly told them the latest updates on what was happening, finishing with Stuart Mason's murder earlier that day.

"Oh my, God rest his soul," Cora said. "He was a good man if somewhat of a recluse. I remember him in the neighborhood where we grew up. Kind of a rough kid who grew into a hard man. A good man, but a hard one."

Henry nodded and rubbed his hand over his face. "I know I need to mourn him, but now I've got to wonder what will happen to us."

Jennifer stared at him dumbly for a few seconds until the reality slowly dawned on her. "Oh my God. I never thought of that. Who will own the building?"

"If he didn't have any heirs, I suppose the building will go into some kind of probate. It could be auctioned off."

"Do you think that will affect us?" Cora asked, concern written on her face.

"Yeah, no doubt," Jennifer sighed. Rubbing her hand across her brow, she looked up into the faces that had been her salvation when her parents died and Ross first came to her. Smiling, she reached out, placing a hand on each of their shoulders. "We'll be fine. We always are."

The two smiled back, agreeing.

"I'll find out what I can about Mr. Mason's funeral and we'll all go together."

She walked with them into the TV lounge, seeing Gabe easily conversing with the men. She glanced around but did not see Tony. Hearing voices from the entrance hall, she moved to the doorway and saw Tony standing there with Sherrie...neither looking happy.

"We're in the middle of trying to keep her safe and I sure as hell don't need you putting yourself in harm's way," Tony was saying.

Tossing her blonde hair out of the way, Sherrie glared back. "I have no intentions of messing things up for Jennifer. I just told her that if she needed me, I would be there for her. And I intend to keep my promise."

"Hmph," was his reply. "I saved you once—"

"You don't have to remind me," she snapped. Glancing behind Tony, she saw Jennifer standing in the doorway. Slipping around him, she hurried over and gave her friend a hug. "I'm so sorry for everything that's happening, sweetie. If you need me for anything, and I mean anything…just let me know."

Jennifer returned her hug, looking at Tony over Sherrie's shoulder. "I'm fine, really. Gabe's going to take me home soon and we'll grab Ross and spend the evening in."

Nodding, Sherrie said goodbye, turned and was walking past Tony without looking up when he reached out and gently snagged her arm. She stopped and looked up sharply.

"I'm sorry I brought up the earlier event," he said. "I never meant that it was an imposition to rescue you. Quite the contrary," he added softly.

Her eyes warmed as she viewed the man in front of her. Ever since the night he had rescued her she had dreamed of him, but he had made it obvious that those feelings were not returned. Calming, she said, "Apology accepted." Smiling, she turned and walked back out of the building.

Gabe approached Jennifer from behind and wrapped his arms around her. "Let's go get Ross, baby." He felt her nod against his chest and they made their goodbyes to the residents. Looking down at her as they walked back to Tony's vehicle, he said, "We'll come back together this weekend and serve the food for breakfast."

She turned that glorious smile up at him, filling him with more warmth than the spring sun.

"I'd like that," she said, realizing that he understood how she felt about this place and the people inside.

A WEEK LATER, Jennifer sat in her cubicle going through emails and writing reports. Her thoughts were filled with her earlier visit to the Senator's office.

His warm eyes welcomed her as he ushered her to one of the plush leather chairs. She took note that he sat next to her, not behind his desk. He asked about Ross and they spent a few minutes chatting, keeping the comments personal.

"I'm going to be honest, Jennifer. The budget is tighter than I realized this year. I don't think your grant will be a problem for at least another year, but now with Mr. Mason passing away so recently, I can't say what will happen when the building is turned over to new owners."

"So our lease could be broken just like that?" she asked, knowing the answer but hoping that perhaps it could be a different one.

"Yes, my dear, it could be over just like that."

Jennifer rubbed her forehead, trying to keep the headache at bay. "Sir, I've looked at the possibilities. If this falls through, then those residents will be out on the street. Some will find housing with relatives, but many will end up in sub-standard housing or in homeless shelters."

"I know, my dear. And I'm trying. Don't give up hope yet, but I wanted you to know the reality I face."

She offered him a small smile and patted his hand. "Thank you for everything you're doing. Really. It means a lot to me and to the residents."

As she walked out of his office, she battled to keep the tears of desperation at bay. Seeing Monty at his desk was just icing on her crappy cake. He turned to look at her as she walked by and she could have sworn she saw a sympathetic look instead of a triumphant one. Shaking her head, she left the building with one of Tony's men who drove her back to her office.

And now she sat and stared at her computer screen. Her phone rang and she recognized Sherrie's number.

"Hey, what's up?"

"Jennifer? I need you to come to my office as soon as you can."

"Are you all right? What's wrong?" she questioned quickly.

"No, I'm fine. It's just that…well…the law firm I work for needs to see you. They were going to send someone to the Center or your office, but I thought it would be better for me to call you since…well, since we know each other."

"Okaaay," Jennifer said slowly. "What's this about?"

"I'm not at liberty to discuss this, but if you can come now, I will clear Mr. Marks' schedule."

Closing the files on her desk, she said, "I'm on my way. It's Marks Attorney at Law isn't it?"

"Yes. Right on the corner of 31st and Courthouse Road."

Jennifer sat for a moment pondering the situation. *What the hell can this be about? A lawyer needs to see me? So much that they were going to send someone for me? Sherrie sounded nervous, so there's no way this can be good news.* Dropping her chin to her chest for a second, she prayed, *Lord, whatever it is, help me deal. I'm not sure I can take much more.*

Walking outside, she hopped in the SUV with Rick, the driver Tony had assigned, and told him where they needed to go. He was new to the agency but seemed very cautious.

"Gabe know about this?" he asked softly, pulling into traffic.

"No, but I'm just going to the law office of my friend, Sherrie. He knows her so it'll be fine."

He nodded but made a call from the vehicle's Bluetooth to Gabe anyway. "FYI – taking Ms. Lambert to the law offices of Sherrie…" He looked sideways again in question.

"Mullins. Sherrie Mullins," Jennifer said in exasperation.

"Call when you leave," came Gabe's reply.

The driver disconnected and they pulled up to the lawyer's office. She was getting ready to get out, when he stopped her with his hand on her arm. "I'm going in as well."

"I know Sherrie, she's a friend of mine."

"I understand Jennifer. But I've got my orders."

Sighing deeply, she agreed. "Let's go."

Entering the old, but well-appointed reception area, they were greeted by a pleasant woman sitting behind an antique desk. "May I help you?" she asked.

Sherrie appeared from the small hall to the left and said, "Thank you, Helen. I have them." Turning to Jennifer she smiled while glancing at the man next to her recognizing that he must be one of Tony's men.

"Jennifer, Mr. Marks will see you now." Looking at her escort, she smiled and offered him a seat in the reception area.

Jennifer followed Sherrie down the short hall, saying, "Girl, you're making me nervous."

Sherrie gave her a quick hug before ushering her into a large office filled with antique furniture. Mr. Marks was an older gentleman, reminding Jennifer of her grandfather. He smiled a warm smile and saw her comfortably settled, offering coffee or water.

Looking over at her, he began, "Ms. Lambert, I have the responsibility of handling the affairs of Mr. Stuart Mason, recently deceased."

At this, her heart began to pound. *Oh shit, he's*

going to tell me that we have to be out of the building to make way for the new owner. She discreetly wiped her palms on her slacks, wishing she could stop the churning in her stomach as easily.

"You may not be aware that Mr. Mason had no living relatives and until recently had no will. He came to me about a month ago and we discussed his affairs."

No relatives. Oh Jesus, the building could be auctioned off to the highest bidder and then we'd definitely be out. If it were a relative, I'd have a chance to ask them—

"Ms. Lambert? Are you all right?"

Startled out of her musing, she blushed. "Yes, I'm so sorry. I just…um…yes."

Nodding, he looked back down at the papers in front of him. "The details of his will for the most part do not concern you, but there is the matter of the property on 21st street that I understand you rent from him based on a grant."

"Yes, sir," she said, barely above a whisper.

"Well, I am to inform you that the property, in its entirety, has been willed to you as sole owner. The will must go through probate, but I can assure you that both my partner and I conversed with Mr. Mason and he was of very sound mind when he wanted you to have the property."

Jennifer sat perfectly still, her numb mind racing to catch up to what her ears had heard. She stared at Mr. Marks, blinking but not really seeing. He looked at her in concern and stood quickly, walking around his desk grabbing a bottle of water from his credenza. Pressing it into her hands, he called for Sherrie to come.

Sherrie, standing on the other side of his door, entered quickly and hurried over to her friend.

Jennifer looked to Sherrie and then to the lawyer. "Me?" she muttered in disbelief. "He left it to me?"

Sherrie smiled as she sat next to her, holding her hand. "Honey, I had no idea until Mr. Marks told me yesterday. I hadn't drawn up the paperwork, but I couldn't have told you even if I'd known. It's yours. Really, truly yours."

Jennifer looked back toward the lawyer, cleared her throat and said truthfully, "I don't know what to do with this news. Does this mean I can keep the Elder Center there? We don't have to move? I've never owned property before so I don't even know how that works. What about taxes?" Her eyes darted back to Sherrie's as her breathing escalated.

"Ms. Lambert," Mr. Marks said calmly. "Everything will be fine. I would advise obtaining an attorney to assist with your needs. We would love to help you, but can give you the names of others equally suited to answer all of your questions. But for now, just rest in the assurance that you own the building. And nothing, except your deciding to sell or your death, will take it away."

Standing, he said, "There is one last thing." He picked up an envelope from the file and handed it to her. "Mr. Mason left this for you. He said it would explain."

With shaky hands, she took the missive from him and opened it. Sherrie and Mr. Marks sat quietly as she pulled out the letter, written in scrawled handwriting.

My dear Ms. Lambert,

"for I was hungry and you gave Me food; I was thirsty and you gave Me drink; I was a stranger and you took Me in"

I have lived alone for many years since my Ester passed away, but meeting you was like seeing her again. She loved people and loved caring for them. She would have made a good mother, but God had other plans.

I have been approached by greedy men to sell the building that houses your good work and have repeatedly refused. To ensure that you can continue doing for others what you offered to me that day...I give the building to you. Use it wisely.

May God bless you for all that you do.
~~Sincerely~~ With affection, Stuart Mason

Tears sprang to her eyes as the weight that had been pressing down on her for months began to recede. Sherrie hugged her tightly as the two women stood. Thanking Mr. Marks as she walked out, she could hear an angry voice from the reception area. It sounded like...*Gabe.*

"I want to see Ms. Lambert right now. If you don't get her, I'll go back and—"

"Gabe, I'm here," she said running to him, seeing

Rick standing to the side, knowing he must have reported to Gabe.

"Baby, are you all right?" he asked, searching her face.

"Yes, I'm great! You're not going to believe it, but Mr. Mason left the building to me in his will!"

Gabe stared numbly at first Jennifer and then at a smiling Sherrie before the realization hit him. *She's got the building. Oh shit. She's now got a fuckin' target on her back.*

"Honey, don't you get it? I can keep the Center!" she said, not understanding the look of concern on his face.

He schooled his expression and gave her a hug. Forcing a smile at Sherrie, he turned and told Rick, "I've got her. Tell Tony that I'll be back in tomorrow for a meeting."

Rick nodded and walked out the door with Gabe and Jennifer following behind. As soon as they were settled in Gabe's Jeep, she began to talk excitedly. Gabe let her ramble and forced himself to smile at the appropriate time and give encouraging nods.

"Gabe, I'm not stupid. You're not nearly as excited about this as you should be. Don't you understand what this means?" she accused.

"Babe, I do. Really I do." Wrestling with how much to disclose to her, he wanted to make sure she was still vigilant. "My concern is that whoever killed Mr. Mason had no idea he had left a will, naming you as new owner of the building."

"But honey, that makes it all better. Once they know, they'll back off. They'll know that it's now in my hands and I won't sell."

Gabe glanced to the side, realizing that she understood the harshness of life but not the nefarious dealings of criminals. "Well, I'll talk to Tony and we're still keeping you on security detail."

"If it makes you feel better," she agreed, but leaned back in the seat with the calm knowledge that her troubles for the time being were over.

CHAPTER 19

TONY AND SHANE were escorted into Michael Gibbons's opulent office. Sharing a quick glance, they both acknowledged that the man was successful and had taste. Pictures on the wall showed him with politicians, both local and state, and at a closer glance indicated that he had been to the White House at one time. Pictures on his credenza showed what they assumed was his family. Well-tended wife and two children.

"Detectives, welcome," came the smooth voice from behind them as he entered. "Forgive my not being here when you arrived; I was just down the hall finishing up a conference. Please, sit down." Turning to his secretary, he said, "Eloise, please bring in some coffee for the gentlemen." She nodded and quietly left the room.

"What can I help the Richland Police Department with today?" he asked, settling down behind his desk.

Matt and Shane, now settled in the comfortable leather chairs, began. "Your real estate company has helped several companies acquire buildings in the downtown area for fairly low prices and then, once they are flipped, assisted them into selling them for a great profit."

Michael beamed proudly. "Yes, indeed. I've built a reputation with my company based on fairness but undoubtedly my clients know that I will seek a low buying price for them and a high selling price." His face took on a concerned look as he continued, "But Detectives, there's nothing wrong with this practice. Any reputable real estate company would do the same, I assure you."

Matt nodded, "Agreed. We're not here to question your company's tactics, but we are concerned about some of your clients."

At this Michael's eyes grew wide in surprise. "My clients? Well, I suppose...I...I don't know what to say to that. What kind of concerns are you talking about?"

"We are investigating the extortion practices where someone threatens building owners into selling at a low price in order to acquire properties to then sell at a higher price."

"Threatens?" Michael said incredulously. "Detectives, my real estate business' reputation is spotless. My realtors are hand-selected by me. Whether they are selling homes or high-end condos or dilapidated warehouses, they must perform to not only the industry's, but my personal, high ethical standards."

"Understood," Matt agreed. "But it's the clients that we want to pursue information on. As clients, they are not bound by your ethics."

Michael appeared to ponder this line of thinking for a moment, and then said, "I'm not sure how I can help you. You see, when a realtor is dealing with selling a home for a family, they get to know the family selling and often the family buying. That's not to say that they can trust them, but they have a face to go with the client's name." Shrugging, he added, "But for our multi-million dollar deals with many clients…we never see them. The dealings are all done through lawyers or company front end people. My realtors and I rarely actually meet them."

His eyes darted between Matt and Shane.

Shane had not voiced any questions yet. It was the tactic often used by Matt and him. Matt asked the questions, smoothly, succinctly. And Shane provided the 'nerve factor'. The quiet, staring, brooding cop that made the interviewee nervous. And possibly slip.

"So in most of these cases, you have never actually met someone representing the buyers?"

"No, I haven't. I will say that as the president of my company, I'm not often in the actual dealings anymore. You are more than welcome to talk to any of my realtors."

Eloise walked quietly back into the room and set the coffee service on the edge of his desk. She fixed a cup for Matt and Shane, handing it to them first and then turned to Michael setting his precisely on his desk where he could reach it easily.

"Eloise, would you please get a list of our realtors

who have sold properties in the downtown area for the past..." he looked at Matt in question.

"Three years would be good," Matt replied.

Eloise nodded and left the room as quietly as she had entered. Within a few minutes, she returned and handed the list to Matt. Thanking her, Matt and Shane stood up and shook Michael's hand. As he ushered them to the door, he added, "Detectives, I have worked hard to build up what I consider to be a reputable real estate business empire. I admit that I love the creature comforts that my successful business offers and do not need any illegal gains to do that. I hope you will be discrete in checking with my clients, but I will also say that I want no part of anyone who you find to be guilty."

Nodding once again he walked back into his office as Matt and Shane stepped onto the elevator. Moving to his desk, he placed a call. "Santo. My office. Now."

In the elevator, Matt looked at his partner, with his eyebrow lifted.

"Prick's guilty of somethin'. Too smooth. Too polished. Had the answers all ready. Don't trust him."

Matt grinned as they left the building. His partner's instincts were generally spot on, having spent two years in an undercover gang. "Good. Now maybe we're getting close." Looking down at his cell, he said, "Got a text from Tony. Seems like there's another meeting."

THE GROUP SAT around Tony's conference table after Gabe had dropped Jennifer off at her work and made sure someone was picking Ross up from school. Filling in everyone on the events of the morning, the group instantly recognized that the news that Jennifer responded to so positively was definitely another reason for needing to watch her carefully.

Gabe looked at the group saying, "I'm so goddamn conflicted. I want to be happy for her 'cause this is huge to her and the Center. But if she had a target on her earlier...it's even bigger now."

"I'd bet that whoever had Stuart Mason killed had no idea that he left the building to the one person who'd never sell," Tony added.

Matt had supplied Lily and BJ with the list of clients and they had been running them through the various databases, looking for more intel on them. He looked over at his wife and as she caught his gaze, she just shook her head. "Sorry, honey. Nothing yet. These companies are buried within other companies. But nothing to tie them back to Micahel Gibbons yet."

"Keep looking," Tony quipped, then turned back to the group at hand. "And keep the rotation schedule up on Jennifer and Ross."

Standing to leave, Vinny clapped his brother on the back. "You okay, bro?"

Gabe turned to look into his twin's eyes. "Got a bad feeling the shit is just getting started."

Vinny nodded, knowing the feeling. It was the

same feeling they all would get before a mission that felt off. As though no matter how much they planned, something major was going to happen.

JENNIFER BOUNDED INTO her office, grabbing Roy and Sybil to give them the news. Chip and a few other social workers came by as well. Smiles and congratulations abounded, as the group knew how important this was to the Center.

"Oh girl, when are you going to share the news with the residents?" Sybil asked.

"I don't know. I haven't even processed how great this is. I'll have to meet with an attorney to have everything put in order, but I'll try to go by tomorrow. They are going to be so excited!"

Chip nodded saying, "Can't believe your good fortune, but you've worked hard for this."

She eyed him, wondering if his words were heartfelt or not. He seemed pleased, but she could not help the niggling feeling that something was off. Just then, Roy walked over carrying a big bottle of Sprite and paper cups.

"Okay, it's not champagne, but it'll have to do," he said laughing.

The group celebrated with cups of Sprite and toasts to an easier future for the Elder Center. As overworked, underpaid social workers, they definitely knew how to celebrate when the news was good. Turning back to the group, Jennifer could not help but notice that Chip had walked back to his office and was not celebrating. Biting her lip in thought, she was quickly pulled back into the celebrations with her co-workers.

A LITTLE LATER a phone call was made to Michael Gibbons' private line.

"Just got the news straight from her. Stuart Mason left her the building in his will. It's hers legally now."

Michael disconnected the line without saying a word. Looking at the woman between his legs sucking him off, he surged forward unloading into her mouth without warning. But she took it. Quickly swallowing, she stayed on her knees until he indicated for her to rise. Realizing his mood had turned with the phone call, she quietly left the room the way she came.

Walking out of the building, one of Michael's men escorted her to an expensive car and she drove away. Eyes bored into her from another car on the street. Theresa took off her designer sunglasses and recognized the woman leaving. The dark-haired beauty caught Michael's eye one night while he was out with her and the flash of jealousy ate at her then and angered her now. Vowing revenge, she held off placing the call until a later time. When it would hurt him the most.

SANTO WALKED BACK into Michael's office having received the message from Eloise to come immediately. He had spoken to Michael earlier after the detectives left and was confident that none of their dealings could be traced back to Gibbons Realties.

He found Michael standing at the wall of windows looking once again at the night skyline. Before he could greet his boss, Michael turned and viciously growled, "I want her signature on a deed of sale or I want her dead."

Santo stopped, waiting for him to continue.

"That goddamn old man left Ms. Lambert the property in his will." Seeing Santo's surprised look, he added, "Yeah. We've covered every angle with this and still that bitch is thwarting me. I want that building and I don't care how. Bury it in a lot of cover-ups, but I want it done with no blow-back."

Santo was quiet for a moment as the thoughts churned in his head. A slow smile spread over his face as he turned to his boss. Michael looked at him with a questioning look.

"We return to the old days," Santo said, recalling Michael's story of his grandfather and great-grandfather. "Grab the brother and hold him over her head. She signs the building over or we kill him. She stays quiet because we'll kill him if she doesn't."

Michael's calculating expression turned back to the windows as he pondered Santo's solution. "Too many ways to trace that back to us. Too much of a chance that blow-back lands right in our lap." Turning to Santo, he said simply, "Grab them both. Hold them and find a way to kill them both making it look like an accident. She's gone and her heir is gone. The building goes on the auction block and will easily fall to me."

Santo smile grew wider as he nodded toward his boss. "I like it. Just like the old days of your grandfather."

Michael turned and walked over to his credenza, pouring two large whiskeys into tumblers. Handing one to his right-hand man who had never failed him, he lifted his glass. "To the old days," he said smiling.

"WHERE'S ROSS?" JENNIFER asked Cora as she ducked by a painter's ladder in the recreation room. The men were trying to clean up for the evening and move their equipment to the side.

"He's upstairs," Cora replied. "When that nice young man from Mr. Alvarez' brought him in from school, Ross said he had homework to finish so that Gabe would have time to teach him how to swim when you two went home."

Jennifer had to smile, the thought of Gabe patiently teaching Ross how to swim in the pool in his apartment building. Vinny would often come along to help but usually did more dunking and splashing than teaching.

Running upstairs and using her special knock, she

entered the old apartment. Ross, looking up with a smile, said, "Are we ready to go yet?"

"Not quite," she answered, bending down to kiss the top of his head. "I've got to take a picture of the residents and it will take a bit to gather them."

Turning back to his homework, he said, "Okay. Just let me know when you are ready to leave."

Hurrying back downstairs, she passed the painters finishing the hallway. "It looks good," she complimented them.

Several minutes later, she begged, "Come on, everyone smile." Jennifer was trying to settle the residents of the Center on the front steps for a group picture. It was almost dusk and she regretted waiting so late to take the picture. When she was in the center earlier, she gathered them into the dining room and told them the good news. Henry and Cora stood to the side as the residents surged forward for hugs and congratulations. As they trickled back, Jennifer saw her two friends, with tears in their eyes, moving forward. Throwing her arms around them she felt their heartfelt relief at the news.

"Oh, darling girl, you've worked so hard for this," Cora cried.

"I know. This is going to make life so much easier. I'm going to have to find a lawyer who can help me figure out how to make this all work, but for now, we don't have to worry about the roof over your heads."

"You're a good girl, Jennifer Lambert," Henry said as his arms held her tight.

Wiping away the tears, she wanted to get a group celebration picture of all of them. They decided to stand on the front steps but the spring sunshine was passing beyond the skyline. It took a while to get the thirty or so residents all on the steps and in position so that she could see all of them.

Finally finished, she led the group back inside. "I'm going to get Ross," she called out. "He's got a swim date to keep."

Jennifer moved through the dining room toward the kitchen when she heard a loud noise from the back kitchen door. Seeing the door standing open, she jogged over to see the painters loading their van. As she continued to watch, her world seemed to alter in slow motion.

As the side panel was closing, she caught sight of Ross being held by one of the painters. Her name, torn from Ross' lips, pierced her heart; his eyes wide as the man's large hand clamped over his mouth.

"Ross!" she screamed as her frozen legs suddenly lurched into action, hurling her down the steps toward her brother as the door closed. *Oh Jesus, I can get him, I can get him.* Just as she was almost to the van another man, deftly leaped out and met her a few feet from the vehicle.

Opening her mouth to scream, she felt a cloth pressed over her nose and mouth as his arms encircled her in a vise grip. A sickly-sweet odor overtook her as she felt her legs slide out from under her. Then black.

SHERRIE'S HEELS CLICKED on the marble floors of the Senate building. She was beginning to feel as though she worked here, as much as her boss had her delivering files to the various Senators. For the umpteenth time she wondered why Senator Reno did not just have the documents sent through currier, but according to Mr. Marks, Monty always said that the Senator did not want his personal correspondences to be carried by just anyone. So, Sherrie made the weekly trip over.

When she arrived at Monty's desk he was not there, so she put the files in the box that he used for incoming packets. She could not help but notice that his desk was neat and orderly—not an attribute that she was able to attain.

Turning, she slung her oversized purse back onto her shoulder, grimacing as it knocked the files off of his desk, scattering them onto the floor. Panicked, she immediately dropped to her knees and began trying to arrange them once again.

As she separated the papers on the floor, she visually scanned them to see what went in her folders. Looking at the notes, she pulled her employer's papers and put them in the appropriate files. As she perused the next paper in the pile, her gaze noted the name *Jennifer Lambert*. Her attention caught, she could not help but read the other words written on the page. *Elder Center Intercept correspondence between Senator and*

Lambert. There were some phone numbers underneath, but her eyes focused on her friend's name. A sick feeling of dread crawled over her, seeping into the suspicious corners of her mind.

She pulled out her cell phone to take a quick picture of the note. She startled when she heard a voice on the phone. Glancing down, she realized that she called the first number on her list with shaky fingers instead of tapping on the camera icon. And she knew who was the first number...Tony. She had never called him but when he rescued her last year he had given her his number and she made it the number one contact.

"Sherrie?"

"Tony? I didn't mean to call, but now I'm glad you picked up," she said, peeking behind her to see the hallway still clear.

"What's wrong?" he asked sharply, hearing her whisper as though not wanting anyone to hear.

"I'm at the Senator's office and I found something strange on Monty's desk. He's the—"

"I know who he is," came the short response. "Do you need help? Can you get out?"

"I'm fine but I was going to take a picture of the note but hit my contact list instead. It lists Jennifer's name and some phone numbers and the instructions to intercept her correspondence."

"Sherrie, get out of there immediately. I'm on my way. Get to the front steps of the building where you're in plain sight and stay there until I come."

"But what about the papers?" she asked, suddenly nervous.

"Leave them and get out now," Tony ordered.

"May I help you?" came a smooth voice coming up from behind her.

Gasping, she twisted around and looked at the man standing close to her. Monty had walked up, admiring the view of the beautiful woman's ass as she was kneeling on the floor by his desk.

She stood quickly, a blush crossing her face, sliding the cell phone down to her side and into her purse without disconnecting the call. Eying him suspiciously, she held out the paper. "I knocked over some papers and was trying to straighten them. What's the meaning of this, Monty?" she asked, accusation dripping off of each word.

His eyes glanced downward and then flew back up to her face, the smile replaced by a grim expression. Stepping closer he took the paper from her hand, folded it and placed it in his pocket. "You shouldn't snoop into things that don't involve you, Ms. Mullins."

"I would disagree. Anything that involves my friends interests me," she retorted.

Glancing around, seeing people at the other end of the hall, he leaned forward again. "I can explain, but not here. Take a little walk with me and I'll give you the answers you need."

She eyed him suspiciously, biting her lip, the indecision visible on her face.

Monty said, "Look, we're surrounded by people here. Let's go somewhere less crowded and I promise you, you'll understand."

She nodded and tossed the rest of the papers on his desk, taking a childish pleasure in knowing it was no longer neat. She moved next to him as they walked to the elevators. Getting off in the underground parking garage, she halted. "The parking garage? That's where you're taking me?" she asked, eyes narrowing.

He took her by the arm, his grip tight but not painful. "For your own safety, you need to come with me. Please."

It was the last word uttered that had her following although the doubt of what she was doing plagued her. Sliding her hand into her purse, her fingers felt her cell phone, knowing the one person she trusted with her life, was listening.

CHAPTER 20

TONY LEFT HIS agency with his trusted men in tow; he, Jobe, and BJ in one vehicle and the twins in another. As he explained the phone call from Sherrie to the men in his SUV, he was on speaker with the others. They would have followed him anywhere without explanations, but Tony was meticulous in mission planning.

As the vehicles approached the Senate building, they made their way through traffic toward the parking garage. Gabe's phone rang and he almost shut it off when he saw **Henry** on the ID.

"Henry? I can't talk now. I'm—"

"We've called the police. Some painters were here and they grabbed Ross and Jennifer!" he said, the words rushing out of him.

Gabe's heart stopped as his brain processed what Henry had said. "Wh…what the fuck? Oh, Jesus."

Turning to his brother behind the wheel, he ordered, "Turn around. Go to the Center. Jennifer and Ross have just been kidnaped."

Vinny, face grim, spoke into the speaker, "Did you copy that?"

Jobe answered in the affirmative. Tony's voice rang clear, "Agreed. Go to the Center. We've got Sherrie covered and then we'll join you there."

TONY PULLED INTO the parking garage slowly, not wanting to alert Monty of their presence. BJ had Sherrie's cell pulled up on his computer giving them directions.

"Fourth floor, east side," he called out from the back seat.

Pulling into a parking place on the third floor, they quietly exited the vehicle, stealthily maneuvering through the cars to the next level. Hearing voices, they crept closer.

"Are you going to tell me anything or are you just going to keep talking in riddles?" Sherrie was asking. Tony moved to the left of a vehicle so that he had a visual of Sherrie and Monty. Jobe and BJ slide around to the right. Jobe's weapon was drawn, ready if needed.

"There are things going on that you don't need to know about and if you want to help your friend, you will convince her to stay away," Monty bit out.

"Is that a threat?" she asked.

"No, but a promise that you won't like the consequences if you get in my way." He reached out and took her arm again, firm but not painful, as he gently pulled her closer to her car. "You need to get in and drive away, now."

"How do you know that's my car?" she asked, surprise showing on her face.

In a flash, Tony launched himself from behind her car and landed on Monty, jerking his hand away from Sherrie's arm. Jobe rushed over to pull her from the brawl as Tony and Monty rolled around, fists flying.

"Who the fuck are you working for?" Tony growled, jerking Monty to his feet.

Monty shoved Tony backward and reached into his pocket. The click of pistols at the ready halted him, then he slowly withdrew his hand from his pocket revealing a…badge. "FBI, fuckers," Monty growled back.

Tony stared at the badge momentarily and then raised his gaze to Monty's. "Jesus, fuck. You're undercover."

"I was until sunshine here," he said pointing to Sherrie, "got so nosey I was trying to scare her off. There's a lot going on here that's bigger than her friend or she understands."

"You…you were trying to help?" Sherrie asked. She had unconsciously moved closer to Tony as she focused on Monty.

"The details of my investigation are not going to be fuckin' discussed in the middle of a goddamn parking garage, but yes…I was trying to keep you and Ms. Lambert from stumbling onto something that was going to get both of you in the line of fire."

Tony rubbed his hand over his face in frustration. He noticed Sherrie's close presence and wanted to pull her closer, but forced himself to keep his mind on the mission. "She's already in the line of fire. Just before we came here, we heard she and her brother were kidnaped."

"No!" Sherrie gasped, grabbing Tony's arms as she whirled around to face him.

Tony and Monty squared off, sizing each other up. "Not asking you to divulge your mission," Tony bit out, but I gotta friend whose woman and brother was just taken and I'm going to do everything I can to help. Now you can either tell us what you know or I'll make sure your cover is blown to hell."

"FBI got a tip over a year ago that Michael Gibbons, the well-known and well-respected real estate mogul, is the grandson of Joseph Gambelini, a local mob boss in the area. Michael Gibbons' reputation and legit business is beyond reproach, but underneath all that refinement is another mob boss who runs an empire based on extortion, murder of those in his way, and he's got politicians as well as police in his pocket."

Sherrie watched the scene unfold in front of her, realization dawning. "The Senator. Oh my God, that's why you're here."

VINNY DROVE AS quickly as he could to the Center,

often glancing at a visibly shaken Gabe in the passenger side.

Vinny's voice was low and steady. "Bro, clear your mind. It's a mission. We gotta get the intel and then plan."

Gabe did not reply, but Vinny could feel the anger begin to pour off of his twin. "That's fine, bro. Be pissed enough to get your head in the game. 'Cause she's gonna need you to have a clear head."

Gabe started to retort, then his brother's reasoning slowly crept in. *He's right. I gotta keep my head in this for her. All for her.* He looked down at his hands that had been shaking, forcing his breathing to slow and watched as his hands became steadier. The fear that had been choking him was being replaced with anger. Cold. Deadly. Anger.

Pulling up to the Center they could see the elderly residents, most visibly shaken, milling around talking to the police. Spotting Matt and Shane, Gabe jumped out as Vinny parked, then ran over to them.

They filled him in on the eyewitness reports of the abductions. Henry made a bee-line to Gabe, grasping him by the arm.

"Gabriel, you have to find them," his voice shook, tears in his eyes.

Gabe stared into the weathered face of the man who had been like a father to Jennifer and held tightly to his shoulders. "I will. Promise," his voice bit out.

He and Vinny met with Matt and Shane to find

out what the police had discovered. The detectives had little to go on at the moment, other than what the residents had told them. "No one got the license number of the van, but several noted that it appeared that white paint covered some former writing on the side. Three men were seen; all with painter uniforms on."

Gabe's heart was pounding as his mind raced. *Where the fuck are you, baby? You gotta hang on until I can get you.* He looked over as Vinny's phone rang and watched his brother take the call. Vinny's eyes came to his as he just said, "Roger, out."

"Tony's got Sherrie. Monty, the Senator's aide, is FBI. They're heading here."

The rapid fire news was more than Gabe's brain could process and he found himself staring dumbly at the others. Matt moved to the side as he took a call. "Got it, babe." Disconnecting, he said, "We may just have a break. That was Lily. She's got a bead on the van from the alley video cameras."

"Does she know where they are?"

"Not yet, but she's working it—"

The squeal of tires sounded as Tony rushed to the scene. The brothers-in-arms met on the sidewalk, eyes staring unabashedly at Monty, who joined them.

Gabe took an angry step towards him but was held back by Vinny. "What the fuck do you know about this?"

"I've been trying to keep her safe," Monty bit back.

"She's been getting too close to our investigation, but she's like a dog with a bone when she's got a crusade to fight for," Monty bit out.

"What investigation?" Vinny asked, still pulling his brother back.

Monty stood silent, staring at the men in front of him.

Gabe jerked out of Vinny's grasp and descended on Monty. The two men were close in build, but Gabe had a couple of inches and at least twenty pounds of pure muscle on him. Leaning into Monty's space, he repeated, "Not asking again. What investigation?"

"Since this one," he said, jerking his head toward Sherrie standing to the side listening avidly, "my cover's been blown to hell. Jesus fuck." He shook his head for a moment then lifted it, taking a deep breath, he continued. "Michael Gambelini. Mob boss. Head of a gang of ruthless extortionists. Has his illegitimate gains so buried in legitimate companies that he's been impossible to trace. And known to most as the real-estate mogul, Michael Gibbons."

"Goddamn it," Shane cursed. "I knew that mother-fucker was too slick to not have his hand in something."

Matt looked at Monty saying, "We've been looking into the extortion claims of the buying of some of the properties around here."

"I don't give a fuck who you all are investigating unless they can lead us to Jennifer and Ross," Gabe growled, holding on to his temper by a thread.

A firm grip on his shoulder had him turning around and staring into Henry's eyes. "Former Air Cav, Vietnam, Sergeant Henry Coghill. Reporting for duty."

Another man stepped up next to Henry. "Infantry, Vietnam, Private Clarence Hardison. Reporting for duty."

Two more, older men joined them, followed by more and more. Each identifying their former military units and all volunteering.

The air whooshed out of Gabe as he battled back the tears. He realized at that moment that his group of brothers-in-arms just expanded. He felt the presence of his friends at his back and knew without turning around that they were just as moved as he.

Tony, knowing Gabe was unable to speak at the moment, stepped forward. "Proud to know you. We've got to plan, but we won't leave you out. Got a room we can use?"

Cora slid next to Henry, tears still streaming down her face as she looked up at Gabe. "I never served in the military, but try to keep me the hell out of this! Follow me gentlemen," she said as she turned and led the group inside to the large dining hall.

Monty followed, already on his phone to his superiors. Tony knew he was letting them know the investigation had taken a turn and his cover was blown. He almost felt sorry for him...almost.

As the police detectives and Tony's men circled one

of the large tables, they listened to what Matt and Shane could tell them about their investigation. BJ worked furiously on his laptop while Matt coordinated on the phone with Lily. Matt looked up, distress on his face.

"The police just found the van about fifteen blocks from here. Empty."

"Goddamn it," Gabe cursed.

Shane looked at Monty as he got off the phone. "You gonna tell us what you know or is the Bureau gonna make us beat the shit outta you?"

Rubbing his bruised chin, Monty replied, "Your friend over there already tried that." Sighing, he said, "I just got verbal confirmation to work with you on this kidnapping.

"Michael Gibbons runs a legitimate real estate company that brings in millions for him alone. Goes to all the right functions. Wife, kids, charity events. The whole package. Several years ago an informant that had just started working with the Bureau turned up dead. Beaten, tortured, and his body found in pieces at the river's edge."

"What had he given you?" Tony asked.

"Info on extortion. It seemed that when an owner of an old warehouse or building resisted selling cheap to whatever buyer was coming along, they suddenly signed gladly or were eliminated." Turning to the detectives, he continued, "You were getting wind of some of this, but by then we had been working for almost two years on trying to find the ties to Gibbons. When his father had their name changed, he did it in a way that really covered his tracks."

Gabe stood up, fists on the table, leaning over toward Monty. "You fuckers knew about this Gambelini for two years. Knew the local detectives were working on the extortion without the resources you have. Knew that it was continuing so innocent people were getting hurt. And you fuckin' did nothing about it?" he roared, veins standing out on his neck.

"Going in early without solid evidence would have done nothing to stop him," Monty bit back. "I do my job just like you do yours."

"The hell you do," Gabe argued.

"You get a mission, you plan it out. Don't fucking tell me that there isn't collateral damage sometimes," Monty yelled back.

Suddenly the eyes of the little boy standing in a room with explosives strapped to his waist flashed back into Gabe's vision. The eyes that wanted to trust that someone would care enough to stop what was inevitable. And the eyes that stared at him as he turned, running away with their mission accomplished as the explosives detonated. His vision began to blur as he held his breath. *Breathe, fuckin' breathe bro,* he heard in the distance.

Taking a ragged breath, his vision began to clear as he felt Vinny push him down into a chair. As his mind cleared of the memory, the dark eyes of another little boy filled his vision. *Ross.* Eyes that looked into his, trusting him to take care of him. And big blue eyes, trusting in his love. Pulling in a huge gulp of air, he looked around the table. Tony, Vinny, and Jobe all knew what was on his mind. Nodding, he stood staring Tony in the eyes.

"Not again. Not happening again, Captain."

Tony nodded. "Then let's do what we can to get those fuckers."

Monty said, "We've been working on the link between the dirty politicians and Gibbons. One of them is State Senator Reno. He's eyeing the White House in a couple of years and has been in Gibbons' back pocket for a while."

"He supports Jennifer. He's always worked with her," piped up Henry from behind the group.

Monty shook his head. "Only on the surface. Behind the closed budget sessions, he sabotages her cause."

Gabe's hand tightened into a fist once again. "So where do we begin?"

"My guess is that Gibbons wants this building and, since he's been unable to persuade the owner to sell, he had him killed without knowing that it was willed to Ms. Lambert."

Tony nodded as Matt said, "We figured that put a target on her back."

"But it's just a building," Cora spoke up from the corner. "I don't understand."

"This is much bigger than just a building. It's money. Greed. But more importantly, power and politics," Monty said.

"Look, this building is on the corner of a busy street that will bring top dollar. If he has the rest of the block without this building, he'll get maybe a million or less for the back part of the block. With this building, he could sell it for tens of millions. It's also about power. He gives up on this, his reputation takes a hit. Right now, he has inroads to politicians who are up and coming. He wants Senator Reno in his back pocket so that when he helps him get to the White House, he'll have a President literally under his thumb.

"None of his tactics worked on the former owner and now he's desperate. Ms. Lambert inheriting this has made him act irrationally." Looking right at Gabe, Monty continued, "That may be the break we need to get him."

"At what cost, you bastard?" Gabe growled.

BJ looked up from quietly working on his laptop. "Tony? Pulling some shit together with Lily. There's a news reporter that Jennifer talked with a couple of months ago who died in a mysterious house fire before the article could be printed."

Gabe looked over sharply, his mind racing with things that Jennifer had told him since they had been together. "Look up some of her co-workers. She said some strange things had been happening. Especially her boss, Chip something. Hell, that's gotta be a nickname.

Try Charles."

BJ went back to work on the laptop, with Lily coordinating. The others gathered around several maps of the city, looking at the possible places Ross and Jennifer could have been taken. No clues. Nothing. Gabe felt the claws of fear creep up this throat as the realization began to sink in that they had no way of knowing where she was.

Matt took a phone call, walking away so that he could hear over the clambering voices behind him. Disconnecting, he hurried back looking at Shane. "We've gotta go. Some woman just showed up at the station, claiming to have information that will take down Michael Gibbons." As he gazed around at the incredulous expressions shooting his way, he grinned, "Disgruntled mistress."

"Thank God for a pissed off fuck," Shane responded, as the group disbanded.

"What can we do?" Henry asked as Gabe began to move out with the others. He turned, his large frame dwarfing the others. Touched by the ravaged look on the elderly man's face, he then looked at the similar expressions on the other residents. "I don't know right now, Henry. But pray. Just pray that I get to them in time."

Cora approached, taking her husband's arm. "That we can do, Gabriel. That we can do."

CHAPTER 21

THE DARKNESS THAT Jennifer had descended into began to slowly recede. Nothing made sense. *I just want to sleep. Just a few more minutes, Ross. Ross? Oh my God!*

As the memories of earlier came crashing back into her mind, she struggled to open her eyes. Blinking at the harsh lights above, she lifted one heavy hand to shade her vision.

She was laying on a pallet and tried to sit up. Nausea rolled over her as a sickly sweet odor drifted by. It reminded her of the scent of the cloth held over her nose. Forcing herself to breathe in through her nose and out her mouth several times helped to quell her rolling stomach.

Pushing herself to a sitting position she noticed that she was actually on a cot with a thick blanket tossed over her. A quick glance downward sent relief through her consciousness. *Thank God, I'm still dressed.*

As the fog lifted slowly from her brain, she saw that Ross was not in the room with her. *Oh Jesus. Where can he be? And where the hell am I?* She rubbed her face with her hands trying to regain her focus. Standing on shaky legs, she grabbed at the wall to steady herself as she perused the room. Large, mostly empty except for the cot and a chair. The window was boarded up with plywood and the only door to the room was on the opposite side.

Exposed wiring and plumbing ran along the walls with drywall finished in some places. *Wherever I am, it's being renovated. Oh shit, that means probably no one is living here to help me.*

Walking to the door, she first placed her ear on it to see if she could hear voices. Nothing. Taking the knob, she gently tried to turn it. Locked. Of course. She quietly slipped over to where the window was, trying to see through a crack between the plywood and frame. Other than a slight hint of air coming through she could not see anything. It seemed to be night time, but she could not be sure.

Frustrated, she looked around to see if there was something to pull the plywood out but there was nothing in the room.

By now her head was clear but that only served to make her fear sharper. *I've got to find Ross. He must be so afraid. Oh Jesus,* she prayed again. *Please keep him safe.*

GABE FOLLOWED THE others into the police department as Matt and Shane gathered information from their chief. Matt turned and said, "Come on. She's being questioned."

Matt and Shane went into the interview room with Gabe and his co-workers going into the observation room.

"What can you tell us Ms. Marconi?"

Theresa tossed her long, dark hair over her shoulder with a perfectly manicured finger. She eyed the handsome detectives in front of her, ever on the lookout for another fuck that might offer her something more. Detective's pay would hardly keep her in the style she was accustomed to, so her eyes moved back to the table.

"I was recently in the company of Michael Gibbons. In fact, you could say that I was *intimately* involved if you know what I mean."

"And this concerns us how?" Shane asked, not willing to play games with her.

She pursed her lips, not used to males ignoring her sexuality. "I know things. Things that you might be interested in."

"You got something to say then say it. You got nothin' then stop wasting our time."

Narrowing her eyes, she retorted, "I can tell you that he buries his legitimate business behind so many companies that it's almost impossible to connect them. I can tell you that he's got Senator Reno in his pocket, and he's not the only politician that owes him."

"Still nothing we don't know, darlin'. Seems like you're just a pissed off ex-mistress who's wanting to cause trouble for a man who moved on."

Slapping her hands down on the table, Theresa leaned forward and bit out, "Yes, but did you know that I can prove it." Pulling a thumb drive from her pocket, her lip curled in a smile. "I'm smarter than he ever thought. He thinks that when he's finished with a woman, he can just put her away in a nice apartment and buy her silence with a few jewels. Well, not me. I made sure I had my own little insurance policy. He throws me over, I take him down."

"What's on that? Anything we can use?"

"See for yourself, detectives. I found some things on his desk one night when he was late getting back from a meeting with his right-hand man, Santo Mancello. Who, by the way, manages most of Michael's dirty work. Well, he and Frederick Gibbons, his nephew. There's stuff on there I didn't know what was, but I saw the names of lots of companies."

Shane took the thumb drive and walked to the door, handing it to BJ who immediately plugged it into his laptop. Tony and Jobe, along with another detective, stood looking over BJ's shoulder as he pulled up company organizations and bank accounts.

BJ looked up saying, "Got plenty here to aid in the investigation, but for where Jennifer is?", he shook his head.

"Figured that making a copy of things would be good if that bastard ever dumped me. If I tried to blackmail him, I'd have to fear for my life. But this," she said while leaning back in the chair, crossing her arms over her ample chest, "would be my way of getting back."

"Tell us about Santo," Matt prodded.

Theresa shivered delicately. "He's...vicious...hidden behind a calm persona. I always thought he could look right through me."

"Did you ever see where they might take someone? Someone they wanted to hurt or question?"

For the first time since she decided to take her limited knowledge to the police, she had a momentary pause. Her mind went back to the times she was in Santo's presence. He was always completely immune to her charms, giving her the impression that he knew she was temporary. Her lips pressed into a tight line as she remembered thinking that Michael would keep her always and not pass her on for the next fuck to keep his bed warm.

"Well, Ms. Marconi?"

"I...I don't know. Michael had buildings all over the city."

"It would need to be somewhere without a lot of people around. Somewhere private," Matt prodded.

Gabe leaned in toward the glass separating his space from the interview room. His heart pounded as his knuckles turned white from gripping the window frame. *Come on, bitch. Think. Give me something. Something to go on.*

She turned her eyes toward the mirror as though

Gabe's thoughts had penetrated her consciousness. "One night when we were out in Michael's limo, Santo was with us. I thought we were heading to a restaurant, but we detoured." She licked her lips nervously as she sought her memories. "I wouldn't have noticed, but Michael had ignored me while talking to Santo so I was pissed. The area of town was…scary. It was dark, with few lights around. I was giving Michael the cold shoulder to make him notice me when we dropped off Santo at a building I didn't recognize."

"Where?"

"I don't know. Um…somewhere over the James River. I remember we drove over the Piedmont Bridge and wound around near some old empty factory buildings."

Gabe turned toward BJ. "You get that?"

"Yeah. Pulling up the list of Gibbons' holding on that side of the river. I've got Lily working on it as well."

Tony moved up by Gabe, telling his men, "We need to head back to the office. Time to plan and suit up as soon as they give us a location."

Matt walked out of the interview room, looking at his chief and Tony. "We're finished in there. Heading out to Tony's place to coordinate."

The men filed out of the police headquarters and into their vehicles. Vinny clapped his hand on Gabe's shoulder. "How're you holdin' up?"

"Better now that we've got a place to go and a mission to plan." Stopping outside the SUV before getting inside, he looked his brother in the eyes, fear mixed with determination pouring off of him. "Bro...I—"

"I know, Gabe. I know. We'll get them."

I'm coming, babe, Gabe thought as they drove to Alvarez Security. *Just hang on for me.*

ONCE THERE, LILY met them in the main room, filled with computers and large screens on the walls. "Guys, I've got some more," she said, the concern over Jennifer's kidnapping overshadowing her excitement in her intel gathering. Looking over at Monty, she narrowed her eyes asking, "Who's this?"

Monty moved toward the beautiful, petite blonde extending his hand. "I'm—"

Matt elbowed him out of the way as he put his arm around Lily. "He's FBI." Looking Monty in the eye, he said, "This is my wife, Lily."

Monty smiled as he nodded, moving over to the table.

Lily's eyes moved to Gabe, sympathy shining from them. "Gabe?" she said, unasked questions hanging in the air.

"Whatcha got, Lily?" he answered with a question, wanting to take the focus off of him and back on the mission at hand.

She nodded her understanding and turned back to

the screen on the wall. "BJ and I've finally traced some of the dummy corporations back to Michael Gibbons. We've also managed to connect the dots between him and the Senator. The Senator's wife is a relative of the elder Gambelini, grandniece or something like that. Anyway, that shows the initial inroads between Gibbons and the Senator's wife. She likes expensive things and has quite a few gambling debts racked up. Cousin Gibbons steps in to help and he's got the Senator now in his back pocket."

Monty nodded, "With what you have and what I've gathered in the last six months, we've got enough to pull the Renos in as well as Gibbons."

"What about Jennifer's office? Chip? Or whoever the hell her boss is."

Lily shook her head at Gabe. "There's nothing there. I've looked into his bank accounts, family, cell phone records, nothing. I did find records of him calling a contact at the newspaper. When I checked into them, the reporter was planning on doing an article on Jennifer and the Center." She looked into his confused eyes. "Gabe, it seems like her boss was on her side, trying to get support."

BJ continued the findings. "Looked into Santo. Works for Gibbons, but his job at the real estate agency is nebulous at best. Not really security. Not really anything for him to be called Gibbons' right-hand man. But if we look at Gibbons as a mob boss...then, yeah, Santo's job makes sense. Santo's name has been loosely tied into some of the smaller companies that come under Gibbons."

Shane added, "When the investigative officers were looking into the possible extortion claims, a few gave descriptions that fit Santo but then clammed up quickly."

Gabe's nerves were stretched taut and he could feel himself ready to blow with the descriptions of Santo. Vinny placed a calming hand on his brother, leaning into him. "You know the drill. We gotta have the whole picture, the whole intel to know what we're dealing with."

All Gabe wanted was to know where Jennifer and Ross were being held. That was it. Just where they were. *Once safe, then the fuckers who took them will be dealt with. 'Cause they will be dead. At my hand.*

He took a deep breath, forcing his mind to clear and focus on the intel coming in. Seeing the eyes of the group looking at him, he nodded. "I'm good. Go on," he forced out.

Lily's gaze landed on his face, understanding his fears. "Gabe, I think it was Santo who took her and as to where, well, Gibbons doesn't have a holding where his ex-mistress said, but two subsidiary companies do. And one of them is owned by a company that's a front and has a hidden owner...Santo."

Gabe's eyes snapped to hers. For the first time since the call from Henry, he felt as though he had a place to concentrate on.

"BJ," Tony said and before he could finish, BJ answered, "I'm on it."

With a few taps on his keyboard, the screen on the wall showed the building in question. Matt was on the phone with the chief as Monty coordinated with the Bureau. Night had fallen, but Gabe realized that it could give them cover. The building was an old warehouse, not large in size, that appeared to be undergoing restoration. Scaffolding on the outside, plastic and boards where some of the windows should be.

BJ looked at Gabe, concern knitting his brow. "I've pulled up the new plans filed with the city as to what it will look like when it's finished and I have the original floor plans, but there's no way of knowing what rooms are there now."

Tony turned to his new hire, a tech equipment manager, and ordered, "Get us ready. Include the thermal imaging goggles." Turning back to Matt and Shane he asked, "We goin' in together or we rogue?"

"Chief says for us to meet him there."

Monty looked confused at the men around suddenly moving into action. "You guys go in with the police?"

Shane looked at him, saying, "Budget cuts keeps our department from having some of the cool toys these guys have. Fuck yeah, we work with them."

The men proceeded quickly and quietly, knowing what needed to be gathered and put on. After suiting up, they each grabbed a large, black duffle bag and headed for the underground parking garage.

Arriving at the vehicles, Tony turned to face Gabe. "Your head on the mission?"

Gabe wanted to tear into him but knew his commander was right. Special Forces always kept their minds on the mission knowing lives were at stake if they did not. Sucking in a huge breath and letting it out slowly, he nodded. Vinny stepped up behind him. "We're good," giving the typical response the twins always made. They were in it together…all the way.

CHAPTER 22

A NOISE COMING from the hall had Jennifer scuttling back from the window to the bed. Sitting down, she anxiously awaited who was on the other side of the door. Licking her lips nervously, she tried to prepare but still startled when it swung open. A dark haired, dark eyed man in a suit came in followed by a huge, bald man whose purpose seemed to be guarding the door. She looked from one to the other, as the first man walked to the chair and sat down.

"Well, well, Ms. Lambert. How nice of you to join us," a smooth voice pierced her ears.

The helplessness of her situation washed over her, realizing that she had no power over one man much less two.

"If we'd wanted to rape you, Ms. Lambert, I assure you it would not have been done while you were asleep. My friend here," the man speaking nodded to the large, bald man next to the door, "likes his women awake, even if not willing."

Sucking in a breath, she stared at the one sitting in a chair nearest to her. Dark hair, neatly trimmed. A tailored suit, fitting him perfectly. Black eyes…boring holes straight into her. Licking her lips nervously, she tried to understand what was happening.

"Where...where's my brother?" her voice shook. Wanting to be brave, she could not help the quivering that radiated out from her inner core invading even her speech.

"He's well. And will stay so as long as you do what you are commanded."

Her eyes glanced around the room, not recognizing their location before being drawn back to the man speaking. "Who are you? I don't understand."

"There is no reason for you to know where you are or to understand anything, Ms. Lambert. My boss wants your signature on the deed, transferring the building you now so fortuitously own into a company that he designates."

Her brow crinkled as she took in his words. *Building? All of this for a building?*

Seeing her look of confusion, Santo continued, "You are but a small pawn in a much larger scheme. My boss will not tolerate anyone getting in the way of what he wants. And your building, combined with the other buildings in the area, will give him the perfect platform. High-end clubs, condos, exclusive gentlemen's clubs. With the zoning commission in his back pocket, all that stands in the way of his next million dollar maker is your little corner of the world."

"Who's your boss?"

"That my dear, is not your concern. But what will

be revealed is this – you will sign the deed over to us and stay out of our business or your brother will suffer the consequences. And if you think of ever changing your mind, we know where he goes to school. Where you live. We know where you stay when you're with your security boyfriend. We will always have one eye on your dear brother and his life will be worth nothing."

Gasping, she saw the grin spread across his face showing even, white teeth. *How can a smile look so evil?*

Pulling her quivering lips inward and pressing tightly, she said, "I want to see him. I want to see Ross."

"I don't think you're in a position to make requests, Ms. Lambert."

"If not, I won't sign. If you've hurt him already, there's no deal. If you've done anything—"

Santo held up his hand, giving her a curt nod. Without turning his head, he gave the order to the man at the door, "Bring him."

The man turned and left the room, leaving her alone with the one in charge. A silence descended between them, uncomfortable and awkward. She wanted to look for something she could use to defend herself with, but his eyes never wavered from her face. Hating to show fear, she found she could not hold his stare. She looked down at her hands for a moment until she heard a sound at the door.

Just as she looked up, Ross came barreling through,

seeing her and launching himself at her. A sob caught in her throat as she wrapped him in her embrace, thankful that he was still alive.

"Jennybenny, what's going on?" he asked, lifting his head from her neck to peer into her face.

"I don't know, buddy, but I'm going to try to take care of everything." *Gabe, please find us. Please.*

Her eyes went back to the men in the room, wondering what would happen next. A knock on the door had the larger man opening it. Jennifer could hear a voice outside the door saying that Santo was needed. *That voice? Why does it seem familiar?*

A furious look crossed the face of the man sitting in front of her as she realized he must be Santo. He stood abruptly and with a last glance her way, stalked to the door. Jennifer pulled Ross in tighter as she watched the door.

She could hear voices outside but was unable to detect the conversation. As the door opened again, she caught a glance of the man talking with Santo just before he looked inside and stared at her. *Roy?* Her breathing caught in her throat as she stared into the eyes of her co-worker.

Roy had the grace to blush as he realized that she saw him. He lifted his hands in supplication, but she saw red as she stood, slowly lowering Ross to the cot. "You? How are you involved?"

"I'm sorry, Jennifer," he said. "It's not personal, honest."

She walked straight over to him stopping just a foot away, her chest heaving. "Not personal? My brother was kidnaped, Roy. What the fuck do you mean 'not personal'?"

His mouth set in a grim line, shrugged as he said, "You have no idea how expensive it is to have twins. They offered money for me to just keep an eye on you and report what you were up to. That's all. Then," he ducked his head, "they said I'd lose my job if I stopped. So that's all I did. Just kept tabs on you and reported when you were going to the Capitol or over to the center."

The loud crack of her hand hitting his face echoed in the empty room. Her handprint immediately reddened his face. His eyes flashed, but he did not move.

"You incredible prick. You have no idea who you've gotten in bed with! You think these kinds of people will ever let you go? You've got children of your own now and you've put them at risk now too. God, what an asshole."

She turned back to the cot, seeing Ross' fearful expression and she immediately felt contrite. Rushing back to him, she gathered him in her arms, crying, "Oh Ross, it's okay."

"You hit him," he whispered. "Is he a bad guy too?"

The air left her in a whoosh as she pondered the question, the adrenaline of earlier beginning to leave. "Kind of," she said over Ross' head, staring into Roy's face. Tears stung her eyes as she thought of the memories of him, Sybil, and her sharing many lunches talking about their families, their cases, their lives.

Roy turned and walked toward the door. He stopped with his hand on the knob and slowly turned back, his eyes glancing at the boarded-up the window. Walking over, he put his hand in his pocket and pulled out his key chain. Slipping off a key, he held it out to her.

She looked down at the key in his hand then lifted her gaze back to his, a question in her expression.

"It's not to anything specific here, but might be useful on that window if you get a chance. The…uh…man that was here may be out for just a little bit."

He tossed the key onto the cot and left the room quickly. She continued to hold Ross as her gaze went from the door to the key and then over to the window.

SANTO WAS ESCORTED into Michael's study by his wife, who had greeted him warmly before leaving the men alone. Michael, not one to mince words, said, "I know you're wondering why I summoned you, but first, did everything go as planned?"

Nodding, Santo said, "No problems. The kid and Ms. Lambert are at my place. She had just woken and I have told her why she is there and what she will need to do to stay alive."

"At least something is going according to plans," Michael said, anger reverberating from his chest.

"What's up?"

"That goddamn, weak link, Reno, called to tell me that his assistant is missing. Didn't make it back from lunch and his desk was somewhat messy, which it not normal for him."

Santo lifted his brow, asking, "You think he's a plant?"

"Don't know, but I don't like the sound of any of it. If he is, how could that moron have hired him? He's had full access to all of Reno's life for the past six months, including his accounts, personal as well as professional."

"What do you have in mind?"

"For now, hold on to your hostages. Get her to sign, but keep her. We may need a little leverage with the good Senator if he starts to get cold feet."

Nodding, Santo stood asking his boss, "Is that all for now?"

"Yeah. Just be smart. I don't need any more cock-ups now."

Santo left quickly and began the drive back to the city. Michael watched him leave and walked back to the liquor cabinet, pouring a tumbler of scotch. Taking a sip of the smooth, amber liquid, he glanced around the room. Elegant. Expensive. Family pictures lining the mantle. Works of art on the wall. Leather bound books lining the shelves. Indian carpets on the polished wooden floor. This was his favorite room, always giving him comfort.

He gripped the glass in his hand so tightly he wondered if it was going to shatter. His empire was shaking and all because of one tiny, meddling woman. Santo would keep her alive for now…just for now.

THE DOOR HAD barely closed and locked before Jennifer set Ross down on the cot, grabbed the key and ran to the boarded-up window. Finding the slight separation between the plywood and the window frame where the air gently blew in, she inserted the key. Working it back and forth, she made a little wiggle room. At one point, the key became wedged tightly and she tugged hard to move it again. *Please don't break off*, she begged silently.

Ross had slid off the cot and stood watching what she was doing, his eyes alert. She turned to him as she managed to get one corner of the plywood loose. "I'm working it, buddy. But I have no idea what's outside or where we are."

The look of utter trust he gave her caused her heart to beat faster and she battled the tears that threatened to form. Turning back to the task at hand, she pushed her curls back and said, "I wish I had something to pull it out with."

Ross looked around and then down at himself and then quickly pulled his belt out of his jeans. "Can you use this?" he asked excitedly.

Jennifer grabbed the belt from his hand while planting a huge kiss on his cheek. "Perfect!"

Looping the belt around the corner of the plywood she used her body weight for leverage and pulled with all her might. The plywood almost bent in half before flying out of the window toward her and Ross. She fell back on her ass, landing hard, but was glad the large piece of wood landed on her and not the floor, realizing too late how much noise it would have made.

The cool air rushed in from the open window and the night sky was littered with stars. Sucking in a deep breath, she felt a rush of adrenaline course back through her. *We just might make it out!*

Grabbing Ross' hand, she ran over to the window-sill and leaned out. *Oh fuck.* They were on the third floor and the only thing on the outside of the building was scaffolding. To their right were some boards lying flat across some of the poles, creating a platform to stand on, and beyond that was more. But directly outside their window was just the poles. *If we can just make it to the first platform, then we can slowly make our way down.* Not knowing how much time was left before Santo returned, she knew there was no time to waste.

"Ross? Honey, this is the only way out and you've got to hold onto me as tight as you can so we can get to safety."

"Is Gabe not coming?" Ross asked peering down into the darkness beyond the window.

"We can't wait right now. We have to try to get away so he can catch the bad guys."

Once again, the look of trust crossed his face and he grinned. "Then let's go. I'm best at the monkey bars at school."

She grabbed the thin sheet off of the cot and wrapped it around his body, then had him climb onto the windowsill, she tied the ends to the long pole leading diagonally down toward the platform.

Crawling out, she carefully put her feet on the horizontal bar nearest her and held onto Ross and the sheet. Maneuvering slowly, they inched their way to the first platform. The muscles in her arms ached as her knees shook. As her feet touched the flat surface, she felt her heart pound a rhythm in her chest.

Dropping to her hands and knees she untied the sheet and slid Ross out onto the platform. Glancing down, she realized that she had only gone about ten feet. The streetlights below appeared to be very far away. She clutched Ross to her chest, beginning to doubt the idea of escaping. He leaned up to peer into her face.

"We did it, Jennybenny!" he said excitedly.

She could not hold back the nervous giggle that erupted at seeing his joy. "Well, we're not quite there, Ross, but you're right. We did get out of the window!"

She sat up and looked at the next platform about ten feet to their right again. "You ready to do this again?"

His grin was her answer, and they made the move one more time. This brought them down to the next floor. *Only two more to go…we can do this.*

THE VEHICLES PULLED up silently to the building that Lily and BJ had pinpointed. It was dark and Gabe looked around anxiously for any sign of activity. Or life.

As his eyes perused the remodeled warehouse, he noticed the scaffolding covered the front and side of the building. The men exited the SUVs, pulling on their night vision goggles. Checking their earpieces, they spread out, each focusing on the mission.

The mission. Who the fuck was he kidding? This was personal. He could feel his heart rate increase and forced it back to normal.

"East side. Single window, light on. All other boarded," came the sound of Jobe through the radio. Gabe and Vinny were closest to that side so they rounded the corner. Looking up they could see the lighted window. His eyes searched the nearby scaffolding for signs of activity.

Toward the left, he saw movement. *Jesus fuck.*

"Sighting?" came Tony's voice over the radio. Gabe realized he'd cursed out loud. Quickly covering his error, he said, "Roger. East side. Thirty feet up and twenty feet from back corner, on scaffolding. Looks to be two figures."

Gabe felt Vinny at his back as he strained to see what was moving. Tony and Shane were on the inside with the police and Gabe heard three men had been apprehended so far. *No sign of Jennifer and Ross inside. Could that possibly be them out there?*

As the larger of the two figures leaned over the side, he saw the mass of curls fall around her head and knew it was her. "Sighting on the scaffolding. Confirm Jennifer." Right then, a small head popped over the edge of the platform as well. *Thank fuck, she's got him.* "Confirm Ross."

The rest of Tony's men converged on the east side. Gabe was already beginning to climb by the time Tony made it around and grabbed Vinny, who was about to climb as well. "I need you back, trained on the window." Vinny knew what that meant – he had been the best sniper of the squad. A quick nod was his response and he jogged to a place where he could see the window clearly.

Gabe continued to climb as quickly as he could. He wanted to shout out to her to warn them he was coming, but knew stealth was imperative. He could hear Ross' voice carrying through the night air and wanted to warn him to not speak, but then heard Jennifer's soft voice hushing her brother. *That's my girl,* he thought proudly.

A shout was heard from above and he looked up toward the window where the light was pouring out. A lone figure was at the edge, with a gun trained down on the platform. A shot rang out and he heard a scream. Hanging onto the metal poles of the scaffolding, his heart leapt into his throat, the pounding threatening to choke him.

Jennifer had just moved Ross over to where she could tie him to the next diagonal pole when a gunshot zipped by and a scream ripped from her lips. Looking up, she saw Santo leaning out of the window with a gun trained on them. Another shot sounded as she tried to throw herself over Ross' body to protect him, shaking so hard she was afraid of them falling off.

A final sound zinged through the air and she saw Santo fall from the window, tumbling down onto the scaffolding, his body banging lifelessly through the metal poles before going out of her sight.

Her heart beat wildly in her chest as she pushed up off of Ross. *More may be coming.* Ross did not move and as her eyes looked down the white sheet, she saw a dark stain. *Oh Jesus, he's been hit.* Screaming his name, she tried to untie the sheet to see where he had been shot, screaming over and over his name.

Below her, Gabe's heart stopped as he realized the reason for her scream. Calling out her name, he continued to climb as quickly as he could. Grab a pole, pull body up. Next pole. Next pole. When he was a few feet away from her platform, he called her name.

"Gabe!" she cried out hearing his voice. "Ross is hurt."

"Jennifer, baby. Move over. I'm coming up."

Unable to move away from her brother, she gathered him in her arms and scooted a few feet away, giving Gabe room to hoist himself up onto the platform. The sight of the woman he loved holding the brother they both loved, covered in blood, had the mission fly out of his head. He no longer cared about stealth, but about getting them out of there.

Taking his weapon, he shot at the plywood window-covering closest to where they were. "Rescue needed. Window nearest us partially shot out. East side, thirty feet from the southeast corner."

He carefully tried to pull Ross out of her arms, but she would not let go. "Baby, you have to let me look at him." Jerking off his goggles, he said, "Jennifer," as sharply as he could. Her wild eyes looked up into his face. "Let me have him."

Slowly his words slipped into her mind and she let her fingers relax one by one. Turning Ross over, Gabe sliced the tied sheet off of him and saw the gunshot wound. On a grown man it would have been more superficial, but on a tiny boy who was losing blood, it was much more serious. Slicing the sheet once again into a strip, he wound it tightly around Ross' body, stemming the flow of blood.

A shout was heard from behind the plywood as it came crashing out of the window and they saw Tony's face peering at them. Vinny was right behind and the two of them quickly ascertained the situation. Vinny's arms reached out for Jennifer, but she was frozen in place.

Gabe, with Ross in his arms, moved closer to Jennifer. "Baby," he said softly, relieved when he saw her eyes focus on him again. "I'm going to lay Ross down for a second and help you get to Vinny. Then I'm getting Ross out of here."

Her eyes filled with tears as she looked at her brother in Gabe's arms. With anguish crying from her every word, she pleaded, "Save him."

"Promise, baby. I promise." *Not again. I'm not losing this child tonight.*

Gathering her strength, Gabe gave her a hand helping her to stand. Reaching her arms up, Vinny and Tony were able to easily grab her, pulling her upwards and through the window.

As he watched her disappear into safety, Gabe looked down at Ross once more, stunned to see his eyes open and peering straight at him. Dark eyes. Unblinking. Seeing. Knowing. Understanding. Gabe felt the tremors threaten to overtake him as he stood with Ross in his arms.

Ross then blinked and a little smile crossed his lips. "I knew you'd rescue us, Gabe. I knew you would."

The tears held at bay spilled forth as Gabe pulled Ross tightly to his chest. Lifting him gently above his head, he felt his squad take the injured, but living, breathing child from his arms to safety. For a second, Gabe turned away from the building and looked out onto the star-sprinkled night sky. Sucking in a deep breath, he let the tears flow. For the children caught in war. For the innocents caught in crime. For little boys who would never live to see adulthood and for those who would. And for the little boy in his brother's arms who would be in his heart forever.

"Gabe," Tony's voice came from above, bringing him back to the present. He quickly jumped up a foot, grabbed the window ledge and allowed his squad to pull him the rest of the way up. Grabbing Jennifer's shaking body into his huge embrace, he enveloped her. Tipping her chin up so that he could peer into her eyes, he kissed her softly.

"Love you, Jennifer Lambert," he said with a smile on his face.

Giving the first smile in hours, she agreed. "I love you too, Gabriel Malloy."

With one final quick kiss, he turned and took Ross from Vinny's arms. Heading out of the room, Gabe looked down at Ross and then turned to Tony. "Mission accomplished, sir."

Tony, flanked by Vinny and Jobe, nodded knowing what this rescue meant to Gabe. "Mission accomplished," Tony agreed.

CHAPTER 23

S HERRIE TAPPED LIGHTLY on the hospital door before opening it, peering inside. She could not hold back the smile as she saw Ross sitting in his hospital bed, playing a video game with Jennifer and Gabe asleep on the uncomfortable sofa pushed next to the bed. Ross looked up with a grin on his face and lay his game down on his lap as Sherrie made her way over to him with her finger on her lips.

"Hey," she whispered, her glance taking in the dark circles under Jennifer's eyes. Gabe's face sported stubble, shaving being the last thing on his mind. Her gaze went back to the little boy in the bed, still grinning.

"How are you?" she asked, handing him a new video game.

His eyes lit up as he said, "Thanks, Miss Sherrie. I'm doing fine. It only hurts a little, but sis won't let me move around much."

At his voice, Jennifer's eyes shot open and she pushed herself to sit up. "Ross? You need something, honey?"

At Jennifer's voice, Gabe also sat up, immediately

alert. "What'd you need, buddy?"

Ross giggled as he replied, "Nothing. I'm just talking to Miss Sherrie. She brought me a game."

Jennifer stood awkwardly, the nap on the uncomfortable sofa made her already achy body feel worse. "Sherrie," she exclaimed as she moved to hug her friend, glancing at her watch to see how long she had been asleep.

Turning back to Ross, she reached to place her hand on his face. Gabe stood, moving to her back and wrapping his arms around her, pulling her close to his chest. Looking over her head, assuring himself that Ross was fine, he leaned down to whisper, "Babe. He's okay. Promise."

Tears sprung to Jennifer's eyes as she tried to hold them back. The memory of that night was still too fresh.

The pediatric surgery waiting room was overflowing to testosterone capacity. While so much of it seemed a blur after Gabe had insisted that she be checked out, she remembered the sight of every seat being filled.

Vinny had walked over, squatting in front of her and Gabe and confessed, "I'm so fuckin' sorry, bro."

Her eyes shot up in confusion and before she could speak she heard Gabe say, "No reason man. You got that bastard."

"But not before he got a shot off. He was fuckin' hidden behind the window frame and I took the first shot I could, but too late."

Gabe stood, pulling his twin up with him, holding him by the shoulders. "You fuckin' got him, bro. You got him. You saved Jennifer and you saved Ross. They owe their lives to you, man."

The two men, separated by only a heartbeat, stared at each other. Vinny slowly nodded and pulled Gabe into a hug. The men felt a presence at their side and realized Jennifer was trying to wrap her arms around both of the massive men. Each taking an arm to pull her in close, the three of them embraced, no longer trying to keep the tears at bay.

Patrick and Maeve, who had entered the waiting room witnessing the exchange between their two sons, joined in the embrace. Patrick moved over to stand with Tony and Jobe while Maeve could not seem to let go of Jennifer.

"You worried you weren't giving Ross enough," Maeve said softly. "But tonight you proved that whether a sister or a mother, you've got what it takes to give him everything he'll ever need. I'm so proud of you."

Henry and Cora arrived, anxious and full of questions. After hugging Jennifer and Gabe, assuring them that the other residents wanted to be there also, they slid to the side next to Vinny to find out about the evening's events.

Matt and Shane had arrived and talked to Tony's crew privately while their wives, Annie and Lily, sat with Jennifer, along with Sherrie. Gabe came back over as soon as the surgeon came through the doors, pulling Jennifer closely to his warmth.

"He came through just fine. The bullet went through the side of his abdominal wall, only passing through some muscle. No internal bleeding. No internal injuries. He'll stay here a day or two on IV antibiotics and pain meds, as well as fluids, then will be able to go home. I'd say he'll be back to low activities in a week and resume normal activities in about six weeks."

Jennifer felt her legs weaken and Gabe's arms were the only thing that kept her upright. He gently set her back down in the chair as he asked the surgeon, "When can we see him?"

"He'll be out of recovery in about two hours and taken to a room. You can see him in recovery in about fifteen minutes. I'll send a nurse for you."

Jennifer covered her face with her hands as she cried unabashedly. Gabe tried to soothe her, but his words only made her sob harder. Finally he picked her up, turned and sat back down with her in his lap as he simply held her to his massive chest, enveloped in his strong arms. Rubbing her back gently, he murmured words of love until her tears were finally spent.

By the time the nurse arrived to take her and Gabe back, she had regained some semblance of composure. Looking around at the faces of the friends and loved ones, she smiled knowing no apology was necessary.

And now, she was in his hospital room, still trying to process the events. The door opened and in walked Tony and Jobe, followed by Monty. Her eyes flew to his quickly and her breath caught in her throat as he approached her.

"Why…what are you…" she tried to question.

"I'm sorry, Jennifer. I'm one of the good guys, I promise."

Her face registered surprise, and then doubt, as she stared at him.

"I'm actually FBI and was on an undercover assignment as Senator Reno's assistant. I was a dick to you because I was trying to keep you away, if possible."

Seeing her look of incredulity, Monty explained his investigation of Senator Reno's involvement with the local crime boss.

"He was working against me?" she asked, voice shaking with anger.

"Not at first. I truly think he and his wife were supporters of yours…it was just when that building was needed and pressure was put on him by Gambelini, well your cause became collateral damage to the Senator."

"I…I don't know…what to say," Jennifer replied, trying to process his words. "I…thought you didn't like me."

Monty brought her hand up to his lips, placing a kiss there and said, "I assure you Ms. Lambert, I have nothing but the highest regard for you. I was trying to keep you out of the line of fire that was growing."

A growl from behind her reached her ears at the same time that a muscled arm circled, pulling her hand back gently from Monty's. Gabe linked his fingers with hers as he tucked her back into his side. Monty grinned and stepped back behind Tony and Jobe, who approached Ross' bed. They stood on the opposite side from Jennifer and Gabe, allowing room for Vinny, who came in with Patrick and Maeve.

"Hey, little man. How you feeling?" Jobe asked.

Ross looked up at his friends and said, "I got shot with a real gun. Did you know that? You can see it if you want." In the process of pulling up his hospital gown, Jennifer tried to stop him.

Gabe stilled her hands, whispering in her ear, "Let him, babe. It's his badge of honor."

She looked over her shoulder, glaring into his face. "Badge of honor, my ass. Gabe...this is nothing to be excited about. He could've been killed."

"But he wasn't. And for him, he acted bravely. Let him have his moment."

Pulling her lips in, she tried to still her pounding heart. "Men," she said, shaking her head as Maeve laughed.

Ross pulled up his gown and showed the bandage on his side proudly. "It went right through. The doctor says that it didn't hit my eternal oregans. It just hit my muscle. I didn't even know I had muscle 'cause I'm not as big as you. But I did and it went right through."

Vinny and Gabe exchanged looks, a secret message passing between them. Gabe reached his hand out and Vinny placed something in it. Jennifer looked on in confusion wondering what was going on.

Gabe leaned over Ross and the serious look on his face quelled Ross' enthusiasm as the young boy looked first into his face and then at the purple cloth in his hand.

"Ross, when a soldier is wounded in action, the President of the United States gives him a special award called the Purple Heart. I was given this many years ago, but it never felt right for me. But now I know why…that's because I was just holding onto it to give to you. For your injuries sustained in the rescue of you and your sister, I award you my Purple Heart." Gabe pinned the medal to Ross' gown and as he stood up straight, he brought his hand up in a salute.

Tony, Jobe, Vinny, and Patrick followed suit, saluting Ross as his bright eyes stared at Gabe with love and adoration, a smile breaking out on his face.

As the men moved forward to congratulate Ross, Gabe stepped back pulling Jennifer with him. He gazed into the huge, tearful, blue eyes that first captured him months ago in the alley. Holding her face in his large hands, he kissed her gently. "I love you more than life itself, baby. You…and that little boy, are my whole world."

Closing his eyes, he then brought her head to his chest as he tightened his arms around her petite frame. Taking a deep, cleansing breath, he let go of the regrets of the past and smiled as the future lay before him.

EPILOGUE

ROSS WAS NERVOUS. He had a job to do and wanted to make sure he did it just right. The doors opened and he looked anxiously to his right at his sister. She glanced down at him, admiring the way he stood so straight and tall in his child-sized tuxedo. *Mom and dad, I wish you could be with us today. You'd be so proud of him.* With a deep breath she said, "Are you ready for this?"

He couldn't keep the grin off of his face, regardless of his nervousness. Taking her hand, he replied, "Absolutely, Jennybenny."

With the music playing, the two of them walked down the aisle toward the man that cared for them. Saved them. Loved them.

Gabe stood at the front of the church, looking out on the crowd of family and friends. Smiling, he couldn't help but notice that there were just as many grey haired guests as younger ones...and he would not have had it any other way. The doors in the back opened as the music changed and his eyes were drawn to the vision making her way toward him.

His breath halted and if Vinny had not leaned over

and reminded him to breathe, he would have passed out on his wedding day. She walked sure and steady on the arm of Ross, looking every bit the princess he thought she was the first time he lay eyes on her.

Jennifer, a vision in her ivory gown with layers of floating lace, kept her eyes on the man at the front. Her giant. Rescuer. Love. With a squeeze of Ross' hand, they continued past their friends toward Gabe.

Reaching the front, she bent to kiss Ross before he moved to stand with Vinny. After saying their vows and sharing their first kiss, she began to turn for their recessional back down the aisle.

Gabe halted her with a gentle pull on her arm. She looked at him in question, but before she could speak, he looked out at the crowd and said, "We have one more part of the ceremony that we wish to have you be a witness to."

Her eyes flew to Gabe, wondering what he was doing. *This wasn't part of the rehearsal!* Just then Ross, his impish grin lighting his face, stepped forward and stood between Gabe and Jennifer.

Gabe's voice rang out, clear and steady. "I have just taken Jennifer to be my wife and now I publicly want to take Ross into the family as well."

A gasp ripped through Jennifer as tears sprung to her eyes. Blinking to keep them at bay, she watched the scene unfold in front of her.

"Ross had wonderful parents and I cannot replace his father. He and I have talked and agreed that he'd like me to become his legal guardian along with his sister." Pulling a piece of paper out of his pocket, he knelt down in front of Ross and said, "Here they are, buddy. The official papers that say we belong to each other."

Ross gave a whoop and threw his arms around Gabe's neck. Jennifer's legs gave out and she fell to the floor next to them. The three, now a family, hugged as the congregation cheered.

Later at the reception, Jennifer danced in the arms of the man she loved. Looking around, she saw Vinny on the dance floor with Bertha and Lucille, swinging them both around at the same time. "Looks like Vinny has his two dates lined up for the evening," she joked.

She felt Gabe's laughter from deep in his chest as he agreed. "This is probably the one wedding where he couldn't hook up with a friend of the bride. At least not one that is under seventy years old."

All of their couple friends were on the dance floor also, swaying to a slow song, each lost in their own world.

As he moved her around the dance floor, she saw Sherrie sitting next to Monty, talking and smiling. And...three tables over sat Tony. Alone. Staring at Sherrie. And scowling.

She sighed and Gabe immediately looked down. "What's wrong?"

"Tony and Sherrie. Why can't they get together?"

A cloud passed over Gabe's face as he said, "Man's

been through a lot. I just don't know that it's in the cards for him."

She peered into his eyes, a question on her lips, but Gabe just shook his head. "Not my story to tell, babe. But I wouldn't hold out hope for those two."

Sighing deeply, she let it go and continued to snuggle close to his chest. Seeing Ross dancing with Cora brought a smile to her face again.

"How long had you and Ross been planning that surprise?"

Smiling, he replied, "For at least a month. But I gotta tell you, babe. Been thinking about it ever since that first breakfast at the Center."

Her smile warmed his heart as he stared at the beauty that had given herself to him. Leaning down, he touched his lips to hers. A kiss promising forever.

THIRTEEN YEARS LATER

"MOM, I DON'T see him," complained twelve-year-old Benjamin. "Why does Lisa get to sit on dad's shoulders?"

"Because your sister is only eight and is shorter than you. You'll be like your daddy and she will, unfortunately, be my height," Jennifer explained.

"There he is. I see him," Benjamin called out excitedly.

The ceremony was over and the soldiers were now

at liberty to find their families. Jennifer could not wait to see him and as she turned around, there he was. Benjamin started forward, but Gabe held him back.

"Hold on, son. Let your mother see him first."

Ross stood proudly in front of the sister that had become his mother. She seemed tinier than he remembered even though it had only been a year since they had been together.

Jennifer stared at the man that filled her vision as tears filled her eyes. Over six feet tall, with his sandy, blond hair buzzed off. Not quite as big as Gabe, but still…a huge man. His uniform was neatly pressed and the name **LAMBERT** proudly on his chest. As her eyes lifted, she saw the Green Beret on his head, signifying the graduation from Special Forces training.

"Jennybenny?" the familiar voice spoke.

Throwing her arms around him, she let the tears flow as she held him close. After a moment, she stepped back allowing Benjamin and Lisa to have a chance at a reunion. Gabe stepped behind his wife, pulling her back into his chest. Leaning down, he whispered, "He's good, baby. It's all good."

Ross moved over to Gabe, sticking his hand out for a shake, when Gabe pulled him in for a hug. "Good to see you, buddy. Congratulations."

The two men hugged, causing Jennifer to cry once again. The rest of the family and friends moved in for congratulations as Gabe moved back a little. Watching the boy grow into a man, one who now took his place in the world, caused his heart to pound.

The eyes of the little boy he could not save had become a faded memory, replaced by the eyes of the man standing in front of him. Smiling, he tucked Jennifer back into his arms, kissing her head, and said, "Let's go everyone. We've got some celebrating to do."

Feeling a pull on his waist, he looked down at Jennifer's teary eyes. Wiping her wet cheeks, he said, "I love you, baby. You and that boy...and now our children...are my world." Her smile was the only response he needed.

THE END

Made in the USA
Charleston, SC
14 April 2016